"I WANT *YOU*, AYLENA. LOOK AT ME; YOU'LL FIND TRUTH IN MY EYES. I INTEND TO HAVE YOU, NO MATTER HOW LONG IT TAKES."

"Oh, God . . . let me go. We can't . . ."

His mouth swallowed the rest of her words, his hard kiss gentling as she yielded, his tongue soothing her bruised lips.

"Ah, my lovely," he whispered, his deep voice shaken. "My exquisite rose . . . your mouth is like sweet wine to me."

She couldn't resist. She drew closer, her arms slid around his shoulders, her fingers inched up and wove themselves into his thick hair, holding him, trembling as he deepened the kiss. . . .

Also by Joanna McGauran

A LOVE SO FIERCE

BY MY LADY'S HONOR

JOANNA McGAURAN

A Dell Book

Published by
Dell Publishing
a division of
Bantam Doubleday Dell Publishing Group, Inc.
1540 Broadway
New York, New York 10036

The trademark Dell® is registered in the U.S. Patent and Trademark Office.

ISBN: 0-440-21368-1

Printed in the United States of America

Published simultaneously in Canada

August 1994

10 9 8 7 6 5 4 3 2 1

RAD

This book is dedicated to Florence Haskell, my mother, who was so sure I would be the writer she had always wanted to be that she bought a typewriter for me when I was twelve.

With gratitude, I acknowledge the
warm, friendly help and useful criticism
given me by my first Dell editor,
Tina Moskow.
(She has a wonderful laugh!)

1

March 6, 1155
Northumbria

 Loud and angry, the voice of old Bruce Stewart roared through the open door of Aylena Stewart's private sitting room and brought her out on the gallery that circled the great hall of the castle. Her six-year-old brother, Ian, whom she was teaching to read, followed her closely. They leaned on the carved balustrade, arms touching, and looked down at the two men standing near the blazing fire in the center of the hall below.

Aylena took in the mingled odors of wood smoke, sweating men, and rank dogs. All familiar, but she was suddenly alarmed by the anger in her father's face. During the six years since her mother had died in childbirth, old Bruce's grief and loneliness had translated into an uncertain temper. Now his rough-hewn features were crimson red, bright contrast against his silver hair and light blue tunic. Veins swelled in his neck as he spit out his fury.

"English dogs! Honor means nothing to them!" The chief of the Stewart clan was huge, even with his bony frame bent with age, and impressive as he raised a knotted fist and shook it at his visitor, John Bretinalle. "What one king gives in an honest bargain, the next on the throne steals away! By God, they'll not take the Stewart castle without a fight!"

John was a scrawny young noble who came here often in the vain hope of gaining Aylena's hand and dowry. His sharp rat's face was greenish pale above a soiled gray velvet tunic, his jet eyes slid away from Bruce's glare.

"Indeed, my lord, I advise caution. King Henry is angered by your refusal to either swear fealty to him or go back to Scotland. He is sending the Baron Thor Rodancott to take your demesne."

"Rodancott!" Bruce's craggy face tightened. He knew the name and the man's impressive reputation. "Another follower of the Plantagenets, damn his arrogant Norman soul! England will rue the day she allowed Henry II to come to power. When does Rodancott arrive?"

John's eyes shifted away, hiding something. "Who knows? Perhaps tomorrow; perhaps not for several days. You've heard of him, then?"

On the gallery above, Aylena tensed. She knew John Bretinalle only too well. His eyes . . . his air of secrecy told her he was looking for an opportunity for himself, one he wasn't likely to admit.

Stewart frowned. "What matter? Normans are as much the devil's tools as the Angevins." He swung toward the gallery, his fierce gaze rising and centering on the slim figure of his daughter. "Get down here, Aylena, and bring Ian with you. I have orders to give."

"Let her travel with me," Bretinalle put in eagerly. "I will take her and your young son safe to Scotland and your brother's home."

Bruce gave the younger man a look of supreme disgust. "Do you think I'd hand them over to a man too cowardly to fight the English? Be off, Bretinalle, or I'll give you a start with my boot in your arse."

Reacting to the anger in their master's voice, Bruce's three big hunting hounds moved toward Bretinalle, growling deep in their chests. Bretinalle slunk away, but not before he cast a pleading glance at Aylena, who was coming down the stairs with Ian's hand clasped in hers.

"If you need me, my lady, I'll . . ." His voice died away. Aylena was a slender and beautiful woman of seventeen, gentle natured and sweet with those she loved, but now her look was as hard as that of her father. Her mass of red-gold hair framed a scornful face. Chin up, eyes hard as blue jewels, and cheeks flaming, her face told him he was vermin, too low to deserve an answer. She turned her back to him and went across the rush-strewn floor to her father, an arm around her brother, who carried the same red gold halo of thick hair and walked as proudly as she.

Bruce waited until the big double doors closed behind John Bretinalle before he spoke, then motioned to Stephen, the seneschal, standing near the fire and listening intently. "Take the boy, Stephen, and make him ready for a trip north."

The young lad gasped, his eyes widening and going toward Aylena and then again to his father's face. Bruce shook his head at him. "You will know in time.

Go with Stephen." He touched the boy's cheek with a rough caress and swung away, waiting again until he could speak to his daughter in private. The seneschal was quick, closing the door of the wardrobe chamber.

"The coward is right, Aylena. I canna win this last battle, yet I will fight. No . . ." He held up a hand as she made an involuntary sound. "I'll not argue with God nor let you do it for me. My faltering heart tells me I am near to death, and perhaps tis a final blessing for me to die as a man dies, on his feet and fighting for what he believes."

Tears filled Aylena's eyes. "Then I will fight beside you, sire. You've taught me to handle a sword. I will use my small skill and be with you until the end."

He put a long arm around her and pulled her to his side. "Your task is much more important than that, daughter. You and your maid Margit will go with my son and his guard to safety in Scotland. Your brother Ian must live to rule the Stewart clan."

"Ian? Surely he'd be safe here. Even the English wouldn't kill a six-year-old child."

"Who knows what the English will do? They have no honor!"

Aylena's golden brows drew together, her eyes questioned him. "My mother was English, and honorable."

Her father's face softened. "Your mother came straight from heaven. Not even an English upbringing could darken that pure heart. When you compare my sweet girl to these Norman barons, you're judging ravening wolves by the soul of an angel. Now get you to your duty, daughter. You and Ian must leave by the coward's way, for the enemy will look to the front gates."

Aylena straightened her spine. "Then I'm off to find Margit, sire, and I'll bring Ian back to you while Margit and I pack. Counsel him, please. Make him see wisdom in your plan. Otherwise, he's as likely as I to refuse to leave you."

In early afternoon a band of hard-riding Normans and Angevins topped the rise of the last rolling hill to the west of the Stewart castle and came thundering down the rough slope toward the castle walls. Sixty big men, black-cloaked on dark horses, they stood out against the snow-splattered barrens, dull as crows except for the glint of steel mail and long shields when the pale sun touched them. They rode at a ground-eating canter and maintained silence except for the rumble of hooves, the creaking of leather saddles. At sight of the castle the leaders glanced at each other and grinned, then slowed to study the ancient fortifications.

"Easy enough," Philip of Anjou said after a moment. "There are few on the walls, and those few moving around to fool us into counting them twice." He laughed suddenly. "The Stewart sent the cowards off. From what I've heard of that old man and his tricks, tis exactly what he would do. He's our enemy in this campaign, but tis easy to like him from the tales I've heard."

In the silence that followed, Philip glanced up at Thor Rodancott and felt the awe he always felt when Thor's strong face changed from the usual half-amused friendliness to a granite mask with searching eyes. Content, Philip faced forward again. Thor's presence alone inspired confidence in his men; his tremendous size, his extraordinary strength was enough to draw them to him. But Philip, who had known him longest, knew Thor's real worth lay inside his cool, intelligent head. Thor was a master of strategy. He would win, but no man on either side would die unnecessarily.

"Durand!" Thor's hand shot out, pointing. "There, near the side wall. Take your men and capture the two women who are riding away. We may be able to use them as hostages. Hasten, for they've seen us and are picking up the pace."

Five men broke away from the group and rode at top speed toward the figures in the distance. Other figures were now joining the women and urging all of them into speed; a mounted man-at-arms and another horse that appeared to carry either a bundle of baggage or a child were passing the women at a run. Thor's attention slipped back to the castle, judging possible points of entry. With defenders, the walls would be hard to breach, but Philip was right—there were no more than twenty-odd men to fight off his sixty. Thor let out his breath in a soundless sigh. He knew the reputation of the Stewart's leader, and while discussing the campaign in London, he had heard the old man was dying on his feet and knew it. Was that the reason he'd refused to leave peaceably? He grimaced, not wanting to be an old man's executioner, yet understanding a warrior's wish to die in action.

"Sire!" Astounded, Philip pointed.

Thor turned, startled, and then laughed. One of the escaping women had whirled her horse around, pulled out a sword from a saddle scabbard, and was charging toward Durand and his four men, waving the blade in glittering slashes and coming on, straight on . . . her hood falling back, her red-gold hair flying loose, her blade whirling close to Durand's neck, then neatly darting toward the next man. . . . Thor caught his breath, stood up in his stirrups, and roared.

"You *fools*! She'll kill one of you!" He dropped back into the saddle and sent his horse galloping toward the milling confusion, the swinging blade, and his knights, who were now dodging the blows as well as they could. He thrust his way through squealing horses and bloodied men, grabbing the woman's sword arm in a powerful hand.

"Enough! Stop or taste steel yourself, you young witch!"

The face that turned to him was as wild and savage as a she wolf. Slitted blue eyes burned the air between them; soft lips curled back from white teeth in a bitter sneer. Then the bright head swooped down and Thor felt teeth clamp hard on an exposed inch of his forearm. Blood spurted, smearing her cheek and golden hair with crimson.

With a curse, Thor wrested the sword from her with his free hand and threw it aside. Then he pried her teeth from his arm and lifted her face with a rough hand under her chin. When she tried to jerk away, his fingers tightened. In spite of the rage he felt, he was amazed by her beauty.

"Look at me."

She looked, and he saw murder in her eyes. There was no fear in her face; there was only fury and hatred. "English dog!" she yelled, and spat his own blood at him. "Kill me or let me go!"

"I will do neither," Thor said, marveling. What a beauty, all fire and flash and heat! "I'm going to use you. But if you bite me again, I will treat you like I treat a hound that bares his teeth at his master. You'll be tied to a tree and switched on your bare bottom."

Her eyes flickered; ice struck by light. "You'd shame a lady?"

Humor eased his strong face. "Never. Is there one about?"

She growled something unintelligible and spat at him again, jerking her arm from his hand. Struggling to turn her horse, kick him into a run, she twisted away, trying to escape. But Thor encircled her waist with an arm and lifted her from her saddle. She shrieked and aimed a blow at him. The blow flailed the air, the shriek ended as she landed facedown across his hard thighs, driving the air from her lungs and leaving her gasping for breath. Seeing her limp and helpless, Thor turned to Philip.

"Ask for a parley, Philip. Tell them we have a hostage, a young, yellow-haired woman from the party which left by the side gate."

"Yes, sire!" Unfurling a parley flag, Philip of Anjou kicked his horse into a gallop toward the gates of the castle.

Catching her breath, Aylena raised her head just enough to look at the clearing between the castle and the forest. There was no sign of Ian and the others. A light snowfall had begun, enough to hide their tracks in the thin scattering of snow. She felt a fierce surge of pride and relief. Ian was safely away. The men on the walls would have told her father by now—and told him, too, that she had been captured.

What her fate would be with these devils was past her ken, but she hoped her father would give in and open the gates. Then, perhaps the old lion could end his years in peace. She shut her eyes and prayed to God that he would; that these harsh Norman devils would let him go; that he'd forget his own terrible anger at the Plantagenet king and go back to Scotland . . .

She twisted violently, shocked as hands grabbed her waist and pulled her up from her prone position. Swinging her like a bag of meal, the Norman devil dropped her into her saddle again and grabbed her reins, tying them to his wide leather belt. Then, pulling her horse even closer to his, he took a silk scarf from his neck and used it to tie her hands behind her. She submitted without a word, conscious of the smoothness of the silk and the warmth it had borrowed from his strong neck. Still, she stared off into the distance with a frozen face, as if in spite of what she saw and felt, nothing that was happening here had anything to do with her. She forced herself to ignore the twisted skirts that bared her slender legs to her thighs, the stiffening blood on her cheek, the tangled hair that hung about her face, and the frequent glances the damnable man gave to those exposed thighs.

"Now," the Norman said, "your fate will be decided by your friends. If you are important enough for the men to open the gates, you may leave for Scotland with them. If not, you'll enter the gates with me when we have won, and share my bed for a time. You seem full of spirit, and I've not been with a woman since I left London."

He meant it, she thought, though his tone was light. She prayed silently for the gates to open.

He kept staring at her, and her skin grew hot. She'd been foolish to fight, yet there was no other way to

make sure Ian went free. Besides, rage had carried
her into the attack. Rage and a sense of unfairness.
When she'd seen the mighty force of men bearing
down on the castle, she'd been angry enough to face
the devil himself. Now she wondered if indeed she
had, and Lucifer was using his wiles on her. Why else
would her breasts prickle with heat when his gaze
touched them? Sitting as still as a statue she tried to
ignore his interest, yet knew immediately when his
attention turned from her to the man Philip riding
toward the barbican that guarded the main gates.

Suddenly her stiffened shoulders loosened, her
throat opened for a full, deep breath. Knowing every
sound of the castle, she knew the faint, muffled creaking she heard for what it was. The drawbridge was
coming down.

Thank God. For once, her father had not thrown
back a challenge to an enemy who wanted peace.
Once he knew Ian was safe, once he discovered she
was a prisoner, he had given in . . . but, oh, dear
Mary, how he must hate it! Still, if these devils would
let them go, they could live safe and free in Scotland.

Calmer now, she studied the man who sat at her
side, her gaze tracing an old scar that rose from his
curling black beard and stopped a quarter inch from
a clear gray eye. Other than that, his face was pleasant enough, even handsome. His big body, clothed in
a knee-length bliaut of dark Flemish wool under a
shirt of mail, was erect and strong; his legs, covered
by heavy wool chausses and cross-gartered above
short leather boots, were long and well shaped. Below the leathern helmet he wore she saw the thick
black hair that protected the nape of his neck. His
skin, though weathered, did not look old, nor did he

look fierce. He glanced at her and she saw from his unworried expression that he also knew the sound of a drawbridge chain.

"You've saved a number of lives," he said carelessly, "by your rash action."

She gritted her teeth. He was so sure of himself, so kindly condescending, as if she were some witless servant. Undoubtedly the man was Rodancott himself; no other would have such an overweening sense of importance.

"I take no pride in that, English dog. One of them may have been yours."

He grinned, and the white flash of teeth was like a slap in her face. "You may be right. So far, I am the only one wounded." He held up his arm and examined it, shaking his head. "Considering the venom with which you bit me, I may die of it." He reached across teasingly, smoothed the golden hair away from her face and traced her lips with a finger. "No, I'm safe enough, I believe. No mouth as beautiful as yours could carry poison in a bite."

His touch had fire in it, a sweet poison of its own that soothed and made her dizzy. Damn him! She watched his slow grin split the glossy beard and she snapped around to watch the drawbridge easing down, the white flags waving on the walls. She thought of her father and sadness assailed her. Giving in, too old and sick to fight . . .

"Come. I'll lead you in." He started off, and with the reins tied to his belt, her horse kept pace, slightly behind his. She was being led as a captive into her own demesne, with hands tied behind, her face bloody, her hair in a tangle, her bare knees impudently showing themselves to any who looked. Her father's pride and hers, she thought, lay in the same dust.

"They'll thank you for it, wench, and be proud of your courage."

Her eyes shot to the broad shoulders, the dropped hood that showed his leathern helmet, still straight, watching ahead. He hadn't turned to look, yet he had known how she felt. She looked up as they neared the walls and saw the white faces looking at her, heads bowing, hands swiftly making the sign of the cross. Her father's men were praying! Why?

They crossed the frozen moat and entered the wide open gates into the courtyard. There were men-at-arms clustered near the keep; the men and women who worked in the kitchens, the stables, the armory and bakery were all out, standing and staring as the column of black-cloaked mercenaries marched in without a single blow exchanged. None of her father's five knights was anywhere to be seen. No sound was heard but the clop of hooves on the stone of the court-yard, the creak of saddles, a muffled cough. They went on, slowly, through the inner gates and to the door of the keep. The big man stopped there, and several of his men formed a circle around him, their weapons at the ready, their hard faces full of suspicion.

Thor Rodancott reached over and untied the silk scarf, loosing Aylena's wrists. Dismounting, he lifted her down from her horse. For once, the look on his face was uncertain.

"Something is wrong here," he said, and grasped her wrist in a hard, suspicious grip. "I have heard enough of the Stewart to know he hews to the code of honor, yet he is not present to hand me his sword. If this is a trick I'll not be the one who suffers. . . ."

"Tis no trick!" Face flaming, Aylena jerked her arm from his grasp. "My father is honorable, but he is ill. Come with me if you wish while I find him, but keep your hands to yourself!"

"Your *father*? You are the Stewart's get?"

A keening wail came from the outskirts of the group, and an elderly woman pushed through the nervously stepping horses and took Aylena's hand, tugging at her. "Oh, Lady Aylena, come quickly! The laird is dying, and the time is short."

"A path," Rodancott snapped, and the path was there, knights jostling each other to move away from the entrance. Leading the way, Rodancott stopped inside and let the old woman and Aylena go ahead, skirts fluttering with the speed of their going. He followed, close and alert, listening to the old woman.

"He went down, my lady, only a moment after you left. Crashed like a felled oak, grabbing at his chest. He's only now able to speak, and that only to ask about you. Sir Roger ordered the drawbridge down so our sire could see you once more. He said these Norman devils would win in any case. . . ."

They were up the stone steps to the gallery and into the solar above. As they turned in, Aylena's face was proud but agonized, chin up, mouth set firm, tears running freely down her pale cheeks. She turned and looked at the two Normans, her eyes blazing through her tears, and waved them back to the door like an angry queen. The laird of the proud Stewart clan would not want his enemy staring at him on his deathbed. She hesitated, watching them, satisfied as they both stopped at the open door and stayed there, the smaller man taking his place behind the big man and facing the other way.

Old Bruce lay on a fur-strewn couch on a dais. Around him stood his five knights in full battle regalia, chain mail and swords over dark woolens. Most of them were as old as the laird, white-haired and thin. But proud. They bowed to Aylena and left the solar, passing the Normans at the door as if no one were there. When they had gone Aylena knelt and touched her father's bearded cheek with a trembling hand.

"Father . . . I am here."

Bruce's big, knotted hand rose, enveloped Aylena's fingers, and then dropped, the strength gone. "I am dying, my sweet daughter. How can you be here? You were . . . to be with Ian."

She looked at him, astounded. Hadn't he heard? "Why, I did as you told me to do, and—and then I came back."

"Ian is safe away?"

"Indeed. I saw to that." She could see the lines in his face relax, a faint smile curve his wide mouth. He spoke again, breathless, forcing the words out.

"Good. Then we have saved him for the clan. I can barely see you now, my darling, but give me your soft hand. Like your mother, you are. What of the Normans? Have they come into sight?"

She gasped, soundlessly. *He knew nothing of what had happened.* For a moment she wondered what to say, and then she knew. Words burst from her throat.

"Oh, yes! They came, a horde of them, sixty strong. They came calling vile threats and throwing lances, saying they'd kill everyone inside unless we surrendered the castle. But, when they heard twas the laird of the Stewart clan who lived here, and when they failed to frighten your knights and men-at-arms, they lost heart and went on. No doubt they are looking for a castle easier to conquer."

From the corner of her eye Aylena saw the dark-haired Norman leader turn and look at the man behind him, his brows rising. The other man smiled, though not cruelly, and said nothing. She felt heat in her face, shamed by her lie but grateful for their silence.

"Ha!" Old Bruce gripped his daughter's hand for a glad moment. A smile illumined the craggy face. "Good," he said faintly. "Good. You . . . all of you have honored me with your actions."

She bowed her head. "As we should."

"I am proud of you. Take care of Ian . . . watch over him. Hold to his heritage, my daughter, put him first before your own wants. Remember that my blood must lead the clan. Promise me, Aylena. Speak loud. My breathing . . . deafens me."

"I will do all, sire. I vow it!" She said it loudly, and saw his faint nod, like a bow to fate. And then his breath rattled in his wide chest, and was gone, his face blank and staring. She knew, and with a shaking hand she closed the wrinkled eyelids over eyes as blue as her own. Bowing her head on her clasped hands, she wept, her slim shoulders shaking. The old woman came to kneel at her side.

Still silent, the two men stepped out onto the gallery and closed the door, leaving the women to their grief.

After the tears and prayers for her father's soul, Aylena thought of the enemy who now occupied her home. She knew any Christian knight would honor the rites of the Church and allow her father a decent burial, but she was not sure she would be allowed to stay and see it done. She decided to act as if she had the right to remain here until the ceremony was finished. Searching silently until she found the old woman Bettina, she instructed her to find a man and send him for a priest from the monastery on the Tweed. After that she straightened her riding skirts as well as she could and went out on the gallery toward the stairs. Looking below, she saw the big man, who she was now certain was the Baron Thor Rodancott, addressing a gathering of servants and her father's elderly knights.

"Your laird is dead," Rodancott was saying. "If you have not already said your prayers for his soul, then you may now. Then get to your duties. There is the body to prepare for burial, and a proper bier to be draped and lighted about with candles." He looked at the five old men. "If you need more knights for the deathwatch hours, I will provide them."

Aylena's answering voice was cold as ice as she descended the steps from the gallery. "We will make do with those who loved him," she said. "We need no help from enemies." She motioned to Stephen, crouched in grief by the fire.

"Seneschal, rouse yourself! There are sixty odd men to feed as well as the rest of us. See that the kitchens are provisioned from our siege stores." She turned, her eyes welling over, and dashed the tears aside. "You, Maxwell, are practiced in preparing a body for the grave. Take whoever you wish to help you."

Both men left the room, Maxwell beckoning to the

old woman who had come down the stairs. Gradually, the other servants were drifting away. There were duties now; there would be a chance to grieve later, to tell the laird good-bye, to say a prayer at his bier. Aylena faced Rodancott again, conscious that this man had held her captive, had handled her body like a sack of meal, had spoken to her of desire, of bedding her!

She burned when she thought of that part, both with indignation and a measure of shame. She was honest; she had to admit that deep inside her there had been some wordless thing that had no thoughts, an insane thing that responded hotly to his touch, as it had to no other man. But she was sure her grief had now conquered it, and only her duties as a chatelaine were on her mind. He would not find her wanting in common decency, even toward a triumphant—and overbearing—enemy.

"There is room here in the hall for your men to sleep," she said, "and enough dried rushes in the storehouse near the east rampart to soften the hard floor. Send your men to bring the rushes here. There are plenty of pallets, but the rushes will add to the softness."

Rodancott's weathered face hardened. "Send the servants, my lady. My knights are noblemen, not serfs."

Her head went up. Even red with weeping, her eyes shot sparks. "Then no doubt they are too hardy and high-minded to feel the cold stone. Since I have few servants and an army of uninvited guests to feed, the rushes will have to stay where they are."

His glance was quick and hard; she saw from the

flattening of his lips inside the black beard that he was annoyed.

"There will be time between the serving of the meal and the end of eating it to bring rushes enough for a comfortable night. See that it's done." He hesitated, and then added silkenly: "You do remember that the castle is now mine, I trust. Or do you believe your own lies?"

Aylena opened her mouth and shut it again. The words that had rushed to her lips would make her no friends, only a worse enemy out of this English dog. She tried to sound a little less haughty.

"I had thought a nobleman would allow me the grace of a few days to bury my father."

"And so I will. All honor will be paid to the head of the Stewart clan. But the castle is mine, and my orders stand. See to the rushes."

Aylena inclined her head and spoke bitterly. "I will tell the seneschal, my lord, and explain to him that it will be my last order. From now forward, you have the task of directing the servants. Please remember that I am not one of them." She turned and hurried toward the door that led out to the kitchen, her back straight, her golden head unbowed.

Thor stared after her, and behind him Philip chuckled.

"You have stumbled over your own foot, my lord. What do you know of managing a household?"

"Damn little," Thor said grimly, watching Aylena's high-held chin disappear through the door. "But I will learn. The Scottish lass will not lord it over me. From the first I knew I must have her, and I want her sweet and obedient when I take her to bed."

The side door had not closed itself; Aylena had

turned back to make sure the heat would not waste in the cold air, and, hearing that last sentence, she herself grew hot with rage. Did that barbarian think he had conquered her along with the castle? Did he truly believe he could make her sweet and obedient? By God's bones, the English dog would never find her so!

2

That night the Stewart lay in state on his bier, the same couch but draped now with black silk and cornered by tall silver candlesticks, their candles burning all night long. He was dressed in shining battle array, his sword lay on his body, his fingers clasped the jeweled handle that formed a glittering cross on his chest. At the right of the bier stood a knight with his sword drawn, protecting his lord for the last time. The five knights who mourned their leader each stood for their share of the deathwatch, and began again during the hours before dawn.

A prie-dieu with a carved ivory figure of Christ was brought near and draped with black silk. The pillow on the kneeling bench had been kept warm all night by the knees of the castle servants, come to pray for the soul of their master. But all was quiet in early morning when Aylena emerged from her chamber and came to the door. She was dressed in a gown of black velvet, unrelieved by jewels or even the silver embroidery allowed. Her bright hair was covered

with a black veil of silk. Coming into the solar, she
went to Sir Roger of Perth and put a hand on his arm.

"Leave us," she said. "The night is gone, and I want
a time alone with the spirit of my father. Thank you
all for the honor you've done him."

The old knight nodded and left, weak tears in his
eyes, never noticing the presence of one of the hated
invaders outside on the dark gallery. When he was
gone, Thor shifted his position slightly so that he
could see a portion of the solar and the black-draped
woman who stood by the bier.

Thor was puzzled by the growing emotion he felt.
Somehow he was beginning to feel Aylena's pain, the
deep sorrow of losing her father and her home. It was
a thing that had never happened to him before; his
sympathy was usually with his own men. He had chosen a bedchamber beside the one Aylena slept in, not
to harass her but from pity and a decision to watch
over her; there were some knights in his band of mercenaries who felt entitled to use any conquered female, no matter her rank or condition, as a prize.
Most of the time, he ignored them as long as they used
persuasion instead of force. But this time, the thought
angered him.

He had heard the woman moving about an hour
ago, and sleep left him. In preparation to attend the
rite of burial, which was to take place at sunrise in the
castle burying ground, he had gotten up, dressed in
black, and left off the protection of his mail. However,
he wasn't trusting enough to leave off his sword.
Some one of these grieving old men might blame him
for the death of their laird and cut him down.

Watching Aylena now, Thor pitied her. She was
aimlessly tapping around the dark walls, hands

touching the icons and tapestries, moving them about, as if action alone would help her grief. He was almost shamed by the passion he felt, the hot desire that grew with every sight of the woman. But he felt sure he could comfort her if she'd let him. Brave as she was, it would be hard to face an empty future. But, once the burial was over, and she had time to think, surely she'd be more responsive to a plan that would allow her to remain at home. In the meantime, he had tasks he'd never done before. Orders for servants, a look at the grave to see if it was deep enough, and a word with the priest if he had arrived . . .

Bettina, carrying her rosary and heading for the prie-dieu in the solar, leaped in fright and squealed as a big form stepped from the shadows and started toward her. Her wrinkled face lost its fear when she saw who it was. He was the enemy, true, but she trusted him instinctively not to injure a harmless old woman.

"Your pardon, sire," she whispered. "I thought you a ghost."

Thor stopped, looking down at her. "Not yet. Are you going in to pray?"

"Yes, sire."

"Then, if you can, comfort your mistress." He turned abruptly and left, his footsteps noiseless in spite of his size. Bettina stood looking after him, amazed. The English dog had pity for his victims, then. It was hard to believe. She went in, finding the Lady Aylena just kneeling at the prie-dieu herself. With a soundless sigh, she settled herself to wait. And to listen. Sins were always interesting.

Some minutes later Aylena crossed herself and rose, pale and tired from grief and a restless night.

Bettina, conscious of the order she'd received from the English dog, fluttered up from her seat.

"That lie you just confessed was no sin," she said firmly. "You were right to say we won and make your father happy as he died. In truth, our Lord Jesus must feel relieved. He would know, as we both know, that the Stewart is terrible company to have around when he's lost a battle."

Aylena's wet eyes opened wide, amazed. Then she smiled tremulously and came to put her arms around the old woman.

"Thank you, Bettina. You have given me back my memories. Both of us have heard the old lion roar in triumph, haven't we? And groan like a sick donkey in defeat. But he never gave up, and neither will I. Some day this castle will again belong to the Stewarts, and Ian will be the laird."

"I pray he will, my lady. I pray he will."

A cold, bright day met them as they marched out behind the oak coffin. Eight men carried the weight of body and oak and puffed under the load. A priest from the monastery on the Tweed River had ridden all night to say the service, and he, bundled in wool and humbly perched on a donkey, followed the coffin. Sir Roger led the black-clad mourners, escorting Aylena, and behind them came the other old knights, two of them piping a dirge. Then, walking alone, came Thor Rodancott, showing respect for a worthy opponent. After him, and watching him warily, came the servants of the castle, the serfs in the courtyard, the husbandmen from the fields.

The burying ground was on a knoll just outside the castle walls, and the men who dug the grave had worked all night, first lighting fires on the ground to melt the layer of frozen earth. It was a great task, for the space between the wall and the grave of the laird's wife was barely wide enough for the men to work. The laird had chosen to lie close to his wife.

Aylena clung to Sir Roger's arm and stared through her veil at the white stone that marked her mother's grave.

Alyse Belmain, Lady Stewart, beloved wife of Bruce, laird of the Highland Stewarts.

She wondered if the Norman would allow her to put up a matching stone for her father. She glanced at Thor and caught him looking at her with deep feeling in his gray eyes. She looked away, fighting the pang in her heart, the thickness in her throat. She didn't need his damnable pity. And by God, she didn't need his permission for a stone, either. She would put one on the Stewart's grave when she got the castle back.

The short ceremony over, the two factions—the conquered and the conquerors—gathered again in the great hall. The Stewart knights came to Aylena and kissed her hand, wishing her well. Sir Roger spoke for them all, which he usually did.

"We are off to Scotland, my lady, and will escort you there if you are willing."

Aylena, hidden within their circle, was able to speak freely. But she kept her voice low.

"Would that I could travel with you, Sir Roger. But the cache of my father's gold and the box of my mother's jewels remain hidden within the walls of the solar, and I am not willing to leave them for the English dogs to find. I looked early this morning, but they were not in the places where I sought them. I will have to look again."

Sir Roger nodded. "The work of the laird, I vow. He was forever changing the coffers from one hidden place to another. But they'll be in that wall, my lady. When they're found I believe the Baron Rodancott will recognize your ownership. He seems an honorable man, despite his Norman heritage."

Aylena looked at him doubtfully, but didn't argue. The old knight was seldom wrong about another man. But he didn't know that the baron had made different plans for her. Perhaps Lord Rodancott would allow her to pack, hand her the gold and jewels, and tell her she was welcome to leave, but she wouldn't chance it. She and Ian truly needed the legacy her father left her, and what was more, she needed to escape the baron's attentions.

"I cannot take the chance," she told Sir Roger. "That gold, those jewels, will undoubtedly be all we will ever have. Claiming my mother's English property is impossible now with an enemy on the English throne."

Sir Roger nodded, his face sad. "You may well be right, Aylena. Still, I hate to leave you here, unprotected."

"I will be fine. Harald will help me escape when the time is right. I must continue the hunt. If others find the money and jewels first, we may never see the coffers again. I will stay and make sure of Ian's future, and mine."

After the knights left, Aylena changed her heavy black wool for a house gown of pale linen and lace, clinging and soft. She packed clothing—as much as she could carry on the back of a horse—and hid it away. Then she sought out the Baron Rodancott. She found him in the storerooms outside the castle, deep in conversation with Stephen of Blaine, the seneschal. Stephen was proud to have been asked to stay on, to continue his task of instructing the servants and buying supplies. But his face fell when he saw Aylena, and he came to her quickly, his gray robes flattening against his bony legs. Aylena reassured him with a nod.

"I hope you will all stay," she said, reassuring him. "There is no reason to leave. The castle needs you." And *I* will need you here later, she thought, bolstering her resolve. Then she approached Thor, who seemed intent on the accounts the seneschal had shown him. He turned and looked down at her, his hard face and steely-gray eyes warming as he noted the low lacy neckline of her gown and the rise of her young breasts, as richly creamy as the Irish lace.

Aylena avoided his eyes. She had meant to interest him, to put him off guard, and it seemed she had done so. That was good. She needed his indulgence desperately. But she had been told often that her own feelings were easy to see in her eyes, and she was afraid to test her own discipline. She felt many things when she was near this man—fury, a desire for revenge, a hurt pride . . . and a pull toward him strong enough to be the black magic of the devil himself. She forced her thoughts to dwell on her plan, swallowed her pride, and asked for what she wanted—permission to enter her father's room and remain there alone.

"I understand, Lord Rodancott, that the castle is now yours," she said, "and the solar is the proper chamber for the new lord. But I wish to—to commune with the spirit of my father. I am not sure I know what he'd want me to do, and I must dream and listen to my heart. May I?"

Thor smiled, as if glad to see that she'd gentled. "Yes. I am comfortable where I am, and in truth I have heard of family members seeking advice from the souls of their parents or grandparents, and receiving it. I wish you good chance."

Aylena hurried away, exulting. Privacy is hard to find in a castle full of servants and nobles, but hers was now assured. The seneschal had heard. No one would open the door of the solar during the rest of the day and night. Not only that, but the secret passage known as the coward's way led from the solar to the bailey and thence outside the walls, through a hidden door in the back of the stable. Her father had shown it to her the day they had taken over the castle and made it their home. He had sneered at it, and named it.

"A coward's way," he had said. "One who would use it to run from danger is no man."

Well, she was no man. Once the jewels and gold were in her hands, she would take them and whatever else she could carry and be off to make sure Ian was all right, that he was happy where he was. He'd never known a mother, and he depended on her, though truthfully he had begun to chafe at her rules. What he needed was a stronger hand.

That night the Normans and Angevins held a riotous wake for the Stewart. He'd been the last of four Scottish rebels who refused to swear fealty to Henry II, and the Norman forces—except for those like Thor who wanted to be landholders—soon would head back to London and Normandy. In the meantime, they'd found the barrels of smoky whisky the Scots made, and they used it properly—drinking toasts to the laird's eventful life, his illustrious campaigns in the Scottish wars, his many victories, and his notorious temper, which some said had burst his old heart and killed him.

Somehow the news had been spread, and from the small town a few miles away singers came, and players. From a castle where the baron had submitted to Henry II, more knights came. The great hall was in a constant hubbub, packed with over a hundred men, drinking and singing, grabbing a crwth and twanging away. The servant girls, caught and kissed, felt and pinched and pulled down to sit wriggling on aroused loins, giggled and gabbled like geese.

Up in the solar with the heavy door closed, Aylena hunted with an ever-mounting fear. She was dressed ready to ride, her bundle set by the panel that opened to the coward's way. She knew loyal men in the stables would see her off. But she couldn't find the damnable coffers! She had found nothing but a handful of gold coins—a good sum, but only what was kept out for weekly use. And one other thing—the testament of her father's English aunt, tucked away for many years. The aunt had owned this castle and little else. Bruce Stewart had seen to it that his aunt had all she needed, and in return the childless Lady Celestine willed the castle to him. King Henry might pay no attention to that, but the praise of her father in the manuscript touched Aylena's sore heart. She stuffed it into her pocket as a memoir. She was now sure in her own mind that the English had found the coffers themselves and stolen them.

Then, as the noise below began to die away, she

seemed to hear a thunderous "Go!" in her father's voice. At once she stuffed the gold coins into her pocket, took her bundle and candle, and opened the panel. There, on the dusty wooden steps that led downward, were the missing coffers. Her father had put them there for whoever escaped from the Normans.

Thrilled, she knelt and opened them, dazzled by the gleam of gold in the candlelight, the sparkle of emeralds and diamonds. Her heart leaped up. Surely, with this wealth, she could make her way and Ian's. She put Lady Celestine's will into one of the coffers, closed them, and tucked them safe into the bundle. She stood, her heart pounding heavily. There would be dangers, and she thought with regret of her sword, rusting on the rocky heath where Thor had tossed it. But she had a dagger concealed at her waist, and she knew how to use it. One step at a time, she told herself, but quickly. Grasping the candle, she pulled the door shut behind her, hoisted the heavy bundle, and, with only the flickering candlelight to pierce the musty darkness, started down the winding steps.

Two yeomen, dozing in the stables, leaped to their feet as the door from the coward's way creaked open and Aylena appeared. The older man stepped forward and took the heavy bundle from her.

"Does the Norman know where you are, my lady?"

"Indeed not." She smiled in triumph and brushed cobwebs from her face. "He thinks me sound asleep in the solar. Quickly, Harald, saddle Star for me. I'm off to Scotland and young Ian."

"Tis as good as done!" The two yeomen rushed to obey, bringing out the spirited mare she usually rode, flinging a saddle on the sleek back, and tying the bundle on behind. Then they both grabbed the heavy panel on the wall behind them and dragged it open, exposing a corridor cut in the stone wall of the castle. It was horse head high, and black dark as it turned and curved, but Aylena knew how to traverse it. She lay forward on her mare's neck and coaxed her through. Harald followed close behind, muttering a prayer for her. He made sure she was out and unseen before he went back into the stable and shoved the rough panel back into place.

Outside, Aylena stayed close to the wall and waited for the sentry overhead to pace the parapet above her. She saw his shadow waver across the rocky ground, blur as he turned and started the other way. She quit the overhang of the walls then, and, keeping to the soft meadow grass, went quick and silent toward the north. She knew the stars that guided night travelers, for she and her father had often taken this heading on their way to Scotland. For that matter, the first leg of the trip was as familiar to her as the road to the nearest village. She'd be across the Tweed and into Scotland by dawn, and perhaps halfway to Leckie by this time tomorrow night.

Barring thieves. That small addition to her thoughts was chilling. But Star was fast. If she kept her senses alert, she should have no trouble. There were few highwaymen in the forests to the north, for there were few travelers who carried anything worth a fight. Thinking of the two coffers inside her bundle, one of gold and one of jewels, she pressed her heels into the mare's flanks and stroked her neck, comforted by her warmth and willingness.

"Run, my friend," she whispered. "We risk much."

The mare stretched into a fast canter that took them

along the familiar path and into dense forest. A young
moon was rising in the east, sailing higher, casting
shadows. They were safe in the forest now. Aylena
looked back, seeing the distant torches flaring along
the castle walls, the silhouette of the sentry still pac-
ing slowly back and forth. They were safe away. By
the sound of the revelry as she quitted the castle,
twould be noon before she was missed. She laughed
softly and settled her strong young body into the saddle, swaying to the mare's steady rhythm.

Hours later the Tweed was icy cold and touched
with the pink of early dawn. Aylena studied the edges
warily, afraid of her mare's unshod hooves slipping
on the ice, but the water in the shallow ford ran fast
toward the sea, too fast to freeze. They were across
and climbing the steep northern bank in good time,
then taking a minute or two to catch a breath. Off
again, finding the meshing paths that joined together
and became a road. In her mind Aylena's father rode
beside her, urging her on. She was tiring, yet she felt
she could go on forever. For Ian. Mother Mary, how
she missed Ian! And for the brave old lion . . . never
to be forgotten as long as she lived . . .

Fog rose with the sun. A thick gray fog that filled
the spaces between the trees, hung in every dip of the
road, circled the tops of the hills. Twice it cleared a
little and she saw over the edge of the road into a
deep valley. One misstep and she and Star would fall
. . . she slowed, straining her eyes to see, sensing
movement nearby, hearing a rustle . . . and then
they were on her, three of them.

They came leaping from behind trees, grabbing the
bridle, wresting the reins from her hands, jerking her
from the saddle. She shrieked with fear and anger,

but cut off the sound as soon as she became aware of it. She gathered her feet beneath her and sprang at the nearest man, a great hulking brute who was laughing with triumph. Her nails dug into his bearded face, she twisted her fingers tight in his dirty beard and shook him. He only laughed harder, reached up and snatched the gold chain and tiny jewel from her neck, slipping it into his pocket.

"His lordship will have a job of it with this one," he roared at the others. "She's stronger than he is! Here, Sims, hold 'er while I catch up with the horse." With a grunt of satisfaction a tall, muscular man dragged her backward into his arms. He smelled of rank sweat and filth, strong enough to make her gag as she struggled to get away.

"No bruises," the third man said calmly. Small and thin, with long, stringy hair, he leaned against a tree and watched the others. "Remember what his lordship said. We must bring her to him in perfect condition."

"I'll not bruise 'er apurpose," Sims said, grinning. "But she may show a blue spot or two if she keeps on bangin' my stiff prick with her soft backside. Not that I'm askin' her to stop . . ."

Aylena whirled and kicked his bulging loins, making him howl, then dove for a thicket, scrambling into it like a small animal pursued by dogs. A hand reached in the other side and gripped her hair, twisting the handful until tears ran down her cheeks, then pulled her through. She looked into the thin man's cold, reptilian eyes.

"That will be enough, my lady. There are three of us —why ask for broken bones?"

"Take what you want of my possessions," she burst

out, "and let me go! I have a duty to my young brother . . ."

"Oh, no, we've a fat purse comin' from a fancy lord if we bring you to him, and a promise of more money after. Hurry now, the man is waiting."

Panting, she looked around at the three of them. Stupid they might be, but she saw no chance of getting away. What noble would hire this filthy riffraff? Not William, certainly. But, whoever it was, he had to be better than these . . .

"Then loose me," she said sharply. "I will go with you."

The thin man spoke and they let her go at once. Taking the reins of her mare in one hand, she led her along the narrow road and around the next long bend. The sun was well up now, the fog lifting and wafting away into a sharp, winter blue sky. When they came to the top of the next roll she looked down into the dip of the road ahead and saw a horse and rider waiting there, the man vaguely familiar in a faded green velvet tunic trimmed with bands of scraggly fur. She stared, wondering, and then as the man saw them and smiled triumphantly, she knew.

"Bretinalle," she said slowly, and glanced at the thin man. "What in God's name does he want from me?"

Lashless eyes as cold as the day looked back at her. The man shrugged. "He said he's to marry you."

"He'll not!"

The big bearded man, slouching along behind, laughed heartily. "Don't fancy John, m'lady? What a shame, when he's so fond o' you. Why, he's been payin' us for three days to look for you on the road, fer fear you'd outrun him. Oh, well, once he spreads you a few times you'll be changin' your mind."

For the first time since she left the castle Aylena remembered the dagger concealed in her waistband. After a moment she raised a hand and rested it there beneath the cloak, as if she had a catch in her side. If John Bretinalle so much as touched her, she'd use it on him.

Bretinalle waited like a tawdry king for his hirelings to bring Aylena to him. Then, with a patronizing smile showing brown and decaying teeth, he dismounted from his horse.

"Welcome to Scotland, Lady Aylena."

Aylena saw the glow of triumph in the thin rat face, patches of red against the pallor of his cheeks. The idiot thought he'd done something clever!

"I was in Scotland for some time before your cutthroats attacked me," she said shortly. "Long enough for a nobleman less cowardly to find and greet me himself. Were you afraid I'd challenge you, John?"

He laughed and waved a hand, dismissing her words as a jest. "These men are much better at watching the roads than I, my lady, and less apt to feel badly if forced to kill a Stewart man-at-arms. I am surprised you rode alone."

Aylena stiffened. "As I will continue to ride, after you call off your three dogs."

"Oh, no, my dear. You will be with me, once we are wed. I have a priest waiting at Stowe Abbey, only a half day's ride from here."

Caught by surprise, Aylena burst into scornful laughter. "Are you mad? I'd no sooner marry you than one of these other thieves. Just stand back, Sir John, and let me ride away!" She whirled and

grasped the pommel of the mare's saddle, sprang up
to balance in one stirrup while she gathered her skirt
to swing the other leg over. Hands grabbed her waist
and pulled her down again. Gasping, she whirled and
looked into Bretinalle's grinning face. He laughed,
and his sour breath made her wince.

"Now, now, Aylena . . . you mustn't play the reluctant virgin. You'll soon be happily coupling with
me in our marriage bed. . . ." His hand swept up
from her waist, fastened around a firm, rounded
breast, and squeezed it. "I look forward to showing
you what women are for. . . ."

Fury straight from her Stewart temper burst like
fire in Aylena's mind, blotting out reason. Her fingers
closed on the shaft of her dagger, her arm flew up, the
dagger flashed once, twice, and then again in the cold
bright air. Staggering back, Bretinalle let out a thin
screech and collapsed on the ground, writhing in pain
and holding his hands over his face. Blood flowed between his fingers.

"She's blinded me! *Blinded* me! Kill her!"

Aylena dropped the dagger and leaped again to her
saddle. This time the hands that dragged her down
belonged to the skinny man with the cold eyes. Jerking her to her feet, he held her arms up behind her,
tensing his hold enough to hurt, but not enough to
make her scream. As impersonal as ever, he watched
the other two kneel beside the screaming Bretinalle
and pull his hands away from his face. It took some
time.

Staring down at the bloody mess, the heavy man
chuckled. "You're blinded by naught but your own
blood, Sir John. She cut you on forehead and cheek

but not in the eye. Shall we let her go, or do you still want the wench?''

"I want her killed! I want her body flung to the wolves!''

The thin man repressed a laugh. "For murder," he said, "we will be flayed if we are caught. The price is double.''

"But what I've already paid you has impoverished me," Bretinalle whined, no longer afraid of death. The cut on his forehead was shallow; the blood ran but slowly now. His cheek was puffing around the cuts there, but he could see. Rising, he gazed at Aylena with pure hate in his eyes.

"Never mind," he said, after thought. "I see it clear. I will be revenged a hundred times and you will be handsomely paid and royally amused. Don't you have a hut, Jock, up in the hills past the next village?''

The big man laughed. "It leaks a bit, but tis mine. Why?''

"Twill hold this virgin treasure," Bretinalle said, sneering at Aylena's angry gaze, "long enough to make you a month's pay and over. I know a man in the village who gives four times over the usual price to break a maidenhead. I'll send him to you. And there'll be many men coming afterward for his leavings, and yours. You, Sims"—he motioned to the muscular man—"help me onto my horse. I'll take along the mare to sell, for you'll not dare to let your whore escape.''

Aylena gasped. "You'll die for this, Bretinalle! Once the Stewarts hear of . . .''

The thin man let go of her arms and knocked her sprawling on the rocky path. "Quiet, woman!" He waited a moment and then nudged her with a foot. "Get up. No one is going to carry you."

Slowly, Aylena got to her feet. The blow had knocked some sense into her. She was numbly aware of the stupid mistake her temper led her into; if she'd gone along with Bretinalle to the Stowe Abbey all would have been well—the priest would have listened to her and protected her. Her temper and pride were stronger, she thought dismally, than her good judgment. She had failed her father, and even worse, she'd failed Ian. Now she must do what she could in the time left. These men would have to kill her in the end.

"I have gold," she said to the thin man, and pulled the bag of gold coins from a hidden pocket. "Take it and let me go."

He burst into delighted laughter, grabbing it out of her hand. "Indeed an we will take it, my lady. We counted on searching you well."

Bretinalle stepped forward hastily and pushed Aylena aside. "That money is mine, Tom. That and the mare."

Tom, the bag clenched in one hand, looked him in the eye. "The money is ours, to be shared amongst us. The mare you can easily sell—which we cannot."

Aylena looked from one angry face to the other, thinking hard. "Yes," she said, risking another blow, "let the coward Bretinalle have my mare. Someone in the village will recognize my saddle and clothes and report it to the clan. You men will not suffer, but he will."

Sims laughed, winking at Bretinalle. "I'll rid you of that problem, my lord. Tis a steep fall here at the edge of the road, and thick growth below. Shall I drop her belongings over?"

Bretinalle grumbled that he might have found some profit in the clothes, but his fear of discovery was clear. He nodded. Sims removed the saddle and bundle from the nervous mare and threw them over; they bounced once and disappeared in the underbrush. Staring down, Aylena wondered if she could find this spot again, and if she would be alive long enough to escape and try. The coffers were closed tightly . . . the gold and jewels safe until the day someone found them. Behind her, the three highwaymen argued about the shares of the gold they held, and Bretinalle tied the mare to his saddle. He rode up to Aylena before he left, his sneer more like a grimace of pain.

"Think of me, Aylena," he said, "when the man I send arrives for his virgin. No woman he's ever mounted will have him in her bed again—not even the whores."

"Strange," she said venomously, "I've heard the same of you."

An hour later, plodding along high in the deserted hills, Aylena's legs buckled with weariness. Jock laughed and threw her over his heavy shoulder.

"Never mind, my lady. Tis only a turn or two and we'll be there. We'll all have some little pleasures afore yer real work begins."

3

 It was near noon of the day following the burial when Thor knocked on the door of the solar, and receiving no answer, opened it and went in. A moment later, he came out and strode along the gallery to the chamber where Aylena usually slept. The door was ajar, the room empty. There were clothes strewn about, a lace-trimmed shift, a gathered underskirt, a woolen scarf. He cursed under his breath and left, running down the steps into the great hall.

"Philip! Go ask if anyone left the castle last night!"

Philip rose from a seat before the fire where he had been nursing a pounding head, and faced him. "Good God, Thor, there was a continual coming and going through those gates. Why? Is anything missing?"

Thor cursed again, luridly. "My woman is missing! Either she left of her own accord, or someone took her away, someone who had time and nerve enough to pack her clothing."

Philip forgot his aching head. *My woman?* Clearly,

Thor was in earnest about the lady. "What do you want me to do?"

"What I said, for God's sake. Find out if anyone knows she left, and in which direction."

"Twould be north, sire." Stephen, the seneschal, spoke out of his own fears for the Lady Aylena. Thor whirled and looked at him.

"Why?"

"Her tiring woman, Bettina, told me the Stewart made her promise to take care of her young brother. Ian is but six years old and the next laird of the Stewart clan. Lady Aylena's handmaid escaped with him while you were . . . ah, capturing Lady Aylena. They were headed north."

Thor was silent, staring at the old man. He had known part of that. He'd heard her promise, and she wasn't the kind to promise lightly. He should have known she'd be gone at the first chance.

"To the Tweed River?"

"And beyond, sire, if she's heading for the home of the clan. The old place is far north, past the southern Highlands and near a sea fishing village on Moray Firth."

"She'll be taken by highwaymen or drunken oafs long before that," Thor said harshly. "No woman is safe alone, certainly not one as beautiful as she. Philip! Find a man or two sober enough to ride and we'll find her. God willing, she'll still be alive and unharmed. . . ."

An hour later, provisioned for several days and with a mounted stable hand leading extra horses, four knights left the castle and started north. Besides quick and wiry Philip, Thor had chosen Nicholas and Martin Reeve, blond as Philip was dark, and heavy-mus-

cled. They were brothers and fought well together.
They were also more concerned than the others; they
had a sister, Martin Reeve said, very like the Lady
Aylena.

Riding ahead with Thor to look for tracks, Philip
was silent and intent, his dark eyes missing nothing.
Late in the day he found hoofprints he was sure were
made by her mare.

Martin Reeve took a long look at them and shook
his head doubtfully.

"Hoofprints are hoofprints," he said. "These are
well used paths we're on, and there are many prints,
both big and small."

"The mare she rides is small," Philip said, slowing
his horse to explain. "And the Lady Aylena is light.
The track is small, shallow, and unaccompanied, for
there are no fresh tracks that keep pace beside them."
He looked ahead, and laughed. "Our sire is convinced. We'd better catch up to him."

It grew dark, but still they went on, for that path
had turned into a road, and the road led straight into
the uplands and then to the Tweed. They came to the
rushing stream, cold and pure; they paused to drink
of it and let their horses drink, and went on hurriedly
in the light of a clouded moon.

At night the wilderness they came to was full of
odd-shaped shadows cast by the hills and the great
rocks that reared from the barren ground. But there
was no thought of stopping nor making a camp for a
rest. All had begun to fear for Aylena's life; all prayed
they would find her, tired and lost, on the other side
of the next hill. . . .

"There," Thor said, as they topped a rise, "I
thought I smelled smoke. There is a cob hut, and in it

a fire. Some sheepherder then, and he may have seen
her passing by. We'll ask, and find out how far we are
from the main road north." The words were calm
enough, but Thor's deep voice gave him away. He was
on a raw edge of fear, taut as a bow. He gave his big
horse his head, dropping down the side of the hill,
and the others scrambled after, seeing as they drew
nearer that there was smoke coming from the roof
hole and hearing men's voices inside, arguing hotly.

Thor raised a hand and stayed his men short of the
dim glow from the windows. "Two men," he said quietly, "maybe three, and none pleased with the others." There was a hoarse howl of pain from inside,
and the sound of a body crashing to the floor. Thor
grimaced.

"I'll take a look and ask a question or two and we'll
be on our way. You stay back, out of sight. We have no
time for brawling with drunken shepherds."

They nodded and stayed in the shadows as Thor
dismounted and went to the door. He knocked, and
there was a sudden silence. Then a rumbling growl
and heavy footsteps toward the door. It was flung
open, the dim opening filled with a bearded, barrel-
chested man in greasy leather tunic and woolen leggings. He stared up at Thor, his face changing from
bullish challenge to a look of caution.

"Are ye lost then, sire? Wanting direction? No noblemen live in this godforsaken valley." He waved an
arm, staggering a little. "Better go back to where ye
came from, m'lord. There's no honest men on the
road at night." From behind him came a stifled laugh.

"Don't raise a downy bird's feathers, Jock. Ask the
customer in." The man who spoke rose from a chair
at the fire and bowed elaborately, his stringy hair fall-

ing over his face. He stepped over a muscular man who lay unconscious at his feet. "Perhaps you'd like a mug of whisky to warm your cold belly, sir."

Thor was staring at the sparkle of a small gem that hung around Jock's thick neck, nearly hidden by the filthy beard. The delicate gold chain, flickering in the firelight, had caught Thor's gaze, and his face went steel hard as he stepped onto the stone floor of the hut, leaving the door open behind him. Looking down at Jock's suddenly wary face, Thor buried a hand in the greasy beard and held him still.

"Where did you get that jewel?"

From the dark rear of the room there was a strangled cry, hardly heard, hardly human. Thor tensed. Then he shoved Jock out of the way and strode toward the sound. Jock laughed with relief and grabbed a jug, tipping it up.

"So, ye've met our master and tis the fancy woman ye came for! Ye had only to say so, m'lord, an' come up wi' the siller."

The thin man had seen the change on Thor's face. He grabbed Jock's arm, spilling whisky down his soiled tunic. "Watch that wagging tongue! He's not the same sort as t'other one. . . ."

Thor no longer heard their voices through the drumming of blood in his ears. On a cot in a dark corner, flickering firelight shone on a slim woman with a wealth of golden hair, a slim, half-naked body. Her wrists and ankles were tied to the legs of the cot, her mouth was stuffed with a filthy rag. Wet blue eyes looked straight at him, begging for help. He felt a searing pain in his broad chest, a wild rage that surged through his huge body and demanded instant death for the men who put her there. He whirled, grabbed up a heavy axe leaning against the wall and threw it with all his strength.

"You *die!*" The axe whistled through the air, burying its thick blade in Jock's chest. Jock went down like a butchered ox, spraying blood, making no cry. The thin man stared, half paralyzed with fear, and inched toward the door.

"And you!" Thor's dagger leaped to his hand, he crouched and sprang, grasping the thin man's stringy hair. The dagger plunged into the narrow belly and swept up to the breastbone, opening a gushing wound as the man screamed and fell.

Rushing in, Philip grabbed Thor, forced his fingers to release the dagger, and shook him. Thor stared down at his friend numbly.

"Let me be. Drag these bodies outside." He looked down at the unconscious man. "Kill that one."

"Listen, Thor. I will help you. Is she here?"

"Yes." He got the word out, but behind it was an anguished fury. "Go, Philip. Give me back the knife, and bring my heavy cloak. Throw it inside. I will call you when she is ready to be seen."

Philip went, dragging the unconscious man along. Thor stood there another moment, wiped the dagger clean, and went back to the cot, his step heavy. Behind him he heard the Reeve brothers dragging out the bodies of the men he had killed. Kneeling, he cut the bonds that held Aylena's trembling body, cut away the gag, then got the cloak Philip tossed in and lifted her slight weight onto it. She made no sound, but her eyes never left his face. Wrapping her in the warm cloak, he covered her from neck to ankle. Then, with her bright hair hanging over his arm, he carried her to the dying fire and sat down, holding her close to his warmth, feeling deep, nearly silent sobs of relief rack her slender body.

Philip and the Reeve brothers came to the door when they saw Thor approach the fire with the woman in his arms. He nodded to them and they came in, bringing bread and meat, water and ale from their supplies. There were no chairs except the one Thor sat in, so they sat on the floor and passed the food around. In time Aylena drank a small amount of water from Thor's leathern water bag but refused the food. She said nothing, looked at no one. Silently she stared into the fire until her eyelids drooped and closed. Asleep, she still clung tightly to Thor.

The stable hand who led the extra horses came in with his own provisions and more firewood. He sat apart, uncomfortable with the nobility gathered in a filthy hut he himself would scorn. He had seen the bodies dragged outside; he saw the white face of the Lady Aylena and the way she clung to the arms that held her; he saw the deep anger in the hard eyes of the Norman. It was plain to him what had happened. The men the baron killed were lucky, he thought. Had the baron a colder nature, they would have been taken to the castle and flayed, screaming on a rack while their skin was nicked and pulled in strips from the raw meat, then another day or so of jeers and agony before they died.

"Was there a sign of the mare she rode?" Thor's voice was controlled when he finally spoke. Philip was quick to answer.

"No. We searched with light from a torch. There are no hoofprints but those of our horses. Someone brought her here on foot."

There was a silence. Finally Thor spoke again. "Perhaps I was hasty in telling you to kill the other man. I should have questioned him first."

Philip glanced at him and away. "He, ah, woke before I cut his throat, and I prevailed upon him to tell us what he knew. I'm afraid your quarry is deep in the Highlands by now, out of your reach."

Thor stared at him. "The man will have to be in hell to be out of my reach. Tell me his name if you know it."

Philip sighed. "Are you sure she's sleeping, Thor?"

Thor nodded. "Yes, thanks to the good Christ, she sleeps. Tell me."

"Remember the little rat-faced man who handed over the demesne with the starving serfs and absent knights?"

"Bretinalle!"

"Yes. This man described him perfectly. Bretinalle hired them to waylay her along the roads, but when they brought her to him she attacked him with a dagger she carried. He received one or two deep cuts on his right cheek before the others pulled her off. He was furious; they had to stop him from killing her. He cursed her and took her horse and belongings. He even robbed her pockets of her gold. When they asked for their pay, he told them to keep the woman. He said he would send men here who would give them money to lie with her."

There was a long silence as Thor wrestled with his rage. Then the woman in his arms moaned in her sleep and trembled, turning her pale face into the curve of his strong neck. He looked down at the bright tangle of hair, his face showing the struggle going on inside of him.

"I make this vow," he said after a long moment. "By my honor as a knight, I will kill John Bretinalle for what he has done. This is my chosen woman, and I will avenge her."

4

Aylena woke to faint morning light, to warmth, to a breathing presence and a soft beard brushing against her forehead. She knew at once where she was and who he was. She clutched the cloak close and stared at the cluttered room. She saw Philip, stretched out in front of the embers of the fire and beginning to move; she saw two large yellow-haired men and a stable hand who had belonged to her father, all fast asleep. Moving, she felt Thor's arms tighten and yielded to them, glad for the security. Then she turned in the arms and looked up. He was awake, and he looked tired but clean and clear-eyed, his black beard glistening. He had saved her; she remembered a fight, a huge axe, knives, blood . . . she shut her eyes and pushed the memory away. It didn't bear thinking about. She spoke, opening her eyes and gazing into his.

"I well know I owe you my life, my lord. Those men . . . those horrible men . . . so dirty and rough. And . . ." She choked, and caught back a sob. "Oh, dear Mary, they *touched* me . . . and I wanted to die."

He caressed her hair slowly, threading fingers through the snarls, coaxing them out. "You will not die, my lady." His voice was sure. "You will live long and happy, and all of this will be forgotten." She had lain in his arms all night long and he had come to terms with what he felt. What had happened to her would ruin a woman for most men, but this woman was his. He knew that now; he knew nothing would change it. Her despoilers were dead; there would be no others, and, passing strange for a man who thought himself invulnerable to women, he knew there would be no others for him, either.

Around them the men were stirring, sitting up, carefully not looking her way. They got to their feet and went outside, giving them privacy. For a moment Aylena wished she could turn and press her face into Thor's warm neck and breathe in his scent, compounded of man, leather, and wool, and safe harbor. She thought how easy it would be to give in to him, to take his protection. To hide behind him . . . then she thought of what she still must do. She had promised her father, and she had lost all; she had failed badly; now she must plan again for her trip. But not today. Today she would rest . . . and tell Thor Rodancott how thankful she was and how grateful to him, her enemy. She stood, and wrapped his cloak tighter around her. "I want to leave here, please."

There were pieces of her clothing thrown down beside the cot, trampled and torn, bloody from the scratches she'd made on the men who removed them. Cursing softly, Thor kicked them under the cot. He went outside, coming back with a clean woolen tunic from his bundle and a small leather slipper one of the Reeve brothers had found. Seeing it, Aylena looked for its mate and found it in a clutter of trash near the door.

"When you are dressed," Thor said, "the hut will be burned with the bodies inside. Leave nothing of value."

Aylena pulled off her stained and torn shift and dressed hurriedly, donning the oversize tunic and using a leather thong she found on the floor to tie it in great folds around her waist. Over that the cloak, wrapped double around her, the hood pulled up over her hair. The slippers on, she opened the door and stepped out, a walking bundle. Thor came to her on his heavy war-horse, reaching down and pulling her up before him in the big saddle, turning the horse and starting away at once, up the slant of hill toward the south.

"You will be warmer with me," he said when she said that she could ride one of the spare horses they'd brought. "Nor will your light weight be felt by my Frere d'Armes. Besides, there is no extra saddle."

"Still, I could . . ."

"No."

She was quiet, biting her lip. He was harsher now, but he had reason. They were in the open; they were traveling enemy ground. He was a man and a warrior, responsible for her. And for his men. She turned, dislodging the overlarge hood, and craned her neck to see if the others were behind them. They were disappearing into the hut below, dragging the last of the bodies. A curl of smoke came from the doorway as they came out.

Thor's gloved hand touched her hair, turned her

face forward, and replaced the hood, kicking his war-horse into a rocking canter. "Think no more of what's past," he said. "Tis over and done."

She looked ahead, firming her resolve. As the daughter of the Stewart she must kill John Bretinalle for what he had done to her. That she would do, no matter how long it might take to find him. But otherwise, the Norman was right. What she had lost was lost; what she had promised to do was all that mattered. That, and the strange debt she owed—would always owe—to the Norman enemy who hunted for and found her. It was truly odd, she thought, that the instant she had heard his voice at the door she knew he would save her and the nightmare would be over. And he the same great, murdering beast of a man she had hated two days ago!

Bettina cried over her, but even while crying she was ordering up a bath, telling a serf to bring wood and start a fire in the Lady Aylena's chamber. Helping her out of the enormous tunic and into the tub, Bettina was scandalized.

"An' the robbers took even your shift and left you naked! Oh, my lady, ye could have died there in the uplands an' never be found. Thank God, thank God for His mercy in guiding our sire!"

"Hush, Bettina. My head is throbbing. But you have it right—Baron Rodancott deserves praise and gratitude from me, and I deserve to be called a fool. I should have taken at least two or three of our own men-at-arms, and I will when I start out again."

Soaping her hair, Bettina frowned. "He'll not let ye go again, I vow. And ye have no gold. Ye took it all along, and now the thieves are rich."

No thieves had gained her parents' gold and jewels, but Aylena did not say that to gossipy Bettina. Even a rumor of hidden treasure would send men of all kinds to comb through the hills. Unfortunately, she had no real idea herself where to start looking on the long, steep slopes of the hills. She sighed and nodded.

"There's enough of the Stewart belongings here to sell and use the money to fulfill the promise I made to my father."

"But, what if the lad wants to stay where he is?"

Stricken, Aylena stared at the old woman. It was possible. She thought of the desolate sea fishing village there near the mouth of the Moray Firth; she thought of the biting cold wind and the hard life, the strong men who went out in their little boats to wrest a cruelly hard living from the North Sea. No woman was ever content there, but it surely appealed to young, hero-worshipping boys. And the men would well nigh worship Ian, too, as heir to the Stewart laird. His small head could be turned. . . .

"Damnation!" she said angrily, standing up to be rinsed. "It would be just like Ian to dig in his heels and refuse to leave! Then, I reckon, I'd be forced to stay, too."

Bettina handed her a towel. "Stay or leave, tis still in the time to come. Now, stand by the fire and dry y'self. I've a potion to mix an' tis one that requires great care." She left the room and Aylena heard her clattering down the steps. Alone, her mind flew to Thor Rodancott. She told herself she kept thinking of him and wanting to see him because she hadn't thanked him properly and wanted to make sure he knew how grateful she was—even to an enemy. Yes, they were enemies, but, as a man and a Christian knight, he had rescued a helpless woman in mortal danger.

Putting on her clothes, she dreamed childishly of repaying the debt by charging into a battle and rescuing him. Then a fragment of memory appeared like a vision in her mind. Thor would never need rescuing. He had thrown that heavy axe as if it weighed no more than a knife. She saw the axe flash through the air and bury itself in Jock's chest, spraying blood. Trembling, she willed the scene away.

She wanted so much to forget. But she'd learned her own feelings in a horrifying way. She felt, she was unlikely to ever forget the shame she'd felt nor ever think herself clean and invulnerable again. She sat down, remembering Thor's haunted eyes as he carried her to the chair last night. . . .

"There, now," Bettina said, coming in again. "Here is the potion. Ye'll not like the taste, nor the cramps in your belly that follow, but ye'll live through it. I've made many a sad woman smile again with this. . . ." She handed the steaming mug to Aylena. "Drink it down, m'lady. You need it all, though the taste would run a dog off."

Aylena sniffed cautiously, pulled a face, and then took a generous mouthful. In the same instant she shot up from her chair and spewed it out with force, spraying it halfway across the room. She threw the mug after it, hard enough to shatter it against the wall.

"By God's bones, you old witch, you gave me poison!" Coughing and gagging, she grabbed a bucket that held a bit of water intended for the tub and up-ended it, sucking the water into her mouth, spitting again, this time in the fire.

Bettina looked at her with admiration in her eyes. "While you live, lass, our beloved laird will never die. He spoke through your lips just then. But still you must drink the potion, or shame yourself and your father's name."

"Ha! It's gone!"

"I will make more. Ye canna refuse, once you think it over. The laird would whirl in his grave if ye bore a babe from the seed of thieves an' murderers."

Aylena turned slowly to look at her. "Who said I would?"

Bettina stared. "Why, no one! But the sire said to make the potion that comes from the blackened heads of rye, an' give it to ye."

Aylena turned and smashed her doubled fists against the paneled wall, then bowed her head and leaned against it, groaning. She knew what that potion was for. All women did. It was whispered about from one to another. She whirled back, red with rage, to face Bettina.

"Damn him! He believes those men took my virginity on that filthy cot! Not one of those animals tried me!"

Bettina stared, and Aylena saw disbelief in her old eyes. "But . . . are ye certain?"

Aylena laughed harshly. "Could I forget such a thing? Oh, Bettina, everyone will believe I was used by those filthy men! But I will tell you the truth of all that happened. I was traveling alone and making good speed when I was waylaid by thieves and murderers hired by that coward John Bretinalle. I attacked John and gave the damned weakling a good cut or two on his ugly face. Then he gave me to the men instead of their pay! I was dragged down a rocky hill and into the filthiest hut I ever saw. The oafs stripped me near naked, damn them! Then I was tied to a stinking cot and told that men would come to pleasure themselves on my body."

She turned away from Bettina's white face, her voice trembling as the memories came. "I would have done whatever I could to stop the men, but thank God Thor Rodancott found me first and killed the men who had tied me down. I owe him my life; I owe him eternal gratitude. But I do wish he'd asked me if I'd been taken by any man before he began telling the story to others."

"He has told only me," Bettina said quickly, "and that after he swore me to silence." She was looking at Aylena doubtfully. "He said there were three men there with you, and you half naked and helpless to stop them from using you." She hesitated. "Don't blame the sire, my lady. I would have thought the same, and so must anyone who saw you there with them."

Aylena's heart burned within her. She knew how men felt about women who were foolish enough to let themselves be raped. She'd heard them speak of such women as spoiled for life, as fools, as loose women, as unfit to marry a decent man. Not that she would dream of marrying Thor, but she wanted his respect desperately. Silent now, she went to a window and looked out. The night was coming on apace, darkening and chilling the courtyard below, as in her chest her heart darkened and grew cold. In a moment she spoke again, slowly forcing words out.

"They did shame me, Bettina, for they looked at my body and touched me with their filthy hands. One man tried to take me, but the others stopped him and told him to wait, because the man who was to come first to the hut was a rich man who would pay four times over for a true virgin. So they panted like dogs and waited their turns." She glanced back, and in the glance was a bitter satisfaction. "Their forebearance was not rewarded. Our sire killed them as quickly as you could swat a fly."

"But thanks be to God they had not mated with you! T'will be a great pleasure to tell our sire that."

"No! He'll not be told unless he asks me," Aylena said. Her voice turned sharp. "He'd likely not believe it in any case. Tell him nothing. My body is not his concern."

"Did you tell him John Bretinalle was the cause of it?"

Aylena shook her head. "I did not," she answered, her voice tight, "nor will you. When I lay there, helpless, I made a promise to myself. I promised that if I lived, I'd find Bretinalle and make him suffer worse before he dies."

"Our sire would do that for you, my lady."

"I know. But he kills in an instant. I want Bretinalle to beg for mercy and be refused."

That evening Aylena sat at the high table with the Baron Rodancott and as many of his knights as there was room for. The others waited a turn. She ate sparingly of venison, stewed dried fruit, and fresh bread. She drank a little wine, but she was careful not to take enough to loosen her tongue. She was very quiet and excused herself early.

Thor rose when she rose and followed her up the steps. None of the men below raised their heads to watch, though Bettina did, and two of the maids. Coloring, Aylena stopped and turned when they reached the gallery. She was wearing a long, narrow gown of light green silk, covered with a deep-cut sleeveless mantle of dark green velvet. The cascade of red-gold hair that fell to her shoulders was topped with a cap of silk net, sewn with pearls. She had taken a great deal of trouble with her appearance tonight. No one was to be sorry for her; no one must think her shamed.

"I am retiring, sire." Her tone was cool, though she still burned inside.

Thor nodded, his gaze puzzled and questioning. "I would speak with you, my lady. Will you come to the solar?"

She bent her head in a tiny nod and when he stood back she preceded him to the door. He followed her in and shut the door behind him. As always a fire flickered in the grate, the bed on the dais was covered with furs. There were two chairs near the hearth, and she took one, sinking into it as if to put more distance between them. Thor stood with his back to the flames, his hands clasped behind him. Even in her anger Aylena noted the flowing symmetry of his big body, the way his broad shoulders sloped into powerful arms, the wide chest narrowed into a taut waist and belly. His muscular legs were encased in dark chausses and gartered in gold. Over a shirt of cream wool he wore a tunic of dark blue velvet that ended halfway down his thighs. It was trimmed in bands of gold, matching the cross-garters. Even with that old scar on one cheek he was handsome, his black hair and beard dramatic against ruddy skin and light gray eyes. Eyes that looked at her with warmth and gentleness . . . and tonight with doubt.

She looked away, her throat tightening, ashamed of

her rush of desire. He'd let his loose tongue accuse
her of being used by those dirty men, and yet her body
yearned toward him, wanted his touch. She hated her
weakness. She also regretted her debt of gratitude,
and yet she could not deny it. She swallowed bitterness and spoke.

"You wished to speak to me, my lord? I am ready to
listen."

"I am wondering if I should," Thor answered. "You
seem different; perhaps you wish to be alone."

An angry retort sprang to her lips and was swallowed. "At times I prefer to keep my thoughts to myself, sire. But say what you want to say."

He didn't hesitate this time. "I want you to tell me
when you plan to leave the castle and allow me to
accompany you."

Her hands clasped together in her lap. "You will
deny me the freedom to go alone?"

Thor turned and looked into the fire, his jaw set.
"Was the last time so pleasant you want to repeat it?"

Aylena jumped up from the chair, too angry to sit
still. "You dare to taunt me? First you spread stories
about filthy men lying with me, now you put me under guard, as if you believe me witless enough to repeat my stupidity! What *do* you want? A shamed
woman creeping around in the shadows?"

He whirled and took her, pulling her close against
his chest, knowing he held her too tightly, but unable
to stop. One big hand grasped the thick golden hair at
the back of her head, holding her still.

"I want *you*, Aylena. Look at me; you'll find truth in
my eyes. I intend to have you, no matter how long it
takes."

"Oh, God . . . let me go. We can't—"

His mouth swallowed the rest of her words, his hard kiss gentling as she yielded, his tongue soothing her bruised lips.

"Ah, my lovely," he whispered, his deep voice shaken. "My exquisite rose . . . your mouth is like sweet wine to me. . . ."

She couldn't resist. The taste of him within the soft beard was the very essence of this man she wanted; the scent of his skin dizzied her, made her weak. Her body softened and clung to his hard strength. She drew closer, her arms slid around his shoulders, her fingers inched up and wove themselves into his thick hair, holding him, trembling as he deepened the kiss. She closed her eyes and felt her swelling heart beat like a drum against his chest.

Finally he drew away, still cupping the back of her head in his palm, and saw the beautiful, dreaming face, lips parted in surrender to him, eyes closed. His own eyes were wet with emotion as he kissed her again, gently.

"I thank a generous God," he whispered against her lips. "You want me, too."

She opened her eyes and turned away, shaken because he was right. She did want him. She *needed* him, like air, like food and water. She couldn't misunderstand her feelings; the tormenting rush of heat clamored for him. How strong passion was!

"No matter," she got out. "I—I have no time for such dalliance. I must keep the promises I've made."

He thought of his vow to kill John Bretinalle. He thought of his fighting men, already growing restive without battles or tournaments. They should be led back to London and dispersed before they started a war themselves. He sighed.

"And I the same. But we'll be together."

She stood straighter, her head up, her tumbled red-gold hair like a bright flower on the slim green stem of her gown. "No! There are places I must go alone, my lord. Oh, not truly alone—I could take my father's men and they would be safe. But for you—a king's man—to go into Scotland . . ."

"I am not easy to kill." He came close, clasping her slender shoulders in his wide palms, looking down into her face. "Where you go, my Lady Aylena, I go also. We will discover together whether your brother is thriving."

But a few days later everything was changed. One of the most important problems resolved itself, at least for a time. Margit arrived from Scotland, accompanied by an uncle, Malcolm of Corvey. Aylena embraced her and led her up the steps to her room, leaving Malcolm to be settled by the seneschal, Stephen. In the chamber Aylena asked if all was well with Ian. Margit's smiles answered her.

"The lad is with your father's brother William and his lady wife, and lording it over the whole village. He misses you very much, but he wants to stay in Leckie." She laughed. "The poor lad asked William if he could order you to come to him. Will told him it might work better if he waited until he grew up."

Aylena hugged her again, laughing. "So then he's happy and safe inside our own clan. Do you stay with me?"

"I do." Margit's fine dark eyes were warm. "Even were Leckie my choice, which it is not, I would still come back to you. I am lucky indeed you haven't yet left for England."

"Left for England?"

"Surely now that you've lost your home here to the baron, you'll go to London and claim your mother's legacy. Tis said the Belmain demense is a fine and profitable place."

"With an enemy on the throne, who would listen to me?"

"Perhaps the enemy will be grateful to the daughter of the Stewart clan. When this castle fell without a battle, the others put away their weapons and swore fealty. Besides, I have heard that the Norman baron here has rescued you from highwaymen and brought you back here as an honored guest. It is even whispered that the two of you are more than friendly."

"Gracious Mary! You've been here an hour, and gossip like that found your ears?"

Margit laughed again. "Would that we had lances that flew as fast . . ." She paused, watching Aylena's shifting eyes, and added slyly, ". . . and as true to the mark."

Aylena stiffened. "Nonsense. A king's man, and a Norman, could be only an enemy, Margit. I do admit I owe him a great deal of gratitude, but that is all."

"Since it is gratitude for your life, I should think it enough. There are those among the men-at-arms who think him the greatest warrior in all of Britain."

"I agree," Aylena said immediately. "There could be no better."

"They say," Margit continued, glancing at her, "he is also a man few women could resist. Is he handsome, my lady?"

"He is . . . not ugly, as I recall. Cease this chattering, Margit. You shall see him soon enough yourself."

"Yes, my lady. Shall I brush your hair?"

"Indeed." Falling by habit into Margit's expert hands, Aylena sat down and handed her the brush. "But if you must gossip, gossip about someone else. I am weary of hearing my own name coupled with scandal." Her tone was bored, lightly humorous, but inside, where she had walled in her hurt and overwhelming shame, she felt the wall crack and winced at what she found there. Memory roared up like a fire and seared her pride. Those filthy hands . . . the drunken laughter . . .

In late afternoon Aylena sought out Thor. She came quietly to the open door of the solar and saw him inside, seated in one of the deep window embrasures. She could see Stephen's accounts spread out before him for study. The embrasure boasted a table and bench where her father had often sat to read, for the sunlight pouring in gave good light. Now it lighted Thor's intent face, giving it a golden tint, and struck dark gleams from his thick hair and close-clipped beard. Thinking of that firm mouth on hers the other night, she felt her pulse quicken; a warmth spread through her. She looked away, angry at herself. What a fool she was to dream about a Norman, one who thought her already sullied and ruined by common thieves and murderers. She hurried to speak.

"May I come in, my lord?"

He looked up, then sprang to his feet, shoving the papers aside. He came to her, smiling, and took her hand. "Tis a pleasure, Aylena. Come, sit with me."

She allowed him to lead her to a chair at the fire. Seated, she waited while he drew up another chair and sat beside her, close enough to touch, like great friends or new lovers. He took her hand, and she let him, marveling at how gently he held it, how warm his hand was.

"Is there something you need, my lady?"

"Yes. I plan a trip to plead my rights before the English king. I hope you'll allow me to sell some of the sheep for the money needed and to take four or five of my father's men along as guards." She was watching him as she spoke, and she saw his thoughts chase across his face. Mostly, she thought, he is pleased. Why? Because I asked his permission? Irritated, she withdrew her hand from his. "If my request to the king is granted, there will be money to repay you for the sheep. And you need not worry about my safety if my father's men are with me."

Thor laughed. "There will be no need for them, my lady. I must take my men back to London, and no one will attack an army. I heard your maid had returned. She must have brought you good news of the lad."

"She did. Ian is safe and content to stay." She hesitated, wishing he'd fallen in with her own plan, yet knowing she'd be safe indeed, she and Margit, with him and his fighting men. "In time he may tire of the sea fishing village where our clan rules. Until then, he's under their protection."

"Then we may leave as soon as you want."

"After I sell the sheep."

"You need not. I have money enough for us both."

"I want money in my hand," Aylena said, staring at the fire. "I will not go depending on you for every obole." She looked up, the fire mirrored in her eyes. "Those sheep are more mine than yours, my lord. I helped to birth them before you ever left Normandy."

He frowned, displeased by her arguing. "And

whose sheep were they when your father stormed the castle and threw out the English who lived here?"

A small, sarcastic smile touched her curved lips. "That question will be answered if your King Henry is willing to listen to me. If not, why, then I cannot pay you." She stood up and moved gracefully toward the door. "Til evening, then."

"Wait." He came to her, uncertain but not ready to let her leave. "Where would you find buyers for sheep at this time of year?"

"At Tynemouth, where the Tyne River meets the sea. There are always traders there, and most Northumbrian men have a taste for mutton."

He stood still and silent, thinking. She was keeping something from him, something she hoped would bring her good fortune when she spoke to King Henry. What it was he didn't know. What he did know was his own firm intention, which was that from now on he would keep her with him and out of harm.

"I came to Northumbria by another way, but if this Tynemouth is truly a market with traders, I'd like to see it. In any event, I will give you the sheep, and go with you when you sell them."

"Thank you!" This time she gave him a cool smile, tinged with surprise. "Then we will be ready when you decide to start the trip. I will tell Margit to see to our packing."

5

 The trip to Tynemouth was slowed by
two wagons, one to carry the sheep, the
other for baggage and small luxuries required by women. Still the party made
good time, and on the evening of the
second day came to a stop on the wild, wind-ham-
mered coast of the North Sea.

Forced to find shelter from the wind and icy spray,
they took over an abandoned Norman castle, built in
the time of William the Conqueror. The outer walls of
the castle were of stone, the inside rooms and floors
of wood, much of it rotted away. The old castle, built
on a sheer cliff, overlooked the sea. Far to the north
were the misty shapes of the fabled Farne Islands,
touched with gold by the westering sun.

Aylena, her hood pushed back, her cloak rippling in
the wind, had come out to stand alone at the edge of
the cliff, breathing in the fresh salt air and watching
the waves crashing on the rocks below. She'd stopped
here as a child on trips with her father and stayed in
the same rough shelter. But there had been peace
then, and quiet. This time she left the noise and smoke

of the cooking fires, the harsh babble of raised voices, to breathe fresh air and remember the past.

Here strong tides carved living rock into intricate patterns, hollowed it out in swirls of changing colors, blues and lavender, dark reds and yellows that shone even in the shadow of the cliff. Her father had stood on this point and told her the story of the most cele-brated of all the Farne Islands, where innocent Scot-tish monks were slain by raiding Vikings centuries ago. The Stewart had always said a prayer for the souls of the monks, and, remembering that, Aylena bowed her head to do as he had done.

Thor had also come from the crumbling stone shel-ter, to watch over her. He knew she was strong—for a woman. She had ridden with him at the head of the column for two hard days, though her maid, Margit, had given up her horse and taken to the rumbling baggage cart, saying she was exhausted. Thor's in-stinct sensed danger for the daughter of the Stewart laird, and now, in a place strange to him, he was un-easy when Aylena was out of his sight. He moved closer, drawn by the graceful figure, the bowed head with the thick braid of golden hair glistening in the sunset light. Aylena heard the scrape of his boot through the rubble of rock, turned, and saw him. The sight of him made her heart leap. She turned back, looking down.

"Good evening, my lord," she said politely. "We've come a long way. Tomorrow night we may well be in Tynemouth."

Her shy look tempted Thor, who fought down an impulse to pull her into his arms. Her lips, soft and parted, brought an instant surge of hot desire to swell his loins. He forced his hungry gaze away and stared north at the islands, hazy now in the deepening shade. Soon, he thought. Soon I must have her. Yet he knew he would wait until she felt the same.

"We will, if all goes well."

"What can go wrong?"

He started to say he'd felt a sense of impending trouble during the hours since noon today. But he'd seen nothing, heard nothing except once a faint, far-off call and later a rattling stone that became dislodged from one of the peaks they'd passed. The call could have been from one shepherd to another, and an animal might have dislodged the stone. Besides, he didn't want to frighten her. He put a hand on her shoulder, not to emphasize a point, only because his desire to touch her was irresistible.

"Nothing, unless you wander away alone. Come back to the fires and the company."

She obeyed, turning from the sight of the tumbling seas and changing colors, but unwillingly. She wanted space and time, away from the noise and confusion of half a hundred men, their cups reaching deep in the ale barrels by now and the voices growing aggressive. Loud laughter and boasting came from the ancient courtyard as they entered. Aylena started to protest but let her words die away as they entered the gates, noting that the sight of Thor brought the noise down.

Thor took her directly to Margit, who was standing near a cooking fire and flirting with one of the Stewart men-at-arms who had come along on the trip. Margit looked up and flinched at the expression on Thor's face.

"You will accompany your mistress when she leaves the company," Thor said evenly, "and remain with her until she returns. That is your only duty. Remember it, or suffer."

"Yes, sire." Margit's reply came quickly. "I won't forget." She came to Aylena's side as Thor turned and left. "Don't slip away from me again, my lady. God knows what that Norman devil will do to me. Even his men fear him."

Aylena opened her mouth and suddenly shut it again. She had been about to defend the Norman devil. "Maybe it's well that they do," she said instead. "Otherwise we'd have no peace. The mercenaries would quarrel amongst themselves all night."

Margit grimaced. "Would that we were back at Stewart Castle and none of this had happened. Full summer will come before we see home again, if ever."

"If ever? Why do you say that?"

"Because his knights have said in my hearing that the Stewart castle was the reason Thor Rodancott agreed to run the rebel Scots out of England's Northumbria. Tis his prize."

"Indeed. He took possession. But things may change when we stand in the king's court."

"The knights said," Margit uttered each word slowly and clearly, "that the king swore to grant Rodancott the Stewart castle and half the plunder from the rest. They also say that Rodancott was favored because the king must have a strong leader in Northumbria."

Aylena shook her head. "No more. Without my father's leadership Scotland is no threat. King Malcolm will never be a real leader. The clans will break into quarreling groups and hold their silly wars amongst themselves."

Margit laughed. "True. Malcolm the Maiden will

forever hide from trouble. It takes a man with an iron
fist and a silver tongue to knit the Scots together and
make them like it. The laird of the Stewarts was that
man. We must pray for another to come along. Ah,
look. Good hot soup and the flat bread is fresh baked.
Come, we must eat. Tomorrow is another hard ride."

Pushing into the same chill wind the next morning,
the party rode past sandy bays and rock on the east
and grassy flats on the west that edged down close to
the beaches. Fresh-shorn sheep grazed there, and out
in the thrashing waves seabirds screeched and dived.
Wrapped in their cloaks, the travelers yawned and
shivered in their saddles, peering through the early
morning fog. Today Thor again rode with Aylena beside him, but changed the long straggle of his knights
into a tight column, so they all stayed in sight. Philip
of Anjou looked at him wonderingly, and then
searched the rolling hills and sharp, looming cliffs
ahead.

"I see," he said softly. "If they come, this would be
their choice spot." He glanced past Thor's impassive
face and saw the Lady Aylena and her maid deep in
conversation. "What of them?"

"Men have been told to surround them."

Philip nodded. The women were small, the mares
too, compared with the huge war-horses. Surrounded, they'd be hard to hit even with a well-
thrown lance. "A good plan," he said, his voice still
low, "though that firebrand of yours might again grab
a sword for herself."

They were coming up on one of the flats where
shaggy cattle cropped the sparse grass. Wild as hares,
two bulls dashed away from the war-horses, herding

their cows before them, and whirled, lowering their
horns and bellowing a warning. Their fighting spirit
aroused, the war-horses rose on their hind legs and
pawed the air, whistling a challenge. Both mares
squealed, rearing and fighting the reins, and rushed
to safety behind the great stallions.

"Coward," Aylena said, and pulled her mare's head
around. "Face the enemy, don't run from him. Go!"
She kicked the mare's flanks to get her started, then
realized that knights had crowded around her and
Margit, leaving no path.

"Make way," she called out, "make way! Those
bulls will break and run—" She gasped and was silent, staring wide-eyed at bearded men on shaggy
horses pouring from a hidden passage in the cliff,
yelling hoarse threats. Their lances were poised to
throw; battle-axes swung from their rough saddles. A
roar went up from the Norman knights as they raised
their shields and brandished their broadswords,
charging the attackers. Aylena whirled and called to
Margit.

"They're Scots! They must think the Normans have
taken us prisoners!"

Margit nodded, white-faced and frightened as a
lance flew overhead. Her lips moved, but the clash of
battle covered her words. Pale and sweating with
fear, she pressed through to Aylena's side and shouted
into her ear. "Should we try to—to join the Scots? To
give them our support?"

"How?" Aylena made a wide, hopeless gesture at
the jostling, swinging circle of mail-clad knights surrounding them, and then gasped again as she saw a
white-bearded old Scot go down, bloody and screaming as he fell from his stocky horse. "They are mad,"

she cried out, and tried to push through the wall of horses and men. "They'll all be killed!"

Margit grabbed her arm, jerking her back. "You'll be the one killed if you get between them. Look! Tis soon over . . . the ones who are left are breaking away and running. The Norman was ready for them, and the attack failed."

Aylena looked. It was true. The Scots were disappearing into the rocky cliffs as fast as they'd come out, except for three who had fallen. Then, as the Normans pursued the deserters, the crowd around her and Margit eased and allowed her to break through. She rode out to the first Scot who she'd seen fall, and slipped from her horse to kneel beside him. He was very old; a once red beard was nearly white now, his face furrowed with deep wrinkles. There was something familiar about him, though she couldn't name him. But she knew at once that he was dying, that there was nothing she could do except to comfort him or pray for his soul. She took his hand in both of hers and his eyes opened and stared up at her.

"Have you words you want your family to hear?" she asked gently. "I will see that they do—" She jerked back, amazed, as the old man spat at her face.

"Traitor!" he panted. "Lying whore! Die and go to hell!" His hand fumbled at his belt, trying vainly to loose the dagger couched there. "God give me strength to kill . . ."

A booted foot came down on the old man's wrist, a gloved hand grasped Aylena's arm and lifted her to her feet.

"Mount your horse," Thor said quietly, "and stay in the saddle. Your life is in danger."

Aylena stared at him. "But *why*?" she burst forth.

"I have done nothing against the Scots, nor would I. They are my people." She glanced down and tears filled her eyes as she saw the old man had died. "Fergus," she said, remembering the name at last. "Fergus Cline. He was a friend of my father's. . . . How could he believe I would betray the Scots?"

Thor shrugged and took her arm, drawing her away and toward her horse. Grasping the nervous mare's bridle in one hand, he held her still while Aylena mounted. Then he answered. "You may have an enemy who has told a lying tale."

Bretinalle. At once, Aylena was sure of her enemy. That miserable rat would do anything, say anything to discredit her. He wanted her dead and powerless. And, had it not been for Thor Rodancott, she would be. As dead as old Fergus Cline, a good man destroyed by a coward's lie. She wiped her eyes and looked at Thor's impassive face.

"I thank you again for saving my life, Sir Thor. I owe you much. I hope in time I can repay you."

A sudden glint appeared in the clear gray eyes; the black beard split and revealed strong white teeth in a quick smile.

"I'll make sure you find a chance, Lady Aylena." He stepped back and took the reins of his own horse, who had followed him. Swinging into the heavy saddle, he motioned her to the front of the rapidly forming square of his knights.

"Come. The sooner we quit the field, the sooner the Scots can come back and take care of their dead and wounded. We want to make Tynemouth before dark."

They came down the long slope that led into the bustling harbor of the Tyne at dusk, and they came in a hurry—horses cantering, wagons bumping and creaking, sheep baaing in fright, and the extra horses milling excitedly and trying to catch up. The city gates were closed at full dark; the men who swung them into place and locked them were already there, grinning, making a show of pulling hard to shut them before the newcomers were all inside.

Margit, again on her mare, rolled her eyes at Aylena and laughed as they gained the cobbled lane inside and slowed, moving aside with Thor and Philip to let the others go past.

"They'd have us believe they'd shut the gates on travelers with money and sheep? I vow they would open them at midnight for this many men wanting food and a bed."

Aylena nodded, looking about, reminded again of trips with her father. There was the Tyne, quiet enough as it flowed, for much of the river to the north was still bound in ice. On either side there were broad flats and boats careened on them for scraping and repairing the thick planks of the bottom. The settlement around the port had grown considerably since she'd been here two years ago, but the mud and wattle houses of workers, the traders' booths, the flaring torches being lit were familiar. And the odors: The air was pungent with offal, the reek of river mud, the smoke of cooking fires, and, above the stench, an occasional, tantalizing whiff of roasting mutton. She turned to look for Thor, and a familiar voice spoke to her, full of surprise.

"My Lady Aylena! What brings you here in the midst of a band of Normans?" A rotund man, well dressed, spoke to her.

"Godwin!" Handing her reins to Margit, Aylena slid

from her horse and took the man's hands in hers. "How glad I am to see you! Have you room at your inn for two women? I will pay well—"

A war-horse eased between them, breaking the clasp of their hands with his powerful chest. Thor looked down at her, frowning. "Mount your mare, my lady, and stay on't." He turned to the man Godwin. "You are an innkeeper? How many rooms have you?"

Godwin's red face bloomed redder. "Enough for Lady Aylena and her maid, sire. No more."

"Find another, then. They'll stay only if I guard them."

The innkeeper stepped forward, staring up at Thor angrily. "What have you done? Taken the Lady Aylena prisoner?"

"Oh, no . . . no, Godwin!" Aylena, back on her mare, called over to him. "The Baron Rodancott is protecting us. We travel to London with him."

"To London! So far? Then . . . why not with your father, the Stewart?"

Aylena looked away, swallowing. "He has died, Godwin, days ago, and was buried beside my mother. His heart failed."

"No! Scotland will mourn the day. No other man but he has roused the old chieftains to their duty." He glanced up at Thor, uneasy. "England will own the Highlands yet."

Thor grinned suddenly. "I doubt King Henry wants the Highlands, innkeeper. They'd be the very devil to conquer, with a barbarian behind every rock, and useless to England once it was done. All England wants is her own back. And all we want is a good dinner and a good bed. Will my men be able to find the same?"

Godwin laughed, reassured. "Tynemouth has enough beds in town for your band and another like it. We are used to many traders and boatmen to be fed and bedded. Give me the number needed, and I'll send a boy around with a torch to guide them. We've plenty of families that take in the one or two for a fair price the night and give them supper as well. Come along now, while there's light enough to see."

Following Godwin's rounded body, dressed in his familiar cloth boots and dark red woolen gown with copper chain and keys round his neck, Aylena sighed with relief. A dark night had fallen and brought the bitter cold, but she had much to look forward to. A bath. A meat pie made by Godwin's wife, Drusilla, and a goose-feather bed. Margit would have nothing to complain about tonight. She turned to peer up through the dark at Thor, hulking like a protective wall beside her.

"How many days will see us to London?"

He looked down at her and smiled. "Six, barring trouble. Seven, more likely—and surely no more than eight."

In the light of the flares carried by his men on either side, Thor's gray eyes reflected the flames like dancing fire on cool water. And, within the clipped beard, his sculptured mouth was still relaxed. . . . Aylena looked away, her breath caught in her throat, remembering how she felt when he kissed her that night in her father's castle . . . as if she were melting inside. She forced herself to think of another question.

"Will we find inns along the way, or must we take provisions and find some rude shelter from the cold?"

"Oh, no, that hardship is behind us. From here to

London there are many places where we will be welcomed. These are the king's men. No one in castle or monastery would dare to turn them away and suffer the punishment."

She gave him another quick glance upward. "Punishment from the king—or from the king's men?"

Thor's jaw jutted forward. "Both, no doubt. Henry has been king but a short time, but all know his wisdom and strength. He is no Stephen, to let the barons of England take over the reins and drive the country to ruin. You will see—we'll have a strong monarchy within a year."

She was quiet then, afraid of what he'd said. Her father had never thought Stephen of Blois man enough to be king, but even more often he'd spoken against the Angevins, calling them the devil's brood. Crafty and proud, he'd said, like the devil himself, and even less pity. If she wanted to persuade King Henry of Ian's right to the Stewart castle, she'd need every bit of her intelligence and pride.

At the small inn, set high on a slope away from the noise and smells along the river, Aylena and Margit had a room to themselves and dinner brought up after the bath she'd wanted. Drusilla, middle-aged and heavy from her own good food, panted up the short flight of steps that led to their room and sat to talk while they ate.

"Godwin an' I grieve with you, my lady. The whole of Northumbria respected the Stewart and will groan with his passing, but tis better for him not to see this Norman baron take over his demesne. He would have felt shamed."

"True, indeed," Aylena replied. "But even if it takes years I'm determined to see the demesne back in

Stewart hands. My young brother Ian will be the lord of Stewart Castle when he reaches his majority. Tis his right, as my father's son." She looked up at a sound and saw Thor standing in the open door, his eyes on her, his dark brows raised quizzically. She felt a cold shock, her heart seemed to shrink with foreboding. His strong body filled the doorway, and there was something in his hard face that told her he'd heard what she said and was only amused by it, as a hawk might be amused by the squeaking of a mouse. The castle, the land, the cattle and sheep, all were his now—as promised by the king of England.

Both Margit and Drusilla scrambled to their feet and stood aside from the table, and, slowly, Aylena put down her spoon and stood up, facing Thor. The inn was warm, and after her bath she had put on a narrow shift of light blue linen and with it a wide chain of gold links woven with ribbon as a loose belt, worn below her waist. She looked very young and very dignified, in spite of the simplicity of her gown and the unbound glory of her hair, falling like a mantle on her shoulders.

"Have you eaten, my lord? There is more than enough for another here."

Thor's face softened into a smile. "I thank you, but I eat with my men. I came only to see if you were properly served, and warm enough. I see that you are."

Aylena smiled coolly. "Always, at Godwin's Inn."

Thor nodded. "Then I wish you a comfortable night. We meet at dawn in the common room. Be ready." He turned on a heel and was gone, his footsteps muffled by the thick mat in the hall. Slowly, Aylena sat down again and looked at the other two.

"I should have been more cautious with my

words," she said. "Our lord moves lightly for all his size. I am sure he heard what I said."

"No matter," Margit said, reverting to her usual air of confidence. "The Baron Rodancott will consider what you said as the mere babbling of a weak woman. He will not feel threatened by your purpose."

Aylena, already flushed with warmth and food, grew pinker still. "Perhaps. But I, as well as Ian, am the get of the Stewart. My father never gave up, nor will I." She brooded a moment and then straightened and looked at Drusilla.

"Tell Godwin the sheep in the big wagon are mine. I would sell them to him if he has need of meat or to any man he knows who will pay a decent price. The wagon we'll pick up again as we return home."

Drusilla rose immediately. "We'll take them, my lady. Godwin told me to ask. I'll clear these dishes away and bring back the money. Then you must sleep. Tis a long and tiring way to London."

6

 A mile northwest of Tynemouth was a heavy ferry, made of large logs fastened together with iron spikes. Fashioned to be drawn back and forth across the fast-running river by ropes and pulleys, it boasted a smooth deck of split logs big enough to hold some eight horses and eight men. It crossed at a spot where a roadway ran south, and most of Thor's mercenaries had risen early and crossed before dawn, lighting fires on the opposite side to keep warm.

Aylena and Margit saw the glow of the fires when they left Godwin's Inn in the faint light of dawn, and knew where they were. Traders came up that way from York, to buy or sell at Tynemouth, but neither Aylena nor Margit had ever crossed to the other side, and Margit feared what they might find in the wilderness beyond. The women were accompanied by the Baron Rodancott and his remaining men, some twenty or more. The men were silent, as was the town around them, except for crowing roosters and an occasional sleepy voice raised irritably in one of the mud or cob houses.

Glancing behind her, Aylena saw streaks of pink light glistening on turbulent water where the Tyne met the angry North Sea. Before her everything except the fires was unknown to her, and strange. Then, passing an old Norman church and seeing the first of the dawn glow touch the crucifix on the tower, she made the sign of the cross and was immediately joined by a flickering of mailed fists around her, rising to helmets, dropping to heart, crossing from broad shoulder to broad shoulder. Norman, French, English, or Scot, she mused, were alike in their reverence for the same God. She glanced at Margit, whose dark hair showed a gold-sprigged halo from the rising sun behind them.

"How do you read the day?"

Margit put on an expression of wisdom. She was noted as a prophetess of weather and was proud of it. "Cold," she said, "and clearing. The air is dry, the mist is rising." She looked back along the line of men and then at Aylena. "No baggage cart, my lady? What if we tire?"

Aylena laughed. "We'll continue to ride. Twas my decision, Margit. Not having to match our speed to a wagon will cut out a full day from the trip, Lord Rodancott said. He had the men pack our belongings on two of the extra horses and they are being led by others."

"Oh." After a moment, Margit added, "Perhaps you forgot that I tire easily on horseback." The "my lady" was conspicuously absent.

"Indeed, and I tire, also. But the benefits outweigh the discomfort. And if you sit straight in the saddle and stop wobbling about, the strain will be less."

"Thank you, my lady," Margit said coldly, "for the

lesson. I will ride behind you and try to learn from your example." She dropped back, and the knights riding as a rear guard opened ranks to let her in.

At the ferry all dismounted. Curious, Aylena looked at the tangle of heavy pulleys and wheels that drew the ferry from bank to bank across the running Tyne. The horses, nickering and plunging, were afraid of the bouncing ferry and had to be blindfolded and led on, trembling. Group after group was taken over by the ferrymen and left on the far bank with the men who had crossed earlier. Then Thor, Philip of Anjou, and the Reeve brothers formed a square around the two women and, stepping carefully through the mud, boarded the ferry, leaving three of Thor's mercenaries to cross over last.

In midstream, Aylena glanced back and saw two Scotsmen burst through the snow-covered shrubs along the bank, and she screamed a warning to the men left behind. They whirled to defend themselves. But one of the Scots dodged their blows and swung his axe, cutting the rope that held the ferry to the north bank. The ferry swung violently, bucking and jerking in the current, then coming to a heaving stop that threw all on it to the deck. Thor pulled Aylena close and shielded her with his body.

"Stay low. They may have lances . . ." But as he spoke the mercenaries downed the Scots, killing them both. He let Aylena go and stood up, staring at the straining line holding them to the south shore where most of his men and horses waited. The men had grabbed it and were pulling the heavy, sloshing ferry to them. Slowly, everyone on the raft stood up, Margit weeping from fright, leaning on Philip. Thor reached out an arm and brought Aylena to his side, throwing

his cloak around her. She was grateful for his
warmth, but her eyes were full of horror.

"Those men thought the line on this side would
break under the strain," Thor said. "Thank our saints
and angels that it held. You've a charmed life, my
lady. They meant the ferry to whirl downstream and
turn over at the curve, which it likely would. Don't
pity them . . . they wanted you to drown."

Aylena nodded but was silent. She watched the men
on the opposite shore drag the bodies of the two Scots
to the river and drop them in. Innocent men, she
thought, dying because of John Bretinalle's false
tongue. Their families will wonder and then grieve,
never knowing the truth of their going . . . nor the
evil lie that caused their deaths.

The world beyond the Tyne was a new world to
Aylena. Some might say that the Stewart castle was
now in England, but it was still Northumbria to her,
an ancient part of old Scotland. South of the Tyne, she
felt herself to be in England, her mother's country.
Still, the land was much the same, with no large trees
or fertile farms, only bleak moors with rocky hills rising above them, higher than those near Stewart Castle. The men seemed to feel it; they kept their eyes
forward on the beaten path and maintained their
speed, as if anxious to get through this barren country.

Thor rode to her right, and to her left was Philip of
Anjou. Margit rode behind her, between the two
Reeve brothers; the mercenaries and the extra horses
with their baggage brought up the rear. This pattern,
Thor had said, would be followed throughout the trip.

Before they left the river shore he'd shown them the tactics if they were again pursued and harassed.

"At the first sign of trouble," he had said, "you and your maid will come to a stop, lie forward on your mare's neck, and our men behind you will come up and form a circle with you in the midpoint." He had stopped, looking at Aylena narrowly. "Do it now, so I may see if you understand."

That angered her. "Do you think me stupid?"

"I will see it before we go."

She glared at him. Then, seeing his jaw tighten, she shrugged and dropped forward on her mare's neck.

"Good. Make no attempt to either run away or fight. You are women and must be protected."

She'd dared to argue. "I am a woman, yes. But I am accustomed to wearing a dagger, and I know how to use one."

He had given her a look that almost made her think he knew how little good and much harm her dagger and her temper had done in the argument with Bretinalle, though he couldn't know any of that. She made no more comments.

Now, well past midday, she still felt guilty riding in the midst of this band of fighting men. It was her presence that brought the lurking danger to them. And death to innocent Scots, all because of a lying tongue. At the first thought of Bretinalle, anger heated her blood again and drew her brows together. She pushed the thought away, instinctively knowing she wasted her strength in hating. Beside her, Thor eased his horse to a slower gait and motioned her to do the same.

"There has been a slide of small rocks from that cliff ahead. The horses must pick their way through."

They had been holding the pace at an easy canter, but even that grew tiresome after hours in the saddle. Aylena was willing enough to rest both herself and her mount, but her thoughts had made her wary. She glanced up at the overhanging cliff ahead and saw sparkling mist in the cold air. Then, as the thunder of hooves around and behind her slowed and turned into a slow clopping, she heard the sound of plunging water. And, as they moved around the face of the towering cliff, she saw it. Brown, peaty water fell down a series of huge rocks into a deep pool, then wandered toward the southeast in a shallow spread edged with ice.

"The falls Godwin described," Philip of Anjou said, speaking to Thor. "This must be the Tees River. We have but to cross it, he said, to be in York. Then another hour of hard riding to the south will see us at Fountains Abbey."

"We have made good time," Thor answered, and glanced at Aylena's tense face. "We are in no danger now. Even if the Scots dared to follow us this deep into England, our horses would have far outstripped them."

Aylena recognized the truth in that. "Thank the good Christ for that blessing. What of your men you left behind?"

Thor laughed. "They are warriors; they can take care of themselves. Why, they may take to the sea and land in London before us. Come, we'll follow the stream and find a shallow ford."

In minutes they'd crossed the small river choked with lacy ice and were riding south in York. Larger trees and long stretches of browned and frozen meadows appeared. This was farmland, with hills in the distance that grew larger and more impressive as the afternoon wore into evening dusk.

Then the huge Fountains Abbey appeared, sprawled between the long, rock-strewn flanks of two mountains and bound round about with thickets of thorn and jutting cliffs. The shadows were long as they came slowly to the gates, the white robes of the Cistercian monks like ghosts in the fields. They were still toiling, digging up and burning the thornbushes, readying the inhospitable land for sheep meadows. Those nearest bowed and made the sign of the cross as the party arrived, and motioned for them to go in through the gates.

The abbot, who had been giving orders to his flock ever since the large party appeared in the distance, made them welcome. Payment for food and beds made up a sizable part of the money needed to keep the monastery. Even women travelers were welcome, though they were not allowed to mingle with the others. Aylena and Margit were given lighted candles and hurriedly shown to a large room, with dry wood ready to light in a fireplace. In it were several beds built in niches of the thick wall, chairs and a table, and a garderobe and laver for relieving themselves and washing.

Margit, who had traveled before, knew the customs women must observe at a monastery. She shut the door at once and locked it. Then she took her candle and lit the fire, as much for light as for heat.

"Someone will knock," she said, rising from the hearth, "and we must wait a moment or two before we open the door. There will be food there, and water. We eat, and place the dishes outside, locking the door again. In the morning, the sire will come to fetch us."

"Well enough," Aylena said. She had taken a chair and was loosening her outer clothes and shaking her hair from its thick braid. Glancing around at the thick stone walls, the shadowy niches, and dark draperies that hid the beds, she shrugged slim shoulders. "If tis a dungeon, tis a comfortable one, and a time apart from the men is welcome."

Margit sniffed. "So you say. But from the soft words and glances you give the Baron Rodancott, you'd prefer him to me as a companion, whether on horseback or in bed."

Aylena's eyes were down, her fingers continuing to loosen her hair, to fluff it out into waving strands. After a moment, she nodded. "That is undoubtedly true. He is much more attractive than you, and certainly more courteous. But I do admit he is not a female, nor a maid. Perhaps I should begin looking about for a new companion. . . ."

Red-faced, Margit snapped back. "Your father would whirl in his grave to hear you praise a Norman baron, and one who is a king's man, to boot."

"Perhaps. But my father ever loved a brave knight, and one who fought well and fairly. Whereas he would certainly deplore a weak noblewoman who allowed her body servant to criticize and insult her."

Margit's face paled. "I humbly beg your pardon."

Aylena looked up and smiled. "And I gladly give it. We are both tired, Margit, but a day closer to our goal. Ah, there is the knock on the door that you prophesied. Hot food and a loaf of good bread will put us into better spirits."

* * *

Later, washed clean of dust from the dry fields and full of thick, hot gruel, bread, and preserved fruits, Aylena slid between fresh, coarse sheets and pulled a wooly blanket over her. Margit was already snoring in the niche across from hers; all she had required to gentle her tongue had been food and sleep. Aylena had been relieved; perhaps a servant woman didn't count as family, but Margit was the only link she had now with the old castle, the old life . . . the only one who would join her in wishing the past back again.

She stared into glowing coals, all that was left of the fire, thinking and hoping. No nobleman nor lady would wish her well when she went before the king to ask for her heritage and Ian's, but Margit would. Margit would pray for her success.

Once more she blamed herself for losing the coffers. The paper she'd saved and put in with the jewels was now of utmost importance. Surely, if it could be found, the king would honor the testament from her father's aunt, the Lady Celestine. Or would he? Laws were made for lesser men. A king needed none—he had absolute power.

The next six days of the trip to London were far easier on the women. The rocky roads had given way to broad lanes, the weather had moderated, and the nights were spent in pleasant surroundings—along the way there were good inns and several wooden castles built by England's robber barons during Stephen's reign. The barons had built them without permission and filled them with mercenaries to war against their own neighbors. King Henry did not approve. He had issued a mandate forcing the barons to send their mercenaries back to Normandy, Italy, and

France, and there was gossip that he intended to take over the castles and tear them down. One sight of the king's red and gold banner over the crowd of mail-clad knights brought the barons out to welcome them. The travelers had the best of beds, the best of foods and wines, and, at midday of the seventh day, they saw in the distance the walls of London. Thor threw up a hand and slowed the pace to a gentle trot, sparing tired horses.

Seeing the great city, Aylena unconsciously drew nearer to Thor's bulk. The first English villages in lower York had surprised her with their cob and thatch houses, bigger than any she'd seen before; then the towns—with their stone walls and Norman churches, the cobbled streets, the houses of the rich burgesses made of sawn wood above the ground floor —had struck her into helpless admiration. Now, the city of London became a glittering lodestone, drawing her on.

Thor looked down at Aylena's entranced face and his own face relaxed. Some of her confidence had left her; he'd noted her edging closer, and that pleased him. He wanted her to put her faith in him, and during these days he'd felt her growing respect. Perhaps he would soon have her in his arms, willing and soft. In a new place, especially one so different from her home, she might be able to forget those men who had taken her virginity—and lost their lives for the shame she had to endure. But Bretinalle was still alive. . . .

Glancing up, Aylena saw the sudden hardening of the jaw beneath Thor's untrimmed beard. In some ways Thor had become an open book to her, and she knew his thoughts were ranging ahead, studying a challenge.

"Have you enemies in London?" she asked, and saw surprise in his eyes. Then he laughed.

"No more than any other fighting man," he said, "and less than most. Londoners are far more interested in games, pleasures, and trade than they are in quarreling and argument."

"I see." Watching the city and the great Thames River unfolding before her eyes, she could believe everyone there was happy. The homes outside of the old Roman walls were blessed by spring gardens and large shade trees leafing out. On the north side were pastures and meadowlands marked by streams strong enough to turn mill wheels. She could hear the faint clacking and swish through the still, fragrant air.

"Where will we stay? Inside the walls, or out?"

"Inside, my lady. We will be given rooms in part of Palatine Castle, which stands in the southeast corner of the city."

She nodded. Even she had heard of that great tower of London, where the king and queen often stayed, where prisoners of a certain rank were held in comfortable quarters. The tower was said to be very strong, the keep and walls rising from very deep foundations and the mortar tempered magically by the blood of animals. There was a royal palace connected with Westminster Abbey, but it was common to hear of the reigning king and queen living at the tower instead. Perhaps they felt safer inside the city walls.

"What of your men?"

"My knights will be housed in comfort in the town; the mercenaries will be boarding ships and sailing by tomorrow noon. I arranged for their payment through the king's chancellor, Thomas à Becket."

"I see." She was astounded that a mere Norman

baron could deal with the king himself and men like Thomas à Becket, and she wondered if Thor was spinning tales. She would hate to discover that he was actually on speaking terms with the king. It boded ill for her chance to keep the castle. No matter. She would try, because she had promised her father.

They came toward the city from the west, seeing the palace of Westminster, its bulwarks and ramparts majestic above the wide, deep flowing Thames River. Then another mile or two through a flourishing suburb and they came to the heavily fortified double gates. The old Roman wall ran north and then east, disappearing in the welter of buildings inside.

They went through the huge arched passage, the sound of the horses' hooves echoing around them, and into a narrow and crooked street. At first only a few other travelers were there, heading in various directions in the maze of alleys and lanes that led off from the gates. Then Thor led them straight east on a gradually broadening thoroughfare.

The wide street was full of hurrying people in the dimming light of day. Hundreds of people, Aylena thought, dismayed. Perhaps thousands. Most were beggars; many were children, shivering in ragged clothes. And the stench of the drain that ran through the middle of the street was awful.

"This is the worst of it," Thor said, noticing her discomfort. "We'll soon leave it behind."

"Thank the good Lord for that," Margit mumbled behind her. "Where are we going to stay, my lady?"

"In Palatine Castle," Aylena said, and marveled at her own confidence. "Across the city." She turned her head and glanced at Margit's white face and down-dropped jaw. "Sir Thor is welcome there, as we will be as his guests."

"More likely his hostages," Margit said, but kept her voice low. "I have heard there are prison cells in that tower."

Aylena didn't answer. She was too busy staring at the lines of close-set buildings on one side, and on the other, peering through narrow, congested streets and markets to see the shine of evening light on the Thames. Half-forgotten memories of her mother's talk came back to her. Lady Alyse Belmain had loved London, had loved England, but had loved Bruce Stewart more. Still, she had talked of London and the Thames, had spoken of fetes and the gaiety at court in Winchester, England's capital. Aylena turned to Thor, looking up at him through the darkening air.

"Will we go on later to Winchester, Lord Rodancott?"

Thor reached out a long arm and twitched her hood forward, to hide part of her face.

"Beauty such as yours should be kept hidden on London streets," he said by way of explanation. He well knew no one would dare attack his group for any reason, but he needed an excuse to touch her, even if only her clothing. Watching Aylena on this journey had increased his feeling for her a hundredfold, and in his heart she was already his. She had been argumentative occasionally and inclined to ask for information no woman needed to know, but she stood the rigors of traveling better than any other woman he'd ever known. He was foolishly proud of her. He fussed a moment longer, settling the hood lower over her smooth forehead, and then answered her question.

"Yes, we'll travel to Winchester once I have seen the

mercenaries aboard ship and leaving. That's where the king will hear your plea. He is building a new hall of justice there, though I doubt it will be ready for your audience.''

She smiled wryly, teeth glistening in the dusk. "I care not where the king sits to hear me—only that he listen.''

Thor laughed. "He will listen, my lady. And after he listens he will do what pleases him. That is the privilege of kings.''

She nodded and rode on. The knights had found torches and lit them against the advancing night. Four of them took the lead now, torches flaming, and behind them in the body of mercenaries other torches flared to life. The streets were suddenly empty; the sounds of slamming doors and windows echoed as the canny Londoners locked themselves in against the many thieves. Once again Thor felt Aylena's heavy skirts brush against his leg and smiled in the dark. She hid her fears well, but one night in Scotland she had learned whom to trust. He smiled in the dark. She would give in to him, soon.

Palatine Castle loomed white and immense before them an hour later. The mercenaries had departed the train when they came abreast of the Lion Quay, where their ship awaited them, and now only fifteen of Thor's knights accompanied them. The gates to the courtyard swung open as soon as Thor spoke; a man-at-arms was sent running toward the huge white tower with news of his coming. Then the tired riders filed in and dispersed, each knight facing Thor and waiting for his dismissal before he left for the stables to see to his horse. Thor dismounted, handed his reins to Philip, and greeted an old man in red and gold robes who came hurrying across the courtyard, accompanied by two footmen with flaring torches.

"Lord Rodancott! King Henry sends his greetings and requires you to attend him immediately."

For once, Thor was surprised. "The king is here? I thought him in Winchester."

"No, no. He is here, and so is the queen. Come! He is impatient."

Thor nodded and turned, grasping Aylena around the waist, swinging her down from her mare. "I have a noblewoman here, chamberlain, who must stay with me until you find safe accommodations for her. Come, Lady Aylena. The king of England wishes to see us."

"To see *you*, Thor." Aylena's heart dropped. It was true; they were friends. Her chances against Thor were indeed small. "Leave Margit and me to the chamberlain."

"As you please, then . . ." But he caught her arm and hurried her toward the open doors and streaming light that came from inside, whisking her up the broad steps and into a hall paved with marble and boasting a soaring staircase that rose to a long gallery above. Margit came after them with long strides, directing a footman staggering under baggage.

Aylena loosed herself from Thor's grasp. "Now, my lord, we are in good hands. Go to the king, by all means . . ."

"Or stay, my dear Lord of Northumbria, and let me come to you!" A barrel-chested man with fiery red hair and large blue eyes was coming rapidly down the stairs, taking the steps two at a time with his strong bowed legs. He wore a cream satin tunic sewn with jewels over a dark blue velvet gown, and though he carried no scepter, wore no crown, there was an aura about him that sent Aylena down in a low curtsy and Margit to her knees, head bowed. Thor dropped to one knee as the king stopped before him, and put his two hands together into the king's firm clasp.

"My hands in your service, my liege lord," Thor said, and stood, smiling. "What brings England's king to London?"

Henry II threw back his head and laughed. "My son!" he said, his voice crackling with excitement. "My strong, healthy son, now nearly four weeks old." He clapped Thor's shoulder with a resounding blow and laughed again. "He was born here on the last day of February. Eleanor has given me an heir—and England has a new prince! Come with me, you and your lady. I'd have you both drink to a long life for the next king of England, Henry III!"

7

 Travel-stained and weary, Aylena would have gladly welcomed a bath and a night in a soft bed before she met the reigning king of England. But as Thor turned and presented her to Henry II as the Lady Aylena Stewart, she knew that the vibrant, joyous man before her was not only the king, he was also the judge who would hear her claim Stewart Castle for her brother, Ian. She must not displease him in any way. . . .

Thor was looking at her, his bearded face proud and encouraging. There was, she knew, no way out of it. She let her hood fall back from her golden hair, and gave the king a brilliant smile with another low curtsy. Rising, she took Thor's arm with as much dignity as possible and went with him up the long flight of stairs, leaving Margit to deal with the footmen and baggage. They came into a great hall, where tall, carved pillars disappeared into upper darkness made darker yet by the contrast of flickering lamps along the walls. On the south wall was an open door where light and soft music streamed forth, and as they approached they heard voices talking and laughing. The king increased his already rapid steps, hurrying them along.

"Eleanor," he said with infinite satisfaction, "is beside herself with joy. After giving Louis only girls, she has proven the fault does not lie with her." He glanced at Thor and winked broadly. "She but needed a better man."

"And found one," Thor agreed. "May she bear many more."

They were at the door, and the talk inside ceased at the sight of the king. The king turned, and in a rare moment of simple grace he took Aylena's arm and drew her inside. Pale with weariness, Aylena still lifted her chin and gazed at the people there with a half smile, her dark blue eyes startled, her mass of golden hair tangled on her shoulders. Coming up behind her, Thor noted the raised chin and smiled inwardly. The Stewart pride was still there.

"The Lady Aylena Stewart," the king announced, "and Baron Thor Rodancott, now to be Lord of Northumbria, are here to see my son."

Aylena was amazed by the scene inside the large room. There seemed to be hundreds of candles lit, the light reflecting on polished wood, on beautiful furniture and paintings. Reflected flames danced in great steel and silver mirrors, doubling the light. And there were so many beautiful women, dressed in wonderfully colored silks and laces, so many handsome men, in satin and velvet tunics, and so many jewels, sparkling from the women's hair, glistening on the sleeves and shoulders of the men's short cloaks. There were troubadours, resting with their crwths and lyres in the corners, who were wearing tabards made of a violet satin richer than any cloth she'd ever seen. Then a tall woman, proud and very beautiful, turned to stare at her. The woman's eyes were large and seemed to stand out boldly from her face. They were pale blue, like a robin's egg, and clear. Her hair was also pale, a lemony blond shade, and dressed in intricate style, held by a coronet of emeralds. She was gowned in silk samite woven of threads dyed the greens and blues of the sea, and over the gown was a sleeveless tunic of fine lace. Studying Aylena from the center of her group, the woman smiled thinly.

"Welcome, Lady Aylena. Come to me, my dear. I would greet you and Lord Rodancott."

There was the faintest rebuke in the assured voice, a reminder that royalty demands instant respect. Aylena went forward quickly, curtsied, rose, and stood with lowered gaze as Thor went to a knee and kissed the queen's hand.

"You have blessed England with an heir to the throne," he said, rising to smile down at her. "And at the same time provided a duke for Aquitaine, Languedoc, and Provence."

Eleanor of Aquitaine laughed. "Indeed. He will rule over half of France," she agreed, eyes gleaming. "And the best half, at that. Who is your beautiful companion, Thor?"

"Lady Aylena Stewart is the daughter of the laird of the Scottish clan of the Stewarts, who has died. She has traveled with me from Northumbria to plead before the king for her young brother's rights to Stewart Castle."

Eleanor's gaze, sparkling with sudden curiosity, shot to Aylena's face. "Then she has more courage than most women," she said, "but, perhaps, less common sense. Does she truly hope to take the spoils of war away from the Baron Thor Rodancott?"

The crowd around them hummed with low laughter, and Thor reached out protectively to take Aylena's arm. Her smile came, her eyes brilliant with resolve, as he drew her closer to the group.

"That," Thor said calmly, "will be the king's decision, not mine."

Aylena managed to get through the next half hour by ignoring her dusty clothes and hair and remembering her own proud heritage. She admired the infant prince as his wet nurse brought him in, and answered questions from the other guests, most of whom were from Aquitaine or from Languedoc, which she knew was a region in southeast France.

Never far from her, Thor listened, watched, and finally won her freedom by engaging the queen's sympathy for a tired traveler. At his request Eleanor called a lady-in-waiting to escort Aylena to her room, where Margit waited to help her bathe and eat a supper sent up to them.

Thor excused himself as well and followed a servant to his allotted room. Readying himself for bed, he knew he should have asked if the royal family was in residence. He could have found another place, perhaps not as comfortable or grand, but fine enough. He had seen the interest Eleanor showed in Aylena and regretted it. He knew the beautiful and assured women who clustered around the queen, and he knew the men—gorgeously dressed, highly mannered, and in many ways foreign to him. And he had followed Henry II long enough to know how easily the queen and her courtiers influenced the young.

Queen Eleanor, eleven years older than the king,

and more worldly, was happy only when she had her favorites fawning on her, with troubadours and poets for pleasure. Eleanor's early life had been spent in Provence and Languedoc, where the French nobility gathered for part of every season. Pleasures abounded in that pleasant southeastern land. There was the blue Mediterranean, there was music, there were naughty comedies in the old Roman amphitheater, and, when all of that grew dull, they played at love together. None of that had ever bothered Thor—until now.

He knew them too well. Most of Eleanor's court were cynics; all of them believed in a life of careless pleasure; and though they kept up an appearance of sanctity for fear of swift punishment from an all-powerful church, none seemed to believe in priest or God. Tonight, he had seen the hot interest in the eyes of the men who had gathered around Aylena—and he had burned with a slow, deep anger.

In her own room, Aylena yawned her way through the bath provided by silent, scurrying maids, and answered Margit's excited questions. Yes, the queen was beautiful, though older than she had thought, the infant loud and lusty, and the handsome king himself had presented her to the nobles gathered in celebration.

"Had it not been for Thor's good sense," she concluded, "I would still be there, filthy and tired. He persuaded the queen to send me to bed." She stood, to allow Margit to rinse her slim body with fresh water, then stepped out and wrapped the big linen square around her.

"There were only two or three English nobles amongst them," she added. "The rest were from Anjou and Aquitaine. Our queen of England remains French in her heart."

Margit's hands trembled with excitement as she rubbed the water from Aylena's bright hair and began brushing it. "Never did I think I would be in a king's palace," she said, marveling, "and see the king himself, not an ell away, talking and laughing! Will he hear your plea soon?"

"I doubt it. Our sire has said he holds audience for his subjects in Winchester, more than a day's trip from here." Her voice was steady enough, but fear thrilled through her body as she spoke. Now that she had seen the power and wealth of a king around her, her own argument seemed weak and foolish. Without that testament from her father's aunt, she had no evidence at all—except for her sworn word. She looked around at Margit's excited face and then stood up.

"Tomorrow," she said, "I will think on't. Tonight I will eat a bit of that supper there, and then sleep."

Summoned in late morning by one of Queen Eleanor's ladies-in-waiting to join the queen in her suite, Aylena put on the best of her few gowns, the same narrow green silk sheath with its sleeveless overgown of dark green velvet that she had worn the night after her rescue by Thor. But she left off the cap of net and pearls, preferring a band of chased gold around her forehead to hold her mass of golden hair.

The lady-in-waiting, Lady Marie de Fermi, was— Aylena guessed—only a few years older than she, pretty and full of news and laughter. "One of our queen's favorite courtiers has asked to talk to you. Sir Charles Halchester vows he can never rest until he discovers if you are related to him. It seems he remembers a cousin whom you strongly resemble. But, I will warn you, Sir Charles is inclined to golden blondes. Perhaps he only wishes to charm you into his arms."

Aylena smiled but said little as she joined Marie at the door and began the walk to the queen's chambers. She had taken the measure of the men who had been in the gathering last evening, and they had seemed different from the strong, masculine men she knew—different enough to make her doubtful of them. Still, she decided to wait and use her own judgment when she knew them better.

"Is Lord Rodancott in the gathering?" she asked, and Marie de Fermi shook her black curls.

"I believe he and his knights are conferring with the king, which our ladies regret. Some solemn business about false nobles—King Henry is denying the separate earldoms, it is said, and taking the lands back into the royal demesne. His new chancellor, Thomas à Becket, has advised it."

"I see." Aylena's heart fell. If the king would take land from English earls, he would never hesitate to take it from a Scottish rebel. Her cause now seemed hopeless, but as she approached the open doors to the queen's salon, she managed a smile, telling herself a dour expression never made friends.

Inside, the same group of well-dressed women and courtiers were gathered, though at this hour they were quiet and less flamboyantly dressed. The queen, at the center of the room, looked up as Aylena came in, her prominent eyes alive with curiosity. As Aylena curtsied, Eleanor waved her to her side.

"Come," she said, taking Aylena's hand in hers, "we have a friend, Charles Halchester, who swears he has the same English blood as you. Mayhap you will find a connection."

A tall, fair-haired man turned from a table laden with fruit pastries and came, smiling and pleasant, to meet Aylena at the queen's side. He was lavishly dressed, wearing a light green velvet cape lined with vair and a short tunic of heavy silk, designed to emphasize his length of slender, well-shaped leg. He bowed and took Aylena's hand as the queen introduced him, holding it as the queen moved on to another group. Then, he turned, blocking stares from the others.

"I have but one question, Lady Aylena. I know you've come here from Northumbria, and perhaps tis foolish to think you belong to the same family in Wessex as I, but the resemblance is striking. Have you known a noblewoman named Alyse Belmain?"

Aylena gasped. "Alyse Belmain was my mother, Sir Charles. What was she to you?"

He laughed and gripped her hands excitedly. "My cousin. Older, of a certainty, but easily remembered for her kindness to a young boy." Then, looking deep into her eyes, he stopped smiling. "From your choice of words, my lady, Alyse is dead. I am sorry to hear it."

"Tis six, near seven years since her death," Aylena said. Gazing up at Halchester's sympathetic face she felt a growing communion with him, a sense of family. "Have you other Belmain relatives, Sir Charles?"

He shook his head. "None. I'm afraid we're the last of the blood."

"No," Aylena said, and smiled. "There is one more. My six—no, now nearly seven-year-old brother, Ian

Stewart. Tis on his behalf I've come to England's royal courts.''

"Oh?" Halchester's voice was less certain. "What plea will you make to the king?"

"To restore Ian's birthright as son and heir of the Stewart," Aylena answered. She was suddenly flushed with purpose. "I gave my word to my father as he lay dying.''

Incredulity, and then doubt, chased over Charles's handsome face. He looked for a moment as if he would protest, but, seeming to soften, he took her hands again.

"You gave your word? Then, as a Belmain, you must honor it. If I can help, you've only to ask."

"So, Halchester," Queen Eleanor said, approaching them again, "you were right. The resemblance must be strong. As I recall, you have believed for some years that you were the last surviving relative of the Baron Belmain." The queen's smooth face wore a look of secret amusement as she met his eyes. Halchester flushed red.

"I did, my queen. I was sure of it. But . . ." He swung back to Aylena and put an arm across her slender shoulders. "I must say I am glad to be wrong."

His arm was warm, holding her to his side, his fingers moving on her arm in light caress. Aylena smiled up at him, surprised and as glad as he to have a living relative. Naturally, she had Ian, but he was only a child, and far away. Having a cousin—a man and older than she—was wonderful. He would be someone to talk to, and trust.

"Come," Sir Charles said, and drew her toward the tables, following the queen. "The pastries are fresh from the ovens.''

* * *

Aylena was talking and laughing with the others when the king and the men who had been conferring with him came in to join the queen and her court. Thor greeted the queen and then came to Aylena, his cool gray eyes touching Halchester briefly and warming as he turned to her.

"You are rested?"

"I am, and I have discovered a member of my mother's family, Thor. I have a cousin!" She turned toward Halchester, smiling. "Do you know the Baron Rodancott, Charles?" Behind her, Thor went suddenly still, his black brows drawing together, his look hardening on Halchester's face. Halchester dropped his gaze and bowed slightly. "Everyone knows the king's right arm, my lady, and admires him greatly."

Turning back, Aylena was flushed with excitement. It was wonderful to discover a relative right in the midst of the English court, one who might help her in her battle for Stewart Castle. Yet Thor took her eye. He was so different from these pale others in their fancy satins and laces, and their weak bodies, with narrow shoulders and thin, birdlike legs. Standing amongst them, she noted the differences.

Thor was more than impressive, he was a handsome giant in this crowd of courtiers. He was wearing a cream-colored silk shirt over his massive chest and shoulders, and over it a golden brown velvet tunic that hung to mid-thigh, belted snug to his taut waist. Dark brown chausses clung to his muscular legs, ending in fine leather half boots. He had taken pains for his appearance in the court, and his black wavy hair and beard were freshly clipped and neat, fragrant with rosemary, an herb often used as scent. Aylena breathed in the fragrance and smiled, noticing that the courtiers and their ladies had moved closer, listening to every word. All were curious about the king's session with his men, as she was, too.

"Have you news, my lord?"

"Not now." The words were clipped; his tone said she'd hear it later. In the short time since they met they had both learned the signals given by the other. "Have you eaten?"

"Enough, surely. More than enough." She gestured toward the still laden tables. "May I bring you some of the fruit pastries?"

"Thank you, but I have no time. Get your cloak and come with me. We'll eat later, from the cookshops along the Thames."

"But . . ." She stiffened, thinking how often Thor ordered her about and wishing he wouldn't in front of others. "The queen requested my presence here, and—"

"I will speak to her, Aylena. Go you and find your cloak."

She started to refuse, then thought it might be some idea he wanted to tell her. She looked around, seeing her cousin in conversation with Marie de Fermi. She went to find her cloak, certain she would see her cousin Charles again, and soon.

London on a bright day offered up a variety of sights. The houses of the plain citizens were ramshackle, dangerously decayed warrens filled with all manner of people of different ages, and held up by other similar houses pressed so tightly together that none could fall without the others. The churches, many of them stone, were beautiful and numerous, and in the northwest part of the walled city what seemed an army of workmen were rebuilding a church, to be dedicated, Thor said, to St. Paul. He said little else, except to mention a woman in the cloth trade who was skilled in sewing.

"We go to France within a fortnight," he added, "with the queen. You will need new and fashionable gowns."

"To *France*? Why?" She saw Philip of Anjou roll his eyes at Thor and grin. "Are you teasing me?"

Thor's serious expression disappeared; his broad mouth relaxed into humor. "No. The trip is the queen's whim. She was criticized for failing to provide a French heir to the throne, for she had only daughters for Louis. She wants the French nobility to see her infant son and know twas Louis's seed that was at fault, not her. Or so she has told the king."

"But royal news travels fast. All Europe would know by now that an English heir is born."

"Indeed. But she would make sure of it. We go."

Aylena frowned. "I had hoped for a quick audience with the king. The trip will take many weeks, perhaps months."

"True. But from what you tell me, your brother is in good hands. And King Henry insists that I accompany the queen. I will not leave you here alone."

Aylena gave him a surprised glance. That possibility hadn't come to her mind, nor did she want to consider it. With no funds, she could not even feed herself and Margit.

"Then I must wait. Take me to this seamstress."

The narrow streets of the traders ran from the wide thoroughfares down to the waterfront and the ships. There was barely space for two horses abreast in the muddy lanes. When they came to the street of the drapers and fur merchants, Thor dismounted and lifted Aylena from her horse, setting her slippered feet on a dry wooden platform in front of a draper's stall.

"Thank you, my lord. When will you return?"

"I will stay. You will need me to help you choose, my lady."

She frowned. "You cannot trust my judgment?"

"You would be beautiful in rags, Aylena. But I have more knowledge of court fashions. Let me lead you."

She swallowed. *Beautiful in rags.* She felt blood rising to her cheeks. Next he'd call her a beggar. "You are very kind, my lord." Her voice was only a little sarcastic. "You may choose, since tis your money paying for the work."

Inside the rough wooden stall a man and a woman came forward to a counter at the sight of them, bowing and smiling. The man spoke eagerly to Thor, asking him his wants, saying he could offer any cloth needed, and at a good price. Thor nodded, but turned to the woman.

"You are the seamstress Martha Rowley? Good! My lady has need of gowns for attending the queen, perhaps as many as four, with changes of lace and velvet overgowns. And cloaks, one light, one lined with vair. Can you hire others to help? The clothes will be needed within ten days."

The woman nodded vigorously, her face scarlet with pleasure. "Indeed, my lord, indeed. It will be as you say. And the price less if you buy the cloth here."

"Good. Then take my lady's measure while I see your husband's wares."

Martha Rowley turned and curtsied to Aylena.

"Come with me, my lady. My sewing room is plain but clean."

There was no doubt, Aylena thought, following the woman, that she had been led into this. She thought of the sum of money Godwin had given her for the sheep and knew it was fearfully small for such fashions. This would be one more debt to be owed to Thor Rodancott.

Martha drew her past the covered rolls of cloth piled in the gloom and into a substantial house attached to the rear of the stall. In the main room there was a line of windows high on the south and west walls admitting light to three women sitting below them. The women were sewing, the bright fabrics lay in folds around them, but each took a quick glance at the stranger as Martha brought her in, then lowered her eyes again to her needle.

Martha ignored them. She brought white muslin strips, draped them over Aylena's slender body, and cut them to the exact lengths and widths. The length of an arm, the width of shoulders, the length from shoulder to waist, the waist to the floor, each carefully marked.

"Queen Eleanor's gowns sweep the floor, my lady," Martha said, "and then trail a few inches behind. We have been kept busy adding those few inches to last year's gowns. Yours will be all new."

Aylena nodded, stood still, and watched. In time, Martha's husband came in and out, bringing varied colors of silks and satin, gauzes and samite, laces and net, deep blue wool for a warm cloak, asking for her opinion on them. She struggled to keep up, then spread her hands and told the draper to allow the Baron Rodancott to choose.

"Except," she added, "I do very much like the blue wool." After he left she looked at Martha. "May I leave now?"

"Yes, my lady. I have your measure. The gowns will fit."

Aylena stepped lightly as she went out. It was hard not to be pleased by new clothes. Never had she seen such creamy silk, such fine, light wool. Never had she thought to own such gowns. Somehow, she'd find a way to pay for them, later.

There was no one in the stall except the draper, busily cutting lengths of gleaming silks. She went on, stepping out on the wooden platform and finding Thor leaning there, staring south through the narrow alleyway at the moving, silvery gray Thames River and the myriad of boats and ships, some tied to the quays, some sailing past, some unloading casks of wine or, in this spring of the year, loading bundles of shorn wool bound for Flanders and Normandy. A fresh breeze blew up from the water, bringing the odors of roasting meat from the cooking fires along the embankment and in the moored ships.

Aylena sniffed the air and caught the unconscious look of longing on Thor's bearded face.

"Are you hungry, my lord?"

He straightened and turned, looking down at her with pleasure, ignoring her question.

"Were you suited by my choices, my lady?"

"I was." Her clear eyes met his directly. "Each cloth and color you chose was beautiful. I had not expected such taste from a Norman mercenary. You are kind to take on the debt, but I will repay you when I can."

Thor stared, surprised. He had bought many a

gown for a lady-in-waiting, but not one had been so frank in doubting his taste, nor, for that matter, offered to repay him. "If you are pleased," he said, hiding amusement, "I am already repaid." He looked back up to the opening of the street and motioned to Philip to bring up their horses. "I am hungry, and so are my men. I'll send them to buy a meal from the public cookshops, and we'll find a place to eat on the embankment."

They rode west along the river and found a spot where the crumbled ruins of the old Roman wall, long ago undermined by the river current, offered a clean and dry spot to sit. Philip and the Reeve brothers came with food and wine and settled down with them to eat. They were all full of high spirits, laughing and talking, relieved, Aylena thought, to be free of the strict rules of the king's court. She felt the same, lazily leaning on a smoothed section of stone pillar, eating pasties and spring berries and listening to the men.

Nicholas Reeve, huge and Saxon-blond, was laughing heartily at his brother Martin's tale about one of the queen's courtiers who had pulled the wool over her eyes and the eyes of the king as well. They had been discussing him as they rode up and were embroidering the story with their own feelings.

"The man has a silver tongue," Martin added. "He not only convinced the queen of his sincere devotion to her, he has fooled King Henry into believing he had never supported King Stephen. But Stephen, according to others, had loaded him with favors, giving him an earldom and the demesne he asked for."

"Which King Henry took for himself," Philip broke in, grinning. "Our king is well aware of its value. I am not at all sure that our liege lord was ever taken in."

"Enough of gossip," Thor said. "There is no proof." He frowned, and they fell silent, glancing at each other. Aylena looked away, surprised at Thor's gruff tone and disappointed not to learn the courtier's name. It was best to know who could be trusted . . . and whom not to trust. But perhaps her cousin would know.

Aylena learned London in the next week. Thor took her everywhere, even to the famous Smithfield, a smooth meadow outside the walls where on every sixth day of the week the horse traders brought their finest animals to show off their paces. There were races, and wagers on the races; there were the earls, barons, and knights of the realm come out to buy fancy saddle horses, sumpter horses, and infrequently, a costly war-horse. They often stopped to confer with Thor and stare at the golden-haired lady with him.

"I will buy you a blooded mare when we return from France," Thor told Aylena as they watched the races, but Aylena shook her head.

"I need no mare, my lord. I can ride any horse in the Stewart stable. In truth, I am far too much in your debt now to allow you to add more."

"We will see."

They were sitting alone in one of the roofed enclosures set aside for nobles and their ladies near the London walls. Aylena's bright hair brought light to the shadows, her dark blue eyes glowed like jewels. Her mouth, soft in a half smile, drew Thor's heated gaze. Without duties or care, with good rest and a constant round of pleasures, wine, and good food, Thor's physical desire for her was growing unmanageable. Nor could he divert it to a less innocent, more carnal woman for relief. He had tried, and left the woman's bed at the first touch of her alien flesh. But when he thought of asking Aylena for her love, he thought of the men in that filthy hut. After being despoiled by beasts, how could she help but hate the act of love from any man? He would wait until these distractions and duties were over and then he would ask for her hand in marriage. Perhaps a ceremony and a blessing from a priest would allow her to bear it . . . and learn to love him.

"Tomorrow," he said after a long silence, "we leave for Winchester. Three ships have come in at Southhampton, a port near the capital; our queen may wish to travel to her duchy in France on one of them."

Aylena gasped and half rose from her seat. "Why, then, shouldn't we be preparing for the trip? My new clothes—"

"Philip of Anjou took your maid Margit to the draper's shop this morning to gather them up. Your packing is being done, as mine is. We will be ready."

She sank back down again, excited yet frowning. "I should have known, Thor. You accomplish much in your life without asking for advice from anyone."

His infrequent grin flashed white in the black beard. "Thank you, my lady." He reached over and took her small hand in his, closing his long fingers gently. "I hope you're a true prophet. There is one passionate goal of mine own that needs more than ordinary thought. I may need a miracle."

Aylena smiled uncertainly. He had seemed to hold himself aloof from her recently; she couldn't credit her first thought that he might be referring to her denial of him. "Oh? In that case, Thor, I shall pray for your success. . . ."

He laughed abruptly and stood, pulling her up with him. Around them, others were leaving the field of horses, most of them mounted, a few leading a newly purchased colt or dray horse. The sun was going down, the air cooling rapidly. "Come," he said, and drew her hand to his arm. "We'll be missed and wondered about unless we hurry."

She knew that to be fact. When the courtiers gathered in Palatine Castle, the main diversion of the evening was guessing why this or that couple came late to dinner—and the laughter was always bawdy.

8

King Henry's party, some seventy-five men and women of varying rank, left London's west gates at dawn of the next day, continuing to ride west until the Thames narrowed and they found a suitable crossing. Then they turned southwest toward Winchester, England's capital city.

The road was wide and well used, but those coming toward them gave way at the first sight of the brilliant red silk banner with the ferocious Plantagenet lions shining gold in the sun. They left the road and stood in the fields to watch the royal procession go by, some of them silent and gaping, others giving a rousing cheer for King Henry.

The royal couple led, as if in formal parade, yet set up a good pace. Queen Eleanor, swathed in a maroon velvet cloak and hood, rode a white Arabian stallion. She handled the fiery animal, Aylena noted, as well as any man. The king rode his handsome war-horse. After them came the roofed and draped wagon in which their son—now a robust six-week-old infant—rode with his two nurses and three ladies-in-waiting. Half

of the queen's courtiers and ladies were making the
trip and were in high spirits, laughing and talking.
It pleased Aylena to see her cousin, Sir Charles
Halchester, mounted on a high-stepping palfrey and
looking, she thought, very handsome. She watched a
lighthearted exchange of compliments between him
and Marie de Fermi and smiled. The two of them
would make a charming couple. . . .

The royal guards, a hard-bitten group of battle-
trained knights, followed the royal party closely.
Henry II was a popular king, but there was always a
man or two in England who would put up a scheme
against the throne.

Riding next in line were Thor and Aylena, with
Thor's knights behind them. Margit, visibly thrilled to
be part of a king's retinue, rode with the knights. Pack
animals in the rear carried the baggage.

The April weather was ideal. Once away from London's coal smoke and open drains, the air was pure
and dazzling bright. There were wild roses beginning
to bloom along the hedgerows, and birds singing their
mating songs in newly green bushes and trees. Aylena
was entranced, tempted to slow her horse to a walk
and enjoy the scene around her. Her home in Northumbria had little to offer in spring glory compared
with this soft and fertile land.

She glanced at Thor, finding his gaze on her. As
always, her skin warmed where his glance touched.
He, too, looked fresh and vibrant, his beard shining
near blue-black in the sunlight, his bronzed skin
gleaming, his smile quick and admiring. She felt the
familiar rush of heat within, the wish to touch him, to
hold him. But—they were close in other ways now
. . . too close. She had to force herself to remember

that he was the barrier that stood between her and her promise to her dying father—to make sure of the Stewart castle and demesne for Ian, and for the clan. Still looking ahead, she spoke of the trip merely to hide her thoughts.

"It takes two days of riding to reach Winchester, I am told. Where will we stop tonight?"

Thor laughed. "Our king was wise in his choices of the outlaw castles to be left standing—he chose to pardon the few within a day's ride of London, and if they swore fealty to him, he let their castles stand. There is one, therefore, halfway between London and Winchester. A messenger was sent to announce that the king and his party would be there tonight and in Winchester on the morrow."

"I see. But . . . is that wise? If the king has secret enemies, that information might help them attack him."

Thor's brows rose. "That is true, though most women would not see the possibility. But with the royal guards and my own men, I doubt his enemies would risk it."

"And will the royal guards also go to France?"

"No, for the king won't. Henry will stay in England. Only the queen and her party will visit Aquitaine— and, naturally, Languedoc."

She shook her head slightly, marveling. "But . . . how long will they be apart?"

"The king has told Eleanor to return by the first of June. Her pleasures in the south of France may keep her an extra day or two, but, though she's very strong-minded, she does give respect to Henry. She fears his Angevin temper."

She nodded, and was quiet. They had come to a

rough stretch of road turning upward over a small rise, a trail gullied by rain and frost, and everyone had slowed and stopped talking while their horses scrambled through it. Nor did they resume the loud laughter and talk when they gained level ground. It was as if the company had taken note of the first difficulty and begun to think of the tiring days ahead.

It was near dark when the company came to Tunbridge Castle and the nervously sweating, bowing baron who tried hard to please the king and his company. There was a great feast, and comfortable beds for the nobility; the knights and servants were supplied with pallets, rushes, and covers. At dawn they were all up and hurrying through a breakfast of ale and hot bread with sweet butter.

Glancing back as they left, Aylena caught a look of great relief on the face of the Baron Tunbridge. The king had told him during breakfast that his castle was safe and would remain in his possession, unless he harassed his neighbors.

Today the courtiers and ladies-in-waiting were tired, and silent except for a few complaints. At the noon rest, Sir Charles came to the shaded glen where Aylena walked, dismounted from his horse, and took her hand, asking how she fared.

She left her hand in his and smiled. "Tis a pleasure to journey in such weather, cousin, and in such beautiful countryside. Are you going on to France?"

"Indeed. I am looking forward to introducing you to the wines and foods of Languedoc, the true domain of epicurean pleasures." He squeezed the hand, his pale eyes alight with admiration. "I will be your interpreter, Aylena. Even some of the French have trouble with the Languedoc speech."

"And with their habits," Thor said from behind Aylena. She felt the weight of his hand on her shoulder, loosed Charles's hand, and looked up at Thor, wondering what thought had made his eyes so hard. He stepped forward to a place beside her, pulling her closer, still staring at Charles.

"You can return to your play with the Lady Marie, Halchester, and stop worrying about your cousin. She will be safe from any harm."

Halchester smiled slowly. "But will she enjoy herself? Tis a shame for a young and beautiful noblewoman to visit the citadels of pure pleasure and never indulge."

Surprisingly, Thor's angry expression relaxed into humor. "You may believe you are tempting Aylena, Sir Charles, but tis I who am tempted now. Do you risk it?"

Lightly, Charles stepped away toward his horse and mounted swiftly, his smile crooked as he looked back at Thor. "I would be a fool to risk tempting you, Baron Rodancott. I will leave my cousin's welfare in your hands."

Around them, other travelers were mounting and riding away toward the road to Winchester. Without words, Thor took Aylena to her horse and held the reins while she mounted. Aylena was deep in thought, but thanked him. He stood still a moment, his hand resting on her slender knee, feeling her warmth through the layers of cloth over it. His eyes on hers, he spoke.

"Your cousin, if indeed he is your cousin, leads a far different life than yours, Aylena. His reputation is well known to English nobles—but is not as well known to King Henry. I would like your promise not to be alone

with him, nor to go with him to any of the—what did
he call them?—the citadels of pleasure in Languedoc."

Aylena's face was sober. "My cousin is dear to me,
Thor. I have no other relative except for my young
brother. But you have my complete trust. If you ask
me to be cautious around him, I surely will do so."
She smiled at his look of relief. "You've protected me
well. I'll not change to other advice now."

"Then you promise not to go with him alone?"

She nodded. "I do so promise, my lord."

Before the sun set the king's party was in sight of
Winchester. They came up and over the surrounding
chalk downs and saw the ancient walled city, bathed
with slanting afternoon sun, sprawled over a hilly site
in the thickly wooded valley of the Itchen River. Raising a hand, the king stopped the long, uneven straggle
of tired nobles and knights that followed along after
him.

"Straighten your backs and get in line," he said,
"before the citizens of Winchester think an army of
sleepy fools is descending upon them. Break out more
banners, and look alive. We go in by Westgate and
head for St. Swithun's Cathedral."

In moments he had what he wanted. Directly behind the royal couple came the wagon, draperies
pulled back to show the infant and his erect and smiling nurses. Then the courtiers and the beautiful ladies-in-waiting, all with their backs straight, gracious
smiles on their faces, riding two by two.

"Miraculous," Aylena breathed as they passed
through the city gates. Thor smiled, but his head
didn't turn.

"They know the manners," he said, staring ahead, "and when to use them. Copy them, my love."

My love. Her face, stiffly smiling as they entered a street lined with grinning, gawking people, turned pink. She hardly heard the roars of approval that came from the citizens of Winchester.

My love? Her heart swelled hugely, filling her chest. She stole a quick glance at Thor, and saw a gradually fading look of amazement on his bronzed face. So, he had surprised himself as well as her. She looked ahead and saw in the lower part of the city a wide and beautiful walled close, and in it a cathedral. They rode into the close through gates quickly opened by men running before them, and dismounted. Then, leaving the horses held by many willing hands, they followed King Henry and Queen Eleanor inside huge doors and marched up the long nave to the altar, where they knelt and gave thanks to God for a safe journey.

The palace, near Kingsgate, was far smaller than Palatine Castle in London, but there was room enough and more for the king's party, and a banquet was set out in the great hall. Those who would travel on to France ate and retired early, for Queen Eleanor ordered them to leave for Southampton at dawn.

"The queen is as strong and tireless as a man," Margit said, amazed. Half asleep herself, she was helping Aylena ready herself for bed. "Her babe not two months old yet, and she as fit as a young maiden."

"She is known for her endurance," Aylena said, and yawned. "And her determination." She smiled suddenly. "But her husband is stronger yet. In time, he will rule her."

"But he is eleven years younger than the queen. Do you truly believe that?"

"I do. Thor says Plantagenet blood breeds strong men, and will breed more before it runs thin."

Margit laughed. "Oh, so the sire is your seer. Do you believe everything he says?"

Aylena smiled. "I do, except in one thing. I do not believe his efforts will make him master of Ian's castle."

Mid-morning of the next day saw the queen's party aboard two large ships, with double masts and lateen sails, in the harbor of Southampton. The craft, sporting both flags—that of England and of Aquitaine—had raised and shaded sterns, offering extra comfort and more safety, for they were made with thicker planks than most. The horses, blindfolded, were loaded into one vessel and tied to iron rings, with knights to handle them; the other took the queen and her company aboard. Thor, not satisfied that the warhorses would stand for rough treatment by strangers, took Aylena aside to explain why they would be separated for the trip across.

"Watch what you say," he added afterward, "if your cousin is about. He is clever in his plans to better himself."

"I will watch my tongue, then. But I wish you would take me in your ship. . . ." She paused, embarrassed, and gazed up at him, her eyes their deepest blue in the morning sun, her curved and slender body sculptured in thin silk by the brisk breeze. "I shouldn't ask, I know, but I would be much happier traveling in the same bark as you."

Looking at her, Thor's face showed his hunger. He reached to smooth back a strand of her golden hair that had escaped the thick braid, and let his hand rest a moment on her shoulder. "I feel the same. But this ship is full of rough men and frightened horses. Stay with our queen and her favorites. With this fair wind, tis only a day and a night and then an early dawn landing in the Baie de la Seine."

A shelter in the stern of the other carvel had been fitted with cushioned seats and pillows for the queen and her women; there was a section in the forepeak set aside for the courtiers. Between them, the sailors went about their tasks and their personal duties as if they were alone, neither staring nor listening as far as Aylena could discover. In all, everyone seemed to take the sailing trip as commonplace. She watched the first carvel leave the docks and make its way slowly down the river, sails flapping, and was glad when the ship she was on moved out and followed.

The river ran clear and smooth, carrying them down into the harbor. There the seamen hoisted the sails and, handling them with skill, coasted out into the salty air of the English Channel, passing a large island on the right. Then the lines to the sails were drawn tight and the boats quickened, cutting through the waves from the force of the wind.

Steersmen, standing on either quarter of the rear deck, handled the two heavy oar-shaped rudders, keeping the ship on course. Aylena was fascinated. She rose from her seat and, gaining her balance on the heaving deck, went forward to lean on the thick gunwale to watch.

"So, my dear cousin, what do you think of sailing?" Sir Charles's pleasant voice came from behind her, and she turned, startled but smiling.

"I think it enjoyable, Sir Charles, but I imagine it would be very different in bad weather."

He laughed and leaned on the gunwale beside her, his fair hair gleaming in the noon sun. "Again you remind me of your mother. Alyse was a woman like you, one who examined all sides of something—or someone—new to her."

That was true. She remembered her mother refusing to make a decision until she saw a problem from all sides. Her mother had been fair, always, a perfect foil for her father's volatile temper. She smiled at Charles, warming to him again. But, she thought, he had shown another side—one she hadn't admired— when Thor challenged him. She must be careful.

"My mother was a wise woman," she said, agreeing. "Would that I be half as wise once I learn the world. In the meantime, I study what I can. Tell me, since you've been on this trip before, how many days will it be until we turn home again?"

His eyes widened. "We have but begun, my lady, and you think of home?" He laughed, genuinely amused. "As I remember, we travel twenty days before we reach Nîmes. Once there, our queen will tarry as long as she can—perhaps a fortnight, perhaps more. When she remembers the king's temper, she will pack and leave—with speed, and great regret."

Somehow, Philip of Anjou had appeared at Aylena's other side, leaning there, watching the waves purl

along the side of the boat. He touched Aylena's arm
and pointed ahead.

"We are overtaking the other ship, my lady. I suspect the horses are proving to be a heavier load than
we."

"Tis likely," she agreed, and laughed. "We must
wave, Sir Philip, as we sail past. Tis not often we out-
distance our friend." She looked around for Charles,
but he had disappeared into the forepeak quarters.
Looking to sea again, watching the other craft grow
larger as they gained on it, she thought of what Thor
might think if he'd seen her in close communion with
her cousin. Twas certain he would dislike it . . . and
perhaps Charles knew that and left rather than cause
trouble. If so, then no doubt he meant it kindly.

"He's there," she said suddenly, and flung up an
arm, waving wildly. "I see his black hair above the
other men. See, Philip? He's standing near the fore-
mast, wearing his red cloak . . . and he . . . oh, he
looks wonderful!"

9

A steady wind and smooth running sea gave the travelers a restful night. Waking early, feeling the easy rise and fall of the ship, Aylena slipped from her pillows and moved quietly through the other sleeping figures. Once away from the others she smoothed down her disarranged clothing and looked out over the water to the east. Behind a misty bank of clouds a pink dawn was rising into a deep blue sky, where a pale star still lingered above the horizon. And —she caught her breath in wonder at the sight—a tall woman leaned on the lee gunwale, her long fingers gripping the weather-beaten wood, her profile pink from the light in the east, her body immobile, waiting. The queen of England, her usual mask of superiority now a naked look of longing, was waiting like an eager child for the first sight of her native land.

Aylena looked away, not wanting the queen to think she spied on her. All the other women were still sleeping; the sailors, with nothing to do, lounged on the bare deck. Only the steersmen were at their posts, tending the rudders. The ship was silent in the calming seas, in the quiet dawn. She coughed a little, her head down, her hands smoothing her skirt, then moved a few feet toward the starboard side. The queen's voice came, filled with the usual amusement.

"So, the young can also rise early. Come, Lady Aylena, and watch with me."

Eleanor's elegant eyebrows were arched, her mouth curved, in either humor or derision, it was hard to tell. Aylena went obediently and stood near the queen, seeing that what she had thought a bank of clouds was solid land. A pristine white beach ran up from the sea to a thickly forested bluff, with morning mists rising like smoke over it and the sunrise tinting the mist with a fire of red and gold.

"If this be France, my queen," Aylena said, her voice soft, "then France is the most beautiful country I have ever seen. Tis no wonder you wish to visit your homeland."

Staring across the water to the land, the queen was silent for a moment, then glanced at Aylena's dreaming young face.

"There are times," she said slowly, "when I would give all I have to be young and free again in Aquitaine, running on the wild shore of the Baie du Biscay. Tis much like this, though the winds there take your breath away, and the waves are huge and glorious, or seemed so to an excited child. My father . . ." She let the last words falter and trail away, as if memories suddenly flooded back, too many to tell. She straightened then and shook her mood away with a question.

"I have heard that your mother was from the noble family of Belmain, a demesne near to Winchester in Wessex. How came she to wed a wild Scot?"

Aylena suddenly forgot the necessity of answering a queen with respect. "My father was no wild Scot! He was chieftain of the Stewart clan, and well educated in the best of England's schools. He was also strong, able, and exceedingly handsome—and he loved my mother above all things, from the moment he first saw her until the day he died."

Queen Eleanor smiled, but faintly. "She was a fortunate woman, then," she said. "There are few husbands who remain constant in their hearts. Where is your mother now?"

Aylena bit her lip. She had remembered at last her lack of proper courtesy to the queen. "She is in her grave, Your Highness. She died giving birth to a son for the Stewart line; my young brother, Ian. Tis in his behalf that I will approach the king."

"That much I had heard," Eleanor replied, and yawned. "Go now to my servants and say that I am hungry. That should waken them to their duties."

That conversation played over in Aylena's mind until they slipped into a Normandy harbor near the peninsula of Cotentin. Then the confusion, the excitement that exploded around the piers, the shouts and cheers from the jostling crowds that ran up from the village streets drove it out.

It was thrilling to have the crowd cheering the unexpected arrival of the queen of England, and she was glad to be with the queen's party, for the knights had to encircle the queen and her women to keep the unruly crowd back. Then she was tossed up into a saddle by Thor, forced to quiet a nervous horse and, finally, escape from the crush.

The knights still grouped around them, the women

and the draped wagon went riding into a fairyland of mist, lush fields, and cattle. Aylena glanced over at Thor in his red cloak, found his eyes as soft as the mist around them, and her heart expanded, filling her chest too tight to breathe.

"I missed you," she said, and felt her face grow hot. "I mean, it seemed quite . . . quite lonely on our ship. This is much better. And tis a beautiful country . . ." She subsided, aware of her useless chatter, positive that she bored him.

"Normandy was my first home," Thor said after a long moment, "but it became beautiful to me only today, when you stepped foot on it."

She met his eyes again, and swallowed. She wanted to say something clever; she wanted to thank him for the chivalrous remark, but she could do neither. She knew very well her voice would give her away. In fact, she was completely entranced by the man who had taken her brother's birthright. Disgusting!

That night they spent in a castle in Fougeres the next, after a long hard ride, they spent in Angers, in the fertile land of the Loire River. There was a large abbey there, and Queen Eleanor stopped their dawn departure long enough for prayer. A respectful crowd gathered to watch her emerge from the great carved doors, head down, hands pressed together, her lips still moving. The silence was profound. No one spoke nor moved until she lifted her head and smiled.

"I have prayed for us all," she said clearly. "May God bless you forever."

They roared their approval. There were cries: "God bless you, Eleanor of Aquitaine! May your star rise even higher!" She walked through the noisy, ap-

plauding crowd without fear; they trampled each
other to clear a path for her.

"They love her," Aylena said, as they moved toward
the east again. "She still rules them in their hearts.
But what do they mean, Thor, in speaking of her rising star?"

Thor shrugged. "She has been the Duchess of Aquitaine, and the queen of France, and she is now queen
of England. There are those among her admirers who
believe she will bring the two countries together and
begin an empire."

"What? Why, that is imposs—"

"Shhh."

"Indeed," Aylena said after a moment, "I do see
that silence is best when dealing with dreams." Her
smile was a bit wry. "Especially now. Where do we
stay tonight?"

"'Tis likely to be Poitiers, and, if the weather holds,
tomorrow night will see us in Bordeaux. There Eleanor will be welcomed again with open arms."

"I am already tired of traveling."

Thor smiled. "And I. I have dreamed recently of a
castle in Northumbria. Wild and lonely it may be, but
it calls to my heart."

And to mine, Aylena thought, and turned away,
mounting her horse and following the queen. What
Thor had said had brought back the problems and
heartaches she'd left in Northumbria. She thought of
the wild and undoubtedly lonely boy even farther
north, in more desolate surroundings, whose dreams
were also wrapped around that castle. And she was
beginning to worry about him. John Bretinalle was a
vindictive little man; it was possible he'd take out his
hatred of her on her brother. Still, if he did, he'd face

the combined fury of every member of the Stewart clan. He wasn't likely to risk it.

One look at her preoccupied face, her downcast eyes, and Thor knew she was thinking of Ian. He set his jaw, knowing he'd started her train of thought with his remark about the Stewart castle. He had taken that castle without a drop of blood on either side, and often that was a fatal flaw. Things easily won were hard to keep, but he meant to keep this one.

After Angers the towns and people, the castles and the broad, lovely rivers and vineyards of France began to flow together in Aylena's mind. Bordeaux turned out with banners and speeches to honor their queen, for Bordeaux was now an English port and governed by homesick Englishmen. The party left the city burdened with cases of Bordeaux wine for their friends in Languedoc, and followed the Garonne River through the foothills of the Pyrenees and on to Narbonne, the first of the cities on the bank of the Gulf of the Lion, a large and shallow piece of the blue Mediterranean Sea. The next day they left the coastline and traveled a smooth and well-made road to Nîmes, a small, ancient city at the foot of the Garrigues hills, barren mounds that protected Nîmes and its treasures from unruly winds. On the highest of the hills there was an old Roman tower, Tour Magne, lived in by monks, giving a hint as to the splendid antiquities found in the town itself.

There were many gates in the city's walls, and most of them open. Riding in, the queen's party passed a tremendous Roman amphitheater of great age, once used for chariot races and still standing, though unused. There was a Roman temple and the ruins of many more ancient buildings. Then they were in the center of the present town and continuing on.

"There," Marie de Fermi said, smiling and pointing, "is our queen's own chateau, built for her by King Louis of France. It's lovely inside, Aylena."

And outside, Aylena thought, enthralled. The news of their intended visit had traveled even faster than they. The Chateau d'Ardeur, graceful, castellated, and faced with white marble, was hung with blue and gold banners to welcome its owner. The train turned in through open gates and found servants waiting to take their horses and baggage and whisk them away. Inside the great hall there were huge bouquets of spring flowers and the tantalizing odors of Languedoc cuisine. The queen swept through the paneled rooms, nodding to the house servants, then turned to her seneschal, Claude.

"As always, you have done well, Claude. Are enough beds ready for my guests?"

Claude smiled. "Indeed, Your Highness. And word sent around to your friends to announce your arrival."

"Very good. Plan a banquet for the third evening of our stay."

"It has been planned, Your Highness."

Eleanor laughed, her eyes gleaming with good humor. "How pleasant it is to be in a civilized country. Will we have our music and other entertainment?"

Claude grinned hugely. "Indeed, Your Highness. Your favorite singers and dancers have been hired, and a new one you will like. Your dinner will be remembered by all."

"Wonderful! Now, find maids to settle my infant son and his nurses, and, naturally, the guests."

Aylena and Margit were given a small tower room with a southeastern view of the plain of Vistre, covered now by acres of grapevines heavy with bloom, and, so far in the distance they looked like smoke, the beginning foothills of the Provence Alps. The ladies-in-waiting changed their riding clothes for simple gowns and trooped down the stairs again, stopping to take Aylena with them. They were excited, happy, but too exhausted to make an evening of it. They ate, their eyes drooping, rose from the table, and went to bed.

The beds, Aylena thought, were the best she'd ever tried. Margit agreed. They slept hard, but woke as usual in early morning refreshed and hungry. Once they were dressed and Aylena's hair brushed and braided, Margit went to the door, stopping with her hand on the latch to look back. "Shall I bring you something to eat, my lady?"

Aylena smiled but refused. "I will wait until others stir. I must learn the customs here."

Margit nodded and left; Aylena could hear her soft footsteps going down the first steps. But she was back almost immediately, quivering with excitement.

"The queen spoke to *me*! Can you imagine? She saw me when I passed her door, and called me in, asking about you. You are to go to her room at once and breakfast with her. She said you are the only guest who rises as early as she."

Rising to her feet, Aylena gave Margit a frightened glance. "Am I suitable? Do you think a different gown . . . ?"

"You look your best in that cream silk and blue overgown. And the queen is not a patient woman. Come!"

Aylena straightened her back and swept from the

room. It had not been such a bad thing, that talk on
the ship. She would listen again, as she had then, and
learn more.

The draperies in the queen's suite on the second
floor diluted the golden sunlight to a soft glow. Eleanor, wearing a lavish robe of pale yellow satin edged
in matching lace, looked rested. She sat at a marble-
topped table near the windows, feasting on pastry and
ripe fruit, smiling as one of her tiring women motioned Aylena inside.

"I would have wagered you'd be up and dressed for
the day, Lady Aylena, though I am sure none of the
other ladies are awake. Come, have some of these
pastries. I despise eating alone."

Aylena thanked her and sat in the chair the tiring
woman brought, hurriedly, to the other side of the
small table. The woman, middle-aged and more confident than most maids, also brought a plate and filled
it for her. Aylena bit into a small pastry hungrily.

"Mmm. This is very good, Your Highness."

Eleanor laughed. "Naturally. Tis a Languedoc
pastry. There are none better in Europe. You will
grow fat on them while we are here."

Aylena smiled and reached for another. "I believe
you. They are filled with clotted cream that tastes of
raspberries but has none in it."

"A Languedoc secret, I fear." The queen motioned
the maid to bring watered wine to the table to fill their
cups, and the maid was there at once, tilting a clay
carafe.

Taking a sip, Aylena studied the queen over the rim
of her cup. Eleanor was always striking, and no less
so now, her abundant lemon-colored hair loose on
her shoulders, her large, well-shaped breasts half ex-

posed by the low neckline of her robe. Her pale eyes suddenly met Aylena's gaze, sharp and clear. Putting her cup down, Aylena felt a flush coloring her cheeks.

"You are more beautiful than I first thought," the queen said after a few moments. "You have been blessed with a lovely figure to match a charming face. But you must learn to display yourself to better effect."

Startled, Aylena put down the pastry she had picked up. "Must I, Your Highness?"

Eleanor stared, and then laughed abruptly. "You mystify me. I have no women in my court who would ask such a question. All want to be known for their beauty and charm."

Aylena felt her face go hot. "But . . . their lives are much different from mine. In Northumbria there is little thought given to appearance or—or elegance. I am able to birth sheep and shear them; I can bind up wounds on either animal or man and I know how to train the dogs we need to herd the sheep and protect them from wolves. Those are the necessary skills in my life."

There was a silence between them that stretched too long for Aylena's comfort. Finally, the queen spoke again, and this time bluntly.

"Those were necessary skills when you were in the Stewart castle, my dear. The necessary skills in my court are far different. They include making the most of your beauty and charm, subtly leading others to think well of me, and—most of all—attracting a strong noble who can be of use to us. I find your air of propriety odd, considering your . . . ah, close friendship with Thor Rodancott. Tell me, why do the two of you persist in sleeping apart? Is he tiring of you?"

Again there was silence. Aylena's face was drained of color, her dark blue eyes fixed in wonder on the queen's irritated face. Why had the queen thought her a bawd? Who had lied to her? Finally she rose from her chair and bowed.

"You have been given false information, Your Highness. Lord Rodancott and I are not—have never been —lovers. He has been my protector and friend, and that is all."

"Are you lying to me, Lady Aylena?"

Aylena flushed. "I never lie."

"A pity, then. I had hoped to gain Rodancott's strength and influence because of you. But there, if he has no great feeling for you, perhaps one of the other women will undertake the pleasurable task of bringing him into our fold."

"Perhaps," Aylena repeated, dazed. "Though he is already sworn to guard and protect you. King Henry gave him the order."

Eleanor gave her an incredulous stare and then laughed, genuinely amused. "I would fain give the baron his orders myself, my dear. Now, if you like, you may go. But remember the banquet tomorrow night. You must look your best."

Aylena bowed herself out of the room and ran up the stairs to the chamber she shared with Margit. There, still amazed and upset, she removed the delicate clothes she wore and put on a forest green samite gown and hooded cloak she often used for riding. She burned with desire to get away from the chateau and into the fresh air. She needed to think, to search out the meanings of what Queen Eleanor had said. Some of it made no sense at all. . . .

Going down the winding stairs again she was glad to see that the door to the queen's suite was closed, and she continued on, turning toward the rear of the chateau. She had noticed that the horses had been led around to stables on the east side. Surely it would be safe in this clean, beautiful city to ride alone, as she always had done in Northumbria. . . .

A quarter hour later Aylena rode out of the court-yard and took the narrow path along a shallow and winding river. Thor's stable man, who had come along to take care of Thor's horses, had helped her with the saddling. He came to the high door of the stables and stood watching to see what direction she chose. Then, his brow wrinkled, he called over one of the household servants passing through the gardens.

"Tell the Baron Rodancott that James of Muir has a message for him."

The servant shook his head. "The baron is sleeping."

"Wake him. He will thank you for it later."

"The blame will be on your head, friend."

"I accept it." He turned and went back in to saddle the horse Thor would want. Behind him, another stable hand greeted Sir Charles Halchester, sleepy-eyed and disheveled, who cut the greeting off with a rough command.

"One of the best horses, Tom, and be quick about it. I'm in a hurry."

In a short time Charles rode out and turned south on the narrow path, too preoccupied with his errand to notice Thor's hurried arrival at the stable. Thor looked after him, noted his tense profile, and shrugged. Halchester had enemies to be wary of in any city, and perhaps most of all in Nîmes. He was a man who took advantage of the tolerance granted to visiting nobles and always went too far. Thor put him out of his mind and went on into the stable, finding James of Muir cleaning a stall, while Thor's favorite mount, saddled and bridled, was tied to a pole beside him.

"What's this about?"

James turned and saw him. "The Lady Aylena Stewart came here, clearly upset and trying hard to hide it. She took a horse and rode off alone. She's on the path along the stream that leads to the city. She may have company you won't like—Lord Halchester is following her."

Thor cursed and grabbed the tether that held his horse, jerking it loose. Mounting, he kicked the horse into a canter, ducking low as they went through the doors. His horse was in full gallop as he turned onto the winding path. Far ahead, he saw the bay horse ridden by Halchester disappear around a bend. He had heard the queen's voice, summoning a maid to waken Halchester and send him out, but he hadn't known why. What lies would Halchester whisper in Aylena's ear? What promises of help with the king? If Aylena knew King Henry's opinion of Halchester, she would never ask him to intervene.

Riding fast and alone in the cool morning air calmed Aylena. The horse she rode was fine gaited, smooth as silk and willing. She stroked his neck with a gloved hand and spoke to him softly, smiling as his ears flicked back and forth. He, at least, seemed to listen when she spoke.

Later, there was a sheen of sweat on the horse's neck and forequarters, and, though there was no sound of labored breathing, she pulled him down to a trot and began to look around. She had come close to the heart of the city, yet except for a few ragged beggars searching refuse piles there was no one else about. It was full daylight now, but still no street cleaners, no shopkeepers getting ready for the day, no priests hurrying along in their robes. Only the ancient buildings and gnarled olive trees, dreaming of the past, cast their shadows on the empty streets. Thor had been right; the customs here were not those of Northumbria, nor like England in busy London or Winchester. This city, with all its past history of strength and art displayed, lived on like a beautiful bawd grown old, still lying abed, glorying in the long ago days of her passion.

There was sound behind her, a horse galloping . . . or was it more than one? She turned to look and saw her cousin Charles bearing down on her. He was waving and smiling, his straw-colored hair glinting in the morning sun. She slowed and stopped, waiting for him, feeling a sudden gratitude. He must have seen her leave and decided to keep her company. In truth, it might well be helpful. Since he was a member of the court, he might know what the queen truly expected from her. Not, she thought, that she would act upon it—if it meant demeaning herself . . .

They were together, talking, when Thor came in sight. One look at his stiff face and Aylena knew he was angry—likely with her. But Thor came up to them and greeted them both with strained courtesy. Then he turned to Charles.

"If you will, thank the queen for her concern and tell her the Lady Aylena is safe with me."

Charles shrugged. "I will. But you put yourself out for nothing. I would have escorted my cousin to such sights as she wished to see, and brought her back to the chateau unharmed."

Thor bared his teeth in a stiff smile. "A privilege I claim, Halchester. The lady is in my care."

Wheeling his horse, Charles laughed. "Then you must cultivate a watchful eye, Lord Rodancott. Your lady tends to fly away while you sleep." He rode off, chuckling.

There was a silence. Aylena studied her folded hands, conscious of Thor in every fiber. She could feel a tension between them like a stretched string on a crwth, humming as it tightened. After a long moment, she raised her eyes to meet his gaze, and found it watchful but warm. The anger had not been directed at her. She took a relieved breath and spoke.

"I did not fly from you, Thor. The queen lectured me on the duties of her court, and . . . then I wanted to be alone."

Thor's face went crimson with anger. "I had hoped the queen would recognize your innocence and leave you out of her machinations. Still, I should have known twas her doing when James of Muir told me you'd fled the place. You would never run from anyone else. Damn her! She is so steeped in court life she can no longer recognize a virtuous woman."

"Shhh!" Aylena glanced around quickly, but saw no one near them. She urged her horse into a walk and motioned to Thor to join her, moving away from the bushes along the path into the empty streets. He seemed almost to know without being told how the queen had intimidated her. But that wasn't important. Twas the queen's plan for him that was worrisome. Somehow, she must convince him of his danger and keep him safe.

"She has power, Thor. Over you and me, as well as all the others. She has said she wants you as part of her court, and will set some attractive woman to lead you in." When Thor's startled eyes met hers, Aylena flushed. "She was interested in me because she thought we were lovers and I might coax you into allegiance to her. When I told her we were only friends, she became angry. Now, if she hears words set against her, she may think them yours."

Thor's look of surprise faded. "She has frightened you," he said, "but she knows too well that my allegiance is with the king and he values it. She'll not dare to do harm to either of us. Come, forget her—and enjoy the day."

Suddenly aware of Thor's strength and her own silly fears, Aylena managed a smile. "I will, then. I will put her out of my mind. What shall we do?"

Thor grinned. "First, find a cookshop. I'm starving. We'll take our food into the olive groves and eat beneath a tree, like the peasants."

Aylena's smile grew warmer. "Tis not new to me, this eating outdoors. We often did so in the shearing times."

The horses were close; Thor's cross-gartered leg brushed against her thigh. He looked down at her, his expression changing, growing soft and hungry. "I would be alone with you, Aylena. On our trip to London we rode together and I was content. But for days now I have seen you only in a noisy crowd, and I feel as if I've lost half of myself."

The look in his eyes, the words he said, robbed her of her breath, making her wonderfully warm and fluid inside. And weak. But she looked away and drew a long breath, determined this time to answer him in a way that would let him know there could be nothing between them, now or later. She would tell him that as long as he held Ian's castle there could be no love or even warm regard for him in her heart—or she could simply tell him she could never love a Norman enemy. Either would do. She considered the choice for a long moment, and then spoke, shakily.

"I feel . . . oh, I cannot lie to you, though I should. I—I feel the same as you do."

He let out his breath. "Good." For a moment his gaze clung to hers, his hand rested on her slim shoulder, touched her hair, and drew a finger along her soft cheek. Then he forced himself away and dug his heels into his horse's flanks. "Come! I smell fresh bread baking in the cookshop there, and there's fruit in the next stall. . . ."

They ended by riding to the northwest gates and setting off toward the hills, their purchases tied to Thor's saddle, and there on the slanting, dry flanks of the Garrigues hills found an old olive grove only a mile or so past the dusty city walls. Some of the angular, broad-leafed trees were thirty feet high, creating welcome pockets of shade. The owner of the grove was working nearby, and for the offered handful of copper coins, he gave them permission to rest and eat there. Jingling the coins happily, he walked away, letting them have the grove to themselves.

Dismounting in cool, rustling shade, Thor lifted Aylena from her saddle and held her close for a long moment. Then, intending to set her down, he kissed

her fiercely instead, as if he couldn't stop, could never
get enough of her. His mouth moved hotly over her
soft lips, crushing them, sucking them in. She was
gasping for breath when he stopped, but clinging to
him, wanting more.

"Kiss me again, Thor."

He looked down at her flushed and passionate face
and shook his head, remembering the coarse men
who had taken her like animals. "I cannot, my dear
love. I would have you here on the bare ground if I
did."

"I will be yours now, if you want . . ."

She stopped, amazed as she heard her own words.
Her face flooded with scarlet, but she didn't retract
nor even turn away. She was willing, why try to hide
it? Thor touched her hot cheek and smiled.

"You are mine, and will ever be, Aylena. But I'll not
take you like a common bawd. Come, sit and eat." His
strong hands trembled as he took off his cloak to
spread on the dusty ground, handed her the bag of
bread and fruit, and led the horses aside, tying them,
thinking he should tie himself. She wanted him, and
God! that made temptation all the greater.

She sat, trying to will away her fiery desire. She
had never before been wholly possessed by passion
and she wondered, watching Thor come toward her
with the wine flask he carried on his saddle, if she
should be ashamed of such strong desire, or was this
aching heat punishment enough? Then he dropped
down beside her and she forgot her doubts at once
and smiled at him. A woman would be a fool to be
ashamed of a feeling as warm and tantalizing as this.

They ate, staying an hour or so, while the southern
sun rose in a dazzlingly blue sky and the birds that

flickered in and out of the olive trees sang their spring courting songs. Then, knowing they would be missed and she would be reprimanded if they stayed longer, they rose, shook out the crumbs, mounted their horses, and rode back toward the chateau, unsatisfied now, but knowing that when the time came right, they would become lovers.

10

Claude, his expressive face taking on a look of caution, opened the chateau's doors for them after they had dismounted and James of Muir had led their horses away. He bowed to them both and then fastened his black eyes on Aylena.

"Queen Eleanor wishes to see you at once, Your Ladyship," he said, and flicked a nervous glance at Thor. "And . . . alone."

"Thank you," Aylena said, and handed Claude her cloak. She was suddenly full of strength. "Where is she?"

"The queen," Claude bore down hard on the title, "is in the solar at the head of the stairs. She has been waiting for over an hour."

"I will go with you," Thor said as they went toward the stairs, but Aylena shook her head.

"No. Tis likely she but requires an apology, which I am willing to offer."

Thor frowned. "Possible. But still . . ."

"No. I am not a child." She went toward the staircase and Thor followed. As she went up, she heard him a step or two behind her. She turned and faced him when they came to the top.

"I will be fine," she said, and managed a smile. "Wait for me." She hadn't meant to add those last words, but they had come out by themselves.

He nodded, and she went on, knocking at the solar door. Marie de Fermi opened it, smiled, and tossed her black curls. "Come in, *ma amie.*" She gave Thor a quick glance and smile, and took Aylena's arm, adding in a tone meant for Thor's ears, "There is no real trouble here." Then she shut the door and whispered, "Ah, Aylena, how he loves you. It is there, plain to see in his eyes. You are fortunate indeed."

"Oh, but we are only friends . . ." Aylena began, and Marie laughed, her green eyes teasing.

"So you say, and I must believe? Then I will, my dear Aylena. Or, I shall pretend I do. . . . Here she is, my queen." She gave Aylena a little shove that put her inside the next room. "Go," she whispered. "I must leave." The door closed, and Aylena was inside. Hesitantly, she went forward in the bright room, open now to the sun and air.

The queen was lying on a chaise longue and listening to a plaintive song of unrequited love, sung by a young boy, a handsome young boy, of perhaps no more than twelve years. His hands, long-fingered and slim, picked out the refrain on a lyre, and his voice, high and pure, was as clear and melodious to Aylena as the song of birds in the olive trees. The queen was, by her silence and deep concentration, enthralled.

Silent, Aylena found a chair and sat down. The queen, turning her regal head, looked at her, nodded pleasantly, and turned back, listening again. The song was nearly over, the poor lover heartbroken, the singer's young throat throbbing as he reached for the high, breaking note at the end, then his voice falling into a sob and dying away as he threw his arms out in one last appeal, and bowed low, crushed by sorrow.

The queen came out of her reverie, sitting up straight and clapping her hands. "Bravo, my dear Rossi! You must tell your father he has made a great performer. You may go now, but be sure you are ready for the dinner tomorrow night. I cannot wait to hear the compliments on my new singer!"

Beaming, the boy bowed again, and again, bowing himself out. The queen turned toward Aylena, smiling broadly. "The boy is but eleven and already a wonderful singer, is he not?"

"I have never heard better, Your Highness," Aylena said, and meant it. "How did you find him?"

Eleanor's pale eyes brightened with triumph. "Twas no more than my usual good fortune. He is my seneschal's second son and was brought to my attention by his mother. He was born with perfect pitch and an entertainer's heart."

Aylena laughed. "An entertainer's heart? What is that?"

The queen laughed with her. "Tis a heart that must have applause offered daily, his father says. He is a very proud boy."

"He has worked hard and has a right to be proud."

Nodding, the queen turned again toward the window and motioned Aylena to come and sit nearer. She rose and took a chair opposite the queen, noticing as she did so that the clear solar light was not kind to Eleanor's face. There were fine lines in the creamy skin, stitched there by time. And her smile, Aylena noted, was rather stiff. But it was there, and friendly enough.

"I fear you took my words this morning to be an insult," the queen said abruptly. "They were not. In my court there are few virgins, and I had forgotten that virginity—in some places, even, perhaps, in most places—is considered a virtue in an unmarried woman. I did not mean to hurt you."

"I know that now. Please, think no more about it, Your Highness."

Eleanor smiled playfully. "I will take that advice, if you take mine. Find Marie, and let her choose your gown for tomorrow night. She is extremely knowledgeable, and fond of you. Now, you may go. I have other musicians to hear today."

Aylena hurried out, finding Thor waiting. He walked with her up to her room, listening to what had happened, looking displeased.

"I would have liked it better had she been angry," he said afterward, leaning against the wall outside her door. "Now I must wonder what scheme she has in mind."

"Scheme?"

"Yes. There will be one. It is rare for Eleanor to admit rudeness even to those who are her favorites. For her to say what she did to you, she must have a pressing reason to gain your regard."

"But I am nothing to her!"

Thor smiled. "There are those who would say you are nothing to me, my love, yet you are all. Believe me, there is something she wants, though surely not as much as I want you. . . ." He swung a long arm around her and pulled her close, fitting her vibrant, yielding body to his. Immediately heat sprang be-

tween them, their mouths sought each other blindly
and clung, kissing, whispering, tasting. . . . Aylena's
arms went around his neck, her lips opened to him.
Her whole body was suddenly afire as his tongue
thrust in, as his hand slid down her back, cupped a
small, firm buttock, and pulled her tight against his
loins. She closed her eyes, feeling the searing heat,
tasting the essence of this man she wanted so
badly. . . .

"Such *good* friends, and so happy to see each other
safe again." Marie's amused voice preceded the soft
fall of her slippered feet and broke the spell of the
embrace. They moved apart, glancing at each other,
red-faced and stumbling over words as they greeted
Marie.

Pausing before them, her arms full of varicolored
silks, Marie smiled at them both. "I have embarrassed
you? I hope not. I was sent here, dear Aylena, to see
that you are more beautiful than ever at tomorrow's
fete. Twill be a pleasant task, but an impossible one. I
can see no faults to hide."

Aylena couldn't help laughing. "What a flatterer
you are, Marie. I cannot believe you, but I put myself
in your hands."

For that evening, and for most of the next day,
Marie de Fermi became Aylena's tutor, lady's maid,
and friend. With the help of a seamstress, Marie
changed one of the prim London gowns into an en-
trancing, low-necked evening gown of glowing emer-
ald satin. Next she tried an intricately knotted hair-
style, but the weight of Aylena's hair dragged it down.

"So," Marie said brightly, "we will leave it down, to
curl in great waves on your shoulders. I have a jew-

eled gold band to go around your head. Will you like it?''

Aylena laughed and shrugged. "I am sure I will, Lady Marie. Now, give me a hint of how to please the company."

"That is simple. You tell all the young women they are beautiful and the old women that they are wise and charming. But when it comes to the men, you must show great respect for the young, inexperienced lords and flirt madly with the old. Tis the safest course for you, and they are all flattered. . . ."

Before evening, Aylena's face ached from laughing. She no longer dreaded the banquet and the noble gathering, nor was she frightened. Marie's humor and stories of the nobles who would be attending had made it seem more a circus than an important social event.

Later, when Margit brushed Aylena's thick golden hair into the deep waves Marie had ordered and placed the jeweled gold band around the top of her head, Aylena walked to a long mirror of silver, so highly burnished she could see every eyelash reflected, and stood there, contemplating a stranger in a revealing gown. After a moment, she turned to Margit.

"What do you think?"

"You look like a member of Queen Eleanor's court," Margit said dryly, "and the Stewart, if he were still alive, would never recognize his daughter. However, there could be no young man alive who could turn away from the sight of you in that gown."

Going back to the mirror, Aylena studied herself for another long moment. It was true what Margit had said—she did look quite like the courtesans, except that they wore amazingly intricate hairstyles. She was not jealous; the golden band of jewels across her smooth forehead gave a sparkling light to her eyes. But . . . she was not sure about the low-cut gown.

"Do you think Lord Rodancott will approve?"

Margit laughed. "Were you meeting him alone, yes. But in this company tonight, he will be bristling and ready to challenge all comers."

Aylena shook her head. "He is more confident than that," she said, "and he knows I pay no attention to flattering tongues." She left the mirror and went toward the partly open door, hearing the chatter of other women coming along the hall. She glanced back at Margit and suddenly felt as if she were walking away from her old life, leaving behind all she had loved and known. Her heart sank at the thought of losing all, then she heard Marie's laugh and quick compliment and went out smiling again, feeling Marie's hand take hers, seeing the surprised glances from the other women. And at the bottom of the stairs, she saw Thor and watched his gray eyes widen and darken, sweeping over her. He came forward as she stepped from the stairs and smiled. "Do you like what you see, my lord?"

"What I see tells me I must guard you tonight," he said, but teasingly. "There will be contenders."

Aylena smiled. She didn't need to worry. If there were any contenders, Thor would handle them. She walked with him through the drawing rooms and saw the wide doors on the north flung open.

Until now, Aylena had not seen the banquet room of the chateau, though she had known it was there. Marie had pointed it out that afternoon when they strolled in the back gardens. It was a large room built on the north side after the chateau was finished. The doors that opened into it were always locked, Marie had told her, because of the queen's fear of thieves. There were, she had said, many treasures in there.

Going into the brightly lit room, crowded with richly clothed, exhilarated guests talking in several languages, Aylena stayed close to Thor, wincing and looking away as a man reached into a woman's low-cut gown and delicately caressed a breast, while those around him laughed softly and the woman swayed toward him, smiling, willing. . . . Glancing down at her own low neckline, Aylena was glad of Thor's company.

There were four high tables, set with silver goblets and plates, enough to seat over a hundred guests; there were gold candelabra and Persian tapestries on the walls, and a raised stage on the west end, made of fine woods, broad enough and deep enough to hold the actors in a Greek play.

Impressed by the beauty and wealth, Aylena was still disturbed by what she had seen, and wondering at the loud laughter and voices. She looked up at Thor.

"Are they drinking too much, my lord? Everyone sounds as if they are drunk. Or, perhaps, mad."

Thor caught her hand in his and drew her aside, dropping his voice. "These are people who live only for pleasure, Aylena, and Eleanor believes her world should be the same. Hers, and that of all nobles. She is much too ambitious to ever be idle, as these wealthy nobles are, but she also lives for pleasure, and has no liking for any virtue that calls for self-denial. Here, among the dissolute nobles she knows so well, she dreams of changing English custom into the same fashion."

Shocked, Aylena found her voice. "But she cannot. Unless—unless something happens to King Henry. Even then, she'd find it difficult to change England. Englishmen have never been happy with a woman on the throne."

Thor's pale gray eyes flickered, glancing toward the queen, circled now by her coterie of smiling, fawning women. "True. But it will happen someday. In the meantime, she . . . bears watching."

Suddenly, as if some inner ear caught a drift of meaning, Aylena knew why Thor was here. Not just as the queen's guardian, as she had supposed, but as the king's spy.

"And you . . ." Her dark blue eyes were huge, frightened. She dropped her voice to a mere whisper. "You are the one doing the watching. Does the queen know that?"

Thor smiled. "I have no doubt that she was sure of it as soon as Henry set me to this journey. But tis nothing for you to fear—our queen is confident that I'll not catch her in some traitorous act. Besides, she believes she will win me over. Come now, we must join in the amusements."

"As a mark of appreciation for my faithful guards," Eleanor said, turning as they approached and smiling at Thor, "I ask the Lord of Northumbria to sit at the head of the middle table." She reached out a hand and lightly stroked Aylena's shimmering hair, as if caressing a child. "And you, Lady Aylena, will sit on my lord's right as an honored guest. Since your cousin, Sir Charles Halchester, has expressed a wish to sit with you, he will be on your right. Does that suit you, Thor?"

There was a look in Eleanor's prominent eyes that seemed almost playful, close to daring as she glanced from Aylena to Thor. Aylena tensed, but Thor smiled and spoke easily.

"It will suit us both very well, my queen. Aylena has had little opportunity to talk to her . . . ah, new-found cousin; and I, when in the same room with Halchester, prefer to keep him in sight."

Eleanor's firm jaw dropped, but in a moment her laughter rang out. *"Le mot juste*, Lord Rodancott! You have said it. One cannot be too careful with a rival of any sort." She turned, her hands fluttering gracefully, gathering her group of favorites to move with her to the first table, raising her clear voice: "It is time, my friends. Take your places."

Color and glitter came in waves as the guests moved to take their seats, and Sir Charles Halchester came briskly through the crowd to smile and bow politely to Thor and Aylena, to turn and take her right arm and fend off the crush of silk- and velvet-clad bodies near them. After they were seated, Charles addressed Thor with an air of respect.

"I want to thank you, Lord Rodancott, for allowing me to sit with my cousin. In the past, I have spoken in such a way to give you reason to think me light-minded and even scheming. I apologize for it, and promise better behavior."

Aylena, surprised and touched, looked up at Thor. Thor's light gray eyes had no more warmth than honed steel.

"'Tis a pretty speech, Halchester. Convince me for a

six-month or more, and you will converse with your cousin at her will. Until then, you first ask me."

Charles nodded. "Fair enough, my lord. I thank you." His handsome face broke into a charming smile as he turned to Aylena. "You have a strong guardian, dear cousin, one who will see you safe wherever you go. But now, tell me of your life in the wilds of Northumbria, and how my delicate and lovely Alyse fared there."

Aylena was thrilled. It was seldom she could talk to anyone about her life and family in the past; no one here was interested. "My mother was the happiest of women," she said, "even on the day she died. She was full of great joy, having at last given my father a son."

Halchester picked up a wine bottle and poured a glass for both of them. "Drink," he said, "and tell me more. I want to hear of castle life in the wilds." He looked at Thor and held the bottle over his glass. "Will you drink with us?"

Thor shook his dark head. "Not yet. Tis a long night of feasting and wine." He glanced at Aylena's brimming glass and then at her alert face, turned to him and inquiring. "As you please," he answered her unspoken question. "Your judgment is good in such matters."

She smiled. "You are right, as always." She took a sip and turned back to Halchester. "Now, Cousin Charles . . . should I begin with the sheep?"

Charles laughed. "Begin with anything, dear Aylena, and twill all be new to me, for I know nothing of the north."

Thor settled back in his chair, amused, and watched the play of pride and love for her Northumbrian home on Aylena's face as she described it to

Charles. It suited him well that she was so fond of it. Once she found out—as he knew she would—that King Henry would bestow the Stewart castle on him no matter how good her argument, her love for the place would help him in his planned courtship.

Dish after dish of seafood and meats, sauced and flavored with pungent herbs, garnished with early fruits and berries, were brought in and served by the chateau staff. A favorite was the lamb pie, flaky-crusted and flavored with rosemary. Wine flowed freely, voices and laughter rose and hummed in the air. And then, with hunger sated and a second round of wine brought in, the entertainment began.

The first of the troubadours put a stop to the conversation between Aylena and Charles and began the continuous show on the raised stage. Gaily dressed, their instruments beribboned and painted in bright colors, the singers and the tumblers with them kept the air full of music and laughter.

Most of the ballads were sung in the Languedoc patois, and many of them were bawdy and comical. There were mummers, who entered the audience with handsprings and whoops, reaching out for women who laughed and dodged away. Then, panting and pretending frustration, they grabbed at their genitals, pumped their loins, and howled in distress. Aylena, at first amazed and then offended, turned her back on the stage and the mummers, not turning around until close to the end of the long evening, when she heard the pure, high voice of the young boy who sang of unrequited love. Then she swung around and grasped Thor's arm.

"Oh, do listen to this, Thor! This is young Rossi, the

queen's newest singer, and he is the best I have ever heard."

Thor straightened and looked toward the stage. "I believe you," he said in a low tone. "Even these fools are quieting down to listen."

It was true. The room grew less noisy from the first, and by the time the boy sang out the lover's broken heart in a last, sustained note, it hung like a star in intense silence, dying away in fainter and fainter echoes, until at the end the whole room broke out in tremendous applause.

The queen rose to her feet. *"Bravo, Rossi! Bravo!"* The room took up the chant, standing and applauding. The boy, who seemed frightened, bowed and bowed again, then went quickly to the steps and down, going toward the seneschal, Claude, who put an arm around him.

"So," Thor said, "the boy is Claude's son. God help him."

Aylena turned, surprised. "Why do you say that? The boy is a born singer, and will go far. The queen herself will likely see to his schooling."

"Yes," Thor said. "I know."

Later, as Margit hung the gown away and brushed and braided Aylena's hair, Aylena told her about the evening, all of it, from the time the queen had settled the enmity that had built up so foolishly between Thor and Charles Halchester, through the wonderful foods and wines, the rude songs and posturings of the mummers, and on to the boy Rossi.

"He sings like an angel," Aylena said, "or so I imagine an angel singing—so clear, so perfect." She was silent for a moment, thinking. "Sir Thor," she added finally, "agreed with me, as anyone would who heard the boy. But he was not happy when he found that Rossi was Claude's son and it was likely that Queen Eleanor would see to his schooling. Surely, that would be the best thing that could happen, don't you think?"

"It will happen," Margit said, laying down the brush and sitting on an opposite stool. "The queen has already made her plans, and the servants all talk of it. Claude—well, Claude is of two minds about it. On the one hand, he, too, thinks Rossi will be a great success. But on the other, he is not sure that success will make up for what is lost. Of course, Claude has the older son and can look forward to grandchildren from him, and the name carried on . . ."

"I don't understand . . ." Frowning, Aylena interrupted. "What has that to do with Rossi? Does the queen expect to keep him apart from his family? Why is Claude uncertain?"

"He is not sure he wants it done, that's all. And, no, the queen doesn't plan to separate the family. What she plans to do is to have Rossi castrated."

Aylena gasped. "Castrated? Like a lamb to be slaughtered? Mother Mary, surely no one would do that to a boy!"

"But they do, my lady. Claude says they often castrate the young boy singers in Rome, to keep their voices high and sweet. Otherwise, when their beards grow and their passion for women rises, their voices break and deepen, becoming ordinary. Our queen doesn't want that to happen to Rossi."

"But he could never be a man, Margit. He could love, but never feel passion nor lie with a woman. He could never have children! Would he want to give up all those things in life just to keep his voice high in tone?"

Margit shrugged. "Who knows? No matter, tis only the queen who will say. Claude is afraid to object to her wishes."

"And Rossi? What does he say?"

Widening her eyes at Aylena, Margit shrugged again. "He has no choice, my lady, as you should know. He is but the son of a servant."

"I," Aylena said, rising to her feet, "will tell Thor of this in the morning and see what can be done."

She was nearly asleep when she realized Thor had known at once what the queen would do. He knew Eleanor well.

Aylena sat up, fluffed her pillow, and lay down again, feeling her heart begin to pound. She knew Thor well. At this moment, she thought, he is stealing that boy . . . and hiding him away.

11

Thinking back on it, when in mid-May the company began the winding trek back to the west and England, Aylena counted that gala evening a turning point, when her anger at the plan to mutilate Rossi burned away the awe and admiration she felt for the queen. Always, now, she saw the woman and her ambitions clearly. There was still much to admire; Eleanor of Aquitaine was learned, extremely intelligent, and charming. Even kind, when it suited her purpose.

But when she was crossed, her temper was monstrous. The day after her banquet, when she discovered that Rossi had run away and could not be found, she screamed like a hungry eagle deprived of its prey. She threatened poor, exhausted Claude with prison. Claude had been out half the night, hunting for Rossi, at first taking only the castle staff to help him, then rousing the stable hands. They had scoured the town and even gone as far as the Pont du Gard, the ancient Roman aqueduct that bridged the Gard River, northeast of the town. Claude feared the boy had heard what was going to be done to him and flung himself in the river. However, the river was nearly dry. There was not enough water to hide even a skinny boy.

Then, when Rossi didn't return the next day, the queen ordered a search of the town, and the townspeople willingly opened their doors. Thor and his knights were welcomed inside and given all aid in their hunting for the boy. They found nothing.

"There is no word, Your Highness," Thor had reported that evening. "No one has seen Rossi since the night of your banquet, and I can swear to you he is not in Nîmes."

They had been in the solar, where a cool evening breeze flickered the candles and ruffled the queen's hair. Several of her younger ladies-in-waiting, including Aylena and Marie de Fermi, were there, enjoying the breeze and an occasional song from the troubadours. When Thor began to talk, Aylena looked away, blushing, as if she felt it rude to listen to the queen's problems, but Marie listened intently to what was said. Eleanor stared at Thor, frowning.

"Then tis one of my guests that night who stole him, perhaps one from Arles, who would realize what a rare talent he has. Naturally, they will have him sing there, in the old Roman cathedral they have—though perhaps not until I have gone back to England. But my loyal friends, and possibly my enemies, too, will see that I hear of it."

The queen jumped to her feet, walked quickly to the balcony ledge and leaned there, letting the wind cool her hot face. "Damn them! I promise the thief shall regret his sin when I discover who he is. I have ways to ensure him of as much misery as he can bear."

"I know." Suddenly Thor's teeth glinted in his dark beard. "I shall pray for the thief nightly."

Eleanor was forced to laugh, though not merrily. "So, you think it a joke, Thor? When I find out who stole the boy from under my nose, the joke will be on him. Or her! You'll see. Whoever did it will suffer."

Behind the queen, Aylena had trembled.

Now, ten days later, riding ahead of the queen's party on a dusty road, Thor and Aylena glanced up at the distant shape of the old Roman tower, Tour Magne, set on a peak of the Garrigues.

"Rossi must see us leaving at last," Aylena said softly, "and is glad he can now go home. He owes you much, Thor."

"He likes being up in the tower, studying and singing for the monks," Thor said, "but he'll be happy to see his parents. Claude has promised to send him back into hiding when our queen visits again."

"If indeed she does visit again," Aylena said. "Marie tells me the message sent by King Henry was very demanding. He wants his heir settled in England."

"'Tis always so, I hear. Until he demands, she stays in Nîmes. And, when she is home, they are constantly at war on one or another issue. Yet, at times, there seems to be warm affection between them."

Aylena glanced up at him and then away. It was hard to meet his eyes and hide her growing desire for him, nor, for that matter, to ignore the constant, hopeful question she saw there. He was patient, but she felt his patience wearing thin, and her own feelings were beating at the walls she had placed around them. It made her cross and sharp-tongued.

"I would not like to be married and always fighting," she said, choosing her words carelessly, "be it to king or commoner. But then I may never wed, since I must first settle Ian's future, in one way or another."

After a moment, Thor answered, now as irritated as she. "Would he not be the laird of the Stewarts even though he had no castle?"

Aylena reddened with anger. "He would be the laird if he had nothing! Our clan is faithful. But I, too, am faithful. And, as I am sure you know, I promised my father—"

"Enough!" Thor's anger rose to meet hers. "I will ask the king to hear your plea as soon as we land in England. But don't expect me to ask him to give you the castle I won."

There was a dead silence that lasted a half hour or so. Finally Aylena spoke in a subdued voice.

"I feel that you and I will be enemies until the king decides, sire, and therefore better off away from each other. I will drop back and ride with Margit. Shall I send Sir Philip up to you?"

"That is not necessary."

Aylena inclined her head as if submitting, but Thor saw plainly the angry pride in her eyes. Later that day, as the column of knights and ladies around the queen rode on into a glorious sunset, he glanced back and saw Charles Halchester riding beside Aylena. They were talking and smiling, seeming in good spirits.

Aylena didn't have to see Thor's frown to know he disapproved, but she knew his pride. He would never act the jealous swain, nor would he intervene between her and Charles as long as they were in company with the others. She and her cousin had talked often at gatherings since Thor had allowed Halchester to sit with them at the banquet, and Thor had admitted that Sir Charles seemed to be honorable and well intentioned, at least toward her.

Now, as they rode, Charles truly intrigued her. He talked to her of Castle Belmain and the Belmain demesne, and his description was of a wonderfully beautiful and prosperous family holding.

"You know, of course," he said, "that King Henry holds it for the crown, since the place lacked an heir. He makes a great profit on it, even though the man who manages it for him takes a full tithe of the monies."

"But *I* am the heir," Aylena said, frowning. "Castle Belmain has always come down to the firstborn, no matter whether the firstborn is male or female. Twas my mother's demesne until she died, though she refused to visit it."

Charles nodded. "So I had heard. Yet no one here— even in Stephen's time—knew of you. In fact, King Stephen gave the demesne over to me, as the nearest relative of the Belmains. I lived in the castle almost two years and enjoyed a good income from it. But when our present king saw how rich it was, and how convenient to Southampton's ports, he said my claim was not valid." He glanced over at Aylena and shrugged. "Only the kings in this world can steal without fear. Henry will not want to give it up, but I will do my best to help you gain ownership of it. Tis yours by right of blood, and you should have the benefit."

Aylena gave him a grateful look, thinking how good it was to have a knowledgeable and helpful cousin. "That is most generous of you, Cousin Charles. I need a champion when I go before the king, for I'm bound to have trouble over the Stewart castle, the heritage of my brother, Ian. Thor is not likely to offer to give it up when Ian comes of age."

Charles smiled ironically. "From what I've heard, it cost him nothing but time to acquire it. No blood was shed."

Aylena was silent for a time, thinking back. There had been blood, and it had been Thor's. She tasted again the salty tang when she bit him on the wrist, and thought, not for the first time, that had it been anyone but Thor Rodancott, she would have been beaten for daring to hurt him. She sighed, looking ahead at his broad, straight back, the thick black hair shining in the sunlight. "However," she said finally, "had there been a battle he would have won. Our men were faithful, but they were not warriors."

Charles shrugged. "I'll take honest yeomen over any paid mercenaries," he said, "for their good qualities. I'm no admirer of murderers."

"Thor is no murderer," Aylena said, her half smile disappearing. "He has saved my life more than once, and I owe him much."

"Ah? If that is true, then I, as a member of your family, also owe him." Charles looked grave. "I will take my duty seriously. What danger threatened you?"

Anger and fear flared in Aylena's eyes; her oval face grew rigid with it. She stared forward, her gaze fastening again on Thor's back, remembering the filthy cottage, the horrible men . . . and after that, the shock on the shore of the North Sea when Scots came to kill her, thinking her a traitor. Her voice was low, almost fierce, as she went on: "I cannot speak of it; fear still holds me in thrall. Fear, and a desire for revenge. But I can tell you I have an enemy who plots my death as his revenge against my father and me. He has tried, with force and with filthy lies, to have me degraded and killed. Thor Rodancott prevented it in each case."

"Then you must tell me this enemy's name! I must know, Aylena, so I can help to protect you."

She kept her face averted, thinking hard about it. Then she gave Charles an abrupt nod. "You are right, for he might try to hurt you because you are my relative and friend. His name is John Bretinalle, and he is the son of a French knight who was killed in a drunken brawl in Edinburgh, his mother a Scottish woman whose father had captured a small holding along the border. John claims the holding as his birthright, though he doesn't work it. He lives by his wits."

"I know him," Charles said slowly. "I met him in London. A miserable little cur, full of pretensions."

"You describe him well."

His handsome face grim, Charles placed his hand on the hilt of his sword, and swore. "An I meet him again, he will answer to me for his actions."

Aylena nodded. "I thank you for your loyalty, cousin. But be careful—tell no one of your intentions. Bretinalle is a man without honor, who would kill you in your sleep if he knew you intended to challenge him."

"I believe you. A cornered rat is always dangerous."

She nodded again. "Nor will I mention telling you my enemy's name, for fear of others repeating it. But for now, let us forget it and be happy. Tis a glorious day and we are heading home."

* * *

In truth the weather for the next ten days was near
perfect, but not everyone took joy from it. The queen,
who on the journey to Nîmes had stopped at every
sizable town to greet her subjects in Aquitaine, who
had laughed and talked happily to all of the gathering
crowds, was now cold and silent, rising early to avoid
the crowds and riding until full dark. Only when they
came into view of the hills on the Cotentin peninsula
one early morning did she relax and call Thor to her
side for a talk. They spoke quietly for some time and
then more openly, about the trip to England.

"The way you divided the travelers on the ships
worked well, Thor. I shall put you in charge again. Be
quick."

Thor nodded. "Yes, Your Highness. The weather in
this season can change in an hour. I'll not take
chances."

The queen's return to good nature ran through the
courtiers and servants like a draft of fine wine. They
brightened and began to talk and laugh. They had
spent the night at a small but comfortable abbey and
were beginning to look forward to the luxurious comfort they would have again in England. Charles
Halchester, riding beside Aylena as he had since the
middle of the first day, looked over at her and winked.

"Our trials are nearly over, Cousin Aylena. Tomorrow we step foot on English soil."

"Indeed we will. But I cannot say my trials are
over. Tis only the beginning for me. Thor intends to
ask the king to hear me soon."

"Then if the king agrees, I shall stay in Winchester
and support you." Charles smiled suddenly, his handsome face alight. "It may be for the best. The king will
be in good humor with his wife and son beside him

again—and I have some little influence with the queen. Besides, when a case is between a man and a woman, Eleanor is always for the lady."

"Ah! Then I hope King Henry consults her."

Charles laughed out loud. "He has no choice in that matter. She speaks on her own, and her arguments are sound. However, he makes his decisions alone, and, at times, after much thought."

She nodded, satisfied. "Then he is wise. Perhaps I have a chance at gaining Ian's future."

"And a chance at the comforts and revenues at Castle Belmain. Do not forget your own birthright."

"I will remember." She gazed at him with gratitude. Many a man, she thought, who had been ousted from a comfortable living and set to earn his money in service, would be too jealous to help another gain his lost prize. Charles was openhearted, pleasant, and certainly helpful. It was hard to understand why Thor disliked him so.

The same two double-rigged ships lay at the port docks, scrubbed clean and victualed for the trip. Below decks, both ships were laden with the wines and brandies of southern France, for Queen Eleanor respected trade—especially trade that put a profit in her pocket. She owned a major part of the vineyards that shipped the wine.

There was a large inn near the docks, and because the docks were narrow and the nervous horses hard to handle onto the ship, the women dismounted and, with the queen's guards around them, went into the common room to wait until that difficult task was completed and the first ship set sail. The news of the English queen's arrival spread over the farms and small towns nearby, and the inn was soon surrounded by noisy villagers straining for a sight of the queen.

Sitting with Marie de Fermi and another young woman, Edda Roumer, Aylena spoke of it. "Our queen is so calm. The shrieks make me jump."

"She is used to it," Marie said. "I doubt she hears it at all." She laughed suddenly, her face impish with glee. "Did you see Charles Halchester's face when Lord Rodancott chose him as one of the knights to accompany him on the first ship?"

Aylena's eyes widened. "No! But I am pleased. Thor has never truly trusted my cousin—perhaps that is changing now."

Marie and Edda looked at each other and laughed again. Edda, a tall, strongly built brown-haired woman with a sweet face, touched Aylena's arm. "Excuse our laughter, my lady. Lord Rodancott was only making sure that silver-tongued Charles has no chance to be with you on the voyage home."

Aylena looked at Marie. "Is that true? You believe he is taking him only to keep us apart?"

Marie nodded. "Yes. But do not resent it, Aylena. Handsome Charles is known to have a lying tongue and a habit of charming women for his own profit."

Anger heated Aylena's cheeks. "Not in this case, I assure you! Tis the exact opposite. My cousin has encouraged me to ask the king for justice. And he intends to help me." She held up a hand as Marie started to answer her. "No! I'll hear no more against Charles. Perhaps he has faults; most men do. But he is loyal to his family."

Again the other two glanced at each other. "Tis possible," Edda ventured, "that family does matter to Charles. We have no way of knowing, because until

Lady Aylena arrived, he seemed to have no relatives at all."

Marie nodded, though reluctantly. "That much is true. And we must have done with this argument, for the queen is rising from her chair. Tis our turn to embark."

The first ship, carrying the horses and a greater number of men than the number on the first trip, was out of sight when the queen and her party came down the docks and were assisted into the ship fitted out for them.

"From the look of the northern sky," the ship's captain told the queen's chamberlain, Sir James Overton, "we'll have a rough voyage. The first ship may miss the worst of the coming storm, for they will be sheltered by England's bulk before night, but we will meet it in open water."

Overton hastened to tell Queen Eleanor what was said and advised her to disembark and wait a day at the inn. She grimaced and refused, her expression sour but determined.

"See that the babe is put in a safe spot and bolstered against injuries. And tell each adult to look to their own safety. I'll not change my plans for a bit of wind."

Once Overton had announced the queen's orders and explained the captain's concerns, there was a great deal of rushing about, everyone trying to find a protected area in which to settle. The oldest of the ladies chose places near the royal infant's nest of pillows and blankets in the center of the rough shelter in the stern; the others huddled around the group. Marie de Fermi, Edda Roumer, and Aylena stayed together, gathering the pallets and pillows assigned to them and waiting for the older women to choose their places first. They sat midships, on a battened-down hatch, and the afternoon sun turned their fresh young faces to gold as they talked and laughed. The captain, passing by in his gartered chausses, short tunic, and hooded cape, stopped to admire them. A smile broke out on his bearded face, and he spoke quietly.

"Choose your places in the shelter of the port side, my ladies. Twill be as rough as any other seat, but high and dry when the spray flies over from the west."

They thanked him and rose, grasping their bundles, and went carefully across the deck, already lifting and falling as the wind freshened. They found space for all three of them between two strong bulkheads, spread their pallets in the gloom beneath the overhead deck, and settled down.

The worst of the storm came at midnight, ripping sails, sending spars flying in the screaming wind. Seamen raced up the masts to shorten sail. Wailing came from terrified ladies-in-waiting and angry shouts from the courtiers in the bow, faintly heard above the noise of the wind. Aylena, Marie, and Edda clutched each other and were silent. Then, in a short lull, the queen's calm voice came clearly to her women.

"Pray for the life of my son, ladies. Ask God to preserve him even if no other soul lives through this gale."

There was an immediate, hysterical babble of voices, praying to God and all the saints to preserve the life of the future king. In the darkness, Edda clutched Aylena's hand and groped for Marie's, finding it outstretched.

"We, too, shall pray," she whispered, "but we will pray for us all. Before God we are equal."

Kneeling, clinging to each other, they prayed for every soul on the ship, and were gratified an hour or so later to feel the wind beginning to abate. Worn out, they crawled onto their pallets and fell into sleep.

They woke to a gray dawn on a rough sea, the waves the color of steel, their blows against the stout bow like a giant hammer. But the sails were patched, the rigging spliced, and the ship calmly plowed through the waves as if they weren't there. Margit, who had stayed with the wet nurses and the royal infant, came looking for Aylena, half afraid something had happened to her. Finding the three young ladies together, she busied herself with brushing their hair, braiding it, making them neat in spite of the pitching and rolling deck. When a sailor went amongst the passengers with a pail of thick, hot gruel, she followed after him into the crowd of women around the queen and fetched back cups of it and small breads.

"The queen," she said, speaking low to Aylena, "told me to say she wishes to speak to you."

"Ah? Did she give a reason?"

Margit gave her a disgusted look. "Queens," she said, grumbling but still speaking only for Aylena's ears, "do not give reasons to servants. They give orders. However, she did say you were to wait until after food was served and eaten, and that you must come alone."

Catching Marie's attention to Margit's grumbling tone of voice, Aylena gestured Margit away. She began to eat, remembering the talk she had with Queen

Eleanor on the voyage out and wondering what the conversation would be about this time. It would not, she was sure, be about her mother marrying a "wild Scot."

"There is something close to impudence in the manner your maid uses with you," Marie said suddenly, her face full of disapproval. "You should have her chastised. A few strokes of the leather across her back would sweeten her considerably."

Aylena smiled. "Perhaps. But punishment with blows seldom works with a hardheaded Scot. Besides, Margit is some ten years older than I and often mistakes herself for my mother. She has tended me since I was three years old."

Marie laughed. "Now I see. What was she saying that you must do?"

Aylena hesitated. But there was no way out of it, for when she rose to go to the queen, Marie would undoubtedly go along, unless she was told to stay. "She brought me a message from the queen. I am to attend her, alone."

That brought the startled attention of both Marie and Edda.

"Why?"

"What have you done?"

"I hope I've done nothing wrong," Aylena answered them. "If I have, twas out of ignorance. Other than that, I am as puzzled as you."

Tall Edda stood up, smoothed her gown around her, and sat down again after giving the quarters a sweeping glance. "It is time, Lady Aylena. The dishes are being gathered, and the queen is alone."

Aylena scrambled to her feet. "Thank you. I'll not keep her waiting."

* * *

Eleanor's calm, arrogant face gleamed with amusement as she watched Aylena make her way past the women and attendants surrounding the bolstered nest of the royal infant. The child was making his discomfort known by screaming with anger, his face brick red and sweating, his stocky legs kicking, fists waving. Aylena glanced at him, hesitated, and came on. She would have liked to try to comfort him, as she used to comfort Ian, but she knew the royal nurses would never allow it.

Approaching the padded and swathed seat where Eleanor sat, Aylena managed a quick curtsy on the pitching deck, then stood before her, smiling. The queen's face softened slightly.

"Come closer," she said. "Sit here, beside me."

Relieved, for the tone was too friendly to fear, Aylena took the seat.

"I am told," the queen said, "that you have put your trust in Sir Charles Halchester, your . . . ah, cousin."

Aylena smiled. "I have, indeed. Charles has been a strong and unselfish friend to me."

"Has he? In what way?"

Aylena felt her face growing hot. "He has promised to help me prove my right to Castle Belmain, Your Highness. He was sorry to lose possession of it to the king, yet he will try to aid me in gaining the demesne for myself. Castle Belmain, as you may know, has always been handed down to the firstborn of the heir, whether male or female."

Eleanor sighed. "You have also put your trust in an unwritten testament. Henry is not likely to give up a richly profitable demesne on your word alone."

"But Charles—"

"The king will not listen to Halchester, my dear. He despises him."

Aylena opened her mouth, then shut it again. Who would know better what the king would do? "I see," she said finally, looking out over the gray, heaving sea. Her eyes grew hot with unshed tears, and she blinked them away. "Then, if I have no chance of receiving my own heritage, I shall fight all the harder for that of my young brother."

For the first time, Eleanor smiled. "You are a brave young woman, Lady Aylena. Thor told me you were, and I see now that he spoke true."

"Thor?" Amazed, Aylena stared at the queen's proud and beautiful face. "Thor spoke to you about my affairs?" She was suddenly, inexplicably angry. "He had no right!"

The queen frowned. "Perhaps not. But tis foolish for any woman, no matter how brave and strong, to scorn the help of a powerful lord. Believe me, he wants the best for you."

Still furious, Aylena had sense enough to lower her gaze and nod, though she certainly did not agree. She was too angry to speak sensibly, and after a moment or so of silence, the queen settled back in her seat.

"You may go, Lady Aylena. I advise you to consider what you have learned."

Aylena rose, suddenly knowing she'd shown a childish anger against Thor. "I will. And . . . and I do know Lord Rodancott is a true friend to me."

12

The patched and battered ship carrying the queen and her party came into Southampton water on the first of the double high tides from the English Channel, that tide coming from the Solent Strait, between the Southampton coast and the Isle of Wight. Inside, the main docks of the port were at the confluence of the Test and Itchen Rivers, and now, in early afternoon, sunlight lay warm and golden on the sturdy stone buttresses and thick planks built to receive the European trade.

The ship eased along the edge of a dock; shouting sailors tossed thick hempen lines to dockworkers who caught them and, without a word or a curse, tied them handily to iron rings and hurried back down the docks, still silent.

"How strange," Edda said, gathering her belongings. "The men around docks are usually garrulous and rude. I wonder what—"

"The king," whispered Marie. "Look! He's come to greet his wife. He looks as if he's been here all day in the sun."

Aylena, who had said nothing, stared. King Henry was, indeed, red faced as he strode along the planks in his splendid red wool, gold-trimmed cloak and be-jeweled satin tunic, his legs encased in knitted silk chausses, his feet in shoes of fine black leather, laced up from sole to ankle with gold cords. He balanced on the edge of the dock and then sprang lightly to the gunwale before stepping down on the deck to greet Eleanor. The queen was smiling and eager. She came to him quickly, bent a knee and straightened, moving into his welcoming arms. The ladies-in-waiting turned away to give them privacy, and busied them-selves with things that must be gathered and brought ashore. But Aylena, intrigued, amazed, glanced side-ways through her lashes and saw the passionate, de-vouring kiss the king gave his queen. They were a remarkable pair, the tall, beautiful woman with her pale blond hair, the even taller man, with red hair that rivaled the setting sun. They seemed perfect, like the gloriously handsome gods of the Greeks. What-ever the differences between them, she thought, there was true desire on his side, and likely the queen en-joyed it, as she herself enjoyed Thor's kisses. . . . She looked up again and discovered her thoughts had conjured Thor's presence. He was stepping down from the dock onto the ship, and his pale gray eyes were on her, searching her as if he feared to find inju-ries.

She straightened and went toward him, knowing suddenly how she would have felt had he been on the storm-wracked ship and she had been safe on shore.

"None of the queen's party was hurt," she said, "though many were frightened. How did you fare?"

"We had a safe crossing," Thor said absently. He

seemed much more interested in examining her small person than in answering her questions. "Are you sure you suffered no injury during that wild night?"

"I am sure." Hesitating, choosing her words, she went on: "Then no one on your ship suffered from the blow?"

Thor's face darkened. "Some were seasick, either from the rough weather or from fright. One of them was Halchester. Is it his possible discomfort that concerns you?"

Aylena touched his arm, her slender fingers smooth and warm on his thick wrist. "He is my cousin, after all. But, he is not as—as dear to me as you, nor could he ever be."

Thor's hard tension relaxed, leaving his bearded face surprised and vulnerable. He took her hand in his and raised it to his lips, his eyes soft as gray goose down. "Then I will thank God for that. Come, I'll take you ashore."

Aylena went willingly and ended by riding beside him as they all traveled back to Winchester. The walls of the city were in view when she finally dared to ask him if he knew when the king would hear her plea, and added that she hoped it would be soon.

"I would be more patient," she said when Thor frowned, "but I know my young brother must believe I have deserted him. He is bound to be lonely and frightened, knowing his father is dead and, if he has heard the tale my enemy has sent around, believing his sister a traitor."

"Would he believe that?"

"I hope not—but he is very young."

Thor rode in silence for a time, studying the radiant reds, golds, and purples of sunset warming into beauty the cold gray stones of the city walls. Finally, he turned to Aylena and asked another, more important question.

"What will you do if the king refuses your plea?"

"Tis only lately," Aylena said, her soft voice tinged with bitterness, "that I have faced the possibility that he might not believe me when I tell him my father received the Stewart castle from the estate of his English aunt. Or, perhaps he will believe and not care. A king, evidently, can do what he pleases."

"You did not answer my question."

She shrugged. "Whether the decision is in my favor or yours, the first thing I must do is travel to Scotland and bring Ian out. The enemy I have is despicable enough to attack a child, even to kill him. He will do anything to exact his revenge on me. I fear greatly for my brother."

"I will go with you then."

"And if I lose," Aylena said wryly, "I will go with you, humbly and thankfully in your train. Though the Stewart castle would be yours, it holds many faithful and willing Scottish yeomen who will ask to go with me and guard me on my trip to Leckie."

Thor gave her a steady look, but said no more. The party of nobles and ladies surrounding the king and queen had tightened and drawn in, preparing to enter the city gates, and some had come closer to the leaders and were within earshot.

That evening, the courtiers and ladies-in-waiting, the titled members of the Royal Guards, and Lord Thor Rodancott of Northumbria dined in the great hall of the king's palace. The king and queen were not present, surprising no one. King Henry wanted his wife to himself.

The next day at first light Aylena was up, dressed in her plainest gown, a long dark cloak hiding her slender figure, and her radiant hair hidden beneath a dark blue wimple swathed about her head and framing her face closely. She left the castle quietly, stepping out into drifting fog, hesitating there inside the gate until an old servant saw her and made haste to open it.

"Be cautious, Lady Aylena. There may be thieves about."

"I have little to lose," she replied, "only my offering to the saints. I go to St. Swithun's church."

"Tis a long walk to the close, my lady."

"I know. But I am used to walking, and in need to pray."

She went on, hurrying on damp cobbled streets, passing through the floating drifts of fog like a slender ghost. No one else was out, and the houses and market stalls, seen through the wavering fog, seemed as insubstantial as her hopes. She was nearly to the gates of the close, shivering and hoping a monk would let her in, when she heard hoofbeats behind her and turned to look.

The first pale tinge of sunlight showed her a big dark figure on a black war-horse she seemed to know. Fear jolted her, but only for an instant. Thor, his face tight with apprehension, slowed as he recognized her, and came to a stop when she waited for him. Dismounting, he led the horse to the path she was on, and spoke sternly.

"Even a good town has its criminals," he said. "There are always men who will kill for a gold piece. You should have asked me to accompany you."

She was dizzy with relief, and suddenly warm with

love. She came closer, wishing she could stand within his arms. "I wanted to, my lord. I would have asked you to come with me this morning. But . . . it would not have been fair."

Her soft look dazzled Thor; her dark blue eyes were warm. He moved, helplessly drawn, and placed his hands on her shoulders. "Not fair? Why do you say that?"

Her smile faded, her eyes stayed locked with his, but he saw that slow tears formed a glittering sea in them. "Because I came here to pray for a victory against you. I must, for my duty is to Ian, no matter how I feel in my heart . . ."

Thor dropped the reins he held and his long arms wrapped her, holding her close, yet not too close. She submitted, and he kissed her, taking his time about it, his mouth within the curly black beard hot and passionate, her mouth opening, offering . . . until she had to breathe. He lifted his head, his eyes dark with wanting.

"And what do you feel in your heart, my love?"

She sighed and clasped her arms around his neck, knowing the time for truth had come. "Torn in two, if you must know. I owe you much; I am happiest when we are together, yet I must try to take your war prize from you."

The advancing sunlight warmed Thor's bearded face, danced in his gray eyes. "Marry me, Aylena."

She caught her breath, dizzied by his words, catching a view of heaven. For a moment she couldn't speak, for her throat was full of tears. "Oh, Thor, how I want to say yes, yes! But I cannot, not until young Ian is free and safe and his future assured. I made my vow to my father and God."

"Surely you didn't vow not to wed in the meantime?"

She pulled away a little, looking up at him. "I vowed to put him before my own desires, his life before my life. I can't change that now. I must hew to my promise."

Thor let her go and sighed. "Tis time for both of us to be on our knees this day. Come, we'll pray together at St. Swithun's altar and ask for God's judgment between us, as we will ask for the king's later." He picked up the reins he'd dropped and tied his horse to a tree in the close, then took her arm to mount the marble steps.

St. Swithun's Cathedral boasted no tall tower, but the length of it was the longest in England, well over five hundred feet from massive doors to the kneeling bench. By the time they were done with prayer and came back to the big doors, they emerged into bright sunlight. They stood on the steps, their spirits rising with the sun and breeze.

"Tis a good omen," Aylena said, her mood lifting. "And I have you to thank for it. The morning was damp and cold, and I was afraid in the fog. Then you came, and the world turned warm and cheerful." She loosened the wimple wrapped around her head and neck and shook out the mass of her fragrant, red-gold hair. She smiled at Thor, adding, "And safe. You need not walk back with me, my lord."

Thor laughed. Taking her hand, he led her to the black war-horse and lifted her to the saddle. "Neither of us will walk, my lady. If you think back, you'll remember that my Frere d'Armes once carried the two of us fifty times as far, and never noticed the double burden."

The memory of that day came, sharp as a blade. She had ridden before him on his saddle, naked except for the warm, woolen shirt and cloak he'd given her to wear. And with the memory came a clear, frightening picture in her mind. A flung axe, shining in a dark, filthy room. A fat, drunken bear of a man as filthy as the room, his barrel chest splitting, showering blood . . . she gripped the saddle with both hands and trembled, remembering more, remembering what the men were like before Thor came. Thor had saved her from an agony of shame, from a sure and ugly death. Thinking of his strength, his care of her, she looked down from the back of the big horse and into suddenly stricken gray eyes. He knew what she saw.

"I have made you remember too much," he said. "I see it in your face."

Aylena nodded slowly. "But I need to be reminded. I should remember always what you have done for me. I am ashamed of myself. How could I think it right to face you in court and try to take away your prize? Even my brother, young though he is, would value my life more than his castle."

"One has nothing to do with the other," Thor said after a startled moment, then swung the reins up into her nerveless hands and mounted behind her, taking the reins again and turning the huge horse toward the palace. "I'd not ask to be paid for saving a life."

She glanced around at him, and saw that he'd brought the memory back into his own mind and feelings as well as hers. His eyes had darkened with it; his jaw had set. He looked as she felt, sickened by evil. She faced forward again and was silent. Neither of them spoke again until they approached the palace walls. Then Thor's deep voice, carefully calm:

"King Henry will hear your plea today, Aylena. I talked to him last night, and he promised a hearing once the sun has passed its zenith. We will meet in the solar, since all of us are quartered in the palace. Are you prepared?"

She froze, staring ahead. "I—I am not sure. But I shall think on't, and attend him when he sends for me." Her face was pale, her eyes veiled behind her long eyelashes as they rode through the opening gate. Then, at the entrance to the great hall, Thor dismounted and grasped her small waist, swinging her down.

"I will say nothing against your claim," he said, "even if asked. The castle was too easily won."

Later, determined to clear her mind and decide what to say, Aylena took her breakfast fruit and bread to her room and sat in a deep stone embrasure, looking out over the courtyard. There was a small wooden table there and a stone bench to sit on, and when she had finished the meal she pushed the plate aside and stayed, elbows on the table and her chin cupped in her hands, watching the swordplay of young boys and yeomen below. It was a scene repeated constantly in every castle courtyard, the awkward young males testing their strength and skill and gaining more, blow by blow. It made Aylena think of Ian, who no doubt was doing the same on the rocky slopes around Leckie. A young noble, she thought, without a home, without family, except for a traitorous older sister who loved the man who had stolen their demesne! Her hands left her chin and came down as fists,

thumping the table. She spoke, her soft voice clear
and determined.

"In spite of my debt to Thor, I must fight for Ian's
heritage until tis either his again or I am dead!"

"Fair words," Margit said from the room beyond.
"The Stewart would be proud of you."

"There is little I can do," Aylena replied. "But what
I can do, I will do. Fetch out my white silk gown and
the overgown of dark Persian blue. I have been given
my chance today to persuade King Henry."

Later, bathed and dressed, Aylena set Margit to
haunt the great hall and watch for the doors of the
solar to open and stand ajar, waiting for those who
would enter. Margit loved nothing better than watching a drama unfold and having her part in it; therefore Aylena knew within seconds that the audience
had, in one way, begun. Margit came running along
the hall to enter Aylena's door, breathless. She closed
the door behind her and then spoke.

"The king has summoned Lord Rodancott, my lady!
And the queen is there, also. The servants say the
queen does as much judging of pleas as does the
king."

None of that news pleased Aylena. "My plea will be
weakened if the king allows his gratitude to Thor to
rule him. Go, see if you can find out if Thor leaves the
king."

Margit left hurriedly. Nervous, Aylena went to the
polished steel mirror set in the wall of her room and
looked at herself. The rich blue overgown, with a low
belt of linked gold, was suitable; the white silk gown
beneath it provided long sleeves, ending with wide
cuffs of falling lace. Her thick double braids of golden

hair were interwoven in blue ribbon and hung to her waist. She looked good, except for the fear in her pale and miserable face.

Angry, afraid of failure, she turned away and sat down near the door, which Margit had left ajar. In the distance she heard a sudden, petulant wail, quickly silenced. Aylena's soft mouth twisted. The king's heir had but to squeak and was given whatsoever he wanted. Always. For the first time, she thought perhaps that the aura royalty carried—that calm assumption of being a mortal god—was not in the blood at all. If everything an ordinary child wanted were given to him at once, might not that child grow to believe himself a king? This child—this Henry III—would surely grow up knowing he was all powerful. He would receive as his kingdom all of England and more than half of France . . . unless, of course, some enemy would arise.

"Lady Aylena."

Aylena looked up into the calm face of Queen Eleanor, then jumped from the stool she sat on and curtsied awkwardly, her face as red as fire.

"I beg your pardon, Your Highness. I was thinking."

Eleanor's smile was sweetly mocking. "No bad thing in a young woman, my dear. Or in any woman, for that matter. We all do too much talking and not enough thinking—or so my husband tells me. Are you ready to speak to the king?"

"I am." And all at once, she was; she had come to a decision in a whirl of connecting thoughts, and the path ahead was straight. Her blue eyes burned, all fire and flash and determination as she stared at Queen

Eleanor. "I know how to say what I want to say now
. . . and win or lose, I'll know I did my best."

The queen's elegant eyebrows climbed, the corners
of her mouth turned up. "Then come. There are few
women who dare to ask a king to change his mind,
and I wish to hear your plea myself."

Until now, Aylena had not entered the solar of this
castle; it was smaller than most and used only by the
king and queen for sleeping. The numbers of the
courtiers and ladies accompanying Queen Eleanor
made the great hall the only gathering room for them,
and, as the queen and Aylena made their way around
the gallery to the open door of the solar, the laughter
and conversation from below billowed up like a prat-
tle of children playing at make believe.

"I am grateful," Aylena said, nearing the door,
"that my plea will be heard in private."

"Not entirely," the queen said. "We have one other
interested party."

"Ah, yes." Aylena's smile was a trifle crooked. "My
Lord Rodancott." She looked away from Eleanor's
knowing eyes. "I expected him."

Then they were in the solar, where the heat of the
nearly midday sun and the fire in the fireplace created
a summer day, and the big dark man sitting with the
king was rising and smiling at her, for all the world as
if he wished her well . . . which of course he could
not.

The queen slowed, finding a chaise heaped with pillows and sitting down on it as Aylena went on, purposefully, and stood in front of the king. She felt no
fear now, but she was careful to give King Henry his
due.

"I am very grateful to you, Your Highness, for your patience. You are kind to allow me to make this plea."

Henry was as charmed as any other man by beauty, and his nod and smile came quickly.

"We will not cut you short, Lady Aylena. Collect your thoughts and take your time."

"Thank you. I will try to make my words count. First I will tell you that the Stewart demesne came in peace to my father, chieftain of the Stewart clan, from an Englishwoman, Lady Celestine of York. Lady Celestine was my father's maternal aunt and a great deal older than he. She had outlived her husband, and she depended on my father for his protection and for her living for many years and was glad to bequeath to him all she had at her death. It may well be, if I recover some of the papers from the castle, that I can show you her testament."

"Twould make your argument stronger," Henry said, and smiled. "However, I cannot say it would change my mind to see the lady's testament. There are many good reasons for that castle to remain in my control. Amongst them, peace on the border of Scotland."

Aylena flushed red. "And I have only one reason why it should stay in the Stewart line. Your Highness, I have seen your happiness with your family, and I know how triumphant you felt—for I was there—when you first knew your queen had given you an heir. You are a young man, with many years and many children ahead of you. My father was old, very old, when my brother Ian was born nearly seven years ago. My mother died at his birth, but she died smiling in my father's arms because she had, at last, given him his only son."

The king's smile had disappeared. "A sad story, my lady. Yet your brother will still be the chieftain of his clan, and likely in his manhood he'll take another castle in Scotland—if he has the courage and strength of his father."

Aylena's eyes met the king's gaze with blue fire. "But not if he also has his father's honor. There are hundreds of battling Scots who prey on each other, but my father was never one of them. He alone of all the chieftains could bring the clans together to fight a common enemy."

The king's dark red eyebrows rose, cocked with humor. "The common enemy was England, I presume."

"Often, but not always, Your Highness. At times it was Ireland or Wales. Now, may I ask you a question?"

"Ask."

Aylena inclined her head, turning toward the fire and gazing into it, as if searching for words.

"Suppose a barbarian tribe rose in the east, came here to England, and overran the land, laying waste to the crops and looting and killing. You would fight, I know, and you would send your family to safety in— in Aquitaine, perhaps. Then—though none of us would will it—it is possible that you could be killed."

The king laughed. "Indeed, I am not immortal. But—"

"If it happened," Aylena continued, swinging back to look into his face, "what would you wish the queen to do? Should she stay safe in Aquitaine and raise her son to be a duke, or should she gather a force and retake England, so that your heir would have all that he was born to rule?"

"By God," Henry said explosively, "Eleanor would

have England back for my son before I was cold in the ground! She is a woman of great courage. A mother of kings! Whoever says differently will answer to me." He stopped, staring at Aylena, his jaw dropping. "I do vow," he went on in a softer tone, "your argument is far more telling than any men have brought to me. Tis true fathers want their blood to reign over all they leave. But Stewart's heir is still a child."

"True, Your Highness. But he will grow, and the clan will uphold him. Ian Stewart will be a warrior chief, and better as a friend to England than as an enemy." There was confidence in Aylena's voice, a calm but serious warning.

Henry studied her quiet young face for a long moment, then looked past her to the queen. Eleanor was sitting erect, her light blue eyes bright with pride and excitement. The king had pleased her tremendously with what he had said. Henry's wide mouth quirked into a wry smile as he returned his attention to Aylena.

"You may be right, my lady. So, I'll take a look at him when he reaches sixteen and can speak for himself. If then he shows promise, we will see to his heritage."

Aylena inclined her head. "Though I hoped for more, I am grateful for that, Your Highness. Thank you for hearing my plea." She curtsied and withdrew, returning to put her hand on Thor's arm. It was far less than she wanted for Ian, but more than she had expected to get. There would be a new chance in years to come. In the meantime, she had done all she could here. Now she must plan Ian's rescue. She tugged at Thor's thick forearm.

"Come," she whispered. "We must pack and leave."

"Shhh. The queen . . ."

Aylena glanced across the big room and saw that Eleanor had risen and was approaching the king. With a regal bow, she stopped before him and offered a roll of parchment, which the king took and unrolled, staring at it.

"This is what you found? Then . . . the story is *true*?"

Eleanor's chin rose triumphantly. "Yes, sire, it is all true. The ceremony was right here in Winchester, at St. Swithun's altar, and this is signed by the archbishop himself. It was given to me this morning by the present bishop, an old man who knew the family well and who attended the wedding. Alyse Belmain was married to Bruce Stewart, chieftain of the Stewart clan, in 1137. They left soon after for the Stewart demesne in Northumbria."

Henry's square jaw jutted out in his suddenly reddening face. "By the blood of Christ, tis a cruel blow to lose Castle Belmain—and to a woman! When will you stop meddling in every case of a female heir? I tire of it!" He leaped to his feet and flung the parchment to a table near to the queen. "Mischief maker! Take it, then, and go! Explain her good fortune to the Lady Aylena and—and send her on her way!"

Confused, half frightened, Aylena found herself swept from the room by the queen and Thor, hurried down the gallery to the room she shared with Margit, swept inside, and after wide-eyed Margit left, led to a chair, handed the parchment roll, and told by the queen to be calm.

"Henry's temper will soon cool, Lady Aylena."

Queen Eleanor's voice was confident, even a little amused. "He has difficulty giving up anything profitable, but even he, who believes no woman should handle her own income, cannot argue against proven facts. Belmain is yours."

"Mine?" Aylena swallowed, her mouth dry. "I—I know nothing of trade with—with Normandy. Or Flanders."

The queen glanced at Thor. "Lord Rodancott can advise you. You will need a trustworthy seneschal, and he is a good judge of men. Once you have moved in, you are intelligent enough to learn."

Aylena took in a deep breath and nodded. That would have to wait, perhaps for years, but she felt thankful to God for the promise of an income for her and Ian, and amazed by the queen's intervention, for it was plain that Eleanor had brought this about.

"God bless you for what you have done, Your Highness."

Eleanor laughed. "It is my true pleasure to aid any noblewoman, Lady Aylena, who needs help in fighting for her rights. In the meantime, visit Belmain, for the staff there and the man who oversees the trade with Normandy will wish to meet the new owner." She nodded and turned, heading for the gallery, and Aylena followed her.

"Your Highness . . ." Steadying herself at the door, Aylena looked up at the arrogant, smiling face once more. "Tell me, did Charles Halchester ask you to act for me?"

Eleanor laughed again. "Indeed. Charles pushed hard for my help. I believe he has wanted revenge against the king ever since Henry took Belmain from

him. If so, this will ease his jealous soul, though not
nearly as well as if he had become the owner again."

Startled, only half hearing all that she said, Aylena
stared at the queen, wondering that she would act so
against her husband. Her king. "But . . ."

"At times," Eleanor added, as if she read Aylena's
thoughts, "Henry needs to learn he is not God. He is
. . . very young."

There was no answer for that. Submissively, Aylena
lowered her eyes and curtsied. "I am forever in your
debt, Your Highness. I promise you I will never forget
it."

Hands clasped, trembling in the aftermath of the
highly charged scene with the king, Aylena watched
the tall figure of the queen move gracefully around
the gallery and into the solar, closing the door behind
her. Aylena sighed and turned, finding that Thor had
come up behind her. She closed the space between
them and, without thinking, put her arms around him
and laid her cheek on his broad chest.

"How can you forgive me, Thor?"

His arms moved around her, held her close. "I find
it easy. In truth, you've done nothing except your
duty, and have done it admirably."

She burrowed closer, feeling the heat of tears in her
eyes and wanting comfort. "But I have not succeeded
in my purpose. Ian still has no home."

"Come, now!" Thor held her away from him and
looked into her wet eyes. "Where is the courage and
sense you showed a quarter hour ago? *You* have a
home—a new home, with a good income. Will you
refuse to take in your own brother?"

Her eyes widened; her quivering mouth curved into
a surprised smile. "Why, I . . ."

Thor made a sound between a sigh and a groan, jerked her against him, and took her open mouth in a deep kiss. His hand cupped the back of her head, his other arm held her tightly against his aroused body. He felt her amazed stillness; then, heart melting, he felt her arms tighten around him, holding him, felt her taut body soften, fit itself warmly to his.

"Thor . . ." She whispered his name against his lips. "Thor, I would be your woman."

Flame ran through him; his powerful arms tightened until she could scarcely breathe. "Marry me, Aylena."

She shook her head. "Not yet. Not until I have Ian safe. But we'll not wait. . . ."

He thought of the filthy beasts who had taken her first. "I'll not take you without the vows."

"Yes. Yes, you will. It may be years, and I canna wait."

The tiny slip of her tongue into Scottish brogue brought a half smile to Thor's stern face. "You could marry me in the same church where your mother married your father."

"No." She slipped away, pushing back her hair from her flushed face. "I will marry you, if you still want me, when Ian is safe and his future assured." She turned away quickly, tears of regret in her eyes, as he reached to take her into his arms again. "If you are angry, I can hire other men to help me find him. I will have the money."

Thor frowned. "We began this together; we will finish it together. How long will it take you to pack and leave for Belmain?"

"If I can find Margit, no more than an hour."

"Good! We'll have one night at an inn I know in

Petersfield, and from what I've learned, we'll be in Belmain by the next noon. The castle is easy to find, close on a small town named Haslemere, and is built in a high valley, overlooking its own land."

Aylena let out her breath. "I had given it up. Strangely, our queen had told me the king would never give me Belmain even if Charles swore twas mine."

Thor started to speak, then turned away. "What matter? She took on the task of persuading the king herself—and did well. Call Margit, my lady. The sooner we leave, the better."

13

At noon on the second day the small band of heavily armored knights, two woolen-swathed women, and a cart drawn by a draft horse driven by one of King Henry's ostlers topped the clean heath of a southeast ridge and looked down at long, heavily wooded slopes slanting into a green valley. In the center of the valley were the shining pink ashlar walls and turrets of a small castle. Light blue banners bordered in silver flew from the keep and the turrets at the gate.

"Belmain," Thor said into the silence, and Aylena drew a deep breath.

"Tis gloriously beautiful," she said softly, and then smiled, a sudden delighted grin that made her look like a child. "I see sheep! They are one thing I do understand."

Thor nodded. "Yes. But you need not learn the labors of the castle staff, my lady. The king hired men who knew sheep, orchards, and grain fields. All you need do is make sure your seneschal is honest and will tend the accounts carefully."

She was not listening. She was pointing, laughing, grabbing Thor's arm. "They have seen us! They are lowering the drawbridge. Someone must have described our party . . . or perhaps the king's banners you carry are opening doors for us. Come, let us show them we appreciate our welcome." She started off, putting her horse at the downward slope and urging it on.

Thor followed and passed, wanting his heavy horse in front if Aylena's horse stumbled and fell. The others picked up their speed. Even Margit's face showed a brighter expression, a look of hope. Glancing back, Aylena smiled. Margit had learned a difficult lesson for a Scot—to be patient. Still, no one would be happier than she when they turned again toward Northumbria.

They managed the slope with no difficulties, arriving on the valley road and settling again into a proper train, with Thor in the van, the Lady Aylena beside him. Stiffly proper men-at-arms came out and over the moat to stand at attention as the company rode in. The courtyard, small but well tended, held a crowd of workers. Cooks stood at the open doorway of the outside kitchen; stable men and field serfs gawked and bowed; more men-at-arms walked the top of the walls. Then they were in the inner courtyard and the carved, heavy doors of the keep were opening. . . .

Aylena's heart was in her throat. Not until now, when she saw the amazed, curious stares from the castle workers, had she truly believed this small but beautiful castle was hers. Not just her home, as the Stewart castle had been, but *hers*. Hers to command, along with the men-at-arms, the servants, the field serfs, and hers to protect in case of warfare. Suddenly aware of these things, she glanced at Thor as they came to a stop and dismounted. She would need advice badly.

Straightening, she shook down her cloak and skirts and put a hand on Thor's offered arm. He smiled down at her and spoke under his breath.

"Your castle is charming, my lady. Well kept and in good repair as far as I can see."

She forced her stiff lips into a smile and allowed him to lead her up the carved stone steps and into the great hall, where the walls were paneled with rich, shining beechwood and hung with tapestries in glowing colors.

The seneschal, the chaplain, the scribe, and the housekeeper, dressed in their best, stood before the household servants, lined up to do honor to the new owner of Castle Belmain. The chaplain, Father Benet, an ancient priest who had served Belmain for nearly forty years, came forward with tears in his eyes to kiss Aylena's cheeks and lay a hand on her bowed head, calling down blessings upon her.

"I would have known you as Lady Alyse's daughter wherever we met," he said, stepping back. "You are very like her."

Aylena took Benet's fragile hand and kissed it, then hugged him impulsively. "You have made me feel at home."

The seneschal, Cedric Wye, was next. He came to Aylena and bowed, but his eyes strayed to Thor as he welcomed them.

"The scribe, Robert, has brought all accounts to final reckoning," he said after his greeting. "They are ready when you wish to study them."

"You have done well to be ready so soon," Thor told

him. "The king's messenger bringing the news of an heiress for Belmain left only an hour before us."

Wye smiled grimly. "He changed horses but never slept. He was charged not only to tell us but also to carry back to the king all of the recent income from the Belmain demesne. There is little left until the monies for our wool come back."

Thor made a dismissing motion with one hand. "That will not matter to Lady Aylena unless you and your people here are in need. She has sufficient funds for the present."

Cedric Wye shook his head. "We are not in need, nor will we be. As you will see in the accounts, my lord, the money we earn is set aside first. Only the profits went to the king." He smiled. "However, once Flanders pays for our wool, Lady Aylena Stewart will be in possession of a small fortune."

"And when do you think that will be, seneschal?" Aylena asked, and felt her heart beat faster. The thought of having a fortune was sweet. She could pay Thor for her gowns . . . she could pay for her trip north . . . and she could hire good, strong men, once she got into Scotland!

"The ship will likely return in less than a week."

"We'll wait for it." Carefully, she did not look at Thor.

"That is not necessary," Thor said after an amazed moment. "We've enough money for your plans."

"My plans," Aylena said, "should be paid for by me. Also my debts." She saw Thor turn away from her, anger in his eyes, and her heart plummeted. He had never before shown real anger toward her, and her face felt hot, her hands trembled. It was more difficult than she had thought to go against Thor.

Behind them, Philip of Anjou laughed abruptly, looked at Thor's dark, frowning face, and motioned to Margit. "Come, maid. Show these servants which bags and bundles belong to your mistress, so they can put them away in the solar."

The housekeeper, a tall, buxom woman with a placid face, stepped forward quickly. Cedric took her arm and presented her to Aylena. "Mistress Blanche is in charge of the household servants, my lady. Whatever you want, whatever you wish changed, she will see to it at once." He hesitated. "She stands ready now to serve a full meal, if you and your company are hungry."

A wave of deep, heartfelt sound ran through the waiting knights. Aylena pulled off her wrapped wimple and cloak, handed them to Margit, and smiled shyly at the housekeeper.

"We are all very hungry, Mistress Blanche. We require only lavers and linens and a laden table at present."

A half hour later the great hall was full; the odors of roast meat and new bread filled the air; wine was passed and voices rose in laughter. Placed at the center of the high table beside Thor, Aylena waited until the others were busy eating, then laid her hand on his thick wrist.

"Please do not be angry with me for going against your advice," she said. "I want to repay the money you have spent on me, and I am glad I can, for it frets me to be in debt. But never could I repay your kindness and care."

Thor's dark brows drew together again. "You owe me nothing, my lady. What I gave you I gave with pleasure."

He did not look at her, and his voice was cold, distant. Her heart clenched in her chest, frightened. To gain a rich castle and lose Thor was no gain to her.

"My lord . . ."

When he heard the fear, he did turn and look at her. She saw past the pale gray ice and found the hurt. "Allow me time this evening to explain myself," she said, her voice low. "Give me that, and I'll not ask for more."

He said nothing, but she saw the unwilling acquiescence in his eyes, and a faint, wary hope.

Castle Belmain was, without a doubt, more comfortable than most. It was small enough to keep the heat of its fires inside on a cold night, and large enough to have room for several guests, though the rooms themselves—except for the solar—were small. However, most of the household servants slept in their own mud and wattle cottages outside the walls, which left the thick pallets in the great hall for the knights. After a day and a half of riding cross-country and a large supply of mutton and good wine at Belmain, the pallets were full that evening, the great hall murmurous with gentle snores vying with drifts of quiet conversation.

In the solar—all of the upper southeast corner of the keep—Aylena stepped from a small wooden tub and took the drying linen from Margit. Wrapping it around her dripping body, she went to stand in front of the fire and dry herself.

"Did you order a bath for Lord Rodancott?"

"Indeed." Margit went on gathering up the clothes Aylena had worn. "Once the maids empty this one, they will begin to fill a tub for him. Do you want me to help him bathe?"

"No."

Bringing Aylena a long, linen shift, Margit laughed. "I would not mind. Shall I brush your hair?"

Aylena nodded, staring into the fire. "Twill dry faster, and end smooth." She put on the shift and sat on a stool, handing Margit the brush. "Be quick. I wish to help Lord Rodancott in his bath, as the duty of the lady of the castle. From the hints, I'd say there are at least three maids who will offer him their services."

Margit chuckled. "No doubt. However, you are the head of this household. Your word must be obeyed."

"By the servants, yes," Aylena said, and sighed. "But not by Lord Rodancott. He . . . may refuse my help."

Margit shook her head, but said no more. She, too, had seen the look on Thor's face.

The sound of shuffling feet on the gallery alerted Aylena to the preparations for Thor's bath. She slipped on a silk robe over her shift, tied a sash around her waist, and stepped out on the narrow gallery. She found Blanche directing the maids with their buckets of hot water, pointing out the room Lord Rodancott had chosen.

"You needn't assist my lord in his bath," Aylena said, noting that Blanche herself was wearing a thick apron. "I, as the lady of the castle, will help him bathe."

Blanche gave her an approving look. "Very well, my lady. Tis good to see a young noblewoman hew to the old ways. I will send Lord Rodancott up once the tub is filled. . . ." She hesitated. "It will take time both to fill and to empty. The tub is one much larger than usual. I thought he'd be uncomfortable in a smaller one."

"Indeed," Aylena said after a startled moment. "I am sure you were right. However, if he seems very tired, we'll leave the emptying until tomorrow. He . . . ah, needs his rest." She turned back to her own doorway and saw Margit standing there, grinning widely. Passing her, Aylena frowned, golden brows nearly meeting over her straight nose.

"If you have nothing more to do than stand there like a grinning ape," she said, "go to bed."

Margit bowed low, still amused. "Yes, my lady. And . . . you, too, should seek a warm bed. I wish you a very good night."

Silent, morose, Thor sat with Philip and the Reeve brothers before the fire in the great hall and lingered over his brandy. Looking back at the last two or three days, he felt that his plans and hopes had been all but destroyed. It was true that he had been declared master of Stewart Castle; his title of Lord of Northumbria was now secure. He had seen happiness ahead of him; his courtship of Aylena could begin once she put her disappointment aside, and he felt a successful rescue of her brother was as good as done. He counted heavily on Aylena's gratitude for that to turn her heart to him. Now, due to that cheat and liar, Charles Halchester, and his influence with Queen Eleanor, Aylena had become a rich woman, well able to finance a fast and strong force of men to raid Scotland and bring back Ian Stewart—without any help from the Lord of Northumbria.

Nor was this disappointment, which he knew was childish, his only problem. A nagging question had risen in his mind. What was the real reason for Halchester's interference? Why had the man gone to the queen and asked her to help Aylena to gain the castle and income that had been snatched from him? Had it been a favor for himself, twould be understood. But . . .

But what? Thor, still silent amongst the conversing others, shook his head numbly. He couldn't believe Halchester would use his shaky position at court to help anyone but himself. He was always careful not to irritate the king, and he'd known how angry Henry would be in this case. It didn't make sense unless Halchester himself intended to benefit from it. . . . Good God! Surely the fool knew Aylena would never marry a relative as close as her mother's cousin . . . or would she?

"Lord Rodancott?"

Thor looked up, dazed a little by the extra brandy, immersed in his gloomy thoughts, and stared at the motherly face of the housekeeper. "Yes?"

Blanche smiled and bent a knee. "Lady Aylena sent me to tell you your bath is ready."

Thor stood. He wavered a little because of the brandy, and because he was tired and heartsore. "Thank you, Mistress Blanche. I'll go up then."

Blanche watched him as he went slowly toward the stone steps that led up to the gallery. A strong, handsome giant of a man, he still walked like a man with great problems. She wondered suddenly if he knew who waited to bathe him. Then she smiled again, ducked her head, and swept out of the great hall. They would settle it, one way or another. She, Cedric Wye, and even Fr. Benet had seen the strong ties between the two.

Standing in the room where Thor was to sleep,
back to the door, Aylena was wrapping a coarse
apron around herself to protect her silk robe from
soapy splatters. She heard the door open and then
close and Thor's heavy tread coming closer. She
turned and smiled, nervously.

"I'll help you with your hauberk, sire. Sit there, on
the stool."

He stopped abruptly, staring at her. "You needn't
trouble yourself, my lady. I am able enough to shed
my clothes and scrub my own hide. Get to your rest.
The day has been long."

Aylena straightened, looking him in the eye. "Would
you rob me of my proper duties, my lord? You are a—
a treasured friend and an honored guest. I am bound
to see you clean and comfortable. Please, sit on the
stool."

For a moment she thought he meant to refuse. Then
he looked at the steaming tub between them and
moved to sit on the stool, letting out his breath in a
long sigh. "If you wish," he said, and lapsed again
into silence, staring at her.

She came to him, ignoring the stare, and lifted the
light chain-mail hauberk from his thick torso. Setting
it aside, she took off his sleeveless wool tunic and
hung it up. Then, when he wore nothing but the knit
shirt, chausses, and half boots, she knelt before him,
took off the boots, and began unwrapping the cross-
garters that held the chausses to his muscular legs,
rolling up the woven bands to keep them straight.
Once she finished and set the bands aside, Thor suddenly stood up. Aylena sat back on her heels and
looked up at him.

"Have I done something wrong?"

"No. But I can finish removing my clothes. Find a scoop of soap, for I see none here."

She reached behind her to a small taboret and brought out a dish of soap made from sheep fat and wood ash, scented with herbs. She set it on the broad rim of the wooden tub and stood, reaching up as Thor bent to pull his shirt over his head. He handed it to her to take to the pile of clothes, then pushed down his chausses to his ankles, stepped out of them and into the tub, sinking down into it with a groan of relief. The hot water felt wonderful.

Coming back, seeing him at last her captive in the tub, Aylena kicked the chausses across the floor to the other clothes and took a spoonful of the soap in her suddenly trembling hands.

"Wet your hair, Thor."

He slid beneath the surface and came up with his black hair and beard wet and shining. Quickly she soaped it, running her strong, slender fingers through the curling mass, rubbing his scalp, massaging his neck and shoulders. The fragrance of herbs rose in the warm air, and he leaned back, closing his eyes, his stern face relaxed. He was lost in a familiar dream of a beautiful, warm woman with long, red-gold hair kissing him in an olive grove, when she picked up a bucket of fresh water and poured it slowly over his head, rinsing away the soap. He ducked and spluttered, hearing her soft laugh as she moved away.

"Here," she said, coming back. "I'll wrap this linen around your hair. Twill keep it from dripping in your eyes while we finish your bath."

"While *I* finish my bath." He meant to sound commanding, but seeing the woman of his dream smiling at him softened his voice. "'Tis easier for me than for you, Aylena."

"I will assist, even so." Her smile broke into more laughter as she stood back and looked at him with the twisted white cloth around his black hair. "You look like a haloed saint, my lord."

"I am no saint." Beneath the water, his body was proving that. The warmth, the intimacy, her hands on him had wreaked magic on his sore and angry heart. He was rampant with desire; his hands gripped the edges of the tub as he fought against reaching for her. "Perhaps I should warn you," he got out. "It would be better if you left me now. . . ."

Aylena's eyes widened, her bright smile wavered, like a candle flame in the wind. "I . . . understand." She turned away, going toward the chair near the fire, lit because even on June evenings the air in the high valley was cool.

Thor watched her, regretting his words. His jaw was set tight, his body on fire. He had frightened her . . . he had reminded her of her shame. No, it was not that. He drew in his breath, hard. She had taken off the apron, but she'd taken off her robe, too. And now she was pulling her nightshift over her head and dropping it on the rest of her clothes . . .

She came back to him, bare skin luminous in the shadows, all shining curves of ivory, full breasts tipped with rose, the tender slope of lower belly veed with soft gold curls. Her head was held high, her mouth curved sweetly. But as she drew nearer Thor saw that her dark blue eyes were not quite as brave as her smile. She was proud, and risking much.

Stunned, he reached for her as she stepped over the edge and lowered herself into the water. He drew her to him, holding her in the circle of his arms, feeling her rounded hips settle on his thighs, smooth and soft as they grazed his throbbing erection. Her breasts, half submerged, brushed his chest as she took in a long, relieved breath and kissed him.

"Why?" His voice was shaken and hoarse.

She kissed him again, shy but wanting more, opening her mouth to him, asking for the thrust of his hot tongue. She closed her eyes, savoring his taste, the pulse in her throat beating visibly against her smooth skin.

"But *why?*" He was insistent. She sighed and opened her eyes.

"I fear you mean to leave me, my love. That I cannot help. But I would have this much . . . if only to remember."

"I will never leave you."

She sighed. "But I may have to leave you. Shhh. We will do our arguing later." Her hands left the back of his neck and ran down his wide chest, smoothing the hard muscles, moving over him, touching him, beginning to tremble. "Oh, Thor, I cannot wait forever. I ache for you."

It was like a dream. He had been sure she'd be frightened by male passion once she was naked and vulnerable. The memory of her ordeal in that hut was sure to return . . . but no. She was burning, full of her own passion. He held her and felt her soft breasts tighten, her small nipples turn hard. She *wanted* him. He bent to her, enclosing her lips with his, thrusting softly with his tongue, his hands stroking her satin, water-slick curves. He was dazed by desire, half convinced he was dreaming.

Then, believing none of it true, he sought the proof

of inner heat and desire with a trembling hand, pressing her thighs apart, gently feeling inside. She moved, slowly, sensuously, to accommodate his fingers, moved against them, tilting her hips. . . . He paused suddenly, dragging his mouth from hers, staring incredulously into her dreaming eyes.

"But . . . you still have a hymen." He sat up, staring at her, disbelieving, then knowing, for there could be no mistake with proof like hers. "You are a virgin!"

She nodded, surprised, and then understanding. She had nearly forgotten that furious night when she'd spat out the potion he'd ordered for her and Bettina had mixed. Now it came back to her, though it brought no anger with it.

"True, my love."

"But . . . I killed the men I thought had taken you."

She saw his dawning regret and spoke swiftly to remove it. "They deserved your vengeance, my lord. Twas only greed that held them from me, nor would it have lasted more than the night. They had sent for a cruel man who would pay four times over for a virgin to torture and despoil, and you, thank our merciful God, came before that man."

Thor gazed into her clear eyes and his own filled with tears of joy. She was his and his alone. She had no real hurt that would haunt her life and cause her pain. He should have known, for she was still so proud. He wiped his eyes without shame and grinned at her, taking the towel halo from his head and tossing it aside.

"And thank Mary and all her angels," he said, and gathered Aylena up like a child in his arms. "You are mine, and will always be. I will now make sure of it."

He stood, and water streamed down from them both. He laughed aloud, stepping out of the tub. "You'll not be a virgin after this night, my lady."

They dried each other in firelight and warmth, caressed each other with their hands and the soft linens, and became nearly incoherent with desire. Thor stumbled over words and laughed at himself, burying his face in her fragrant hair.

"I am no poet nor troubadour. I must speak with my body."

"And I will listen to it."

He hesitated. "There will be pain."

"I know. I will bear it."

He nodded and picked her up again, still bare, but now warm and dry. "Then come. We begin a life together."

The bed, intended for the visiting lord, had been carefully made with the finest of linen and down pillows and covered with a light, fine spread of vair, the soft fur pelts sewn together with invisible stitches. Thor tossed it back.

"We'll not need the warmth yet," he said, easing her into the bed. "Not with the fire we carry between us."

Aylena believed it. She felt well nigh choked with desire. A thick pulsing low in her belly had taken her over, the heat of it scalding, the tightness inside making her ache. Even her breasts felt swollen with shooting pains. . . . She reached for Thor, urging him closer, urging him over her.

"Now." It was a mere whisper, but frantic, for she was caught in a storm of passion she didn't understand. Thor acted at once. He covered her, fitting his muscled flanks between her slender, welcoming thighs, pressing his shaft into the hot, slick wetness waiting for it, pressing hard, and then harder. He eased, letting out a deep breath, propping himself on his elbows. He looked down at her flushed face, her dazed eyes, and saw the fear that had come with the first pain.

"Twill not be easy, my angel, though you are ready. Some virgin guards are easy to break; yours is not." His voice held a deep reluctance to cause her hurt.

She nodded to show him she heard, and whispered, "It must be done, Thor, and quickly, before I lose my courage. . . ."

He knew she was right. He lifted her hips and used his strength, his powerful loins driving his shaft into the tight heat, straining, breaking through at last. He winced at her soft, anguished cry and was still, stroking back her hair from her sweating face. After a moment she opened her eyes and saw the pity and tears in his.

"I am sorry to hurt you, my love. Would that I could take your pain."

She managed a smile and wound her arms around him pulling him down, kissing him again and again.

"Someone has granted your wish, my love. Now . . . I want more."

He knew she lied, but he gave her more, as gently as he knew how, and when he could no longer hold back his own cry of shuddering pleasure, he felt her arms tighten triumphantly around him and heard her whisper.

"Now . . . now you are mine. I'll share you with no other."

14

"Mistress Blanche."

The housekeeper, tall and firmly rounded in her striped gown and white apron, turned from inspecting a faint layer of soot on the fireplace wall and saw the new Lady Aylena of Belmain Castle coming purposefully down the stairway, wearing a light green wimple over her red-gold hair and a cloak with a riding gown beneath. She went to her, smiling as she noted the lady's clear-eyed and confident—and yes—happy look. The night had gone well.

Aylena stopped in front of the big woman and, in spite of a sudden wave of color rising in her cheeks, kept her head high. "You, Mistress Blanche, or a maid you trust not to spread gossip, are to put clean linens on Lord Rodancott's bed and have the bloody ones washed. Oh, and when that is done, the bath must be emptied. I—well, I am sure you will understand." She spoke clearly, but her voice was low, in deference to the men still sleeping on the pallets.

Blanche inclined her head, though her eyes held surprise. A virgin, then. She had thought them sea-

soned lovers. Now she wondered if that giant of a
Norman had been tempted to put his mark on the
beautiful Belmain heiress once he'd seen the wealth
of her inheritance. Somehow she doubted it. There
was something in his strong face that hinted at con-
quest by force of arms, not seduction nor pretense. "I
do understand," she answered. "Tis nothing unfamil-
iar. There will be no gossip."

"Good. Now, if I may have a basket of fruit and
bread to carry along, and a skin of ale, Lord
Rodancott and I will ride out. I wish to know all I can
about my mother's home." She smiled, her eyes as
warm as a summer sky. "And mine."

In less than the week Aylena and Thor had seen the
orchards, heavy with fruit; the burgeoning grapevines; the fields of barley, wheat, and rye; the high
pastures of thick green grass where the sheep grazed
in warm weather. High in the hills they found a clear
stream, leaping boisterously from a rock cavern and
careening down the wildest slopes of the ridge. It
leaped a series of falls, settling into deep pools that
yielded up fat fish.

Here no shepherd brought his sheep, no vineyard
worker planted vines. There were no fields to sow the
barley or wheat. The place was theirs, and they spent
hours beside the pools, lounging on the crystalline
banks and making love.

The first time Thor saw Aylena rise from the deep,
clear water of a pool and come toward him silvered
with shining drops, he knew that as long as he lived
he would be able to close his eyes and see her there
. . . naked and laughing, holding out her arms to
him.

After the first two days of exploring, Thor left off his armor, though he still carried his axe and sword. He rode in light-knit chausses and an ivory linen tunic without sleeves or collar, open halfway down his chest. Just looking at the crisp dark hair curling out along the opening and watching the roll of muscles across his huge shoulders made Aylena's blue eyes go darkly slumberous, her lips part, the tip of her tongue move delicately just inside. Strangely, she had found that the whispering touch of those springing curls against her breasts made her nearly faint with passion.

At night, wanting the cool wind that came through the corner windows of the solar, Thor joined her in her room. All in the castle knew they were lovers; there was no difficulty about it. It was taken for granted by the people who cared about such things as marriage vows—Margit, Fr. Benet, and, surprisingly, the Reeve brothers, who thought Aylena too like their sister to flout convention—that they would marry soon. Thor spoke of it, but only to Aylena.

"If there is a sign of a babe, we will marry at once whether you want it or not. My child will bear my name. But I promise you this—married or not, I'll not rest until your brother is safe."

She believed him, but she knew she could never give him her whole heart, her whole loyalty, until she had satisfied the promise she had made to her father. He knew it, too. Neither of them spoke of it; neither wanted to ignite a quarrel.

Then a messenger came from Portsmouth. The ship bringing the gold the Flemish merchants paid for the Belmain wool had docked and awaited the seneschal and his guards to come fetch it home. Thor went with them, and Aylena thought to do the same. But the seneschal sided with Thor, who forbade it.

"Only men, my lady," Wye said to her. "If a noblewoman was seen in our party the thieves that haunt Portsmouth when a ship comes in would risk their lives to capture her and hold her for ransom. No, leave it to us. With Lord Rodancott along, thieves will show us great respect."

Aylena didn't argue. The thought of being captured by thieves brought back nightmarish fears she thought she had conquered. "I should stay here," she admitted to Thor. "I will be leaving soon—with Scotland as my goal. I will spend the time preparing for it."

"We both will be leaving," Thor said, "for Northumbria. But we will stop in London. The monies you realize from the wool will be far more than you need for the present, and surely more than should be carried into the wilderness. You should place the bulk of it in safety."

Her brows arched. "And where would that be?"

"In London there are honest moneylenders who will keep your gold safe in their coffers. I have used them often."

"Then we go to London. But—we do not tarry there."

He smiled. "No, we will not tarry. I am as anxious as you are to go home."

The gold traveled from Portsmouth in two heavy leathern bags tied across the broad back of Thor's Frere d'Armes, and after food and a night's rest for the men and horses, began a long day's journey northeast to London, guarded by Thor and his knights.

Now they were accompanied by the Lady Aylena of Belmain and her maid, Margit. Arriving at night, they went again to the Palatine castle and were welcomed by the chamberlain.

"The king and queen are not in residence," the chamberlain said, "but several of the queen's courtiers and ladies are here. They are in the upper suite on the north if you wish to join them."

"We are at the end of a long day's ride," Thor said. "We will rest instead." He noticed Aylena's quick look upward, and, remembering her fondness for Marie de Fermi, added, "Perhaps tomorrow . . ."

Thor left Aylena at the door of her room. First, for a few moments, he leaned on the edge of her doorway and talked in a low tone, unwilling to let even Margit hear what he was saying.

"I'll not have those painted fops our queen keeps for amusement thinking of us as like themselves," he said. "Nor will they pull us into their games. They are useless and vain. And amongst them are those who would spread the knowledge of what we carry with us, perhaps to murderers and thieves who would pay them for the information. Others, perhaps, would simply love the gossip. Whatever you say to anyone, make sure you never speak of the gold."

Aylena nodded. There was enough Scottish blood in her veins to keep her mouth shut when it came to the treasure they carried. "When will you visit your, ah, honest friend?"

"At dawn, or soon after. In the meantime, Philip, Nicholas, and Martin share my room."

She smiled. "Tis enough."

Thor's white teeth glinted in his black beard, his hand smoothed her hair and traced her parted lips with one finger. "Tis too many. I prefer the company of one."

She wondered if he knew the power of his teasing touch and hoped he didn't. That roving finger heated her blood and struck a melting warmth down through her belly. She bit it in revenge, and he laughed, drawing it away.

"I'll return early tomorrow. If you like, we can leave then. If not, we'll stay another night."

Aylena's eyes changed. The pupils, huge in the dim light of the gallery, grew darker yet, not seeing Thor, not seeing what was around her. She was seeing the past, and in it a small boy she dearly loved.

"I would leave now if it were possible," she said. "I fear for Ian."

Thor's face grew serious. "Then be ready. I, too, wish to put this journey behind us."

At dawn Aylena was up and sending Margit down to bring up food and drink so they could breakfast while they readied their clothes and supplies for packing into a wagon. It would be necessary to stop at the public cookshops for food to take with them, and to have money on hand to buy more as they went north.

"Thank the good Christ for the blessings of Belmain," she said to Margit. "This time I will not be depending on Thor, like some beggar."

Margit shrugged. "He doesn't mind, my lady. In truth, I believe he likes taking care of your needs."

"But I prefer to take care of myself."

Margit laughed and went on sorting clothes into bundles marked with names. "Did you manage to make him take money for the clothes he had made for you?"

"Not yet. But I will." She turned at a discreet knock on the door and went quickly to open it, hoping it would be Marie de Fermi. But it was Charles Halchester, splendid in pale blue velvet tunic and yellow chausses, looking down at her with his friendly smile. She took his hands, happy to see him. He glanced at Margit, busy with clothes, and stayed outside.

"Have you time to walk with me in the courtyard, Cousin Aylena? I want to hear of your joy in your new home."

"And joy it is, Charles. Tis a wonderful home, and I thank you again for your intercession with the queen. Wait, I can spare a little time . . ." She grabbed a cloak and slung it around her shoulders, told Margit she wouldn't be long, and stepped into the gallery beside him. "Come. I could do with a whiff of fresh air."

"And I." He took her arm and went quickly around the gallery and down the wide stone steps, turning to the rear of the great hall. Ahead of them was an arch with two big doors that led them into a garden, full of herb beds and roses. "Now tell me," he said as they walked out into pale sunlight, "how does my beloved Belmain fare? Was all in order?"

"In perfect order. Cedric Wye showed us through the records."

"Us?" He saw her eyes shift, color coming to her cheeks, and laughed wryly. "So, the dark Norman warlord is watching over you and your new possession. I had hoped he'd be content with the Stewart castle, without profiting again at Belmain."

Aylena dropped his arm and stepped aside, anger leaping into her eyes. "Enough, Charles! Thor is the finest, most generous man I have ever known. If you think him trying to profit from me, you are wrong. He would not."

"Then I beg your forgiveness. I spoke too quickly— no, I will admit the truth—I am jealous of the man. I would be your chiefest friend, Aylena."

His handsome face was flushed and worried, like that of a reprimanded boy. Her temper died away; she remembered again that he shared her blood. Turning to walk back toward the arch and enter the castle, she took his arm. "You are a friend, and my cousin. But I'll hear no insults to Thor."

"I'll hold my tongue." As they mounted the steps to go in, Charles stopped again, a frown meshing his sandy brows. "I nearly forgot—I have seen your enemy, the man called Bretinalle. He is in London."

"In *London*?" Even the mention of the name shocked her. "Where did you see him?"

"At Smithfield. He was pricing a horse. I went to him and challenged him to a battle. He asked why, an I told him. Since he was not armed, I could not force the fight, but he agreed to meet the next day. I should have known the liar wouldn't honor his promise. I haven't seen him since."

"Tis like him." Aylena's tone was bitter. "He has always been an arrant coward. Why, if it had not been for his men who captured me I could have killed him myself. He will not fight, even in his own defense."

"I see. Then if I meet him again, I will force the fight. He is an enemy of our family." He looked up at the sound of a footstep in the great hall and smiled bleakly.

"Good day, Lord Rodancott. You are up and about early."

Coming up to them Thor nodded, then stretched a

hand to Aylena, who took it and moved quickly to his side. "Your pardon, Halchester. The Lady Aylena must ready herself to ride. We leave in an hour."

Halchester's eyes widened. "But you've barely got to London. Surely there is nothing so important—" He turned suddenly, looking at Aylena. "No, I need not ask. You are off to find your young brother and bring him to safety. God speed you, Cousin Aylena. I may travel that way myself and help in the rescue."

Halfway up the stone steps to the gallery, Thor spoke quietly. "Twould have been better not to tell Halchester of Ian."

Aylena's brows were knitted in thought. "I told him of Ian long ago, but I said nothing of bringing him to safety now. He may have taken it for granted that we meant to do so, since Ian is there amongst the quarreling clans. However, it was kind of him to want to help."

Reaching the top of the stairs, she hesitated before turning toward her own room. She would have been glad to tell Thor of Charles's challenge to John Bretinalle, for surely it showed that Charles took his duty to his family seriously and was not the careless courtier Thor imagined him. But each time she thought of Bretinalle her anger returned full force. She burned to keep the vow she'd made to revenge herself on the man. She still felt that if Thor found out Bretinalle's name he'd kill him as soon as he saw him; and, in spite of the good Christ's admonition to forgive your enemies and do good to those who hurt you, she still wanted Bretinalle to suffer the fears and pangs of death long enough to make up for the horror of what he had done to her.

Thor saw the emotion and indecision in her face.

"Is there something you want to say, Aylena? I will listen."

She smiled, and her mind eased. It was something she valued in him—he did listen, though certainly he didn't always agree. Nor would he now, she decided. He would never believe Charles had that much family loyalty. "No, I have no questions nor complaints for you, only gratitude. When will we leave?"

"I have hired guards and a wagon waiting at the main gate. We have but to pack and go."

Aylena drew in a long breath, feeling a deep excitement. At long last, she was off to Scotland and Ian. Off to carry out the promises she had made to her father. She looked up, into the pale gray eyes set like liquid silver in Thor's dark face. Wonderful eyes, full of concern for her. Emotion swelled in her heart. She took his hand between hers and kissed it.

"I will never forget how much you have done for me."

He laughed and turned her toward her door. "If you do, I shall always be close enough to remind you. Come now, tis time for action."

The train, led by Thor and Philip of Anjou, passed through the city and emerged from the west gate hours before the sun touched its zenith. Once away from the heavily populated fields outside the walls, they made good time, the hired guards as eager for speed as the rest of them. In spite of a late start, they made it to the usual first stop out of London, riding into the courtyard of a small monastery known as St. Simon's at full dark. Cowled monks welcomed them, carrying flickering torches to guide them in. There were three other travelers in the courtyard, already dismounted and going into the monastery hall. A flaring torch at the door revealed their faces as they passed. Watching them, Aylena gasped soundlessly and twitched her hood forward, hiding her face.

"Well done," Thor said, nodding to his guards. "Put up your horses and take your rest. The food here is plain but wholesome." He swung down from his own mount, handed the reins to Philip, and came to lift Aylena from her mare, noting her white face.

"Tired?"

Bracing her hands on his shoulders as he swung her to her feet, Aylena stood on the cobbles, head down, straightening her skirts, staying in his shadow as the other travelers, all men, disappeared inside. Then she managed a small smile. "A little, sire. But see to yourself. Margit and I are safe."

"I'll go with you to the door of the women's quarters, and make sure of it. Come, Margit."

Margit came, yawning behind her hand. But tired or not, she was content. They were going home.

That night Aylena wrestled with fear and hatred. One of the faces she had seen in the light of the torch was that of John Bretinalle, and the other two were men who, by the looks of their features and the patterns of their woven wool cloaks, were Scots. John had changed; his clothing was as fine as theirs, his thin face thin no longer, but pinkly plump from good food and wine.

Then what she had thought was true: Bretinalle had poisoned the minds of other Scots against the Stewarts and made friends for himself with his false tales of treachery. There would be Scots now who were likely to hunt her down and kill her. Worse, they could turn against all the Stewarts, from Ian through

William. Twas no uncommon thing for other clans to resent the Stewarts, if only because they were better fighters and harder working than the rest.

Still, she would not tell Thor who her enemy was. Not yet. He could be charged with murder if he killed a man in St. Simon's monastery. All churches were sanctuaries for thieves and murderers.

Early dawn on a midsummer day found Lord Rodancott's party leaving the monastery and heading due north. The other three travelers had left before them and were still in sight on a road leading northwest. As prudent Scots, they aimed to the west of the Pennines and then Carlisle and Hadrian's Wall. Once there, twas a skip and a hop into Scotland, avoiding the warlike English who had taken over Northumbria.

Seeing them in the distance, understanding their purpose, Aylena was eased. But still she was worried. In spite of the rumors, in spite of the attack on her near the North Sea, she had felt that time would solve most of the problem. Surely, she had told herself, the Scots who knew Bruce Stewart well knew also that he would never betray his people. But the sight of Bretinalle, well dressed, well fed, and confident, had made her doubt. It seemed likely now that he had been successful with his vicious lies.

On the seventh day they came in sight of the River Tyne. Riding with Aylena, Thor pointed it out, glistening in the distance.

"Tonight, you will sleep again in Godwin's Inn, with your old friends celebrating your return." He said it to brighten her pale face. It seemed to him that the trip she had waited so long to make had done nothing but worry and sadden her, and he wished her happy.

Aylena nodded, still morose. "I will be glad to see them. Godwin and Drusilla are true friends. I wonder now if perhaps they are the only ones I will have here."

Thor's face showed a sudden doubt. "Will your other friends condemn you for traveling with me?"

"No, tis not that. But there was always strain in our clan because of the English. My father's life was bound up in the lives and fortunes of the members of his clan. In turn, they did their best to forgive him for marrying an English woman. I am afraid they will now consider me a traitor."

Thor was silent. He knew Aylena now; he knew she'd just told him why she feared for Ian. It seemed impossible to him that men would take out their foolish anger at a woman on a small boy, but she knew them better than he did.

"I am not sure I'd care for your Scottish relatives," he said, "nor am I fond of your English one. They all seem dangerous, in one way or another."

She laughed at his wry tone, but soon sobered, her face falling into frowning determination. "The Scots are stubborn, and once they make up their minds the door is closed. You will not accompany me into Scotland, my lord. You would be set upon and killed."

Thor raised his thick black brows and smiled. "An what band of angels with flaming swords will prevent my entry into the purgatory of Scotland? Listen to me, my lady, and listen well. Where you are, I will be. In the meantime, the river is now before us." He turned and looked back along the double line of guards, raising an arm and shouting. "Dismount! The horses ride this ferry first."

That night, sitting to supper with Godwin and Drusilla, Aylena found her own fears and suspicions were only the beginning. After a few glances at Thor, a few leading remarks to test his temper, Godwin told them what he knew.

"The Stewart's nephew, Robbie of Sudbury keep, was beaten and thrown out of his home for defending the Stewart's honor. It is believed by many Scots that your father escaped to England and is living there, his every wish granted by King Henry for his help in getting the English into Northumbria."

"Good God!" Thor was red-faced with anger. "Every man in his castle saw his dead body, stood for the deathwatch, and followed him to the grave. Doesn't their testimony count?"

Godwin shook his head. "Not they nor any others have been able to stop the lies. The clans are like mad wolves. We have heard that William Stewart, now acting as laird until young Ian reaches maturity, has been driven to cover in the Highlands near the Moray Firth. The Stewarts are now under the curse from three other clans."

Aylena shuddered. Under the curse. All Scots knew what that meant. Unless it was lifted, every male Stewart must die, no matter how many years it took to find them. The bloodline must be destroyed, the name forgotten.

15

With two wagons—for the one they'd brought south from Stewart castle, full of sheep, was rattling along empty—the train of eighteen riders left Tynemouth in early dawn, stretching a long, winding way along the rock cliffs and broad beaches of the North Sea. Now, in the middle of July, the sea air was pleasant, the sky clear, the salt-marsh meadows along the way green and thick with growth. Aylena's heart lightened now with every mile taking her closer to the sprawling castle where she was born. Having heard the worst, she felt her hope rising. It was impossible for her to believe that those men who had known Bruce Stewart all their lives could think him a traitor. Twas gossip enlarged ten times over into lies, and surely the old friends would soon recognize the truth.

By late evening they came to the ruins of the old Norman castle on a cliff, the same one they had slept in on their way south with the mercenaries. This time there were two young shepherds huddled around a fire in the empty courtyard, sharing a scanty meal. Startled by the arrival of armored and mounted knights and men-at-arms, they retreated hurriedly to a far corner. Nicholas Reeve went to them and told them to be calm.

"There is room for us all," he said. "Rest well. No one will bother you."

They thanked him, but long after dark the firelight would catch the glint of their wide, wondering eyes, peering at the warlike interlopers.

Aylena and Margit slept in a small cubicle, half roofed over, half open to a black night sky full of stars. Thor slept on a pallet just outside the cubicle's entrance. Toward dawn, a quiet scrabble of sound woke Aylena, who sat up to listen. A frowzy head of hair appeared over the wall above her, and there came a whisper, frightened but determined.

"Are you slaves or captives, you women? We will help you get away from these murderers."

Amazed, Aylena held back laughter and answered in the same low tone. "These men are our friends and guardians. They'll not hurt us, nor you."

The head disappeared and Margit chuckled. "An ignorant boy, but brave. Not many would offer."

At breakfast the young shepherds were still there, sitting alone and gnawing on chunks of cold bread. Margit took mead and pasties over to them, which they downed at once. Then they left, ducking their heads and smiling. Aylena watched them go, thinking that the last time she saw Ian he was nearly as tall as these older boys . . . or even taller, perhaps. Ian had already shown the length of bone that would make him challenge the height and weight of his father.

Later, as they left the ruins and took the path north, she saw them again, rounding up their sheep and driving them to a greener field, west of the path. She glanced at Thor and laughed.

"Our rescuers," she said. "One of them offered to help us get away from you murderers."

"I heard him." Thor's grin broke out. "Had I spoken, he might have broken a bone on the rocks below. Strange, how our appearance frightens the innocent."

"Tis your weapons, not your face, my love."

Thor turned and looked at her. "My love? Do you tease me? I am having a devil of a time staying apart from you."

She smiled, flushing pink. She had felt the same since the trip began. "I also," she said softly. "My love for you burns hot in my veins. But soon we'll be home."

Home. A great hope leaped up in Thor's chest, but he was afraid to ask if it would still be her home, as well as his. He was sure she would tell him her duty still lay in her promises to her father, and he was not ready to hear it again. Then he felt his horse nudged by another and turned, looking into Philip's lively face.

"Lonely and barren country though it is," Philip said, "these rolling plains have rocks to hide behind and glades that can hold men hidden behind their stunted trees. Should we have outriders?"

Thor shook his head. "No one knows we are traveling here, and surely the place has few visitors. Just keep a sharp eye."

"I will." Philip turned to drop back, but Aylena stopped him with a remark to Thor.

"I think Sir Philip should set the outriders. News

travels fast in a place that hears so little. And remember that ignorant men are quick to anger."

Thor shrugged. "You know these people better than I. Set two, Philip, to course the road ahead. If they find a man hidden, they are to bring him to me."

Philip chose two of the guards, sending them forward but not out of sight. They circled clumps of the dwarfed trees that grew on the rolling, barren hills, dropped down into the glades where a man or two might hide, and led them on to the northwest, following the occasional sweep of Thor's arm for direction. Late in the day, as they neared the spot where they had camped on the trip south, the guard on the left flushed two men and a snarling wolfhound from a briar-filled gully along the path. He drew his sword and disposed of the hound, then he and the other guard brought the cursing, arguing men to Thor, who stopped the train and rode out to meet them.

Coming back, the guards each led a man with his arms bound behind him. When they reached the train they dismounted, flung the captives into the empty wagon, and bound their legs.

"They'll not tell us why they are here or who sent them," Thor told Aylena as they rode on. "But the guard was alerted by their attempt to leave quietly. He believes they were set to watch and tell someone of our arrival."

Aylena, sober and pale, nodded. "The place where we mean to camp is well known—all use it, because of the spring water. We are expected, then. How did they know?"

"Only God knows. But if the clans are wilding, as Godwin believes, they may have been watching for us ever since the curse was handed down."

"Watching for me, Thor. You are not a clansman."

He frowned. "Nor would I be if a clansman must war on women."

"Tis not me they want to kill," Aylena said, "though they will if they must. They want Ian." Her voice wavered, and Thor shot a quick glance at her face. Her eyes were full of tears, but her slender jaw was set hard and tight, her hand on the saddle was a fist. "They won't have him," she said, low and fierce. "They *won't!* These enemies are no better than mad dogs. No decent man hunts and kills a child."

Thor was silent, riding on. For the first time, he shared Aylena's depth of feeling. Before this, the trip into Scotland to bring her brother out was more of a challenge or a dare instead of a task, a trip he knew he could make successful. He had not thought it necessary, as long as the boy was with his uncle, but he had thought to please Aylena. Now he saw the danger. The boy could be killed before they could rescue him.

"There is the valley where we camped that night," he said, pointing to the north, then flung the hand up, stopping the train. "You and Margit will stay here, with the guards around you. Philip and the Reeve brothers will help me rid the camp of vermin, if it be infested."

The shallow valley held no real camp; there was shelter there from an overhanging cliff and a wall of cut tree trunks set up around one part of it. Besides that, natural outcroppings of scored stone thrust up from the barren earth and created bulwarks against the wind. Loosing their axes in their sheaths, loosening their lances, Thor and his knights set their horses to an easy canter down the slope. They were nearly to the wall of cut tree trunks when a dozen or so

bearded Scots in breastplates over wool tunics came
from hiding and ran toward them, howling war cries,
yelling insults, and flinging their war axes.

They were met by lances. A thrust through a shoulder, a yank, another thrust for the man who came
next. The war-horses, mountains of squealing, wild-
eyed fury, whirled from the thrown axes, reared, and
struck at the Scots with their front hooves. In minutes
those who could were running away, some dragging
another, some leaping over the bodies of those who
were dying.

Margit, white-faced, was whispering prayers. "Receive the souls of these innocents, Mother Mary. The
devil has lied to them."

Aylena hardly heard her. She was frozen in fear,
staring at the scene with horror. She had seen an axe
flashing silver, whirling in the air, flying in a perfect
arc toward Thor. Graceful as a dancer, he had leaned
away to let it glitter past and fall behind. In an instant, his Frere d'Armes had reared and crushed the
Scot that threw it, stamping him into the ground. But
for one blinding moment Aylena saw a world without
Thor. She had been certain the axe would kill him—as
his axe had killed for her.

"My lady?"

She turned and looked at Margit, who seemed dis-
traught. "They won," she said. "Thor . . . none of
our men is hurt."

Margit stared at her. "But you, are you feeling
faint?"

"I am all right." She was faint, but she was all
right. She was deep in thought as they rode down into
the camp and dismounted. She felt as if she'd had a

revelation. She had seen death for Thor and she knew she could never bear it. She must go alone into Scotland and bring Ian out. Some of her father's men would be loyal to her. She would ask their advice. Surely the Scots would be less likely to kill a woman, less likely to notice a woman and a child. It was impossible not to notice Thor.

The night passed without trouble. The guards had dragged the bodies of the dead to the far end of the valley and left them there for their friends to take care of. When they rode out in the morning the bodies were gone.

"Killed," Aylena said, dropping her voice to speak to Margit, "because of me."

Margit snorted. "Killed," she answered, "by lies. You have done nothing wrong. Stop blaming yourself."

They were riding north again and were passing some of the lower pastures for Stewart sheep. The pastures were all empty as far as Aylena could see, though she had dropped back to take a better look. Another hour, she thought, and they'd see the castle keep, flying the Stewart green and gold banner. No, they wouldn't. Not the Stewart banner. She drew up beside Thor and spoke.

"I know that when you ride for the king you fly the Plantagenet red and gold banner, but what banner will fly on the castle?"

Thor reached over playfully and twitched the cowled hood that hid her eyes and hair. "I may have a new one made, gold for your hair, blue for your eyes."

She tried to frown. "But now? What are your colors?"

"In Normandy my banner is silver and black."

"You have a demesne in Normandy?"

"I do. It is small, compared with this, but very profitable."

"Is it a vineyard?"

He threw back his head and laughed. "No, no wines. That takes patience and care and all of your time. I breed war-horses."

"Oh!" She looked at his stallion's strong, intelligent head, the thick neck and wide chest, the black hide gleaming with health under the fine dust from the path. It seemed right that a man like Thor, extraordinarily strong and skilled in warfare, yet kind, should own superior animals like this. "Are your other horses like your Frere d'Armes?"

"He is my chiefest stallion, but there are many more. You will go there with me, and see it all."

"Do you trust the men who are in charge now?"

"They are my brothers."

She was silent, wondering, thinking that if she married him she would have another part of the world to visit, to see. And another family. Brothers. Mayhap sisters, also, who would mourn if he died. Who would hate her for allowing him to risk his life and lose it. . . .

"Aylena."

She glanced up, seeing the gray eyes soft on her face, the glint of his smile in the crisp black beard. He had left off his helmet in the midsummer warmth, and his wind-tousled black hair made her wish to smooth it. He looked like a god, glistening in the sun.

"Yes, Thor?"

He laughed. "Thank the saints for that smile. You've

seemed sunk in despair for much of the day, my lady.
Why?"

"Oh, no. No despair, my lord. Only thinking."

"Then you found heavy thoughts. Look to the north
and your spirits will rise."

She looked and cried out, turning toward Margit
behind her. "Look, Margit! The air is so clear you can
see the castle keep! We are nearly home."

Aylena was not prepared for the emotions that overwhelmed her as they came in full sight of the castle
where she had been born. Memories came, swirling
thick in her head, thick in her throat. She couldn't
speak, not even to the men-at-arms who had served
her father and now removed their helmets as she rode
in through the gates. She nodded to them, to the
workers in the courtyard. She smiled, but tears ran
from her eyes when she saw the anxious question in
theirs. When she dismounted and handed her reins
to an old groom, she answered as well as she
could.

"It is not over, Rolf. Tell them all I mean to bring
Ian home again."

The old man nodded. "He is in grave danger, my
lady. All has changed in Scotland."

"I know. But I will manage."

"May God help you, then."

She thanked him and went inside. She had not
thought to weep more as she went up the stone steps
to the gallery, but tears dropped. She wiped them
away and smiled at Bettina, who had rushed to greet
her and was shedding a waterfall of her own. But
Bettina's tears were happy tears. She was delighted
to have both Aylena and Margit back again.

Below the women on the gallery, the seneschal, Stephen of Blaine, came to greet Thor and stand ready for orders, though there was too much noise to hear if Thor spoke. The knights Thor had left to protect the castle were greeting him uproariously. Aylena turned away, motioned to Margit and Bettina, then went swiftly along the gallery to her old room. For a time, she told herself, she would hold herself apart from Thor. When they were close, he seemed to read her thoughts. For her plans, that might be ruinous. . . .

Unpacking, Aylena put away most of the elaborate silk and satin gowns she had worn in London and Languedoc and took from her wardrobe the simple ivory and brown linens and the thin wool gowns in dark blues and greens that she had always worn here. Plain gowns in their simplicity, yet fitted to her young body in a way far more becoming than the trailing sleeves, ties, and ribbons of the fashionable styles.

During the first week Aylena had complete freedom. Thor thought he understood why she put distance between them. These were her people; she wanted their respect. But he knew her passionate nature and felt she would soon be with him again. Now, seeing her going in and out of the bailey and the stables, Thor was satisfied that she was, as he was, making sure that supplies for the winter were being stored, that the livestock was thriving, that all was in order.

There were no such thoughts in Aylena's mind. She knew—had always known—that Stephen of Blaine would see to those things better than she. What she

was doing was making plans. She had gone first to
Harald, chief ostler of the stables, and after asking
him out into the horse pens with the excuse of inspecting a new young mare, talked to him about rescuing Ian. Harald she could trust with her life—with
Ian's life.

Harald, a strong, solid man in his thirties, was immediately caught up in the plan. But, even though he
was burning to see the young laird safe and returned
to his family, he was dismayed when she told him it
must be secret from Lord Rodancott.

"Do you mean the Norman is against the attempt?"

"Oh, no! Far from it. But he would insist on going
along. Can you see that great Norman hulk in Scotland? He would give the whole thing away." She tried
to sound scornful, but she was not sure that Harald
was convinced. He looked at the ground, as if he were
thinking hard.

"There are few men here who would refuse to help
you, Lady Aylena, but fewer yet who could keep their
mouths shut if Lord Rodancott were asking the questions."

Aylena knew that was true. Anyone would find it
difficult to hide the truth from Thor. She herself had
trouble there. "Then the two of us must make the arrangements ourselves, find a boat, and then choose
the men we need at the last minute, so that they have
no chance to gossip about it."

"There will be no trouble about a boat. My brother
is a trader, with a boat of his own. His run is from the
Tweed to the Moray Firth."

Aylena drew in her breath and nodded, her smile
breaking out. "An answer to prayer, Harald. No one

will take a second look at a boat they see often in their port. Can he deliver us to Black Isle?"

"He can, and pick you up again on his next run, if the weather holds."

"I will make it worth his while. In the meantime, choose four or five men to escort us."

"First I must go to Tweed harbor and find my brother. Then all will wait on the weather."

Aylena nodded, her smile fading. All did wait on the weather when the North Sea was the road to be taken. A more capricious sea lane than any other, the North Sea had ruined many a plan before this one with its perpetual storms. "I will be ready, Harald, at any time. I will take Margit, but she will not be told aforehand. Her tongue slips."

Harald nodded. "We must all be careful of that."

Suddenly, Thor noticed, Aylena spent most of her time in her room and the rest of it on the young mare's back, riding her every late afternoon, sometimes staying out in these shortening days until after dark. He taxed her with it, calling her into the solar one evening as she came up the gallery steps and passed his door on the way to her room. She came in, her cheeks pink from the exercise, her hair loosened and in curling wisps around her face. She looked up at him doubtfully.

"Have I displeased you, Thor?"

"No, but isn't gentling the horses a duty your ostler performs?"

She looked at the floor. "Yes, it is. But I enjoy it. Moreover, the mare had begun her training, and Harald is, ah, visiting his family. It seemed a shame to let her forget what she had learned."

Thor had known that. He had asked when he saw Harald was missing, and one of the stablemen had told him. But he had needed an excuse to talk privately with Aylena. He came to her now and put his hands on her shoulders, pulling her closer.

"I am hungry for you, my love."

She was silent, fighting the surge of hot desire that came from his touch, his scent, the soft look in his half-lidded eyes. "I know," she said, her breath tight, "I have the same hunger. But I—I need more time. Being here, in my father's room . . ." Her eyes strayed to the bed.

Thor's hands dropped away, his face flushing. "Then take the time," he said, and turned back to the chair where he had been sitting before he stopped her. "I'll not beg for your favors." He was as angry with himself as he was with her. He should have known how she'd feel, surrounded by her memories of her father—and of her father's pride in her. She might well believe she hadn't deserved that pride if she crawled into her father's bed with a Norman invader.

He stood with his back toward her, trying to control his thwarted passion, his hot temper. If she truly loved him, he was positive she could put those memories and feelings aside. But it was evident that the love she had for him was not equal to that task. He had lost her, then, by bringing her home. Bitterness filled him.

Aylena stood still, knowing in every part of herself the pain she caused him. Had caused herself, for the feeling of being cut off from him was agonizing. If he turned back now and held out his arms . . . No! It was better like this. When she left, he would be safe.

She swung around and left the room. Thor stood like a statue and listened. The sound of her small feet on the gallery floor faded rapidly. She was running—running from him.

16

 A week later, riding into the bailey after a day spent in judging the condition of sheep in the far pastures, Aylena slid from the back of the young mare and handed the reins to a stable boy, who had come from the stables with a quicker step than usual. He took the reins from her hand but grasped her fingers, holding her from turning away. She looked down at his excited face, wondering.

"A messenger has come, Lady Aylena," he whispered. "From Tweedmouth. Harald said you would want to know."

"Yes." She turned and went quickly into the stables, holding her full skirts aside so they'd not hinder her quick step, and looking around for Harald. He was there, and a man with him. She went to them, excited and expectant.

"Is it time?"

Harald nodded. "Good weather, and a small load for Black Isle, sailing tomorrow night. We must leave here at the first sign of dawn. This man will be our guide."

"Wonderful!" She laughed, amazed. "The good Christ is looking after us, Harald. Lord Rodancott left this morning on a trip of his own; he'll not be here to ask questions of me. What other men here are going?"

"None," Harald said, glancing at the other man. "James here says we will have all the help we need."

"Fine. The less men we are forced to hide the better. The Scots are suspicious of all strangers. All right —Margit and I will be ready."

"I don't think you should leave until Lord Rodancott returns," Margit said for the fifth time since Aylena had wakened her in the dark. "You need his advice."

"Finish your bundle, Margit, or go without it. We leave soon. Don't you want Ian home and safe again?"

"I pray nightly for his safe return, as you well know. But—"

"Come! They will leave without us!"

Margit regarded her in the dim light of a lamp. Aylena had put on a brown linen gown and a long brown cloak with a deep hood. Her hair was braided and wrapped around her head, and over it a brown wimple hiding every wisp of hair and most of her face. Only the deep blue eyes showed, and once she pulled up the hood, they, too, would disappear. Margit's fears eased. Aylena looked like a peasant. No one would ever guess who she was. Perhaps, then, they would be successful.

Stepping to the edge of Aylena's bed, Margit blew out the spirit candle. "Patience," she said, and hoisted her bag, peering from the window. "They are not in the hurry you are. They have yet to light the signal. No, there it is . . . now we must hurry."

They were down the gallery steps and through the great hall in a rush, through the courtyard and into the stables, where their horses waited, saddled and ready to go. Harald tossed them up, tied their bundles behind them, then mounted his own horse and nodded at James. James was silent, looking them over, his eyes going from Aylena to Margit.

"Twill be a long ride, ladies, and a rough voyage."

It was the first time Aylena had heard him speak, and she was surprised by his accent. No rough Scot, no laborer. But not a noble. A man, near middle age, but no hint of his occupation. She gave a small shrug and smiled. He was a man sent by Harald's brother, and so a man you could trust.

"We are used to traveling, James."

He smiled back at her, brightening his face considerably. "You'll not change your mind?"

"Indeed not."

He looked at her and then at Margit, who stared back at him boldly, her dark eyes challenging. He inclined his head, accepting their decision. "In that case, we'll begin." Then, turning, he led the way through the opening gates and turned east, heading straight for Tweedmouth and the sea.

Only once Aylena glanced back, and, seeing the castle changed and gentled into beauty by long, pale rays of light coming from the east, she wondered if she'd ever see it again. No matter how brave she acted with Margit, she knew it was possible that she would fail in her attempt to rescue Ian. If they were caught, Ian would be killed by the clansmen who had put them under the curse. And she would never forgive herself.

In all, the ride was long but not difficult. Mostly the lay of the land dropped gently toward the sea, the beaten paths along the Tweed were shaded by thick trees that grew on the banks. At noon they stopped under the trees, rested the horses for an hour, and ate the food Margit had brought along. James filled a skin with the clear, purling water of the Tweed.

"Once we're on the salty North Sea, this water will taste like a fine wine," he told them, and laughed at Margit's frown. "Never mind, maid. The fast current will see that our trip, though perhaps uncomfortable, will not last too long."

His teasing increased Aylena's mood. Once started on the trip her confidence had gradually disappeared. She had been so sure of herself; now she was stricken with doubts. She realized—at last—that in trying to rescue Ian, by even appearing on Black Isle, she could call attention to his hiding place. She was nearly ready to tell James she'd reconsidered, and would have, except that she could think of no other plan that would be better.

She was pale and silent as they mounted their horses again and rode toward the east. There was nothing for it but to go through with it and pray to all the saints for help. Twas the only scheme that had come to her; she had to trust her own judgment. At this moment, that was hard to do.

It was coming on dark as they rode muddy streets into the straggle of shops, huts, and warehouses called Tweedmouth. The docks, uneven and rotting, held a number of boats of all kinds, mostly small fishing boats or boats that plied only the river. But there was one larger craft, with a single lateen sail, at the furthermost dock.

"That is our boat, then?" Margit asked, looking at James. "That little sailing vessel? Is there room to sit down?"

Dismounting, James laughed and came to grasp her waist and swing her from the saddle. "And what great ship are you used to, maid?"

Margit, swung down with easy strength, shook down her skirts and stuck her nose in the air. "I sailed to France and back with Queen Eleanor. The ship was magnificent, naturally."

"Naturally," James agreed solemnly, and turned to help Aylena down. Already on the ground, Aylena laughed at his surprise. There was something about James that she liked and trusted. Trusted enough to confide in him. She motioned him closer, and spoke.

"Now that we're on our way," she said, "I am . . . well, a bit shaken. You know our plan?"

"Yes. A good one, my lady."

Aylena breathed easier. "I hope so. I still believe tis the best, but I am not sure I can carry it off. If you have advice, I'll listen to it."

James's eyebrows lifted. "No advice, Lady Aylena. No one can say where this plan will lead you, nor what enemy you will meet. But . . . action, yes. Help when it's needed. You will have that, heaped up and running over."

She had to smile. "You are confident, James. But it is good to hear. And you are right—no one can say where and how my enemies will find us . . . if they do. Now, when do we sail?"

"As soon as we board. The tide is ebbing."

"Oh! Then we must hurry . . ." She turned to Harald. "What of the horses?"

"I will lead them home tomorrow, my lady."

"What? You are not going with us?"

"No, my lady. I know nothing of sailing. James is taking my place."

"Oh." Bewildered by the change of plans but not objecting, Aylena was silent. The two men untied the bundles of clothes and the basket of food from the saddles and carried them toward the sailer. She and Margit followed, careful on the rotting planks, in the falling darkness. Torches were lit on the boat as they drew near, flaring into brightness and blinding them momentarily. Then they were there, and Aylena could see the sturdy, high-sided shape of the boat, could smell the tarred rope and the odors of fish and wool, heard the sail flapping loose on the mast. Men were moving about on the shadowed deck, and hands were outstretched to help them aboard. Aylena took a large hand, looked up to nod her thanks, and froze.

"Welcome, Lady Aylena," Thor said stiffly, "you've come a long way since morning."

"No!" Words burst from Aylena's throat. "No! I will not risk your life! I could not bear it if—" She cut off the telltale words and turned to run back down the dock. But Thor's hand held her, pulled her around.

"So, that is why. You have little faith in me, Aylena." His words expressed disappointment, but there was a great, soaring relief in his voice. "You think me too stupid to include in your plan?"

She tried again to loosen his grip on her hand, but failed. Looking down, she shook her head. "I don't think you stupid, my lord. I think you too brave. And too . . . too noticeable to take into a country of angry men." She looked up, and from the depths of her fear for him, said what she truly believed. "Ah, Thor, they will kill you. I know it."

He shook his head. "I have told you, I am hard to kill. Let me into your company."

"I cannot. I will not. I have a feeling . . . a premonition. I'd rather not go with you in my party."

"What? You'd leave your young brother to find his own way home because of a silly fancy? Come—your plan is excellent, Aylena. I could have done no better. It will work."

She stood looking up at him, trying to hope, trying to believe. Behind her, Margit was praising God, thanking Christ and all the angels for their help in bringing Lord Rodancott to them for this dangerous trip. Aylena turned and looked at Margit, glanced at Harald, whose face was a mixture of guilt and satisfaction, then back at Thor.

"I see I must, after all. I am surrounded by well-meaning traitors. If I am to bring Ian home, tis time we started."

He grasped her waist and swung her up and over the gunwale, stood her on her feet on the tilting deck, and smiled at her. "We will bring him home, Aylena. I promise you."

They slipped from the port at full dark, catching the ebb at midpoint. Harald's brother, older and silent, was at the tiller; two younger men handled the sail. At first no one spoke, except for the captain giving orders. Thor and James, wearing dark woolens like the boatmen, stood with the captain and, as they left the port behind, conversed in low tones. Aylena, tired from the trip and tension, sat on her bundle of clothes and leaned back against a bulkhead. Margit sat beside her and, after a time, spoke.

"Did you bring Bettina's dye to cover Ian's golden locks?"

"I did. And the peasant clothes." She sat up, staring over the gunwale at the choppy dark waves, showing white where they foamed. "I can hardly wait to see him."

"I know. He's a bonny lad is Ian. Though not so bonny once you dye his hair, I suspect."

Aylena's smile was faint, but there. "He'll not mind. He calls his hair fit for a lass and hates it." She leaned back again, her eyes on Thor's huge, shadowy figure standing beside the captain. "Were you my traitor, Margit?"

"Twas Harald, my lady. He feared for you."

Aylena sighed. "Men. They cannot believe a woman can accomplish by guile what they must conquer by brute strength. I knew Harald was doubtful—but I thought him faithful to me."

"To his mind," Margit said practically, "he is. He did what was best for you and for Ian. Most of the men of the castle have turned toward Lord Rodancott as master."

Aylena turned and looked at her in the dim light of the boat's lanterns. Margit's face was placid, accepting. Thinking back, Aylena wondered how she herself would feel if she had been part of the castle workers. Very like the rest of them, she thought. Thor was a good master, strong but fair. She composed herself for sleep, pulling her heavy cloak about her.

"Rest if you can, Margit. We have a long, tiring voyage ahead of us, up past Aberdeen and Rattray Head, and then into the Moray Firth. Even with this tide and wind, we'll not reach Black Isle before tomorrow's midnight.''

Margit answered with a gentle snore.

17

It was cold. No matter the season, the North Sea was always cold at night. Its narrow strait, wedged between the coast of Europe and the islands of Britain, was far too deep to be warmed by a summer sun. But this night, at least, the elements conspired to aid the invaders. Both wind and tide drove them north, drove them so smoothly that not even the captain could assess the speed. He swore in amazement when, long before dawn, he saw the light at Rattray Head.

"We've come more than half the way," he told Thor, "and the rest of the run falls in the lee of the land and the firth. An easier trip I have never made. God must be with you."

"May He stay with us," Thor answered, "long enough to get us safe at home again. How long do you tarry at Black Isle?"

"Not even till morning. We'll load fish for Aberdeen and head out. There I'll pick up a load of wool for Tynemouth. But I'll be back in a for'night or so, barring bad weather."

Thor nodded. He had expected the answer, had hoped for a better one. But there was no use in asking the man to stay; there was no certainty that they could find Ian without a long search. He turned, looking through the darkness to the darker bundles, the cloaked figures leaning against the bulwarks, with pale faces gleaming in the faint light. At last, it seemed, Aylena had gone to sleep. He felt a lightness, a happiness, there in the cold night, that made up for all his doubts. She cared for him, enough to try to keep him out of danger. When this is over, he told himself, we will marry.

Aylena woke to a chilly gray dawn and the sight of sand dunes to the south, alternating with red sandstone cliffs, rearing from the sea. The mist was thick, hovering over the water, beading on the mast, running in rivulets down the taut lines that held the sails. She shivered; the mist had gathered in her clothes and hair, her skin was damp with it. She rose and went toward Thor, instinctively hunting warmth. He swung his cloak open and wrapped her against him, his arm holding her there. His warmth, his scent, the hard strength of his muscular body brought a rush of emotion to Aylena, thickening her throat. Mother Mary, how she had missed him!

They stood in silence, watching the light grow, staring at the changing shore. Numerous small rivers, few of them appearing to be navigable, cut through the beaches and cliffs. There were only a few fishermen, some on shore and others on boats, and none of them interested in the sailer. Behind them, Margit had begun to hunt through the bundles and boxes for food and drink for them all. James went to her and

helped; they spoke in low tones and laughed softly
together.

That evening they slid quietly into the docks of a
village on Black Isle. Still dressed in the dark
woolens of a seafaring man, and with James helping
him with the baggage, Thor hurried the two women
ashore and into an inn. James gave Margit a reluctant
farewell and went back to the docks.

"Let Margit answer questions, if any are asked,"
Thor told Aylena, and left them standing off to the
side while he approached the innkeeper. "My sisters," he said, motioning to them, and put down
coins. "See that they have a clean room. And one for
myself." He hesitated. "How far is it from here to
Leckie? I hear the clan I seek is living near there."

The innkeeper shot a surprised glance at him.
"Why, this is Leckie. There is no clan living here at
this time, though tis true that once the Stewarts made
Leckie their home. But are ye kin to the Stewarts? Ye
haven't the look of them."

"My mother was a Stewart. Tis her wish that I meet
with them and give them a message. Why do you
ask?"

"They are under a curse. No one here at Black Isle
would harm them, but, naturally, they do not welcome strangers into their midst. I will give ye the directions to their camp, but see that ye tread slow and
careful until they recognize your intent."

"That I will. Show us the rooms, so we may rest."

The rooms they were given were at the back of the
inn, small rooms with low ceilings. Thor's head
brushed the top of the door frame as he entered. He
threw off his rough woolen cloak and hood and sat
with them to tell them what he'd learned.

"The innkeeper says we are safe here on the island. He says no one who lives here is against the Stewarts."

Margit frowned. "The same is not true of the men in the northern Highlands, sire. And this island is not truly an island, though at this end it appears to be. It connects with the mainland some miles southwest. I came that way when I brought Ian to William."

"Tell me of it. Is the road broad and open?"

"At its beginning tis narrow and winding, amongst hills. However, William had heard of my coming and came there to greet me and take Ian, so I know little of the rest of it. I turned back then, with my companion, and we made our way home, tarrying only in Perth, when we stayed for a time with my friends and family. We had no enemies in Scotland then."

"Tis possible," Thor said slowly, "that if there is talk of our arrival there will be some who will come to make trouble. We must be ready for them."

Aylena, listening, was also taking in what Thor wore beneath that coarse woolen cloak. The clothes were ordinary enough: a shirt, under light mail, and a thigh-length tunic, dark chausses, cross-gartered with leather, and leather half boots. But his weapons were far different than those he carried when he rode his war-horse. He had a dagger as long as his forearm, sheathed at his belt. A small, two-bladed axe in a double leather case. And a light chain, hung on the same broad leather belt, with a small metal sphere at each end. She wondered at it, but only momentarily. Ian was on her mind.

"We must find Ian at once, disguise him, and then pray for Harald's brother to return," she said, summing up for them all. "Time is our enemy, for once the clans settle their plans, they will begin to search."

When asked, the innkeeper provided dinner for the three of them, served in the room. A fish soup, a roast of pork, apple pasties, and thick slices of dark bread, covered with new butter. They ate like hungry wolves, and afterward found the beds superior to the deck of the sailer, but just as lonely.

Thor was up and gone by the time Aylena wakened. She woke Margit, and when Thor returned with a wagon and horse they were ready to travel. They had bought food from the innkeeper to take along, and a skin of ale. They set out, leaving the broad shore of the isle, where the townsmen had their houses and most of the shops were built. The innkeeper had told them the direction to go—northeast by east—and they hewed to it, though the path through the high midlands was scarce wide enough for the small wagon.

One thing the innkeeper had said to Thor showed the man trusted him on sight. "You will see tree trunks, scarred in a certain way, along the path. When you have not seen one for more than a half hour, go back and look in other directions."

By noon, they had lost the way twice; twice they had gone back and picked it up again. Once they stopped and ate a hurried meal before going on. The wagon crawled slowly up and then down again, approaching the shore on the northeast side of the point. Then, when they could smell salt spray in the air, a young man stepped out from behind a tree and challenged them.

Holding a lance poised to throw, the man was tall and angular, wearing skin leggings and slippers, a long, blue woolen tunic and a cloak. His hair was a fiery red, his eyes as blue as the sea. Aylena leaped to her feet as Thor brought the wagon to a stop, snatched her hood from her hair, and called out.

"Roderick! Tis Aylena!" She followed that with a flood of excited Gaelic, none of which Thor understood. But the tall man came bounding toward them and swung her out of the wagon, kissing her cheeks resoundingly and setting her on the ground.

"Aye, and William set me here to watch for you, for he'd had a dream. Ye ken William's dreams, do ye not?"

Aylena nodded vigorously. "Uncle William has the sight, tis true. What of Ian?"

Roderick burst into laughter. "That cocky lad is more the laird now than he'll be when grown, though he had a sad time of it when we first brought him here. Ye ken there's a curse laid on?" When she nodded, he burst into speech again. "Some liar has told tales of treachery done by the old laird, and now he's offered a bag of gold for the old laird's son, dead or alive."

"Now may the mother of Jesus protect Ian," Margit broke in, turning white. "The stories are not true, Roderick, none of them. Tis the man telling them who is false."

"Aye, we all ken that, Maggie. Now come on, both of ye. Tis not likely ye are followed, with the size o' this guard ye hired, but we take few chances here in our camp." He turned, leading the way. Thor grinned at Aylena and followed.

The wagon rumbled down through stunted trees that bent to the sea winds and emerged on a slope that led down onto a beach, where sturdy fishing boats were pulled up on the sand and nets were hung on long racks, drying in the sun. Farther along, in a huge clearing cut out of the woods, were a series of stone and turf huts, each with a stone chimney and a pen that held a cow or a couple of goats.

Roderick ran before them, silent until they came to the beach, and then hallooing. The sound brought the Scots tumbling out of their houses or running in from fields that stretched east behind the settlement. Off to one side a group of children was working over a pile of flax and tying it into bundles; they tossed their work aside and ran in with the rest of them. Aylena's quick eye caught a familiar red-gold mop of curling hair in the midst of them, and she was off the wagon, grabbing up her skirts and running, running and laughing, falling to her knees with her arms outstretched and tears rolling down her cheeks . . .

Ian was tight in her embrace, his face turned to her neck, his strong, wiry arms straining around her shoulders. She murmured to him, blinked away tears, laughed, and tousled his hair. After a time he drew back and looked at her with a wet-eyed scowl.

"Why did you take so long to come for me? I want to go home."

She hugged him again. "An you will, my brother. But it will take even more time. Oh, Ian, I am glad to see you. How you have grown!"

There were footsteps behind her, and a voice. "Aylena! We wondered if you could find your way here in these times of trouble."

She rose to her feet and went into William's arms. A softer man than his brother Bruce, he was younger by ten years and gentle. He had the same craggy features, the same silver hair, even the same blue eyes.

She kissed his cheek, her memories of her father flooding back. Then came the women: her Aunt Laurie, her cousins, the young bride Roderick had claimed, the children. . . . She looked around from the clamoring crowd and saw William grasping Thor's arm, taking him down to the edge of the water to sit on a bench and talk. The men who headed the other families of the clan followed. Aylena looked over at Margit, who had her arms around Ian, and laughed.

"My lord will learn more about the Stewarts than he wishes to know. But there, who but William would be the best to tell him of the Stewart stubborness?"

Margit snorted. "Lord Rodancott needs no examples of Stewart stubborness, my lady. You have given him all the truth of it he needs."

That afternoon Thor took the wagon and horse back to the stable in the town. He was hardly out of sight when William came looking for Aylena in the hut she and Margit were to have, asking questions about the Norman.

Aylena looked him in the eye and answered with the truth. "Aye, as you suspect, he is the Norman invader who took our castle at King Henry's order, and he intends to keep it. But you will, I hope, treat him as a friend, for he has been more than a friend to me. He has taken me to Winchester and I have talked to the king, who wants Thor in the castle to keep peace on the border. But the king has promised to give Ian another chance to have his heritage restored to him— if, when he is sixteen, the king believes him worthy."

"Are you saying *you* have talked to the English king?"

"Yes, and Thor was the one who made it possible."

She went on, telling all. How Thor had rescued her. How they had gone to Aquitaine and Languedoc. How the queen had intervened and got her the demesne her mother had left her. And then, swearing William to silence, she told him of John Bretinalle.

"I, and I alone, should revenge myself on him, uncle. Had it not been for Thor, I would have been as ill-used as any captive slave, and died of it, alone and never mourned, for none of you would have known the place nor the time of my going. Bretinalle must die a painful death, as he planned for me."

"An I capture him," William growled, "he will know hell. Tis he, then, who has told the lies and caused the curse."

"Indeed. He and his cronies. I hear there are more, but what clans they are I do not know."

William rose from the bench he sat on, his heavy frame seeming to swell with his anger. "I know. The knowledge was sent in by friends, the Cuchlans and the MacLeods. The clans against us are the Kenlochs, the Renfrews, and the Barwicks."

Aylena shrugged. "To be expected, then, except for the Kenlochs. Poor clans, and jealous."

William nodded. "We will talk again, niece. I take it you want to keep this talk between us from Lord Rodancott, an I hear him riding in."

At the stables, Thor had returned the wagon and horse and taken instead three of the shaggy horses. Riding one and leading the others, he had gone to the inn and left word with the innkeeper for the captain who had brought them to Black Isle.

"Tell him to send a man to us as soon as he docks, and we'll be there before he finishes unloading. Twill mean a good profit for him, and a gold coin for you."

The innkeeper's eyes gleamed. "I'll not forget. But ye'll have a wait. There is bad weather coming."

Disappointed but not surprised, Thor shrugged. "The North Sea is never calm for long. We must wait, then."

Back in camp, he told Aylena what the innkeeper had said. "So," he added, "we should take part in the clan's work. The time will go faster for us, and they will benefit from it. They've spent time and money taking care of your brother."

"True, though they'd never count it up. I will help the women, and Margit will help with the children. Ian is already working—he's with the boys who are bundling the flax to be retted."

Thor nodded. "I know nothing of fishing, but I can help pull the nets in."

In a matter of a few days the clan closed around them. The men fished now in Cromarty Firth, a slim body of sea water on the north side of Black Isle, nearly enclosed by land. On the other side the Moray Firth went wild with the strong north winds, battering the coastline, flinging foam halfway up the cliffs.

"Tis the Cromarty gi'es us food an coins in bitter weather," Roderick told Thor, "an though the fish grow bigger an more numerous in the Moray, tha Moray is home to a strong wind. The Cromarty is like havin a wee pond of yer own."

After a week or two on the boats, Thor acknowledged to Aylena that the men of the clan were true men, strong and willing to undergo hardship. When on a Sunday afternoon the young men set up target games to test strength and skill with the battle axes, Thor took part with the weapons he had: the long dagger, the small, double-headed axe, the weighted chain.

Impressed by his skill with the axe, the men gathered around to look at the chain. Roderick ventured a guess.

"Ye throw it, I ken. But what does it do?"

Thor pointed at a sapling growing near the shore. "Say that tree is your enemy, and above that first long branch is his neck. Send him a necklace, then, like this. . . ." He whirled the chain over his head and let it go. It whistled through the air and caught the tree where he'd pointed, wrapped it tight and stayed, the two balls twisting together. Roderick let out his breath in a whistle.

"Where did ye find it?"

"In Spain. But one could be made."

Roderick cocked an eye at him. "An one could be taught?"

Thor laughed. "Perhaps, if one tried to learn."

An hour later, Roderick spoke in private to William, and then disappeared into William's house. When he came out he carried a sword, the biggest of any Thor had ever seen, and shining as if it were polished silver.

William took the sword from Roderick and accompanied him as he came up to Thor.

"This is the clan's pride," William said, displaying the sword held in both hands, the gleaming blade in the palm of his left and the chased handle in his right. "Tis the *claidheamh mor*, a two-edged broadsword few men can swing in battle. Roderick would like to see you try it."

Thor raised his black brows. "On what man? Is there an enemy about?"

"Attack the tree, Norseman," Roderick said, grinning. "If ye dare. Do ye think you can raise this great sword o'er yer head wi'out falling backward?"

Hesitantly, Thor reached out for the sword, taking the hilt in his right hand, examining the blade closely. It was like two broadsword blades fused into one, wide and heavy, both sides ground fine. "The weapon is fit for a king, William. But I'd not like to nick such a blade."

"Twas honed by a master," William said. "You'll not nick either edge." Suddenly paling, he stepped back, grasping Roderick's arm. "Don't stand near, Rod. The sight tells me the blade will fly from someone's grasp one day and do murder."

"Not from my hand," Thor said and smiled. He put no stock in second sight. He whirled and faced the sapling again. "Have at me, tree! Roderick has thrown down your gauntlet."

Aylena had moved closer, drawn by the appearance of the *claidheamh mor*, and other women had followed. Aylena had no doubt that Thor could handle the great sword; she knew his strength. But now, as he hefted the sword and swung it, she saw something more. A man and a weapon made for each other, a perfect match of muscle and steel, of balance and strength. She saw the look of amazement on Thor's face, heard the keening whistle of the sword, and watched the limbs of the tree, clean cut from the bole, falling in a flickering mass to the ground. The last limb fell, and Thor stepped back, looking down at the shining weapon as if it had suddenly come alive. Behind him, the other men broke into excited talk.

"Glorious!" William called out, red-faced and

beaming. "The *claidheamh mor* has found its master."

Roderick looked stunned. "One hand," he said, wheeling to stare at the other men, and said it again. "One hand! No man in the clan has ever swung tha sword with *one hand* . . ."

"Nor so well, even with two hands," William said, still grinning. "I'd not choose a fight with ye, Thor Rodancott."

Thor drew a long, reverent breath, as if he'd witnessed a miracle himself. "Tis a weapon more deadly than any other, William. It nestles in the hand and becomes part of the arm."

"Your hand," Roderick said, half jealous. "And your arm. Tis too heavy and awkward for the rest of us."

Thor looked him in the eye. "Ah, but I was trained as a warrior from the time I could walk. And, as you have often pointed out, I am a useless fisherman, tangling the nets with my boots and getting in the way."

There was a roar of laughter, for what he had said was true. No one but Roderick had ever mentioned it, but all knew how awkward the Norman was around fishing nets. Roderick joined in, laughing and clapping Thor on his shoulder.

"For that truth, we give ye leave to stay ashore, Norman, and let the fishermen do the fishing. Ye can guard our approaches."

Thor turned his head and looked at Aylena, seeing the joy and pride in her eyes. Roderick had just given him final proof of the clan's trust. She came to him with Ian clinging to her hand, and stood beside him. Ian dropped her hand and took Thor's, looking up at him with awe.

"Will I ever swing that sword with one hand, sire?"

Taken by surprise, Thor looked down at him. "Why, that will be as you wish, Ian. The training for a warrior is hard."

Ian's eyes, so like Aylena's, sparked a sudden fire. "Then I say I will. I'll not mind the work if it makes me strong and able."

William came up and rested a hand on Ian's head. "Well said, Ian. I believe ye'll master it." He took the sword as Thor handed it to him and turned toward his hut. "Come along, Ian, and help me clean and polish it again. Twill be yours, in the days to come."

18

"William told me that the place to stand watch is above the trail," Aylena said. "He said we would know the spot when we saw it. Tis unseen from below, he said, and gives a long view of the rising land. Also, he swore that the sound of a whisper or a step on soft ground carries upward as visitors climb the slope."

She and Thor were riding two of the small horses up to the spot where Roderick had hailed them that first day. She had been talking nervously ever since they left the busy settlement below, for she was very aware that this was the first time since they left Tweedmouth that they were alone together. Neither had wished to cause gossip in the clan. And she thought it likely now, here alone in the thick woods, that Thor would want to have her. Her heart beat wildly.

Glancing up at an overhanging bluff covered with small, gnarled oaks, Thor's eyes sharpened at the sight of an outcropping of granite.

"We may be close," he said. "That looks much like

the spot William described. The trail, he said, goes up on either side, but the one on the right is easier. Shall we try it?"

"Yes." She heard the quiver in the one word, and added no more.

Thor led the way, disappearing and appearing in the thicket. She followed, her small horse scrambling to keep up. Branches caught her clothes, and when her wimple slipped to one side, a limb reached out and tangled itself in her hair. She stopped and spent time untangling it and wrapping the wimple around her head again. Looking up, she saw that Thor had stopped farther along and was watching her struggle. His eyes were on her low-cut bodice, on the firm, rising curve of her breasts as she lifted her arms, and his gaze was heated. She folded her lips in a straight line and urged the little horse on, feeling blood warm her cheeks.

"You need not look after me," she said, coming up beside him. "I am able to take care of myself, at least here on my uncle's part of the island."

"I believe you." He smiled as he said it, turned, and went on. She followed and saw that he was entering a small glade in the oaks, which dipped down and away from the overhanging rock formation they had seen from below.

"Ah, yes," she said, riding up on the rock. "Just look how much you can see. Almost all of the winding trail we came up that first day is in sight, yet we saw nothing of this. Roderick must have seen us and come down before we got close enough to see him descend. This is a wonderful spot for spying." She slid from the woolen pad she used as a saddle and turned, taking the horse across the glade to tie him on a line long enough to allow him to graze. Coming back, she offered to do the same with Thor's horse, while he studied the trail below. He dismounted and handed her the reins.

"Are you my servant, then?"

She laughed. "No. I am no one's servant. I am half of the watch, my lord. While you are watching, I will do whatever needs to be done. Then I will take my turn."

"I see. Then, when you come back, bring the roll of heavy woolen cloth tied to my saddle pad."

She brought it and handed it to him. He shook it out and laid it, doubled, on top of the smooth, sun-dappled rock, careful not to leave wrinkles in it. "Now," he said, reaching for her, "I'll have you. And high time it is. Tis a cruel torture to be close to you night and day and never touch that silken skin."

For appearance's sake, Aylena protested. She said no. She said it was indecent to do such out in the woods, though she hadn't thought it indecent at Belmain. She reminded him that some enemy might come along the path and they would miss him because they were occupied with lovemaking. But she was taking off her clothes the whole time she argued, and so was he. They came together on the thick cloth like thunder and lightning, like shooting stars, like two desperate lovers, kissing, murmuring incoherently, burrowing into each other. She wound her slender legs around his muscular buttocks, and when he pushed into her, hot and huge and hard, she thought she would faint from passion and pleasure. She bit him, fastening on his massive shoulder muscle, laughed unsteadily and soothed the red mark with her tongue. Then, as he increased the tempo of their mating she arched her slender, writhing body into his, closed her eyes and swung, all the way up to heaven.

"Aylena."

She stretched, feeling her damp skin sliding sensuously against his, feeling the crispness of the springing hair on his chest teasing the tips of her breasts. She smiled and slowly opened her eyes, looking upward at the green leaves of the branches over them, moving like fluttering lace in the breeze. "Yes, my dear love?"

Thor rolled away from her, gazing upward as she had done. "I need more."

She laughed and sat up, leaning over him. "And so do I." Easing onto his broad chest, she kissed him, her loosened hair a golden veil around their faces. "What do you need the most?"

His hands came up and clasped her head, holding her there so he could look into her eyes. "I need your love, but I also need your trust. You must trust in me, Aylena. I will never hurt you."

She knew at once what he would ask, and she drew away. "I do trust you, my love."

"Then marry me." He watched her eyes and saw the joy in them disappear, the light go flat. She loved him; he knew it. But she would deny him again for the sake of her promises to her father.

"I cannot, Thor. I made my promises—"

He jerked her down and covered her mouth with his, stopped her voice with his tongue, pulled her slender body over him, and began caressing her roughly. "You are mine," he said, "mine. You belong to me, not to the past."

Aylena said nothing more, only gave to him, caressed him, showing him in every way she could that her love was his, and would ever be. But there was still doubt in his pale gray eyes and a sadness there that she could not drive away.

They came down to the village of the clan at dark, still at odds with each other about their future, and having seen no strangers on the path. None of the clan worried that their village would be found and attacked in the night; the path was hard enough to follow during the day, and their dogs barked.

"By the law of the clans," William told Thor that night, "a man who comes here with intent to kill may be killed himself, without blame. Tis only when a cursed man enters the land of another clan that he is fair game. Since we never visit the clans against us, we should be safe here. But those men are devious and vindictive." His eyes went to Aylena. "As are their friends. Not all Scots are honorable."

She nodded. She had certainly known that. "Thor and I will continue to watch, uncle. We—and Ian—are the targets for these devils, we know that well. But if the wind continues to blow as hard as it is now, we have decided to find another way home. Margit can travel anywhere in Scotland without fear; we may send her home to say we want a force of men to meet us as we come down to the southern uplands."

William frowned. "Be patient, Aylena. The wind will abate, and ye are welcome here."

"Thank you, uncle." She meant it; but there were problems William didn't know. Thor was restless, wanting to leave, ready to take his chances. And her mind kept going back to her presentiment of tragedy; her fear of his death. She had made him promise, up there in the woods, that if he decided to go overland, he'd wait for Margit to summon his knights to the border, and even beyond the border, into Scotland.

For another week, Thor and Aylena continued to watch the trail. Finally, aware that their differences could not be solved until the troubles were over, they put them aside. To make love again after the long abstinence following the visit to Belmain was wonderful, healing their hearts. Then, riding up to their woodland glen one early morning, they heard—for the first time since the weather worsened—the sonorous bell buoy in the Moray Firth, steadily tolling the good news that the violent storms were past for a time, and the North Sea waves were only rocking chairs.

Excited, Aylena was all for turning around and going back, her mind on the packing and readying themselves for the trip home.

"Give the man time," Thor said, amused. "It could be two or three days before he brings his boat here. We'll start packing and saying our good-byes tomorrow. Today I want my time with you."

Thor was right; it was three days before Harald's brother brought his boat into the port, and that afternoon before they knew it was there, for it was Harald himself and James who came to tell them the news. They saw the two men on the trail and rushed down to hear what they had to say.

"Ye canna go home by boat," Harald said after greeting them. "Someone has talked, and there is an army of ragtag Scots camping at Tweedmouth, waiting for you to return. They are sworn to kill the lad

and all males in the Stewart clan. I've brought James
to give you a hand in an overland trip home."

White with shock, Aylena asked questions. Without
giving her thoughts away, she listened to Harald
mention Bretinalle, apparently the leader, and the
names of two clans, the Barwick and Renfrew. She
turned to Thor.

"What can we do?"

"There is only one way to get through now. When
Harald goes back he must tell Philip of Anjou to
gather the knights, come to the hills north of the
Tweed, and, when the signal is given, fight their way
in if they must." He turned to Harald. "Tell Philip I
said to take the same trail we took before. We will set
out at once to meet them there. Knowing our enemies
are waiting at Tweedmouth gives us a chance to
travel without being attacked. And, when you land
there without us, give out at the docks that we're on
our way in a bigger boat, due to arrive in a few more
days."

Harald was smiling, relieved. "That I will do, sire."
He turned to Aylena. "There is a man—a noble—who
has arrived at the castle asking for you. He has said
he is your cousin, on the Belmain side."

Thor cursed, his face going dark. "Halchester!"

Aylena looked distressed. "He means well, Thor.
He had said to me in London that he'd visit, that he
wanted to see where his cousin Alyse lived. He seems
very fond of her memory. And he would want to help
us with Ian. Let him stay."

"He is a thief and a liar," Thor said, and turned
away, trying to master his anger. "A useless, vain
fool. There is nothing to the man but his own desires.

I am tired of him. He is only looking for a profit of some kind."

Aylena lowered her eyes and was silent. Thor was set in his opinions, that was easy to see. But he hadn't told Harald to put him out, either, though she had expected it. Thor was right in one way—it was possible to become very tired of Charles Halchester. Cousin or not, he could have waited to visit until he was asked, since Thor was the sire now.

Harald came on into the village with them, offering respect to William, introducing James, and explaining what had happened. He stayed the night and set off with Thor and Aylena at early dawn when they walked back to their post. He stopped, there on the trail, to tell them that James, who had visited the docks, had heard a strong rumor that the Kenloch clan had broken with the Barwick and Renfrew men and called off their curse on the Stewarts.

"They say the old laird of the Kenlochs found too many stories that wouldn't fit together, and called a council. Once he showed the young hotheads the lies upon lies that were being told to them, they went back to tending their sheep. Now, some think the Renfrews are ready to do the same, but the Barwicks will never give up. They have hated the Stewarts for years."

Thor's eyes grew hard, like gray steel. "Then perhaps the Barwicks will soon find a curse on them, Harald. Revenge can be sweet."

Going up to their post after parting from Harald, Aylena was quiet. John Bretinalle was a bastard Barwick, for his mother belonged to that clan. He would be part of the crowd waiting at Tweedmouth for Harald's brother to bring in his boat. She thought of

how he looked now: self-important, bloated with
pride. And though she tried to stifle it, pure hatred
coiled like a snake in the dark memory of what he
had done to her; the fate he had planned for her. . . .

"Aylena."

She jumped, though Thor had said her name gently
enough. She looked over at him as they came into the
glade and managed a pleasant expression. "I was
deep in thought," she said. "What do you wish to
say?"

"Tell me his name."

Her face went red as fire. "I . . . don't know who
you mean."

Thor reached for her, drawing her into his arms.
"Your enemy, my love. The man who hurt you; the
man who sent you into that filthy hell."

She turned her cheek to his chest and fastened her
arms around his sinewy waist. "Why do you ask? The
less I think of that time the happier I am, Thor. I need
to forget those men, not talk about them."

"Those men are dead. Tell me the name of the other
man."

She went stiff in his arms, jolted by his knowledge,
wanting very much to deny it. What had he heard?
Was he guessing? She drew a deep breath and
stepped away from him.

"Who told you that there was anyone else?"

"You did, Aylena. When you think of that hut, when
we speak of that night, he is there in your mind,
laughing at the hurt in your eyes, sneering at your
pride. And your hatred of him burns like blue flame."

She shrugged, avoiding his gaze. "Perhaps I do feel
hatred then. But"—she turned back to him and
looked up—"most of what I feel when I think of that

terrible time is my gratitude to you. Even so, I don't like being reminded of it. Can we talk of something else?"

Thor had hoped they were close enough now that she would confide in him, would say openly that the name of the man who had caused her to be captured and held as a slave was John Bretinalle. It puzzled him that she kept it secret, for he could think of no reason. But now, with a trip through Scotland to plan and enemies to outwit, he let it go.

That night Thor asked William for advice on getting through the Highlands to Perth, for Margit had told him excitedly that her family in Perth would welcome them, hide them, feed them, and let them rest as long as they liked. All of them, she had said, glancing at James, would be welcome.

Margit had lapsed into a garbled confusion of words at the very thought of her beloved family.

"They," she had added, "are not afraid of these skulking liars and thieves that call theirsel's a clan. The Barwicks are naught but murderers an beggars who canna hang t'gither so must hang alone on various gibbets. To which I say hurray an good riddance." She had slapped her knee and grinned at James, who grinned back, as confused as she, but happy.

Now, with all of them sitting in William's house— Ian at Aylena's side, a different Ian with dark brown hair and a look of fascination in his eager eyes when he watched Thor—with the light of the fire shining red on all of their faces, they listened to William.

"You'll go by the rivers," William said, "unless you must take to the high road for safety. First, cross

Beauly River to Inverness, go south up the Findhorn and then into Perth. High ground around you every step o' the way, so keep an eye up. Trouble can fall on you when ye walk the valleys of the Highlands."

"An then Callandar," Margit broke in, still excited about her family, "an the Gowries. Ah, we will be safe there. An full of good food. We may rest as long as it takes to get tired of sitting an eating."

"Then, after that?" Thor was eager to know the extent of the journey. He had never traveled in Scotland, but from what he had seen around him since he arrived on Black Isle, it was a land where an enemy could surprise you at any turn. There were more places for a man to conceal himself behind rocks or trees than there were open spaces.

"After that," William picked up the thread of his talk, "turn south into Stirling. The Cuchlans there are friends; they will help if they can. Then, along the Firth of Forth to West Lothian, an then down, through Lanark to Dumfries."

He hesitated, as if he must say something he didn't like saying, and then went on. "I believe you can expect both your enemies and your own men, either or both, in Lanark, because before you are there your enemy will know you are not coming by sea." His voice trailed away on that, his wrinkled face turning toward Aylena and Ian. "It might be best," he added awkwardly, "to ask the Cuchlans to take in Aylena and Ian until after the battle is over. I'd not put it past the Barwicks to rush you without warning and kill or capture the woman and child."

"No." Aylena's voice was soft and sure. "That will not happen. The men you speak of are not brave enough to rush even one Norman, let alone a party of them."

William looked up, seeing the huge dark outline of Thor standing in the firelight. He smiled a little and then rose, going to a cabinet on the back wall of the room. Opening it, he drew out the *claidheamh mor*. Then, holding it across his palms in the ceremonial way, he took it across the room to Thor.

"You will take this," William said, "and use it well in the defense of our clan. There is no glory for our sword if it stays hidden away when the clan needs its strength."

The next day a group of five peasants appeared on the road, a big man in coarse brown homespun, cloaked and hooded, riding a shaggy Scottish horse, a woman dressed the same and on a horse beside him, an older woman, and a brown-haired, scowling child riding in a mule cart. The cart driver was a lean, sinewy man in gray robes who brought them through the winding, narrow road at the southwest end of Black Isle and turned toward the Beauly River. Crossing it, they went on silently, plodding into Inverness, then disappearing amongst the crags and hollows toward the east.

Much later, finding a green valley and a rushing stream, James turned south and followed it, knowing from William's description that the stream was the Findhorn River and would lead them to the Monadliath Mountains. From those peaks they would be able to see first the rising of the River Dulnan and then the bigger River Spey, which rose at Laggan, a settlement in the far southern part of Inverness.

That night they spent in a forested mountain valley, glad of the thick pallets packed in the bottom of the cart and the woolen throws that covered them. They made a fire of dry wood and heated a kettle of soup the clan had made and given them, along with loaves of bread. After supper, James set the wheels on the wagon, tied the mule to graze, and took a pallet under the wagon, leaving the rest of them to talk.

"Two days," Margit said, and there was a yearning in her voice, "an we come to my old home in Callandar."

"Aye, an soon after," Ian said, his light voice unsteady, "we will be home again in my father's castle. I would fain see my sire ride out to greet me. But I—I know I will never see that sight again."

When Aylena moved to put an arm around him, Ian stood up and moved away. "I'll not cry, my sister. My father was brave an strong, an so will I be." He walked out into the darkness, a small figure but straight, his head up.

"Go with him," Margit whispered, but Aylena shook her head.

"No. He is seven, and beginning to know himself. He'll not wander away, nor be foolish, for he knows twould worry me. Let him grow, Margit."

Thor had listened, but said nothing. Later, he rose and stretched, yawning.

"I'll look about, though I expect no enemies, nor for that matter, anyone else. There has been no movement in the woods, nor any sound except for burrowing animals seeking food. You can feel safe here—and you need your sleep, ladies." He disappeared, and a few moments later Ian came into the circle of firelight and climbed under the cart, pulling a pallet and cover with him.

"We men," he said, yawning widely, "are sleeping

underneath. You and Margit, Aylena, are to sleep in the cart."

Two days later, coming through a pass in the Grampian Mountains and following the River Garry down to the River Tay, the party came to Callandar and the homes of the Gowries, set together in a fertile valley and full of men, women, and children, all shouting and laughing when they saw who it was.

Overwhelmed by the noisy welcome after days in which even their own voices seemed loud in the silence of the Highlands, Aylena and Thor took themselves out in a meadow and sat there, watching Ian frolick with the young Gowrie boys.

"How long do we stay here?" Aylena asked. "One night or two?" She had gotten into the habit of asking Thor what he wanted to do; the trip was hardest on him and on James, so she gave him the right to choose. She, Margit, and Ian had always the choice of riding or of sleeping half the day in the jolting cart.

"One," Thor said. "This is a time when the Barwicks may discover the trick we played on them, and every hour counts. We can trust that Philip and the Reeve brothers have a trick or two also and will use them, but we must depend on ourselves. The longer we wait, the better chance our enemies have to find us traveling and mount a surprise attack."

Aylena was silent, realizing anew their dangerous position. One man against a crowd from two clans, and in those two clans could be someone who would know Margit, and Margit's family. The whole force might be traveling fast, right now, toward Callandar, expecting them to do just what they were doing—stop for a rest at the home of friends. She jumped to her feet.

"Why hadn't I thought of that? Mother of God, we could bring down the whole pack of them on the Gowries! Come, let us leave; let us warn them—and let us leave Margit here. She will be safe, as long as we are gone."

Thor unfolded his long body and stood, looking down at her. "I have already suggested to Margit that she stay here in safety. She has refused. But the rest of it, yes. We leave at dawn and take a devious route. They will expect us to avoid the eastern part by traveling down through Selkirk and Dumfries and will try to catch us there. But, once we are through Stirling and West Lothian, we will do something else. We will move east into Midlothian and come straight down to the River Tweed. That was part of the message Harald carried to Philip, for I told him to come in the same way we did before."

Halfway through his discourse Aylena's eyes dropped; she turned away slightly. "Yes," she said now, "it is. We will be traveling down the same roads you traveled up the first time. Tis not a place I care to remember. Or to see."

"But yet the safest place, because they do not expect us to be there."

"But . . . what if they see your men, traveling that way?"

Thor gave her a look of amusement mixed with sore tried patience. "My men," he said, "are trained in war and the art of war. They will not be seen by the men of the clans until they are ready to be seen, and even then twill prove to be far too soon for the clansmen."

19

The party was up and gone before dawn, disappearing into thick morning mist with only the creaking of the cart on the rocky road to mark their passing. James and Margit sat on the seat in the cart with Ian between them, and Aylena, riding her horse beside Thor and watching them through the drifts of mist, thought how much they looked like a family threesome, now that Ian's hair was dyed. She said so to Thor, and added:

"If they continued down to the border as they are, and without us, they might go straight through the gathering of the clans without being noticed."

Thor shook his head. "We cannot take the chance. James is a good man in a fight, but those clansmen looking for a boy of seven would never let them go without questioning—nor would it be surprising if they recognized Ian even with the dark hair. His features are much the same as yours."

"True, though most of the Barwicks would never recognize me. Their clan and ours were not friendly enough to visit back and forth."

"Twould only take one to recognize you."

She looked at him quickly, wondering if somehow he knew of John Bretinalle, deciding that he couldn't. "I know," she admitted, "twould be too dangerous to chance it. You say James is a good man in a fight. How do you know that? Have you seen him fight?"

"At times. He is part of my castle staff in Normandy."

"Oh? How is it that he has come here?"

"I sent for him, when we left London. I needed a man I could trust for this trip. He has a quiet and humble air about him that is useful in dealing with angry fools. Later, I would say he'll want to return to Normandy."

Aylena was silent, riding on. Thor's constant, silent thoughtfulness for everyone never failed to surprise her. Then, looking at James and Margit in the brightening day and seeing their faces turning to each other with soft glances, she smiled to herself. Those two would not wish to be parted.

Late that evening, when darkness hovered in the valleys and they had come as far as the River Forth and crossed over into Stirling, they found a small village with an inn. Their spirits rose when they found baths were offered and the odors of cooking drifted in through their windows from the kitchen outside. Again, the women slept in one room, the two men and one boy in another, and all rose early to start the rest of the journey.

Thor bought a sack full of meat and fruit pasties, a round of cheese, two extra skins of ale, and enough fresh-baked bread to feed them for two days. Outside, putting the provisions in the cart, James was approached by the innkeeper.

"By the look of things," the innkeeper began, "ye mean to travel toward the borders. Did ye know of the trouble there?"

James shook his head. "We have heard no news, for we have been traveling. What is it?"

"Tis the Barwicks, threatening friends and enemies alike, damn their souls! Some fifty or sixty men have been running the border from Tweedmouth on to the west, setting small farms afire an molesting the women. Until two days ago they were only threatening one clan, the Stewarts, whom they had cursed. The Renfrew and Kenloch clans were with them, but first one and then the other changed their tunes. That was when the Barwicks began this destruction of the poor. Out of anger, they say, or out of meanness. But I am only telling you this so you can be careful. Who knows who is right?"

James listened and then answered calmly. "I know nothing of it, innkeeper. But if some are setting farms afire and molesting women, I would say they are the ones who are wrong. In any case, we are grateful to you for the knowledge."

"I am glad to give it," the innkeeper said, and bowed. "Stop again if you come this way."

When Thor came out James told him what the innkeeper had said. Thor nodded. It was what he had expected, he told James.

"They will course back and forth, make forays into the hills, and try hard to find us. William said they are quick-tempered and greedy men who have been told lies about the Stewart clan and have been promised a share of the plunder if they kill off all the male Stewarts."

James hoisted an eyebrow. "From what I saw on Black Isle, most of the Stewart men will be hard to kill." He turned, seeing Margit and Ian leaving the door of the inn and coming through the morning mist toward the cart. He smiled at them, and Margit smiled back, her fine dark eyes luminous as her glance met his, then turned to Thor.

"Lady Aylena is bringing your horse from the stable, sire. We are both excited this morning, thinking of tomorrow and the end of our journey."

Thor swung around and headed for the inn, but Aylena appeared around the side, her hood back, her bright hair glistening in the mist. She was riding her small horse and leading Thor's. She laughed as she saw his expression.

"Did you think me too weak to take a share of the work?"

"Pull your hood forward," Thor said angrily, "and keep it there. If some stranger asks the stable boy if a woman with golden hair and a young boy have passed here, what do you think he will say?"

Aylena's laughter died away, her face reddening. She jerked her hood forward and pushed her hair back into it. "I am sorry," she said stiffly. "I should have taken more care." She passed the reins of his horse to Thor and turned away, looking to the southeast and the fog-shrouded road they were to take. It was yet a long day's ride before they would come to the southern Midlothian hills where John Bretinalle's outlaws had captured and shamed her, yet the twisting road ahead and the heavy mist reminded her of it sharply, and also of the fact that once again she had been too careless for her own good. Head down, she waited until the cart jolted forward and then followed it, silent and subdued.

Twice in the next quarter hour Thor looked around at the slender, hooded figure on the small horse, then finally stopped his own mount and waited until she came abreast of him. He fell in beside her, and the horses matched their pace, glad to be together. After some little time, Aylena raised her head and looked at Thor. Her eyes were shamed, and angry.

"I said I was sorry. Isn't that enough?"

"No."

Temper flared in her face. "What else must I do?"

"Come ride with me, at the head of the party, and keep my spirits up. I am not happy alone. Nor do I fancy riding in the rear, with the dust kicking up from the cart."

She had to laugh. There was no dust. The road was mainly rock, and the air so damp that beads of moisture settled on every surface, including their clothes. But she was adamant. "I have been foolish, as you noted. As my punishment, I choose to ride in the rear. Until noon, this is my station."

"You are acting like a child."

"Nevertheless, I—" She heard a sound and looked ahead. For a moment she was frozen, unable to speak. Then her eyes came back to Thor. "Keep your eyes on me, my lord. Grab my arm, pretend you are angry; shake me hard and growl. *Now.*" She put her head down, as if frightened by violence, shrank back from him and felt his quick grasp, heard him cursing at her, felt his hand shaking her, hard . . .

There was a growing rattle of rock, of pounding hooves and creaking of saddles, and then coarse laughter, billowing out from a half dozen throats. Hoots and jeers . . . "Tak' her to the woods, goodman, an lay her down. Twill help both yer feelings." "G'ie tha bawd a shakin', then, if she displeases ye . . ." And then they were gone, all fifteen to twenty of them, crowding past and putting their horses to a gallop.

Aylena stared after them, conscious of her fast-beating heart. "Some of the Renfrews," she said softly, "by the color of their tiretaine banners. And on their way home . . . thank the good Christ and the Virgin Mary." She turned her head and saw the stiff figures of James and Margit facing forward, saying nothing, and between them a brown-haired boy, as quiet as they. The cart was rumbling on, gradually regaining the middle of the road, and as it did the small horses increased their pace and came up behind. No one else spoke. But Thor made no move to the front of the cart. It was plain that the peasant family bumping along in the cart attracted no real notice, nor did the riders, following the cart in coarse clothes and mounted on little Scottish horses.

Twice more a group of the Renfrew men passed them, cursing the cart for taking up half the road, shoving past without looking at anyone, intent on the open road ahead.

"They'll not side with the Barwicks again," Aylena said. "They've been led into this by lies, and they won't forget."

Thor had told James that there would be no stop for eating until it was dark. So when the sun was at its zenith Margit climbed into the back of the jolting cart and handed out meat pasties, fruit, and berries to be eaten as they rode. A skin of fresh water was passed around afterward.

The mist of the morning had given way to a brilliant blue sky; the rock-strewn fields had become green fields of grain. They were in the southern uplands and the road now turned tightly around rising hills. An occasional glint of rushing water appeared between forests of pine, and all of them had begun loosening their heavy cloaks. It was hard to believe that at the end of this pleasant trip there would be grown men waiting to murder a child.

As evening drew near they saw the abbey at Stowe shining rose-colored in the late afternoon sun and turned away from it, heading up into high, rolling hills. They rode an hour or so, and Aylena believed they were still north of the place where she had been attacked. She had begun to feel sick, to feel the hatred and fear she had felt then. She thought it must show on her face, for Thor spoke of that time.

"We'll not stop near that burned-out hut, Aylena. I know you have bitter memories of it."

She looked at him through the gathering gloom of evening and gave him the ghost of a smile. "There is one memory of it that I treasure, Thor. The sound of your voice at the door. I knew when I heard it that I would be saved."

"Strange," Thor said. "All you knew of me then was that I was your enemy."

"Not true. I also knew you were an honorable man."

"How?"

"I was raised by an honorable man, and so find it easy to judge other men by him."

"I see." Thor lapsed into silence as he rode on. It

was growing darker, and in the seat of the cart he could see Ian's head drooping against Margit's shoulder. The child was tired, all of them were, but he wanted to pass that damnable hut before he stopped . . . ah, there. There were the ruins of the hut at the bottom of the slope; the only recognizable part was the blackened stone hearth where they had sat in front of a fire most of the night. The rest of it was no more than charred wood, a pile of debris mostly covered by blown leaves. And, he supposed, unless they had friends who cared enough to bury them, there would be human bones under the debris.

"It looks so . . . small."

Thor turned his head and looked at Aylena, who was staring past him at the scene. Her eyes flicked to him, surprised and somehow relieved, and then flicked back, fascinated. "Small, and very old. Like a thing in the past."

"It is in the past, my love."

After a moment, she nodded and turned her attention toward the road ahead. "For me," she said after a silence, "it—it kept on happening every time I thought of it. As if I were there. But now I see tis gone, and no more than a bitter memory fading away. I'll not think of it like that again."

"Then twas good that we came this way."

"Yes." She smiled a little. "Very good. How much farther will we go for this night?"

"No farther than the next space along the road that will hold our cart."

They pulled off into a glen no more than a half mile from the ruins of the hut, ate well, and, protected from view by a copse of small trees, rolled up in their woolen covers and slept.

* * *

Toward morning Aylena dreamed, and the dream
seemed to relive the ending of the cruelty and horror
she had undergone in that destroyed hut. She could
feel the warmth and strength of Thor and his great
horse as they carried her away, she could even sense
the pleasant odor of Frere d'Armes's warm breath,
compounded of sweet hay and oats. It became so real
to her that she finally opened her eyes and, in the first
pale light of coming dawn, saw the great black head
bent over her as she lay in the cart. She heard him
whuffle out another breath and saw him bend to
breathe in again, identifying her. Half awake, she
reached up and stroked the smooth, silken forehead.

"If you want your master," she began drowsily,
"he's under . . ." Reality came to her and she sat up,
half frightened, and looked around at vague figures in
the mountain mist, gradually making out who they
were. Thor and James were standing in the middle of
the glen and talking to Philip of Anjou. The Reeve
brothers were feeding their war-horses but staying
close enough to hear and join into the low-voiced
conversation. There were other men, perhaps six or
seven, moving on the edges of the glen, appearing
and disappearing like ghosts in the mist. Her gaze
came back to the cart and found Ian sitting on the
driver's seat and staring at Frere d'Armes as if at a
holy vision. When he saw her looking at him, he
spoke, carefully.

"Is that your horse? I've been watching him ever
since the men came, and he acts as if he is."

She swallowed a laugh. "His name is Frere
d'Armes. He is friendly to me, but he belongs to Lord
Rodancott. He is a Norman war-horse."

"Oh."

Beside Aylena, Margit yawned. "It's barely light," she said. "Why chatter so?" She caught sight of the black horse and was abruptly silent, sitting up and looking around.

"Gracious Mary, look at the bellies to fill. . . ." She had slipped off her heavy tunic before falling asleep; she reached for it now and jerked it down over her head. "Come! We'll put a kettle on to boil for gruel." She glanced over at Aylena and grinned. "We've men enough to look after us now, my lady."

While the men ate, Philip of Anjou came to talk to Aylena. "Your cousin wanted to come with us, Lady Aylena, but we had to refuse. He has not had the training to come through the night without alerting the enemy. He asked me to tell you he would come once the battle is joined."

Aylena shook her head. Charles Halchester was beginning to irritate her as much as he seemed to irritate Thor. "How could he know when the battle is joined?"

Philip's quick grin seemed to understand her disgust. "Perhaps he means once the battle is over and we come riding back to the castle. In any event, we were glad not to have his company. The Barwicks were on guard, as if they knew we were coming."

"Oh! No one was hurt, though?"

"None of our men, my lady. However, the enemy lost two sentries. Fortunately for us, neither managed an outcry."

Aylena flinched, but only a little. If men must have their throats cut, twas better for Barwicks to suffer than for honest men. "How many are against us?"

Philip hesitated. "I cannot be sure, but I would say no more than fifty."

"Fifty! And we have only ten or so?"

"Twelve, I believe. More than enough."

"A dozen against fifty is more than enough? How can you say that?"

Philip's narrow face broke into a wide grin. "Experience, Lady Aylena. When Thor rides, the odds change."

An hour later they were on their way. Margit took over the cart, driving the mule. With Thor on his warhorse and James riding a good horse from the Stewart stable, young Ian demanded the shaggy Scottish horse Thor had ridden before.

There was no hurrying. Thor pointed out that the two dead sentries would show the Barwicks that the enemy had passed their lines last night, and their trackers would soon find the fresh hoofprints crossing the broad, shallow valley on the north side of the Tweed.

"They will come up to us," Thor added, "and I prefer it." He glanced at Aylena. "You, Margit, and Ian will not be part of the battle, nor even observe it from a distance. Philip has his orders and will obey them. You will obey Philip."

Aylena's face went white, mirroring shock and fear. Somehow she felt Thor would be safer if she stayed. "What are you saying? Do you think me stupid enough to dash into the fray and get myself killed?"

"I think you might. I remember your valiant effort to join the fight when we came to conquer Stewart Castle. The Barwicks might not be as gentle with you as I was when you attacked my men. And I don't

want a Barwick to lay an eye on Ian. I thought you'd
agree on that count alone."

Aylena stared at him, color seeping back into her
face. "I do," she said. "I hadn't thought. I will do
whatever Philip says. But I hate to take away one of
your best men." She wanted very much to warn him,
to tell him she had seen him killed by an axe. But she
knew well enough that he'd only shake his head and
accuse her of fancies. If only she could erase it from
her mind. . . .

They kept their speed to little more than a walk, for
the mule pulling the cart was slow. James, watching,
went back after a time and took over the reins from
Margit long enough to show her how to keep the mule
at a trot.

Thor was himself again. Gone were the coarse
peasant clothes, the long cloak that hid his muscular
legs, the hood that covered his shining black hair and
beard. He wore his own fine chausses and golden-
brown tunic, covered by his hauberk of glittering
mail, and more impressive by far than his other
weapons, the *claidheamh mor* hung from his broad
belt. Aylena watched the growing sunlight strike light
from the blade and felt confidence healing her fears.
Who could defeat him?

They had reached the height of the highest mountain of the beginning ridge when Aylena suddenly recognized the place where the three highwaymen had
waylaid her and pulled her from her horse. There
. . . . there was the thicket she had crawled into,
only to be dragged out by her hair. . . .

"Thor!" She heard the sudden urgency in her own
voice as she looked back the way they had come.
Down there John Bretinalle had waited for them, had

pulled her away from her horse . . . and there Sims
—was it Sims?—had grabbed her . . .

Thor had answered her, had seen her turn back,
not hearing, her eyes a burning blue, searching. . . .
He came back to her.

"What is it?"

She pointed with a shaking hand. "Down there,
where we were only a minute or so ago . . . there is
the slope where the highwayman threw down my
bundle and the two coffers in it. Do we have time to
search?"

He threw up a hand and stopped the horsemen and
the cart. "More than enough time. But there is always
a chance that someone else has found that bundle."

"I know." She looked up at him and he saw that
she truly believed she would find it. Her face was
transformed by hope and determination. "I will go
down myself, my lord. I am the smallest . . . and I
will recognize the bundle. Let me go."

He could not refuse her. When they went back
down to the place she thought most likely, he tied a
line around her waist and another line to a heavy belt
she could sit in. Philip watched him, horror-stricken.

"What if she falls? I can do that, Thor. I am
light . . ."

"She won't fall."

"You can't be sure of that."

Thor was laughing. "But I am sure, and she wants
to do this herself. Be ready to help when we bring her
up. You can hold her away from any rocks with this
long branch."

Going down was not frightening. The first part of
the slope, though too steep to walk on, was mostly
smooth; when she swung into it, she eased away with

a gentle push. And then she was in the trees, and the slope was not nearly as sharp. She braced her feet against the ground, hung on to a small tree, and kept on looking, looking, her heart beating like a drum, her mind a constant prayer. Then, having seen all she could see from where she was, she unfastened the lines that held her, got out of the seat, grasped the next tree, and then the next, slipping and sliding along the curve of the hill.

"Aylena! Put those lines back around you and tie them tight!"

She flung back her head and looked up, her hair blowing in the wind, a golden banner. Thor was not so sure now. He was pale, frightened for her.

"Don't worry, tis neither slippery nor steep. An I will, once I find that bundle. I know it's here."

"Aylena!"

She looked up again, frowning. "Trust me. I can do it." Her foot slipped and she fell, but the trees were thick; she caught herself with a quick grasp at the next one, pulled herself up, and continued on, arms stretching, tree by tree.

Thor and Philip followed along, looking down at her, holding the dangling lines. She fell, but each time she struggled to her feet again. Then, after what seemed an hour of searching, she saw something dark and different in a bank of thick shrubbery, higher on the sloping land and half covered with drifted leaves. Trembling, for she was immediately sure it was her bundle, she climbed through the trees and came to the thick shrubs, grasping their strong limbs. Brushing the leaves away, she felt the familiar soft, smooth wool the Stewart weavers made, now damp and smelly from mold and dead leaves. Then, probing, her fingers touched a hard metal corner. This time when she looked up she couldn't speak.

Thor, gigantic against the clear sky, threw back his head and laughed aloud. "You found it! Then twas meant to be."

She wiped tears from her eyes and nodded, gesturing toward the lines. Thor swung them to her. She tied the single line around the bundle, making it secure, and sat in the wide belt, arms around the lines and around the big bundle in her lap. By now the whole party had gathered along the edge of the road to watch. Margit closed her eyes and prayed as Thor and Philip pulled.

Once on the path above, Aylena refused to give up her heavy bundle. She was full of excitement, full of triumph as she carried it to the cart, put it in, and threw a woolen cloth over it. "I'll not hold us up to search through it," she told Thor. "It is tied the way I tied it; what I put in it will still be there. Let us be on our way."

20

 It was afternoon when one of the Reeve brothers, acting as a lookout in the van of the group, came back to say that the Barwicks had begun crossing the valley and entering the beginning hills.

"They appear to be heading east of us," he added. "And most of them are on foot. A ragtag army, Thor, but the ones I saw first are well armed."

Thor nodded and motioned to Philip, who came near to listen.

"'Tis time to take the women and child out of this, Philip. Take them due west, and when you can see the valley clearly and no one is in it, take them down and across the Tweed. Then, when you think it right, head for the castle."

Philip gave a quick nod. "Where is the cloak you wore, sire? I'll use it as a disguise."

"In the cart." Thor turned, looking at Aylena, riding beside him. There was fear in her eyes, but not for herself.

"Take no chances, sire. God be with you."

He touched her cheek with a rough caress. "And with you."

She turned away to follow Philip, then turned back again, meeting Thor's gaze. "Be wary of axes, sire."

He laughed a little, seeing her haunted look. "William is your clan's seer, my love. Would you usurp his claim?"

Aylena shook her head. "Not I. But I fear for you. Please. Remember what I said."

Touched by her concern, Thor nodded. "Then I will. Follow Philip, my love. There may be little time."

When the cart left, Margit was driving the mule with Ian on the seat with her, and Aylena and Philip, mounted on the Scottish horses and wearing the peasant clothing, plodded along with them.

"Straight west, into the sun," Philip told Margit, and she took the first wide trail she came to that headed west, a trail well marked by wheels and hoofprints. Philip regarded the trail suspiciously.

"From whence came these travelers?" he asked Aylena. "I have seen nothing of farmers or peasants who might use this path."

"They came from near Tweedmouth, Sir Philip, or so I would think, and were moving west. You remember we heard of the Barwicks overrunning the settlers near there and burning their farms."

"True. I had forgotten." Philip's lively face was full of scorn. "Brave men, the Barwicks, to harry the poor peasants and take their livelihood. I would fain help Thor punish them for it."

Aylena glanced at him. She knew how he felt, a man always in the forefront with Thor, now forced to herd women and a child to safety.

"Once we are out of harm's way," she said, choosing her words carefully, "I see no reason why you can't return to the battle. Margit and I know this land better than you do and can keep ourselves out of sight."

Philip laughed. "I would return to a battle, true. But twould be between Thor and me, and I would lose. He would never forgive me for leaving you without a guard."

She knew he was right. Yet she wished Philip at Thor's side. Philip was quick and loyal, the best of Thor's men. "Perhaps," she said, continuing along the same line, "if we see an early chance of getting across the Tweed, then Margit, Ian, and I will be safe enough alone for the rest of the way to the castle. You could return before the battle was over."

Philip bent a quizzical look at her. "I would fare no better, Lady Aylena. Believe me, Thor would have my skin. Isn't this far enough west to drop down into the valley? I have seen no one along here."

Aylena gave up and turned to look down for the rest of the Barwicks. But none were in sight. She followed Philip as he started down a beaten trail toward the water meadows near the Tweed.

"The battle must be joined," she said, looking east. "I see no stragglers hurrying to strengthen the enemy. Damn them all! Thieves and murderers, that's what they are."

"Look, Aylena!" Ian pointed another way, to the southwest. "Are they stragglers?"

Aylena craned her neck and stared, shading her eyes from the bright sun. "No! Those are honest men, wearing our own castle garb. Men-at-arms, by the look of their lances. And the tall man with them is my cousin, Charles Halchester. Your cousin, too, Ian. He is related to the Belmain family."

"Oh. Then we are safe, aren't we?"

Aylena whirled and looked at Philip. "Oh, Philip, we are! With my cousin and four of the castle men-at-arms, Thor will know we're safe. Go! I am sick with worry about Thor. He needs you and I do not. Go, Philip."

On the seat in the cart, Margit had bowed her head over the slack reins and was loudly and volubly thanking God for their deliverance from the Barwick clan.

Philip grinned. This time he could see she was right. "I will," he said. "Halchester is no fighter, but your men-at-arms are loyal to a man. Thor will be pleased to know you are with them." He whirled the little horse, kicked him into a gallop, and headed for the hills without even a glance back. Aylena laughed at his eagerness and then, turning and seeing the party of Halchester and the men coming steadily on, stood up in her stirrups and waved. At last, Charles was doing something useful, and at the same time, helping Thor. Thor depended on Philip.

"Go toward them, Margit. The sooner we meet, the sooner we turn them around and start home."

Margit left off her prayers of thanksgiving and took down the whip, waving it at the mule and encouraging it with chirps. The mule broke into a trot and sent the cart jolting and swaying toward the slowly advancing men. Margit laughed. "Wait until I tell James how fast the mule ran . . . oh, Aylena, I could run myself, thinking of being home."

"And I," Ian said, kicking his small horse into a

trot. "No one will ever take me away from my home again."

Aylena ignored Margit's lapse of manners. Margit was always more a friend than a servant, and leaving off the title before her name was never important to her. But what Ian had said burned her heart. Ian would learn soon that the Stewart castle belonged to Thor Rodancott, by the decree of the English king. Then his small heart would burn—and break. But that was in the days to come. First, they must reach the castle . . . and Thor must defeat the Barwicks.

The battleground was chosen. Thor had sent the Reeve brothers looking for an open vale amongst the thickly forested hills that separated them from the Barwick clan, a vale with a grassy, gentle slope that would offer him the advantage of high ground yet provide safe footing for the war-horses. Martin Reeve had found a choice spot, and once Thor had approved it, he and Nicholas Reeve made enough stealthy noise to bring the Barwick clansmen to investigate.

Watching from the forest, Thor was in full awareness, conscious of the clean odor of pine, a cool, fitful breeze stirring his hair, and the sounds and sight of the clansmen, stocky and muscular, coming into the vale. Beneath him he felt Frere d'Armes tense, his heavily muscled haunches gathering to the ready. Thor gentled him with a hand on his neck, a soft word. "Wait, my brother."

The other Normans watched also, but their eyes went often to Thor. They, mounted and trained, knew they were more than a match for the men slipping into the lower end of the vale. Most of the clan carried lances and axes, but some had no more than long knives. Once they were all in sight, some fifty strong, they stopped, looking around. There were no mounted men, and that troubled Thor. He had thought Bretinalle would be leading them, and perhaps a clan chief. But from the way they acted—aimless and confused—no one was leading.

For once, Thor hesitated. If Bretinalle wasn't here —where was he? He glanced at Nicholas Reeve and saw the same uncertainty on his broad face. Then he looked back at the motley crowd below.

"Wherever Bretinalle is hiding," Thor said, "we've got to take these men first. It won't last long." He looked around at each of his men, nodded and slowly drew the great, glittering sword from the loop of leather that held it. Full throated, he roared out a battle cry:

"To me, to me . . . for the Stewarts!"

The men below were also alerted by the hoarse cry. They milled in circles, looking up, unhooking their axes, holding their lances at the ready, then setting up a loud warning as Thor and his men burst into sight from the trees.

"Beware! Tis Norman mercenaries! Kill them!"

The men on foot rushed them as they came down the slope, throwing their lances, flinging axes. What skill they had disappeared in their wild anger, their fear. They had expected clansmen, men like themselves, on foot, carrying what weapons they had. They had known they could be speared by a lance, cut horribly by an axe, but they had not expected a swift and sure death by a Norman wielding the Stewart *claidheamh mor*. Each time the huge sword rose and swung, a man went down, dead or dying. Those close

enough to see the wounds screamed with supersti-
tious fear of the great blade.

Thor led the charge straight through the clansmen,
turned, and drove back up the vale. His path was
marked by rows of bodies, strong men whose last
sight was of the shining, bloodstained emblem of the
Stewart clan. Thor's men were doing their part,
swinging their axes at any man who ran toward them,
dodging the thrown lances. The mass of men held
bravely, attacking at first, but then, as the knights
turned again, as they saw their clansmen still falling
to the great sword like stalks of grain to a reaper, they
scattered from the mounted men, flinging down their
weapons and running east, into the woods.

Thor slowed and stopped, looking around. A full
half of the clansmen lay dead, dying, or too badly hurt
to rise, on the soft summer grass in the small vale.

"Fools," he said, his mouth a grim line in his black
beard, "to listen to lies from a man too cowardly to
lead them in battle. Come. We will leave the field and
give the Scots a chance at aiding their brothers." He
turned his horse and looked at his men, coming up
around him. "Who is hurt amongst us?"

"Only two men an one horse," Martin Reeve answered, riding up. "An they are bruised but scarcely
bleeding. Philip is staunching them."

"Philip? Where?"

Martin waved a hand. "There, near the woods."

Thor rode across the vale at a gallop. Sliding from
his saddle, he strode toward Philip.

"How are you here? You have not had time enough
to get to the castle and back. Where are your
charges?"

"They are on their way to the castle with

Halchester . . ." He flinched at Thor's sudden, lurid oath and held up a hand. "Wait til I finish the list, sire. They are accompanied by four of the Stewart men-at-arms."

"Oh. Even so I would have rather you continued on . . ."

"The Lady Aylena begged me to return and be with you. She was possessed by a vision she had."

"I know." Thor's taut body relaxed. "As you can see, she was wrong. No axe has done me harm, thank the good Christ."

Philip smiled, looking Thor over. "An you have bloodied the *claidheamh mor* in defense of the Stewarts. Give it to me; I'll clean it as shining clean as ever it was."

Thor nodded, handing over the great sword. "Perhaps it will continue its purpose as well. I'll take your horse to drink with mine. Once the wounds are treated we head for home."

Within an hour Thor led his men down the last of the rolling hills and onto the wide valley of the Tweed, turned and headed west, finding almost at once the wheel tracks of the cart.

"Good," Thor said. "The men-at-arms will know the best of the fords. We'll follow." He was smiling, happy as he had ever been in his life. The troubles were over, and Aylena would be waiting for him. He had no fears, now, that she would change. He knew she loved him.

Margit, who knew the castle staff even better than Aylena did for she went amongst them constantly and learned both their problems and their skills, had been

surprised as the cart drew near the men-at-arms
wearing the Stewart livery.

"I canna see a familiar face on the first two men,
my lady. They must be new since we left."

"Perhaps. It doesn't matter. Stephen would hire
none but the best. He may have felt with the threats
we received that he should hire more."

"True."

After a moment, Ian spoke. "If that tall man is our
cousin, Aylena, why isn't he fighting along with
Thor?"

Aylena smiled. "He is not trained to fight, Ian.
Some people aren't . . . suited for it."

"He is one of those who are called cowards, then?"

"Yes," Margit said firmly, "he is. Look again at
those men-at-arms, my lady. I have never seen any of
them before."

"Nor I," Aylena agreed. "But, as I said, Stephen is
a good judge of character. He'd never put the Stewart
colors on inferior men." They were only about forty
yards apart now, and she was hiding a smile at
Charles's gay apparel. He was dressed for a party
rather than a fight, wearing a lemon-yellow tunic
over a white silk shirt with long sleeves, a pair of light
green chausses cross-gartered in gold ribbon, and a
pair of maroon leather slippers that buttoned up the
sides. Looking at the other men, the castle guards recently hired according to Margit, she saw that they all
looked solemn; there was not even a smile on any of
the four faces. But, as they met, Charles stopped beside her, swung an arm around her waist, and leaned
to kiss her parted lips—except that she evaded the
kiss neatly and it landed on her cheek.

"So wonderful, my dear cousin," Charles said, "to

see you looking well and in such good health. This lad is your brother and the next laird of the Stewarts, is he not?"

"Indeed," Aylena answered, pulling away, puzzled and a little wary. "He is Ian, and my father's heir. I am sure you remember my companion, Margit. We are all in need of an escort across the river and to the castle."

"But where are the others? I was told you were with Lord Rodancott."

"And so we were, Charles. But there is fighting going on back in the foothills, and Thor sent us away from it for our own safety." Watching him, Aylena saw a flicker of triumph in his eyes and wondered at it. "No doubt," she added quickly, "he and his men will follow once they have put down the clansmen."

"You mean if they put down the clans, don't you? I was told that the clans numbered more than seventy-five men strong, while Rodancott had less than a dozen. Perhaps that is why he sent you away, my lady. Not just for your safety, but to keep your brother alive . . . if only for a little longer."

Shocked into silence, Aylena took in the sudden, remarkable difference in the man. His superior tone, his cocked eyebrow, the smile that was now an amused sneer, were at great variance from his usual affectionate and warmly approving air. And that last remark about Ian exposed him. At the very least it was cruel, even vicious. So, a friend had become an enemy. She opened her mouth to demand an explanation, and then shut it again, realizing the truth.

Charles had always been an enemy. It came like a searing light to her reasoning that Thor was right about Charles, and she had been flattered into a foolish affection. A stupid affection. She set her teeth and motioned to Margit.

"Come, Margit. We must find a ford ourselves and head for the castle. It seems my cousin would rather continue on his way." Her glance at Charles was cold and full of scorn. "Perhaps he wishes to find Lord Rodancott and offer him help."

"Oh, not at all!" Halchester's smile broadened. "We will be only too glad to guide you. You need not hurry, you know. Our men-at-arms are good protection. Come, then. We go west, for the shallowest of the fords lie in that direction."

Aylena looked around. There was no chance to get away. The men-at-arms had stationed themselves around the cart and the women. Looking into their hard faces, she knew even suspicious Margit had been wiser than she. They were not men hired by Stephen of Blaine; they were more likely to be criminals hired by Charles Halchester, and the livery they wore stolen from the castle wardrobe for this purpose. What plan was in Charles's devious mind?

After a few moments, Aylena looked over at Ian, riding beside her. The boy was pale, whether with anger or fear she didn't know. Clearly, he had felt the animosity between his sister and the man who was their cousin, and he didn't like it. She spoke to him quietly, dropping into the old Gaelic language of their clan. After a moment, he answered her with a calm question in the same language. She raised her brows in surprise and nodded. Halchester, riding proudly in the van, didn't hear the low-voiced conversation, nor could he have understood it if he had. Whether any of the stone-faced men-at-arms knew the language was questionable, but the chance had been there and was taken.

They were riding within clear sight of the Tweed, and, after passing two good fords within an hour, Aylena knew Charles had no intention of taking them to the castle. Instead, he was gradually leading them away from the river and into open forest on the Scottish side. Once they were out of sight of the river she spurred up beside him.

"Why are we back in the forest? Had you good reason not to take one of those two fords?"

Charles raised his sandy brows. "Indeed. We have been traveling a good part of this hot day, and I want to rest in the shade. I also wish to explore a bargain with you."

A bargain. Something given, something taken away. What did he want? What she wanted was time, and bargaining itself took time. She nodded.

"I will listen."

He laughed, enjoying her submission. "I thought you might. Here, up this bank, now. There are shade and privacy ahead. Have you a skin of ale there in the cart?"

"Two," Aylena said calmly. "I'll get them out once we stop."

Margit gave her a wild look but said nothing; urging the mule up the sloping bank was trouble enough, with everything in the cart sliding and bumping and those coffers of gold and jewels there to be found by these thieves and murderers. . . . She heaved a sigh of relief when the back wheels scraped up onto level land, stopped the mule, climbed down to tie it, and got up in the seat again. Everyone was dismounting, stretching, looking toward Aylena, who was rummaging in the supplies in the back of the cart. She turned, then, with two skins of ale, handing one to Halchester and one to the nearest man-at-arms. Halchester immediately upended the one and drank. The man-at-arms grabbed his and turned toward the other men.

Halchester handed back the skin she'd given him, wiping his mouth with a lace-edged kerchief. "Put it in the shade, Aylena. Tis too warm to drink. Then come back to me, for I've the bargain to talk about."

Aylena, one eye on Ian, who had drifted to the far edge of the clearing to help tie up the horses, took her time about finding a cool spot of damp earth and laying the skin on it. When she finished, she straightened and turned in time to see another horseman approaching them through the open woods. Her heart leaped at the thought of help; she stood still, staring, hoping to recognize a familiar face . . . then all hope was gone, all sensible thoughts, all reason. Her hands curled into fists at her sides, her lips pulled back from her clenched white teeth like a cornered wolf.

Watching her, Charles Halchester noted her expression and turned to look. He gave a quick laugh and strode toward the edge of the woods, taking the bridle as the horse came up to him. "My Lord Bretinalle! You are welcome, indeed. The battle is won?"

Bretinalle, staring at Aylena, seemed hardly to hear Halchester. "Yes," he answered, climbing down from his horse. "The battle is won, the Normans defeated, an you have captured the bitch who nearly blinded me. I'll have her now, here on the ground, with all of you as witnesses." He looked around at the startled faces and laughed shrilly. "An after me, whoever wants may crawl onto my leavings and hump her."

Margit's voice burst forth in earnest prayer, half shouting at God to prevent this violating of a woman by a madman possessed of the devil. The men-at-arms murmured amongst themselves; Charles Halchester stared at Bretinalle, who, sweating and eager, was removing his clothes. Aylena had not moved nor changed expression since Bretinalle had said the battle was won. Thor was dead, or twould be him here, not Bretinalle. For her, soon to die herself, there was one thing of value left. . . . Her lowered eyes slid toward Ian and saw him untying the reins of the horse Halchester had ridden, the tallest and strongest horse in the Stewart stables. Ian knew the horse, for his father had ridden him, often with Ian before him in the saddle. No one else saw the boy now, for Bretinalle had them all staring at her, half in shock and half in lip-licking expectation. She looked up and spoke clearly, no longer afraid of death.

"An you allow that beast to touch me, Charles, you will have nothing of me, whatever your bargain is."

Charles frowned. "I'll not allow it, Aylena. It . . . doesn't suit." He turned toward Bretinalle. "Enough, John. I realize you are only trying to frighten Lady Aylena, and surely you have reason to make her miserable. But she is my cousin, and a member of the nobility. Cease your disrobing."

Bretinalle whirled, half undressed, his fat belly hanging like a filled sack over the top of his chausses, his puffy jowls quivering with anger. "What are you saying? I am the master here!"

Charles smiled. "I don't agree, my lord. This was my part of the scheme, and I have played it perfectly.

You could never have taken this woman away from Thor Rodancott, and you well know it."

"And you well knew what I intended to do to her! You never spoke against it until now."

"You never said you'd make a show of it, John. Leave that part of your revenge for another time and place." Charles's gaze dropped distastefully to the fat, sagging belly. "And in the dark, for God's sake."

One of the men-at-arms laughed. Splotches of red formed on Bretinalle's neck and crept upward. "God's blood! How dare you insult me? This whole scheme was mine, and you but agreed to it. I was the one who roused the clans, and you have done nothing to help. Where were you when the battle was waged?"

"For that matter," drawled Charles, "where were *you*? You've told me the battle is won, and I believe it. Not even Thor Rodancott could best the Barwicks and the Renfrews with ten men. But you weren't there."

"The Renfrews weren't there, either," Margit said, her voice shaking. "They went home two days ago."

Both men whirled and looked at her. Margit, paper-white, nodded. "They did. They passed us on the road. There were none left to fight but Barwicks, and not many of them."

"Tell them nothing, Margit." Aylena's voice was full of contempt. Her mind was beginning to function again; she had felt a small hope rising when she saw, from the corner of her eye, that Ian had led the tall horse away from the others and toward the road below. Later, glancing again while the men flared up into noisy arguing, she saw that Ian and the horse had disappeared. If he managed to get himself up on the horse's back and if he could stay on it, he just might get away. Surely he could find the way home . . . if no one from here hunted him down. And if the Barwicks didn't find him first. She knew Margit had seen him go and was probably doing enough silent praying for them both.

"If this is true," Charles was saying to Bretinalle, "you cannot be certain the battle is over."

"They were within a half mile of each other when I left," Bretinalle blustered. "And neither Rodancott nor the Barwicks would have run away. It has to be over."

"But was it won?"

"Even if this handmaid is telling the truth, there were over fifty men to go against Rodancott's dozen. Do you think he could win? The Barwicks were all armed and more than ready to fight."

"We will see." His handsome face worried and displeased, Charles turned away from Bretinalle and motioned to Aylena. "Come. I would have words with you."

She went gladly, for it meant she could turn away from Bretinalle, who was putting on his clothes again. The sight of him was making her sick. Charles was still an enemy, and she knew now he was dangerous, but he had kept Bretinalle from making a soiled, pitiful thing of her, and for that she was thankful to him. She followed him to the edge of the clearing opposite from the horses and sat with him on a large rock.

"I am sorry to have put you in the way of insults from Bretinalle," Charles said. "He truly is disgusting. I hadn't realized how disgusting until today. I promise you he will never touch you again."

Aylena was silent, wishing she could believe him, knowing she couldn't. When Charles got what he wanted, he would forget her. She watched him burrow into a leather pouch he had fastened to his belt and bring out a square of parchment. He handed it to her.

"If you don't read, cousin, I will tell you what it says."

Dumbfounded, Aylena stared at the parchment, a testament that began with her own name, and, in the event of her death, gave all of her properties and monies to her brother Ian Stewart. Then, in case that they both died in a disaster, she chose to give all to her beloved cousin, Charles Halchester. There was a place for her signature below. Slowly, she raised her eyes to Charles.

"I am sorry to say that I have very little education, Charles. I have no idea what is written here."

Charles smiled, pleased. "Women have little need for education, my dear. This is just a simple agreement between us, two cousins of the Belmain blood, to share and share alike in our estates, no matter what they are or become. Since I helped you in acquiring Belmain, I am sure you will agree to my right to ask. Can you sign your name?"

She looked down again at the paper, hiding a flush of anger. What he wanted—doubtless had always wanted—was the return of Belmain to his hands. She sighed, but only at her own stupidity. She could sign it now, and these two men, Bretinalle and Halchester, would then do to her what they wished to do. Bretinalle would rape her; Halchester would see that she died. And then, when he realized Ian was gone, Halchester would hunt him down. With both of them dead, Halchester would lay the blame on the murderous clansmen, and show great grief as he took over Belmain. . . .

If she could be sure Ian would find his way home she would escape her enemies here by killing herself —better by far than to be shamed and dirtied by John Bretinalle. Without Thor life held little but duty. But . . . was Thor dead? The shock of hearing that the battle was won had frightened her, but she realized suddenly that her own superstition about his death had convinced her. Even cocky Halchester had looked worried when Bretinalle admitted he hadn't been there—didn't know firsthand that the battle had been won. Suddenly she felt the first faint wave of warmth in her frozen heart. Perhaps it was a futile hope, but Thor's words came back to her in that moment: *I am not easy to kill.* Suddenly words poured from her mouth.

"I am so ashamed, Charles, to have to tell you this. Not only am I unable to read, I have never learned to sign my name. There has been no reason to learn until now." The lie tripped from her tongue sweetly and full of sorrow at not being able to do as he asked. Charles looked pained.

"Ah, well, we can return to the castle long enough to have people there swear to your mark. Your seneschal, for one, and no doubt your priest. You will tell them you fear for your life because of the Barwick clan and wish to make sure of a legal heir."

"Indeed, tis a good reason, and one I should have thought of myself."

Charles smiled and stood up, looking around. "Where is your brother? Bretinalle will never agree to me taking you to the castle without leaving the lad here as your ransom."

Aylena got to her feet, feeling her heart pounding as she pretended to look around. "I don't see him, cousin. The child was tired; he may be sleeping in the cart or in the thick grass. He can sleep anywhere, and never mind it."

Charles looked at the men-at-arms, who had settled at the base of some trees and were lounging there, talking in low voices. Bretinalle was with them, and from the lustful glances they gave Aylena as she stood up, they were talking of her.

"Henry!" Charles's tone was peremptory. "Where is the lad?"

One of the men-at-arms jumped to his feet and looked from one end of the big clearing to the other, turned and looked through the woods behind him, then went to the cart. Margit sat like a stone statue, staring ahead, while the man looked inside, moving the bundles about, finding nothing. His hard face flushing red, he went back to kick up the other men. "Come! While we've been listening to this fat-bellied whoremonger, the young Stewart has wandered off. Look sharp!"

21

Thor and his men rode at an easy canter, heading into the golden light of late afternoon. It would be an hour or so before they crossed the Tweed, and hours more before they entered the castle walls. But the horses, used to hard campaigns, were scarcely winded from the easy ride yesterday and the short but violent engagement this early afternoon. And the men the same. They were almost ashamed of their strange involvement in a clan war, but those who knew the reason—the Reeve brothers, Philip of Anjou, and James—were not sorry, nor were they through with it. John Bretinalle had not yet shown his cowardly head in the war he had incited.

"We'll get him yet," Philip said to Thor as they rode. "Someone will know how to find him."

"If not," Thor replied, "we'll learn. I vow we'll not see him with either the Kenloch or Renfrew clans. They'll kill him as quickly as we would, for the blame will land on him, first for the lies they caught him in, then for the trouble they have made with the Stewarts."

James, riding on the other side of Thor and listening, made no comment on that. His eyes were on the tracks of the cart, ever going west. A little later, he slowed and spoke, pointing. "Here is where you met Lady Aylena's cousin, isn't it, Philip? The tracks are plain enough. Five horses coming from the west, meeting the cart and mule and one of your small Scottish horses. A lot of tracks, moving around as horses do when people talk. You must have had a long conversation."

Philip laughed. "Not I, James. I saw them only at a fair distance, though close enough to recognize Halchester and the livery of the Stewart castle. When Lady Aylena saw who it was coming toward us, she sent me back to aid Thor and went on to meet them."

Thor was studying the tracks. In a moment he turned away, brows knitted in thought. "Come. Evening is nearly here and we're wasting time. The fords are still ahead and we'll want the light to see which one they took."

But the tracks went past the fords. Neither hoof tracks nor wheel ruts turned toward the Tweed, but continued on, veering again to the north, staying in Scotland. As the twilight began to darken, Thor picked up the pace, now feeling a cold apprehension he could not dismiss. Then, as he watched the mark of the cart wheels growing fainter and twisting off toward the woods, he heard the sound of pounding hooves. He threw up his hand to stop the column just as a horse burst from the forest and came on at a hard gallop. Thor recognized the small figure on the horse's back and called out a warning.

"Pull him in, Ian! Pull him in!"

Ian strained to stop the horse, but the animal was

frightened and bolting. Thor spurred into his path, swung his horse to run with him, reached and lifted Ian over into his saddle, letting the frightened horse gallop on. Turning back, Thor saw four mounted men-at-arms burst from the woods, slide to a stop at sight of the Normans, and whirl, disappearing again. He looked down at Ian's white face.

"Who were those men chasing you?"

"We thought they were our men-at-arms, sire, but they are not. They were hired by our cousin, Charles."

"Where is Lady Aylena?"

Ian pointed, back toward the woods.

"Right in there?"

"No. Farther that way. . . ." He pointed west. "They made us go with them. My sister told me to get away if I could, and I did. Charles was riding my father's horse, and I took it while they argued, and then I stopped and hid in the woods, to see if I could help Aylena an Margit get away, too. But Charles and the men-at-arms found me and beat my horse to make it run."

"Beat your horse? Why?"

Ian drew a deep breath, setting his jaw. "They wanted me killed. Charles told them to see that I took a hard fall from the horse and if the fall didn't break my neck to break it themselves. Then bring the body back to show to Aylena. That's when I tried to get away."

Thor's arm tightened around the boy. "You did well, Ian. You will stay here, while I hunt for their camp." He handed him over to one of his men and motioned to Philip and the Reeve brothers. They looked at his steel-hard face and said nothing. They had heard; they knew Thor was ready to kill.

"Come," Thor said. "We'll not keep those men-at-arms waiting. Be quiet. They know we'll follow them."

"Those men may be smart enough to go another way. They ran as soon as they saw us."

"Not far, Philip, and we only need one of them."

Philip nodded, understanding. "I'll take the left, sire. We'll find them."

Martin and Nicholas went to the right and found three of the four easing away up a slope covered with heavy growth. The brothers attacked them with ferocity, leaving one dead and two wounded. The fourth man came out of the brush on foot, dropped to his knees, and begged for his life. They took him to Thor when he explained that Halchester had taken his horse because the child had taken the one Halchester had been riding. He was very humble before Lord Rodancott.

"We were leaving them, my lord. We didn't like the task of killing a child and shaming a lady." He saw Thor's face change and added hurriedly, "One of the lords was set on having the lady, but t'other one stopped it."

"Where is their camp?"

The man pointed west. "There, if they haven't left. Lord Halchester was planning to take the woman across the Tweed, and if Lord Bretinalle has heard you're here with your men, he'll be gone."

At that name Thor whirled and mounted his horse. "Set him loose to lead us, Martin, and warn him. If he takes us astray, he'll regret it."

Martin had tied the man's arms behind him and let

him walk, while he led the other three horses, which
were all from the Stewart stables. Now he cut his
bonds and handed him the reins of one of them.
"Lead on to the camp, then. You heard what Lord
Rodancott said. Lead straight or die."

The man was sweating with fear. "Yes, sire. I'll take
you right there." He set off at a fast trot.

From this section of forest the camp was not easy to
find, but within a quarter hour they were there, riding
into the clearing from the forest itself and finding
nothing but the mule and cart, with Aylena and Margit lying in it, bound with straps and gagged, to keep
them from crying out and guiding the men to them.

Thor and James were off their horses, cutting the
bonds that held the women, and the rest of the men
spread out into the woods to the north, walking carefully, hunting for hoofprints. The man who had
guided them asked to go back to his wounded com-
rades, and Philip let him go, afoot. James, who joined
the hunt once Margit was free, found a few tracks.
But the ground rose sharply behind the camp and
was studded with rock, showing only a scrape here
and there, too few to follow.

"Damn their rotten souls," James said, returning to
the clearing. "If we had a dozen good trackers with
dogs and a month to seek for them, we might suc-
ceed. This land was made for cowards and villains.
There are hiding places everywhere."

"Bretinalle will return," Aylena said, and said it
with conviction. She was seated on the driver's bench
in the cart, leaning into Thor's arms. Margit, frightened even yet, sat at her feet. Aylena's face was white
with weariness, yet her eyes were still intensely blue
and thoughtful.

Thor's arms tightened. "Why do you think so? He will know now that you will be well guarded."

"The man is mad," Aylena finally confessed tiredly. "He is possessed of a devil. Had you been here, you would know that is true. He lives to see me raped and shamed and then dead. Twas all he came for, and Charles stopped him. He will try again."

She glanced up at Thor's dark face. "He wanted to kill me before he left, so you would find me dead. Charles jerked him away. Not out of mercy, Thor, only out of fear of you. He told Bretinalle not to be a fool—you'd hunt them down and kill them both if I was injured."

"I believe you," Philip said. "I have thought him mad from the beginning. From what I have heard from other men he lashes out without reason in a frenzy of hate."

Aylena sighed. "Charles knows now that he will never have Belmain, and Bretinalle must know he's lost his chance to kill off the Stewart clan. Doubtless Charles will let it go and look for an easier way to take money from others. But Bretinalle will never give up his vengeance. He will try again to shame and kill me—even if he must find someone braver than he to do it."

The moon, nearly full, lighted their way to the fords. The glitter of silver light on water purling over the shallows kept them out of the deeper water on each side. James drove the mule, with Margit beside him and Ian asleep in the cart, snuggled comfortably amongst the bundles. Halfway from the Tweed to the castle, a tall horse, saddled but riderless, joined his stablemates and followed along with them. The cuts from whips were visible on his hindquarters. Riding together, Thor and Aylena saw them.

"An I meet Charles Halchester again," Thor said, "I will show him no mercy."

"Good," Aylena said. She had realized that Charles's scheme proved he had intended from the beginning to kill Ian and allow Bretinalle to kill her, leave their bodies to be found, and blame it all on the Barwicks. Then, armed with the testament he had wanted her to sign, he would have gone to the king and asked for Belmain. And likely he would have gotten it. She was ashamed of how easily he had fooled her with his friendliness and praise. But then, he'd fooled Queen Eleanor, too . . . or had he?

"I am not always a good judge of men," she said after a few minutes. "Charles also would have killed me—once I signed the testament he carried. He wanted Belmain."

There was a short silence. Finally, Thor spoke. "Then I will make sure I meet him again; I'll not leave it to fate."

The castle gates opened when the moon's light shone on the lances of the knights and the gleam of their armor. It was a still night, and the Stewart castle yeomen had heard the rumble of hooves before the column came into sight and were watching for them. When the flaring torches at the open gates shone on Aylena's white face and golden hair, a cheer went up. But then, as Ian woke and stood up in the cart, blinking, holding on to James's shoulder and waving, the men on the walls burst into a roar of welcome, and in the courtyard people came running. This was what they had waited for—had prayed for—the son, the old laird's son, safe at home again, where he would grow

up and carry on the blood of the clan. And the courage of the old lion.

Aylena had known what the welcome for Ian would
be, but Thor had not. Even the serfs, the field workers, sleepy-eyed but gloriously happy, ignored the
knights, pushing past the riders to crowd around the
cart. The ostlers, the workers in the armory, the
kitchen, came out half dressed, laughing and crying,
to cheer for Ian. It was a miracle to them, for they all
knew of the curse and had been cold with fear for the
boy.

Aylena let the noise go on and finally die down to
an ordinary level. Then she mounted the steps leading
into the keep and spoke.

"You owe thanks to Lord Rodancott," she said, "for
he and his handful of men brought Ian through the
uplands safe and now unthreatened. The Renfrews
and the Kenlochs have called off the curse, and the
Barwicks have been soundly defeated."

Brought back to reality, the castle staff, from scul-
lery boy to Stephen of Blaine, put up a polite cheer
for Lord Rodancott.

Thor bowed to them and thanked them for their
praise. But later, going up the gallery steps inside, he
gave Aylena an ironic smile and spoke his true feelings.

"I have been defeated by one small boy. I am not
the king of this castle."

Aylena frowned, her neck stiffening with pride.
"They love him, Thor. He is their future."

He saw the frown, the unconscious arrogance of
her lifting chin, and paused at the head of the steps,
determined to make her give him his due.

"If it weren't for me and my men," he said, "neither of you would be here. You'd be in your graves. There would be no hope then for the Stewarts to remain a clan, for who would be the next laird?"

Aylena had stopped when he stopped and listened to him, carefully. Then she answered him. Coldly.

"William."

He stared at her. She was perfectly calm, as if the only thing that mattered at all was the clan and the line of succession. *Why* was it so damnably important? In all of Europe and most of Britain, strong rulers came from first one royal bloodline and then another, often ending as king of a country they had never lived in nor cared about. At times they were unable to even speak the language of their citizens.

"I see." In fact, he didn't. "And after William?"

"His son."

"What if he had none? Could someone conquer the clan and take over as ruler?"

She cocked her head at him. "Are you thinking of doing so?"

"Sainted Mary! I can imagine nothing worse!"

Blood ran up her cheeks at the implied insult. "Be at rest. Twould be impossible. You have no Stewart blood; therefore you could not lead the clan. They would die defending Ian from you."

Thor nodded, his face grim. "I see that now. As you said, he is their future, or so they believe."

Aylena looked at the iron set of Thor's black-bearded jaw and was silent. After a moment he turned abruptly and left her there, heading for the solar and his bed.

Subdued, Aylena went on, hoping Bettina had ordered a bath for her, hoping for a truce tomorrow with angry Thor. She had been tired and angry when they quarreled, but she loved him; she knew she always would. No other man would ever be in her bed or in her heart. But still, when the nine years were up, she would journey to London to go before the king and beg that the Stewart castle be returned to Ian Stewart. She might find it hard, even impossible, but she would honor her heritage and her sworn word.

Entering her room, she found Bettina there, waiting beside a tub of warm water. There were tears in the old woman's eyes, but a smile as broad as her face could hold proved they were happy tears. Bettina rushed to help her disrobe, and after Aylena eased into the water, began clucking like an old hen over the ugly, coarse cloth of her gown and cloak, the shapeless shoes.

"Like some beggar, an you the lady of the castle," she said. "An these great bundles here, sent up to your room! Why, one of them is filthy with damp an rotten leaves. I canna see why Margit insisted on leaving it here."

Aylena's eyes, half closed in the bliss of warm water and fragrant soap, flew open. She raised herself slightly and looked around, seeing the bundle near the hearth, still tied as she had tied it. It seemed an eon ago, or in another life, that she had tied those knots and escaped from this castle.

"Never mind," she said, sliding back down into the water and closing her eyes. "Margit was right. I want it here."

Later, gowned in fresh, smooth cotton, with her golden hair lying in damp waves on her back, she sent Bettina back to bed for the short time remaining before dawn, and went to bed herself. Lighting the spirit candle beside her, she glanced at the bundle and yawned. Tomorrow would do.

Afterward, lying in the semidarkness, she began to laugh and weep a little and, for a while, couldn't stop without erupting again. John Bretinalle would sell his soul for half of what was in those coffers, and yet he'd had Sims—was it Sims? She still couldn't remember —throw the bundle over the cliff. Then, again presented with a chance of finding something valuable in her possessions while she was held captive, Bretinalle had never thought to look in the bundles. He had thought only of his hatred for her. She and Philip were right; the man was crazed by hate.

Aylena awoke at noon, rested and immediately happy as she looked around her at the familiar icons and tapestry on the walls, at the sheepskin rug beside her bed, the sunshine pouring through the open window. Familiar scents came in with the fresh air; had she not opened her eyes the scents alone would have told her she was home. She slipped out of bed and took deep drafts of it as she hunted in her wardrobe for something to wear, settling on a green silk gown with insets of lace and ribbon bordering the deep square neckline, a tight bodice that fit like a glove, and a gracefully draped skirt.

"Lady Aylena? Are you awake?" The door swung open, and Margit's face appeared around the edge, followed by her solid body. She stood staring at Aylena with all the pride of a mother hen watching a fine feathered chick. "So, you did not need me to help you dress. Are you hungry?"

Aylena laughed. "Starving. I'll come down to eat."

"Let me braid your hair, then. It will tangle if I don't."

Hesitating a moment, Aylena handed Margit the comb she held and sat down. "One braid then, not two."

Margit sniffed. "One braid? Twill be bigger than Thor's wrist, my lady. Two would be more proper."

"I am at home. I need not be proper here. Now, hurry. Has Lord Rodancott come down yet?"

Separating the mass of hair into three thick strands and braiding them rapidly, Margit nodded. "He has come down, he has eaten, and he has gone to the stables to see to the horse those men beat so cruelly. Ian followed him out."

"So I am the only lazy one?"

"Indeed. I see you did not open the bundle last night, either. How can you be so sure those coffers are still within? Someone more clever than you might have slipped them out."

"By the saints, Margit, you sting like a bee! Tie off that braid and go bring me my breakfast while I open the damnable thing."

Finishing off the braid with a ribbon wrapped and tied, Margit left hastily, closing the door, remarking to no one that she'd bring up fruit, fresh bread, and cooled ale.

Fearful that Margit's needling remark might have some truth to it, Aylena dragged the damp bundle onto the stone hearth and, working hard with her slender fingers, untied the knots that held it together. It opened slowly, splaying out ruined garments at her feet and disclosing both coffers, their brass covers blackened by damp and mold, their colorful enamel sides still bright as ever. She knelt, her heart beating hard, and unlatched and opened them. Dragging in a full breath, she settled back and sighed in relief.

Margit's frightening remark had no substance. Everything was there: the brimming gold pieces in the one, the flashing, glittering, glowing jewels in the other, and, tucked down one side, the testament she counted on to regain the castle for Ian. She snatched it out and opened it, reading it over. It gave the former Yorkleigh castle to "my beloved nephew, Sir Bruce Stewart, laird of the Stewart clan." And then, to prove it was no mistake, it continued on to speak of the faithful service and protection Sir Bruce had given devotedly to his aunt, the Lady Celestine of York, for the many years that had passed since her husband had died.

"Ah! Tis true, then, my lady." Margit swept in with a tray and placed it on a low table near the hearth. She went down on her knees, clasping her hands in pleasure, and stared at the sparkling gold and jewels. "Tis a blessing from God, Aylena. Twas meant to be."

Aylena smiled, taking a piece of fruit, biting into it, savoring the taste of home. "That is what Thor said, there on the mountain. 'Twas meant to be.' And I believe you both. Tis enough to see to the needs of the clan until Ian is ready to take over." She glanced toward the door and then sprang to her feet. "Thor! Come, see what you helped me find. A treasure I had thought gone forever."

Thor, his beard and hair freshly trimmed, wore a white silk shirt under a sleeveless black tunic, black knit chausses cross-gartered in silver, and a silver chain around his neck, with a stalking heron carved from a pale blue, translucent stone. Surprised, Aylena came close, taking his hands and admiring him, wondering why he seemed so quiet. "You look wonderful," she said, "and your heron will bring you the best of luck. Perhaps it brought mine. . . ." She turned and swept a hand to take in the soggy bundle and the coffers. "See? I have lost nothing but a few old clothes."

"I do see," Thor said. "I know you are happy." His eyes lit on the parchment. "Is that the testament you mentioned to the king?"

She picked it up and handed it to him. "It is, and you will see why I think twould make a difference. But I have learned there is truly no way to be sure, for kings are kings, and do as they will."

Thor read it through and handed it back to her. "It will be hard for Henry to rule against it," he said, "but you are right. He has the power to rule us all." Staring down at the coffers of gold and jewels, he shook his head in wonder. "Have you a place to keep them safe, Aylena?"

Aylena laughed happily. "I do, but tis in your room, not mine. Will you allow me?"

Thor's unsmiling face didn't change. "I will, if you will trust me not to steal."

"I have trusted you with my life, Thor. Surely I can trust you with gold. Come, I will show you the places we have always used. Mayhap you will find use for them yourself." She reached for his arm, but he moved away. So he was still angry, too angry for the slightest show of affection. She felt a dull ache in her chest, a premonition of sorrow.

They went into the solar, leaving the coffers behind, for Margit had dumped out the contents and was polishing the discolored brass tops. Aylena shut the door and took him on a tour of the walls. There were small indentations in some of the fitted stones that, once firmly pressed, yielded and allowed the stone to swing open. Behind them were spaces where the coffers fitted neatly. They were all empty.

"Why so many?"

"My father's aunt, the Lady Celestine, had many jewels and jewel boxes. Over the last of the years before my father took over her expenses, she sold them for her needs. Now, here . . ." She opened the door to the hidden stairs and stood back. "This is the secret way out of the castle, which my father called the coward's way." She turned, looking up at him and wondering again why he was still so angry. "I took the coward's way myself, the night I ran away from you —and ended in that hut."

Thor looked down the dark and dusty stairs and back at her. "Twas no coward's way for you, my lady. It took courage and more to make that attempt. Had it not been for Bretinalle and his plotting, you might well have made it to Black Isle."

"True." So his anger at her was not great enough to change his opinion of her character. Suddenly thoughtful, she stepped back from the opening and closed the panel that hid it from view. It *was* true. Had she managed to get even as far as Midlothian, she would have found the rest of it easy. There were many Scots in the uplands then who would help any clan member along the way—especially those the English preyed on. And, had that happened, she would have never truly known Thor Rodancott.

Now she was suspect. She had consorted with a Norman mercenary and allowed him to fight for her clan. There would be many Scots who would view her as a traitor, others who would say she had done what she did only to save Ian . . . and both would be wrong. She had stayed faithful to the Stewarts, she had done all she could to save Ian. But she loved Thor . . . and always would.

"Aylena."

She came out of her thoughts and looked up at him. "Yes?"

"I give you a week to rest, my lady, and then we ride again to Winchester."

She was amazed. She watched him as he moved around the room, restless and avoiding her eyes. "Why?"

"I believe it best." He turned then and came back to her, still not touching her, but looking at her squarely with an expression she understood at once. Male pride and hot desire battled for dominance on his hard face. "You left me to sleep alone last night," he said. "I'll not have that happen again. If you try it, I'll drag you from your room and into mine. Save yourself the laughter that will bring."

Color swept her face. "You left me, Thor."

"You should have followed."

Suddenly, she was angry. "I am not so meek as that! I'll not follow a man who insults my whole family and then walks away without even saying good night." She whirled toward the closed door and felt his hand grasp her and pull her back, turning her into his arms.

"Aylena . . ." What he had intended to say was lost as his mouth covered hers, his tongue licked her lips open and slid inside like warm silk. Her anger was gone, as if it had never been, the heat in her blood turning it into mist, floating away.

For an instant she yielded all to him, knowing only

the way his desire thrilled through her, slipping down her slender body, tightening her breasts, bringing fluid fire deep in her belly. Her thoughts suddenly whirled. Was that all he had to do? Kiss her, and she forgave and forgot every insult?

Angry at herself now, she pushed at him, twisting her face away, and felt a hand grasp the thick braid and tilt her mouth to his. His arm slid down and drew her closer to his loins. His tongue teased her lips and the inside of her soft mouth, slid in and out, in and out, coaxing, demanding, and all at once her body forgot who owned it. Helplessly she moved against him, her slender loins hunting his hot arousal. Her hands ran up to his shoulders, moved higher to thread fingers into his crisp black hair and hold his lips to hers. Eyes closing, she reveled in his warmth and scent.

He swung her up in his arms and carried her across the big room to the dais and bed that had once belonged to the laird of the Stewart clan. He well knew she was as full of passion as he, and he lay with her on the bed, kissing, caressing, reaching up under her skirts, pulling her bodice apart so that her firm, pointed breasts were freed. He suckled, feeling her arch up, feeling her thighs widen. He moved to the other breast and heard her moan. Then he made himself move away and looked down at her, breathing deeply.

"Are you going to tell me you cannot love me on this bed?"

For a moment she didn't understand his urgent whisper, then she smiled and shook her head. "Never. My father would have been proud to call you friend, had he known you. Nor would he have blamed me for loving you. He was ever fond of a fearless and honorable fighting man."

Thor heaved a sigh and sat down, lying back on the bed, pulling her on top of him and running his hands over her back. "But I am not fearless, Aylena. I greatly fear losing you."

She laughed and sat up, untying the laces that held his white shirt. "I will not allow you to lose me, my lord. I love you much too well." She saw the doubtful gray eyes change to soft warmth, his firm mouth soften in the glossy beard. It tempted her, and she leaned to lick it, teasing him, making him purr like a great cat. Laughing, she moved away.

Standing beside the bed, her breasts gleaming in the half-light that came in the small windows, she loosened the ties that held her tumbled clothes to her waist. He rose, took off his tunic and loosened shirt, and bare to his chausses, began to help her to take off the layers, his fingers awkward with buttons and ties. She let him do it alone, and played with him, threading her fingers through the springing black curls on his chest, touching the flat nipples and drawing circles around them. Then, as her loosened clothing dropped to the floor, Thor grasped her, lifted her high with his arms beneath her buttocks, curled his tongue around a nipple, and sucked.

She gasped, wrapped her legs around his waist, and held on. When his mouth moved to the other breast she gasped again and wriggled, wanting more. "Let me down, now . . . I want—I need— more . . ."

He laughed a little, deep in his chest, pleased by her eagerness. He let her slide down his body to the heat and hardness bulging in the soft knit chausses and felt her legs tighten, her hips sway and circle. When he heard her moan softly, he put his mouth to her ear and bit it gently.

"My lady is greedy?"

She sighed, giving in. "Starving," she whispered. "Please stop teasing me."

He kissed her mouth and put her down, strode across the room and bolted the door, came back and stripped himself of his chausses. Standing naked beside the bed, she toed off her soft slippers and held out a hand to him.

"Come," she said, "we will make up for the loss last night."

"A moment," he answered, and reached for her thick braid. Unfastening the ribbon, tossing it aside, he thrust his fingers through her hair, cupped her head in his palms, and leaned to kiss her. Then, as their mouths clung, he drew the shimmering flood of hair out to freedom, letting it drape her shoulders and breasts with silken gold.

"Like an angel," he said, and she smiled, dazed, her eyes dreaming in a softened face.

"No angel ever burned with the passion I feel, my love. Take me to bed, for I can wait no longer."

He threw back the woolen coverlet from the linens under it and invited her in with a sweep of an arm. She came and lay in it, opening her arms to him. Immediately he covered her, pressed into her in fiery desire, and felt her slim hips rise and take him in, felt her hands slide down to his buttocks and hold him there, motionless, while her swollen, throbbing flesh locked around him in a rush, a tightening, pulsing heat that he couldn't resist. In a moment they were on the heart-stopping peak of consummation, helpless to hold back the wild beat of their blood, the soft moans and cries of pure pleasure.

Coming back to reality, they murmured to each other, touched gently, kissed, admired. Then, yawning, they slept and woke later to touch and kiss again. Desire returned in an unexpectedly strong rush of passion shared between them.

"Twould seem sensible, considering that we're still in bed and naked, to take advantage of our readiness," Aylena said, and laughed as Thor rolled her up on his massive body. "Tis foolish to let an opportunity go by. . . ."

"Yes," Thor said, "yes. But this time I would have it last a bit longer."

"Greedy?"

"For you, always."

22

A week later, after a wonderfully satisfying time of being together night after night, day after day, happier together than ever they had been, Thor had surprised Aylena with his plans for the trip to Winchester, by including Ian. When asked, he refused to say why they were going, only saying that the Reeve brothers would be their guards and Margit would be Aylena's companion. Hearing that she was included, Margit objected in private.

"If you and Ian must go, my lady," she said to Aylena, who was going over a lesson with Ian, "then I must go. But why should any of us make another trip to Winchester when we've scarcely had time to rest from that harrowing, dangerous trip to Black Isle and back? Truly, our sire seems too restless to ever make a good sheep baron. The sheep have been sheared, their wool bundled and tied. Who will see to the shipping?"

Aylena sighed. "The same man who has seen to the shearing, the bundling, and tying, Margit. Stephen of Blaine. Stephen has seen to the wool for the past ten years. Do pack some of my old gowns, please, so that I can be less fashionable and more at ease astride a horse. However, I will also need a court gown or two."

"Why? Didn't you tell me you'd not be going back to court until Ian is sixteen?"

"I did. But Thor says we'll almost surely be invited to attend the king. And there is something he intends to do that requires a trip to court, though he hasn't explained it."

"As close as you two are lately, I canna believe that."

"Believe it, Margit. Thor is good at keeping his secrets. But then, I can tell you one thing that will brighten your dark eyes—James is going with us."

"Oh. Well, in that case . . . after all, tis a pleasant time of year to travel. I'll get out some leathern bags to hold your best gowns."

Aylena and Ian waited until Margit left the room and then smiled at each other.

"Twas James that turned her about, was it, then?" Ian asked, and Aylena laughed.

"Indeed. She enjoys his company and does not want to lose it."

"As you enjoy Lord Rodancott's company?"

She looked at him quickly. "Who told you I did?"

"One of the grooms. Was he wrong?"

She wouldn't lie, not to Ian nor to anyone she loved. "No. He was right. What else did the groom say?"

Embarrassed, Ian looked down at the illuminated leather volume of sayings he had been reading aloud and traced a letter with one finger. "He said the cas-

tle now belongs to Lord Rodancott, who—who allows
us to live here because he fancies you."

Aylena rose abruptly from the table where they sat
and turned away from Ian toward the window. She
hadn't thought of their presence there in just that
way; the castle had always been her home and she'd
given little thought to the way others would regard
her staying now. She'd always known that gossip
about the nobles was part of castle life, but this time
the loose tongues were hurting Ian, and at first she
was angry enough to take vengeance on the talkative
groom. She quieted herself with logic: what else
would a groom think? Besides, it was no lie.

"That is true, also," she said, still at the window.
"He does own the castle, and the demesne. He was
sent here by the king of England to take our home
and return it to English rule. I know you will find that
hard to understand, but tis nothing out of the ordinary. All kings try to guard the boundaries of their
country, and King Henry wants no trouble with the
Scots."

"But we were giving him no trouble, Aylena."

"I know that. So does the king. He was making
sure it didn't happen in the future. Oh, there is no
way to explain it, Ian! Kings are kings, and they do as
they will."

Ian smiled. "Never mind, Aylena. I will take it back
again when I am old enough. Then I will have the
claidheamh mor and the strength to use it. Lord
Rodancott has promised to teach me all he knows."
He slid from the bench and came to put his arms
around her waist and hug her. "Twill be the Stewart
castle again—and the clan will gather about it. And,

in the meantime, I want to see this tremendous city of London and the king of England."

Aylena smiled and ran her fingers through his hair, now a brindled color of dark brown and bright red-gold. At seven, now going on eight, Ian was old enough to be sent to another clan to learn the beliefs and skills of the Scots. Had things gone differently, her father would now be choosing the clan and the laird who would best train Ian. But Aylena—suspect amongst the Scots now—had no such choice. That part of it suited her well. In her opinion, Ian would learn all he needed to know from Thor, if, as time went on, Thor was willing to teach him. She sighed, thinking of it. How long could she hold the dauntless Thor Rodancott? In the last few days, he seemed to be distancing himself from her; perhaps he had begun to feel she would never marry him and he must look elsewhere for a wife. A wife who would put him first in her heart and bear his children now, not in some future time. . . .

The day they left for Winchester brought unseasonably cold winds from the north, keening and whistling through the thickness of their hoods, chilling their hands on their reins. The horses and men leaving the gates turned south gladly, putting their backs to the wind. Thor ordered the women and Ian into the center of the column, where they were protected from the worst of the blasts. The baggage and the clothes and food brought along for the first part of the trip were distributed in bundles and boxes lashed onto the spare horses instead of being carried in wagons.

"This trip will take half the time of the first one,"

Thor told the women, "if you can take the hard riding. If you tire, we'll slow our pace."

Margit looked relieved when he mentioned slowing the pace, but when Thor resumed his position in the lead, Aylena gave Margit something to think about.

"No complaints, dear Margit. Do you want James to think you too old to keep up?"

Margit straightened in the saddle. "Have I complained? Why, a good day's ride doesn't tire me at all. I'm not so old as that."

Aylena smiled. "I believe you. Lately, you seem younger every day. Soon you'll be no older than I."

Ian laughed. "Nor I, for I am growing very old." He was riding his father's tall horse again. The cuts on the horse's muscled rump had healed over and Harald had said the exercise would be good for him, especially since the lad was light. Aylena had agreed to it—she knew Ian's feelings about the horse. He cherished the memories of his rides in the big saddle with his father. And, after a week of training from Thor, Ian's skill with a horse was much improved.

They rode hard the first day, and after a stop in the evening and a hot meal over a fire, took advantage of the full moon rising and rode on, continuing until well past noon of the next day, when they found themselves again at the ruins of the old Norman castle on the seacoast.

"We'll rest here," Thor said to Aylena, riding with her in the van, "until tomorrow. Then we'll leave before dawn and by evening we'll be in Tynemouth. After that we'll be in York and safe from those who would hunt down and kill a child."

She glanced at him quickly, shocked by what he

said. "Do you believe the Barwicks will try for Ian again?"

"They well might. Martin and Nicholas found two of them near the east pastures three days ago, watching a path Ian took the day before. They were armed and ready."

Aylena drew in her breath, dizzied by sudden fear. "May the saints save my brother from those cruel murderers! Do you think they will return?"

"Those two won't. They were last seen, bloodied by deep wounds, trying to cross the Tweed where the water was deepest. Neither made it to the far side."

"Two more gone, then. The clan war against the Stewarts is killing off the Barwicks. Surely, they will see that."

They were inside the crumbling walls of the old courtyard now, and James behind them with Margit, then Ian, riding with the Reeve brothers, and Harald, who, having been taken with desire to see a part of the world he had never seen, had come along with two yeomen to take care of the horses.

Dismounting, Aylena helped Margit to take the rolled pallets from the backs of the sumpter horses and spread them in the small sections of the stone building that were still of use. Then, since there were some hours of daylight left, she went out and onto the cliff over the sea as she always did.

Thor followed, though first giving her a few moments alone, for he knew the pull of the memories she had of her father in this place. They stood a few feet apart, the spray from the breaking waves on the rock below flying up, wetting their faces with salty mist.

"Tomorrow," Thor said, breaking the silence, "we will be again with your friends in Tynemouth. Then, four or five days after that, we will be in London. That will be an excitement for Ian."

"Yes." She was very conscious of him, of the space between them. She was remembering the time he had come here after her on that first trip together and had not been able to keep from touching her. Now he stood apart, as if by choice, and spoke calmly of excitement for others. It was strange, she thought, for all of this past week he had taken every chance he found to make love with her. She moved closer.

"You are quiet, my lord."

He swung around to face her, stepping back, putting distance between them again. "Does it offend you that I fail to constantly court your touch and your kisses?"

Aylena reddened. By the anger in his gray eyes and the rude tone of his voice she knew he had no intention of explaining his savage mood, nor did he wish to hear more on the subject. "No, my lord, it does not. Now," she added, "if you will excuse me, I will return to the others." She left, hurriedly, not waiting for his answer.

At the ruins, she found Ian in joyous combat with the two shepherd boys who had offered to save her and Margit from the Normans. They were taking turns wrestling, and though the shepherds were two to three years older than Ian, they were close to the same size. Until now, she had not thought of how tall, how long-legged Ian was for his age. He would be as big as their father, then. Stopping to watch them, she was conscious of Thor coming up behind her. He put a hand on her shoulder and spoke for her alone, his deep voice soft in her ear.

"Forgive me, my lady, for my rudeness. I, too, am

wrestling, but with a question I do not wish to answer. Tis not your fault, but mine."

Aylena turned to him, and, without taking note of who might be watching, put her hand on his cheek in light caress. "All of us give you our hardest questions, Thor. If you wish, I will listen to yours."

Thor's smile was crooked, as if he laughed at himself. "You are my hardest question, my lady. You and that stalwart boy there who has just won his match, fairly and well. Another week or so, and you will hear my decision, right or wrong."

Ian came running up with the two shepherd boys and slid to a halt in front of Aylena. "Tell them again," Ian ordered, "that we have enough food for two more."

Aylena smiled at the three of them, though what Thor had just said frightened her badly. She knew, somehow, that he'd come to the end of waiting for her to make up her mind. She might have to make a decision, too.

"We have enough food for twenty more," she told the lads, "and you are welcome to share it." She turned away then and looked for Thor, seeing his broad back between the Reeve brothers as the three of them disappeared outside. Another week, he had said, and his decision would be made. She wondered if that meant she would have to marry him or lose him. She went toward the fire and Margit, who was tending the flat breads, knowing she had to hew to her vows. She must lose him, then, and break her heart.

They were all hungry, all tired after the day and a half of riding. Harald, fearful of the horses wandering close to the cliff, had the yeomen tie them inside at the rear of the courtyard and feed and water them there. There was little talk during the meal, and all but the shepherds and Ian found their pallets early. Margit, annoyed by the constant whispering of tales of adventure and witches, went to them after a time and told them to be quiet. They moved, finding a safe spot away from the others, and continued their stories.

The full moon was at the zenith before midnight, shafts of moonlight made a pattern on the stone floor of the old castle, and, in the room where Margit and Aylena were sleeping, one of the shafts played on Aylena's face. It woke her, and she turned from it restlessly, bothered by its brilliance and by a still-whispering voice that seemed to come from above her. Margit, across the room, growled threats of violence. But the whisper kept on, becoming more urgent.

"Aylena! Aylena! Wake up!"

Aylena opened her eyes and looked up. There, like the time when the shepherds offered to save them from the Normans, a head hung over the wall, frowsy and urgent, looking down at her and whispering. "There are men outside, Aylena, and they're creeping closer. They're carrying axes and knives and motioning others to follow."

Ian. Aylena sighed and stood up, pulling on her cloak. "Are you sure your stories haven't made shadows into men?"

Ian flung a leg over the wall and dropped down beside her. "Look for yourself, my sister. They are not large or strong from the look of them, but they are well armed."

She stared down at him and saw that he meant it.

He was frightened, but hiding it well. She stepped to a wide crack in the nearest wall and looked outside. At first she saw nothing, then a man slipped from behind a clump of windburned bushes and raised an arm to someone in the shadows, motioning him on. Her heart jumped into a double beat and slammed into her ribs. It was true. Turning, she left the small enclosure and went looking for Thor among the men sleeping on pallets in the courtyard. Finding him, she touched his shoulder. His eyes opened and immediately he was on his feet.

"What is it?"

From behind her, Ian's voice. "Men, sire. They mean to attack us."

Thor whirled and went to peer over a break in the old wall, taking a long look. He came back and began gathering his weapons, speaking in a low tone.

"Help me waken the others, Aylena, but be quiet about it. There are more men out there than we have here, and, with no room to use our horses on these cliffs, we have lost our biggest advantage." He turned again to Ian, seeing behind the boy the thin, frightened faces of the shepherds listening and watching. He went to them.

"Is there a quick way out of here that you know? A way to the fields you tend?"

They stared, and then one nodded vigorously. "There is, a path no stranger ever sees. Shall we leave?"

"Yes, and take Ian with you. Stay with your sheep until we come to you."

Aylena heard him but she went on waking the men, cautioning them to be quiet and to arm themselves. She could see the boys running through the moonlight that pierced the old castle and toward the steep cliff at the rear that fell away into a valley. She saw Margit, kneeling on the stone floor, praying for Ian's safety, and yet knew Thor had done what should be done. Ian would be safer in the sheep fields than here. By now the men were gathering in the middle of the courtyard and listening to Thor, who spoke to them quietly.

"Every blow must count," he was saying. "Keep your weapons in your hands. If you throw and miss, tis a weapon for them. And don't stand foursquare and challenge them to prove your courage. This is a time for using shadows as your shield. Remember that, even if you remember nothing else. Tis skill, and the sense to use your advantage, that will bring us victory."

The men, most of them watching the invaders edge closer as they listened, were silent. They had the advantage now, for standing in the shadows of the ruined walls they could watch the others moving about in brilliant moonlight. But they were caught in one place, forced to wait for the enemy to draw near enough to attack.

Silent, and drawn tight as a bow, the young yeomen crossed themselves; the Reeve brothers fingered their swords. James stood quietly, a coil of hempen rope in one hand. But there were so few, Aylena thought, and counted them to herself. Martin Reeve, Nicholas Reeve, James. Harald. Two yeomen, willing to fight but untrained. And Thor. Seven. There were twice that many men outside, and likely more. Who were the attackers? Barwicks, surely, but if they were all Barwicks, then the whole clan was here, for news had come that there were less than twenty of them

left—and some of those too crippled to fight, or far
too old.

Thor had moved from man to man, talking softly,
seeing that they were armed and ready. Now he took
a place at the tumbledown entrance to the courtyard,
hidden by the shadows but able to see outside. He
motioned to Aylena, and she came, quiet and ready to
listen. Standing beside him in the cold air, she felt the
solid warmth that always came from his big body and
moved closer, seeking reassurance.

"Take your handmaid with you," Thor said, "and
stay in the inner room where you sleep. In the heat of
battle a woman can be mistaken for a man."

She nodded slowly, her eyes searching the space
outside, seeing a man crawling toward the entrance,
a dagger in his hand. She pointed at him, and Thor
loosened his own dagger.

"Go," he whispered, and she was gone, touching
Margit on the way, motioning to her to follow.

In the room, they could still look into the courtyard
through a space where a large stone had fallen.
Aylena watched the moonlit opening where Thor had
been standing and held back a cry of warning as she
saw the crawling man ease to his feet with the dagger
held ready. Then a quick flicker of steel in the dark,
and the man stepped back, groaned, and fell forward.
Hands came out and dragged him inside. Immediately five men leaped to their feet beyond the walls
and charged the entrance, yelling at the top of their
voices.

"Down with the Normans! Kill them!"

Watching from the inner room, Aylena brought her
hood forward to hide her bright hair and white face.
She could see most of the circle of rocky cliff outside,

and more men were leaping up and running toward the walls, brandishing knives and clubs, shouting "Kill them! Kill them! They carry stolen treasure!" Listening, Aylena heard a note of frantic fear in their voices.

One, faster running than the others, plunged through a wide crack in a side wall, club held high, and turning toward a light patch in the darkness brought the club down smartly on Martin Reeve's Saxon yellow hair. Martin bellowed with rage and tore the club from the man's hand. He swung it hard and caught the interloper fairly across his face, dropping him in his tracks. The man lay in a pool of moonlight, bleeding from one bulging eye but not conscious. Martin stooped and looked closely.

"This is no Scot," he said. "I'd say he's—" Hearing a noise behind him, he swung again at a dim figure and tossed the club aside when it broke across the man's head. Grabbing the arm of the sagging attacker, he held it high, the dagger in the hand gleaming in the darkness. Then he kicked the man in the belly, caught the knife as it fell, and stepped back. Doubled over, the man crumpled to the stone floor, groaning.

"—a dock rat," Martin added, and, seeing a form slowly rising at the window, grabbed him and dragged him, screaming with fear, into the darkness, shoving the dagger into his narrow chest to quiet him. Behind Martin, Thor spoke calmly.

"I agree. The six men Nicholas and I have under our feet smell like bilgewater. How in God's name did London rabble find a way here? And where is James?"

From the room where the women were came a sudden rapid mumble of prayer for James. And, from the back of the courtyard, a quiet voice.

"I'm here, sire. Harald and I have captured two of the enemy behind the castle. Shall we bring them to you?"

"Yes, if you will. Are you hurt?"

"No, but Harald was bloodied by the first man we met." James's voice grew closer as he marched the men forward. "One of the yeomen killed the man and bandaged Harald's arm."

"Good. Bring the men here, in this patch of moonlight."

James pushed them forward. Thin, their faces marked with grime and dissipation, the men wore the short, cheap gowns of fustian the poor wore in the city. They looked old, well past their mid thirties, and they each had weapons concealed in their clothes. Thor had the yeomen search them, and they found knives in hidden pockets. Thor asked both of them questions.

"You are city men. Why are you here?"

"We were hired to catch thieves, my lord."

Thor's laugh was without humor. "Set a thief to catch a thief? Who hired you? Tell us the truth, or take a beating."

"A liar," the older man said, his tone bitter. "He said he would take us to a band of thieves who had stolen his gold from Scotland. He said taking it back would be an easy job for us, and well paid. We were fools to try it; the man talked wildly. But he gave us money, saying it was all he had left."

"How did you get here?"

"He brought us, aboard a sailer, to a river called the Tyne. He left us aboard while he sent spies to watch for your party. Once he heard you were on the way, he hired a wagon an driver to bring us here, for he said twas a spot where you often stayed. We've waited here for two days, an tis a wild and miserable place."

"And the liar's name?"

"He calls himself Lord Bretinalle."

Thor cursed under his breath. "Where is he now?"

The man shrugged. "Who knows? He carries a knife and an axe, but he is too cowardly to use them. He hid himself behind the castle walls when it was time to begin the attack. I stayed with him to hear his orders. Then three boys came running past and took a hidden path down to the valley. He followed them, telling me to see to the fight."

Thor turned and went swiftly across the stone floor to pull the *claidheamh mor* from his saddle scabbard. Turning back, he saw Aylena come from the small room, her face white with fear. She was carrying a dagger, one he hadn't known she owned.

"You stay here," he said to her. "I will find him."

"I am going with you," she said, "or if not with you, then alone. John Bretinalle's quarrel is with me, not Ian. I'll not let the boy suffer for it."

Thor turned again to the older man. "What is your name?"

"Tom, my lord."

"You've lost half your men, Tom, and you'll lose the rest if you don't call them in to surrender."

The man shook his head. "They're on their way to Tyne now, an I wish myself with them. There'll be no more trouble here from this one an me."

"Show us the hidden path the boys took."

The man hurried to obey, going before them out

through the ruined walls, pointing down to a steep path. Even in the bright moonlight it was nearly concealed by brush and small trees. Thor stared, his eyes narrowing.

"There is someone coming up." What he had seen was a dark form, a flash of steel. He put a hand behind him and touched Aylena's arm. "Move into the shadows," he whispered, and she stepped back into the tumbled ruins. He joined her, and in a moment so did Tom. They watched as Bretinalle struggled up the path with an arm around Ian's muscular young body and a knife held against the boy's neck. Bretinalle was panting with the effort, his breath audible and hoarse, his hands shaking. A thin smear of red blood marked a line on Ian's white throat. Aylena's hand grasped Thor's wrist, warning him. If Bretinalle was startled, even alarmed, he could jerk the blade and kill the boy.

They watched him gain the top of the cliff and stand there for a moment, breathing hard. When Ian moved to ease his bent arm, Bretinalle swore at him and tightened his grip. His breathless whisper to Ian came to them where they stood in darkness.

"If you want to live, listen to me. We go to the cliff over the sea, and you will call out for your sister. I will do the rest."

"I understand." Ian's reply was faint, and Aylena's eyes filled for him. He was only a boy, she thought, and he must be terrified. Then Thor's hand took hers, for Bretinalle and Ian were heading toward the path around the wall.

"I will be ready for him," Thor whispered. "There will come a moment yet when I can down him without hurting Ian."

They went quickly into the courtyard again and to the entrance. Thor went out, crossing the beaten ground swiftly, and sprang over the cliff, disappearing in the rubble of rocks just below. Tom joined the other dock rats who were still alive and spoke in low tones. The knights and James gathered around the entrance with Aylena.

"What has happened?"

Aylena's hand was clenched on the doorway, her throat dry with terror. "He . . ." She swallowed and tried again. "John Bretinalle has Ian and is holding a knife to his throat. He will ask for me in exchange. Thor hopes to down him when he lets Ian go. There . . ." She lowered her whisper to a breath of sound. "There they are, coming around the courtyard and going toward the cliff."

The men stared, tense with sudden anger, growling under their breath, moving restlessly. The scene was stark black and white, black rocks silhouetted against a moving, muttering sea, the full moon in the west giving a glare of light that picked out Ian's white face and neck, glittered on the bright steel with the smear of blood beneath it. Then, climbing clumsily onto the highest rock, Bretinalle turned toward the castle entrance and tightened his hold on the boy.

"Call your proud sister, boy! Call loud, or I scratch you again, and deeper."

Ian was silent. Bretinalle waited, tightening his hold.

"Do you hear me, boy? Do you die now?" The knife moved, and Ian's head jerked. The boy was still stubbornly silent.

"Stop that!" Aylena burst from the entrance, her cloak flying out behind her, her feet thrusting forward, carrying her shaking body straight toward Bretinalle. "What in the name of God are you thinking of, Bretinalle? How long would you live if you killed that boy?"

Bretinalle giggled, a high, hysterical sound that raised the hair on the back of Aylena's neck. "But I don't need to kill him, do I? Once you are in my hands your brother is free to go. Thor Rodancott won't risk your life, either."

She came on, her face frozen with fear and anger, her hands reaching out for Ian. Bretinalle turned, still making that sound, that bubbling hysteria in his throat, keeping the boy away from her. "Oh, no. Oh, no. How do I know you've no weapons hidden about you? Take off your cloak an your gown."

She took them off, the cloak blowing up in the cold wind as she tossed it aside, the riding gown dropping into a pool of silk at her feet. She was so hot with anger, she barely felt the cold. She stood there in her thin, nearly transparent shift and put her hands on her hips. "So, coward, can you trust me now?"

Bretinalle's jaw dropped open, his arms loosened and let Ian go, his hand reached for her hungrily. Ian grabbed him and tried to pull him back.

"You let her alone!"

Bretinalle threatened him with the knife, jabbing the air. "You'll die yet, you young fool!"

"Ian," Aylena said, and he looked up at her. "The bargain was made. I promise you twill be right. Go to the castle."

"This—this is *not* right!"

"Go to the castle. Run!"

Ian broke into frustrated tears. "I canna leave you with him, Aylena!"

Frantic, Aylena snapped at him. "Thor said you must!"

Sobbing, Ian turned and ran toward the courtyard where the others waited. Bretinalle giggled and started toward Aylena again. But, behind Aylena, Thor stood up on the rocks below and stepped up on the cliff, the *claidheamh mor* shining like silver in his hand.

"Move out of my way, my love," he said. "I have a madman to kill."

She grabbed up her cloak and ran past him, hearing a shriek of awful fear, turning in time to see Bretinalle's shaking hand grab the axe from his belt and fling it up in a crazy spiral. She screamed, seeing the axe whirl down and hit Thor's wide chest, knocking him flat on his back. The *axe*. She remembered the vision and was swept with a wild rage. She swung around, yelling at Bretinalle, her lips pulled back from her teeth like a wolf.

"You killed him! You killed Thor! You *die!*" She ran to Thor's unmoving body, heaved up the *claidheamh mor* with both hands, and ran back, awkwardly swinging the great blade at Bretinalle with all her strength. Then the weight of the sword and the force she gave it pulled it from her hands halfway through the swing and she staggered, sitting down hard, staring, mesmerized by the sight of the sword glittering through the dark air, cutting a wide and jagged swath through Bretinalle's sagging belly and then dropping, clattering on the rocks. A fountain of blood spurted upward, black in the night, and Bretinalle sank to his knees, dying, falling sideways without a sound. Aylena looked at the huge, gaping hole in him and burst into hopeless tears. He was dead, but so was

Thor. She crawled toward Thor's body, her heart breaking. . . .

Thor sat up, rubbing the back of his head and muttering. Aylena gasped and sat back on her heels. Pure joy and utter amazement flooded through her, and she cried harder, trying to get words out.

"Oh, Thor! Oh, Thor . . . you're alive! And . . . I killed him."

"What?"

"I *told* you to be careful of axes, didn't I?"

"Well, yes. Several times. What do you mean, you killed him?" He looked past her at the sword, the body, and all the thick blood, black in the moonlight. "By the saints! You could hardly lift that sword. How did you give him such a wound as that?"

She wiped her eyes. "I thought he'd killed you. I was . . . very, very angry an I wanted him dead. I canna remember how I did it. But I did."

"As I recall," Thor said, "I've seen you like that myself. Tis a good thing you hadn't the *claidheamh mor* that day I took the castle. As it was, you merely bit me."

She frowned, ignoring the tears that ran down her cheeks. "Tis nothing to laugh about, Thor. His axe slammed into your chest and you fell like a dead man an never moved until now. It was awful!"

He rubbed his mail-covered chest thoughtfully. "I see. But it was a light axe, with little force behind it, and no aim at all. It hit me broadside and I slipped and fell. Twas my head hitting the rock that made me lose my senses." He looked at her and smiled. "It aches. You should have warned me about rocks, not the silly axe."

She glanced up at the circle of silent men that gath-

ered around them, reached for her cloak, and put it
around her. She had never felt so foolish and full of
tears in her life. She stood, picked up her gown, and
took Ian's hand.

"It's over," she said to him, "and we're going to
bed." Walking, she searched her mind wildly for
something good to say to Ian. "Tomorrow we'll be in
Tynemouth with Godwin and Drusilla."

Ian smiled, matching her steps. "An Drusilla's meat
pies. You were brave, Aylena. An the *claidheamh mor*
did what William said it would do."

Aylena wiped her wet face with a sleeve and
glanced down at him. "What are you talking about?"

"Don't you remember? On Black Isle, when
Roderick handed it to Thor, William grabbed him and
pulled him away. He said his sight told him the sword
would someday fly from someone's hands and do
murder."

Aylena shuddered. "I do remember, now. But you
needn't think on't."

"But I like it! It's magic, Aylena. The sword knew
who to kill."

She looked down at his moonlit, excited face and,
slowly, smiled back at him. "You also were brave,
Ian."

He nodded and squeezed her hand. "I know. We
Stewarts are all brave."

23

The big stone kitchen at Godwin's Inn was warm, full of the odors of cooking, full of tempting platters of pastries made with cream and the last of the summer fruit. When Aylena and Margit came in with Ian, and Thor behind them, Drusilla ran to them, embraced Ian and then Aylena, stood back, and despite her size and ever-mounting weight, curtsied gracefully to Thor.

"So, you have saved them both from the Barwicks, Lord Rodancott. May God bless you for that. Is Godwin seeing to the needs of your men?"

"He is, Drusilla. He has called a boy to take them around to the boarding houses."

"An I," Margit said, taking Ian's hand, "will take this boy up to his bath an then his bed. He has missed a night's sleep an so have we all."

"I'll send up two good suppers, then," Drusilla said. "No one sleeps well on an empty belly."

Thor's tired face relaxed as he looked around, breathing in mouth-watering fragrances lifting in lazy swirls from huge cook pots. His gaze centered on the high-backed settles and table before the open fire and then moved to the kegs of wine stacked below the north windows.

Drusilla watched and smiled. "Sit, my lord, and I'll pour you some wine, and some for Lady Aylena. You can eat here with Godwin an me, an find your way to bed when you like. I know Godwin will want to hear all your news."

Thor dropped into one of the settles with a sound of satisfaction, watching Drusilla tap a keg and fill a cup. He reached for it and drank it in one gulp. Handing the cup back, he asked Drusilla to fill it again.

"And one for Lady Aylena, please. Come, Aylena, and sit. We will tell our news when Godwin returns, and mayhap he will have news for us. This is the one place where our plans and problems are heard but never told again."

The four of them sat before the fire for an hour or so after dinner. Thor and Aylena told the story of the first attempt against Ian—and against Aylena—to leave them dead and blame it on the Barwicks.

Godwin, hearing the name of Charles Halchester, cursed him roundly.

"He came here from London with a handful of hard-looking men, and John Bretinalle was with them. Halchester acted as if he did us a favor to stay in our rough inn. He insisted on having the best room an his supper served in it. Then he complained of the coarse sheets and the plain food and left early the next morning, taking the whole bunch with him, without paying the bill. If he comes this way again he will complain even more of the treatment he gets, and

and the mark of my boot will be on his silk-covered buttocks."

Thor laughed. "Then he's not come through Tynemouth again on his way to London?"

"No. But he may have traveled by way of Carlisle, to avoid his debt here."

There was a silence. Then Thor shrugged. "Nor Bretinalle will come through Tynemouth again, either. He came here not long ago by sailer, bringing with him a party of dock rats to ambush us at the old castle as we traveled through. Instead, he went over the cliff and into the North Sea last night, an none to save him."

Godwin leaned back, laughing and holding his wine cup high. "Hurrah! An none to mourn the bastard, I vow."

"True." Thor's answering smile creased the lines of fatigue around his eyes. He yawned, glancing over at Aylena, noting the paleness of her cheeks, the droop of her slim shoulders, the tears in her eyes. She had never killed before, and it was coming to her, as it did to others who loved their fellowmen, that she had taken a life. She was full of sorrow and regret. Thor pushed back his chair and rose, huge in the low-ceilinged, cozy kitchen, and reached for her hand.

"Come, my love. We need Drusilla's soft and comfortable beds."

Upstairs, when she turned to the room where Margit and Ian were sleeping, Thor turned her into his room instead. Inside, he held her loosely in his arms. "I know you've tears to shed and you'll not want Ian to see them."

She pulled away from him and lifted her chin. "Af-

ter what he did to me I'll not cry over that—that evil
fool!" Then she burst into tearing sobs. "Oh, Thor,
you are right. I canna forget what I did. That awful
wound! He . . . he might have changed . . . but not
now. I *killed* him. I took away his life!"

He pulled her back into his arms. "And I am grateful for *my* life, my lady."

She wiped her eyes and looked up at him. "Why do
you say that?"

"He had a dagger in his hand, and I lay helpless,
my head spinning. It would be the work of a moment
to thrust that dagger into my heart. He was a madman, yes, and a coward, but he had sense enough to
take the opportunity, had you not prevented it. You
saved my life with your quick action."

She sighed, easing into his arms. Her hands moved
up and over his powerful shoulders and curled
around the back of his neck, her fingers weaving into
his thick black hair. "If there is even a chance that he
would be brave enough to try that, then I am glad I
killed him. Take me to bed, Thor."

He was still, but she felt him tense. Then, gently, he
stepped back. "Forgive me, my lady, but I must refuse. There is a problem in my mind that must be
resolved, and until it is done, I will sleep alone."

Embarrassment turned her white neck and face a
brilliant red, but she kept her temper. She inclined
her head in a tiny bow, turned on her heel, and went
to the door. "In that case," she said, looking back in
tear-stained dignity, "I am sorry to have bothered
you. Good night."

The rest of the trip was easy and pleasant—the
ferry across the Tyne, a stop at Fountains Abbey

again, and then the days growing warmer, the fields
in the south still lush and green, the small towns
dreaming in the last of pleasant weather. Then they
were in sight of London, with its great walls and its
forest of church steeples. And, inside, the poor beggars, the walls of tumbledown houses, and the nause-
ating odor of the drains. They rode through that part
of the city holding cloths wet with vinegar and rosemary to their noses.

Again they stayed at the Palatine castle, though
there was no one there except for the noble wrongdo-
ers imprisoned in their comfortable cells. There was,
also, the full staff, which numbered some forty servants. The chamberlain gave Lord Rodancott the luxurious suite of rooms usually kept for visiting royalty.

"King Henry and Queen Eleanor are in Southampton," the old man told Thor, standing in the hall while
the housekeeper unlocked the doors and the footmen
brought in the baggage. "They are there to enjoy the
last warm days near the sea. However, tis not all pleasure. More loaded carvels are arriving from Normandy every day, and the king has a share in most of
them. Trade is bursting its own seams, they say, and
he makes the most of it. When will you bring over
your great war-horses, my lord?"

Thor shook his head. "I have no thought of that. Tis
easier for me to let the buyers come to Normandy and
see the horses on their own home ground. After
they're sold, the buyers can take them where they
will, but the horses themselves thrive in their early
years because of our oats and hay."

"It has been some time since you've been there, my
lord. You'll be going back soon, I take it."

"Yes, soon. I look forward to it."

Listening, Aylena thought how few times she'd heard Thor speak of his place in Normandy and how little interest she had shown in it. Inside their rooms, standing in the small sitting room that centered the rest, she asked Thor to tell her where his demesne was.

"East of Rouen," he said, surprised, "and on the south bank of the Seine. Often we bring the horses to port on barges. Why do you ask?"

She felt her face redden. She had been wishing to travel there with him, but there was such strain between them now that she wasn't sure they would travel together anywhere after this. "I was only curious," she answered and turned away, moving toward the room given to her. She was losing him; she felt it strongly. Nor could she blame him. What other man would let a woman and her young brother turn his plans upside down? All she could do was to take the loss bravely.

"Aylena."

She turned back. "Yes, my lord?"

"You needn't unpack more than enough for a day. Tomorrow we go to Winchester, and if necessary, on to Southampton. It is important to me to see the king as soon as possible."

Meeting his clear gray eyes, she found it impossible not to ask again. He did not look angry, but still she chose her words carefully. "Do you wish to tell me why?"

"No." He was half smiling, but determined. "You have no part in it. Now, if you plan to show Ian some of London's delights, I suggest we do it this afternoon. He would enjoy seeing the boats and ships and eating the roast meats and sweet cakes at the river cookshops. Then, I suggest we take him to Smithfield. Tis the sixth day, and he will like seeing the races."

It seemed to Aylena that the rest of the day flew by in a bewildering array of pleasures that Thor and Ian found together. The small village of Tynemouth had been the biggest town Ian had ever seen until this trip, and he was amazed by London and the number of its people. Though tired, Aylena caught his mood and enjoyed it with him. It was a pleasure to her to be with Ian and not worry about the next rider coming by. No one here knew him as the next laird of the Stewarts—nor would they care if they did.

"It is wonderful," Ian said as they left Smithfield in twilight. "All of it is wonderful. When I become a knight, I will return here and see it all again. And perhaps I will buy that cream-colored Barb from Persia. He runs faster than the falcon flies."

Riding on either side of him, Thor and Aylena exchanged a smiling glance. They were easier with each other than they had been for several days, for Aylena had accepted his withdrawal. She told herself she should have known it would come—no man would wait nine years for a woman to agree to marry him. Thor was in his prime, and there were many beautiful women who would jump at the chance to wed the king's right arm. She sighed as the white tower of the Palatine castle reared up in front of them and thought to herself that this might well be the last time she would be with him within those wrought iron gates. But still, there was another castle, another set of gates . . . she turned to Ian again.

"Wait," she said, buoying up her own spirits, "until

you see Belmain. Tis the loveliest castle in all England."

The last time they rode from London to Winchester had been in the spring of the year; now, in the late summer, the lush fields of ripe grain and trees heavy with fruit were tended by harvesters, men wielding scythes in the grain or filling baskets from the trees and berry bushes.

"Tis a rich land," Margit said, watching them as she rode. "In Northumbria the harvest is small and early. But then we do have plenty of meat. Where do we stop tonight, sire?"

Thor answered, amused. "In Tunbridge Castle, with the nervous Baron Tunbridge. I sent a rider ahead yesterday to tell him we were coming. The next day, we'll see Winchester before dark."

He was in good humor, Aylena decided, and was glad for it. Whatever his decision brought, she wanted him happy. None of the problems between them were his fault. She smiled at him, finding good humor infectious.

"Will you come with us to Belmain after your day with the king? It would be pleasant to have your company."

Thor looked startled, as if he'd taken it for granted. "Indeed. Twould be hard to keep me away."

Dinner at Tunbridge Castle was made an event by the good harvest. There was fruit and nuts in abundance, fresh bread and roast mutton. The Baron Tunbridge, a large and portly man, was less nervous and much more the genial host when he discovered Aylena was the owner of Belmain.

"Better by far to have you in that perfect spot than

that pretender Charles Halchester," Tunbridge said. "Did you know him?"

"I knew him," Aylena said, "but—as it turned out—not very well."

Tunbridge frowned. "You lost nothing by that. He was a thief and a liar. He persuaded King Stephen of Blois that he was related to the Belmains, when in fact he was from an entirely different family, a family without a dram of noble blood. Stephen believed him and gave him the use of Belmain for his lifetime. But King Henry is no fool; when he was crowned he took it for himself."

"And then gave it to me, the rightful heir." Aylena's voice was suddenly happy. For the first time since she discovered Charles's murderous scheme, her heart was light. Whoever he was, he was not of her blood! She turned to Thor.

"Thank the good Christ, Ian and I are not related to Halchester after all. That is wonderful news."

"I agree." Thor glanced at Tunbridge. "You say he 'was' a thief and a liar, as if he had changed, or died. Do you know aught of him recently?"

"Only word of mouth, Lord Rodancott. I heard he went to Scotland to recoup his fortunes, but failed. Then, on the way back to England, he was caught robbing the till in the Carlisle Inn and was hanged. Whether the story is true or not, I cannot tell you, but the man who told me is honest."

Subdued, though not unhappy, Aylena finished her dinner in silence, then rose and excused herself, leaving the men to finish the wine and talk. It seemed to her that her whole world was changing, and, going toward the bedroom given to her, she stopped in Ian's

room and studied him in the light of a spirit candle.
His father's strong features were beginning to show
through the rounded contours of a child's face; his
hair was nearly all red-gold, for Margit had been
faithful in cutting away the brown. Aylena sighed. Another year, and he'd need a strong hand to guide him.
All she could do would be to send him back to William; and William, a wonderful man in his heart, was
far too gentle and vague to guide a boy like Ian.

Coming into Winchester the next afternoon Aylena
laughed inside. In topping the rise of the surrounding
hills she had remembered King Henry's admonitions
and found herself straightening in the saddle, holding
her head up, smiling graciously. She looked over at
Thor and saw the humor in his eyes.

"Still," she said, laughing with him, "tis a fine
habit, looking the world in the eye and smiling."

His grin broke out. "Agreed."

She looked ahead again, but her attention stayed
on Thor. He was suddenly at ease, as if Winchester
had been his goal for some time, as if he were heaving
a sigh of relief inside. Whatever it was that he had to
discuss with King Henry must weigh heavy on his
mind. She was consumed with curiosity, but too well
used to Thor's stubborness to ask again what problem
had forced this trip.

Beside her, Thor let out a held breath. "Thank the
good Christ," he said, "the king's flag is flying over
the castle. He's here, not in Southampton. That saves
a day or two."

Aylena smiled. "Ah! We will be in Belmain all the
sooner." She glanced over at Ian, atop his father's tall
horse, and added, "You never knew our mother, Ian,

but you will feel her gentleness and beauty when you
see where she was born and spent her childhood. You
will be proud of your Belmain blood, English though
it is."

Ian laughed. "Tis no great trouble to me to have
English blood, my sister. After all, you and I have
more of it than any other kind. Our mother's blood
was all English, and our father's half. James told me
that, didn't you, James?"

James looked embarrassed. "I did mention it, I believe."

There was a silence, lasting until they arrived at the
castle gates. Seeing Thor, the guards made haste to
open the gates and let them in. The chamberlain
came from the keep and crossed the courtyard to
greet them, bowing to Thor. Still in the saddle, Thor
replied courteously and then asked to be given information.

"I would speak to the king," he said, "on a matter
of consequence. Ask when he will listen."

"Yes, my Lord Rodancott. But first let me accommodate you and your party."

Thor shook his head. "I thank you, but we will take
rooms in the town."

"But my lord, the king will expect—"

Thor's jaw tightened under the black beard. "At this
time I prefer to be outside the castle walls. Tell King
Henry I offer fealty to him and pray for an audience."

The chamberlain hurried off, his face pale. Thor
was silent, sitting Frere d'Armes like a statue. None of
the rest of them spoke, though Ian took his horse on a
circular path around the courtyard, looking everywhere, his young face inquisitive. After a time, the

chamberlain appeared again, hurrying down the stone steps of the inner keep.

"The king sends this message, Lord Rodancott. He says that you may attend him tomorrow in the new halls of justice, where he intends to inspect the work in the morning. The building is close, only a hundred ells from here, and tis far from complete. But, the king is already proud of it."

Thor's tight expression eased. "Very good. I thank you. Tell the king we will be there." He turned toward the gates, motioning the others to follow.

We. Aylena's heart leaped. Was she to hear the plea Thor would make? Or did he intend to take James along? He seemed closer to James than to anyone but Philip of Anjou. "Or me," she whispered, turning her horse to ride out, "or *me.*" But she knew he had shut her out of this.

They found rooms in an old inn that had once been the town house of a wealthy burgher. It was clean and comfortable, and the dinner served to them was accompanied by good wines. Thor made the sleeping arrangements. Aylena and Margit shared a room; Ian, this time, insisted on sleeping on the first floor of the inn with Thor, James, and the Reeve brothers.

"I asked," he told Aylena, "and Thor said yes. He thinks it right."

When he was gone, Aylena asked Margit if she thought it wise to allow Ian so much freedom.

"Ian wants to be with men," Margit said, shaking out their night shifts and laying them on the beds. "He misses his father."

Aylena sighed. "So do I. When the old lion was alive I always knew what to do."

Margit laughed, but there was a rueful note in the

sound. "Everyone in the castle did. The Stewart made sure of that."

After a moment of surprise, Aylena nodded thoughtfully. "Indeed, Margit. He was forever giving out orders. Twas the last thing he did before he died. He said I must see that only his blood was to lead the clan; he ordered me to protect Ian's heritage and keep the castle for him, and made me swear to it all, promising not to think of myself til the vow was done."

Margit sniffed. "An order like that is fit for a company of Norman mercenaries like Lord Rodancott's, but not for a seventeen-year-old woman. You could not possibly live up to it. Why, he himself could not have won the battle if he had been in good health, for in the years of peace he'd gotten rid of most of his men-at-arms."

Aylena was silent, staring at Margit. "That is true," she said finally. "He had told me earlier there was no hope that he could win, but he meant to fight anyway." She sighed. "Twas my fault that he thought we had won. He was dying, and I wanted him happy—so I lied. I told him the Normans had not been able to take our castle—and he believed me! He thought he was giving orders that could be obeyed. And I have tried. However, I have found that miracles are rare."

"Ah, well, forget the old mistakes. You have done well in protecting Ian, and the Stewart would be proud of you. So cast aside the impossible things— and do what you can with the others."

Aylena smiled and came to Margit, putting her arms around her and giving her a hug. "Faithful Margit. What would I do without you? Your advice is sensible and I am listening well. I'll try to take it to heart."

Margit laughed. "Oh no! Take it to your mind instead. Tis foolish to give advice to the heart, my lady. The heart always expects miracles."

24

The innkeeper, a thin, smiling man with a white beard and apron, greeted Aylena as she came down the stairs early the next morning.

"Food is laid out in the public room," he said, "hot and fresh. Lord Rodancott is there, along with the young boy."

"Thank you." Remembering the simple philosophy she'd thought of yesterday, she kept her head up and her smile bright as she went on, opening the door to the public room and easing her full skirts inside. Thor and Ian were at a laden table near the open windows.

Ian saw her first, and came to take her hand. Leading her back to the table, he told her they had already eaten. "But Thor will wait," he added, "for you are to go with us to the halls of justice."

"I see." She did not see, but she felt a leap of hope. And why was Ian going? But there—Thor believed in giving children all the knowledge they could hold. Her smile began to feel natural. Thor had not cut her or Ian out of his life completely—not yet. She ignored the admiring stares of other men as she walked through the room with Ian. She had been ashamed, this morning, of her desperate efforts to look truly beautiful, better than her usual best. She had known it was useless. Thor was not a man who let clothes change his mind. He wasn't light-minded or frivolous. But, just the same, she was wearing an undergown of white silk, striped with woven bands of colorfully embroidered satin, with narrow sleeves that widened at her wrists into long, hanging cuffs that nearly reached her knees. Over the gown she wore a sleeveless violet tunic of samite, fitted tight to her waist and breasts, springing free in luxurious folds of skirt, but allowing only a single ruffle of lace around the deeply cut, square neckline. The tunic was almost as long as the undergown, but parted on the sides to show the graceful white silk. Her long, shining golden hair, held by a circlet of gold and multicolored jewels around her forehead, lay on the violet samite in sweeping waves that flowed like a waterfall down to her waist.

Thor had risen and brought back food from a chest near the kitchen door, putting it in place at their table. Aylena thanked him and sat down to eat. Thor sat with her, but Ian left, going through the busy room and then outside. Aylena saw him through an open window, talking to James.

"He is safe enough," Thor said, noting her glance. "He has no enemies here."

"Thank God for that."

"Yes." He went on looking at her, and sighed. "You are more beautiful every day, my lady. The king will enjoy seeing you in that gown."

She put down her wooden cup of mead with a

trembling hand. "So you have decided to take me with you today?"

"Indeed. I planned so from the first."

She wanted to kiss him. Instead, she frowned. "Then why the secrecy? If I am to hear your plea explained to the king, why not to me?"

"You will know, once it begins."

She met his eyes and found them crinkled at the corners with amusement. He looked as he often looked in their bed—as if he had wonderful secrets to share. And often he did. She laughed a little at her own thoughts and bit into a fruit and cream tart, to hide the sudden rush of desire she felt.

"Then"—she picked up a napkin and wiped her creamy lips—"then . . . if I have objections, will I—"

"No." Thor's expression stayed warm and a bit more than friendly. "Not at this time. But you have the right to ask for a hearing yourself if you so decide. Our king, no matter what you may think, is fair in a court of law."

"I see." She didn't believe it, but she wanted to. Perhaps she should have asked to see Queen Eleanor first.

"If you've had enough to eat—" Thor began, and Aylena broke in.

"I have. I am ready to go." She hesitated. "Will the queen be there?"

For a moment Thor's pale eyes were full of laughter, then they were serious again. "Tis possible, I suppose. However, this is not part of a day in court. The king has given us permission to approach him during his daily inspection of a new building. Tis not a formal meeting."

"I see." She did see. Warned by what happened to him the last time he gave audience to Aylena Stewart, the king was making it impossible for the queen to interfere. Aylena thought about it for a minute or so and then nodded. Twas fair. This time Thor was asking for something he wanted.

Only the three of them mounted their horses and set out for the huge new building going up near the city walls. The building was part of stone and part of fine woods, and while one section had been completed except for furnishings, the rest of it was in complete disarray, with stonemasons and carpenters vying for space. They found the king in the middle of a shouting match between the builder and the architect who had drawn the plans. King Henry was glad to leave.

"They'll not listen to reason until the heat of their temper cools," he said to Thor, and then laughed. "I know that from the study of mine own. Now, what is this favor you need, and how long will it take you to tell me about it?"

Thor smiled. "Once we are settled, it shouldn't take more than a few minutes. First, show us your prize."

Watching the king, listening to him, Aylena lost her awe of him, though not the awe she felt when she thought of his power. Following Henry's tall and imposing figure about in the unfinished rooms, stepping over blocks of stone and great beams of wood, she clung to Ian's hand for support and listened to Henry explaining the work. Then, when the king led them into the section that had been completed, she found a bench for herself and Ian and sat down.

King Henry, dragging out a chair and pointing to

another one for Thor, sat down and fanned his red
face with a large handkerchief.

"I'd not want you to think my judgment today is
not binding," he said, "for it is. This is the first case to
be tried in my new halls of justice. We are making
history, Thor."

"Perhaps we are," Thor answered. "If so, you may
be setting a precedent that can be used again." He
was still standing, though he'd brought the chair near
when the king pointed at it. Thor, Aylena had often
noted, never looked awkward either standing or sitting. He stood at ease, yet always straight, always
ready to spring into action. At this moment, he faced
the king and watched his expression, as if pondering
when the man would be ready to listen.

Settling back, Henry waved a hand. "Speak, my
lord. I would hear you now."

Thor spoke clearly. "I petition you for the guardianship of one Ian Stewart, seven-year-old son of the
deceased Bruce Stewart, laird of the Stewart clan,
and also the son of Alyse Belmain Stewart, who died
at his birth. I, having taken over the boy's home, am
ready to assume the duties and rights of a guardian
and mentor for him and continue acting as such until
he is of age."

Aylena gasped and began to rise, but Ian pulled her
back down, his eyes huge. "Let him!" he whispered.
"Oh, Aylena, *let* him! He can teach me so much more
than William. And I'd like to learn all he knows."

The king was staring at them. "Have you aught to
say, Lady Aylena?"

She gave him a wild glance. "Why, yes, Your Highness. I . . . ." She felt Ian's strong young hand grab

her wrist and squeeze. "I . . . ah, approve. And so does my brother."

Henry nodded benignly. "Good! Tis a problem settled. Now, Lord Rodancott, is there more to your thoughts?"

"Much more, sire. I want my ward, Ian Stewart, to be named as the heir of Stewart Castle in Northumbria."

The king jerked in his chair. "For the sake of my sanity, Rodancott, tell me you're joking!"

"Indeed not, sire. If you want peace on the border, you'll have it under the new reign of the Stewart clan. The Stewarts will be friends to the English."

Henry II leaned forward in his chair and spat out words. "The Stewarts are *Scots!* There's no English blood there!"

Ian let go of Aylena's hand and stood up, glaring at the king. "You are wrong, Your Highness! I have more English blood in me than you have in you!"

With a smothered groan, Aylena leaped to her feet, grabbed Ian's hand, and pulled him after her, leaving the room as rapidly as possible, leaping gracefully over the beams and blocks that lay in her path. Outside, she paused, panting.

"Where did we leave the horses, Ian?" She looked around, too frightened to see, only imagining a young throat in a noose. Or on a chopping block.

"There they are," Ian said, "right in front of you. Are we leaving?"

"You and I are. Get on your horse. Now!"

They rode through the crowded streets as if the devil himself were after them, though from the delighted grin on Ian's face, it was well worth it just for the ride.

Margit was horrified at the news. But she managed to help Aylena pack up their clothes and Ian's. Still they were forced to wait there at the inn, for neither of them knew the way from Winchester to Belmain well enough to undertake the trip alone.

Finding himself at blame, Ian was clearly puzzled. "I only told the truth," he said, "and I addressed him properly, calling him Your Highness. How could he take that amiss?"

"One must wait until one is asked to speak directly to the king," Aylena said. "And for a child—heaven help us—to insult a reigning English king by pointing out his lack of English blood is likely grounds for banishment. Or worse."

"But tis true," Ian said, suddenly laughing. "My father said this king was a Plantagenet, which he said is a cross between the devil and a French noblewoman."

"Ian!"

"That's what he said."

"We must make certain," Margit said, "that Ian is never in the presence of royalty again. He hasn't the proper reverence."

"He will learn," Aylena said, "if he lives. Was that a knock?"

Ian was already at the door, opening it. "My lord! Are you my guardian now?"

Thor's gaze swept the room as he came in. "I am. I am now allowed to beat you at my will. And I will beat you—if you ever again address a king before being asked to speak. You were extremely rude."

Ian hung his head. "Then I am sorry."

"Remember what you have learned. Tis easier than having to learn the same thing again. Find James, and tell him we spend another day or two here before we leave for Belmain.''

Ian was gone, and Margit, seeing the look Thor gave Aylena, followed him out.

As soon as the door closed, Aylena burst into speech. "The king will not punish Ian, then?"

"No, no punishment." Thor came to her, taking her into his arms, holding her loosely while he searched her frightened face. "The king was shocked, but soon laughing. And, after I told him what I know about the lad, he agreed to make Ian heir to his father's castle. When Ian comes of age, tis his."

"Ohhhh!" Tears sprang to Aylena's eyes, whether of joy or sadness she would never know. "But . . . tis *your* castle, Thor. You took it fairly."

He laughed. "You can't make it both mine and Ian's, my love. Twill still be mine to run and protect until Ian is old enough to take over. But you do have a part in this. I need one thing more to make this work well for us."

Aylena wiped her eyes. "Whatever it is, if I can help supply it, tis yours now."

"I hope you mean that. I am in need of a wife."

Aylena's jaw dropped. "You want to marry *me*? I thought you'd tired of me and were looking forward to escaping to Normandy once this damnable trip was over. I mean, well—you've been very cold toward me recently."

"Only because when you are in my bed I lose the power of reason. Besides, I found it very hard to give up the castle. I wanted it, and I wanted you, an you wanted it for Ian. At the first, I meant only to ask for the guardianship of the boy, for he is your brother and both strong and intelligent. He deserves a guardian, and no Scot would apply."

He glanced at Aylena, his brows furrowed. "That, of course, was due to my presence in Stewart Castle. I admit I was glad of it—I wanted the guardianship of Ian. He is a fine boy. I thought it would be a pleasure to work with him, to teach him." He looked away, swallowing. Aylena was silent, seeing his emotion, wondering at it . . . listening as he spoke again:

"Then, in the middle of making up my mind, I changed. That night when Bretinalle held a knife at Ian's throat and told him to cry out to you, I knew I had never seen so brave and faithful a child in all my life. He was willing to die to keep you safe. How could I deny his heritage from a father who taught a seven-year-old boy to hold to his courage, even in the face of death?"

Aylena went to him, wove her arms around his neck, and kissed him, taking her time about it. Then she leaned back and looked at him with tears glistening in her eyes.

"I know," she said shakily. "We Stewarts are all brave. Therefore, I will not hesitate to marry you."

Thor laughed, but his steel gray eyes were as wet as her own as he brought her close again, his hand caressing the deep waves of her red-gold hair, the slim softness of her supple back.

"Thank God. I hope . . . no, I pray, that you are giving yourself to me because you want me as I want you. I would not like you to submit to me out of gratitude."

"I am more grateful to you than I can ever express," Aylena said. "You have been more generous to me than I would have thought possible from any man. And I love you for it. But if I am to be honest—not one of those wonderful qualities draws me to your bed."

He leaned back to look into her eyes, his face doubtful. "Then what will?"

Her smile was slow and sweet. "I think you know," she said softly. "It's the love we make together. I canna do without it if I am to be happy."

He laughed out loud, swinging her up into his arms. "Ah, my darling, you'll be the happiest woman in all of England, then. When shall we marry?"

"Whenever you wish."

"Where?"

She laughed. "Wherever you wish!"

"Good! We will marry tomorrow at St. Swithun's Cathedral, at the same altar where your parents were wed. And after that we will leave James and Margit and Ian at Belmain, and we will travel to Normandy."

"Oh! We will have a wedding trip?"

"Indeed. We will begin our marriage in *my* castle, so that you learn the proper respect for your husband."

Aylena smiled, looking at him with great pride. "I already respect you, Thor. You are a wonderful man."

"Then I can count on your good behavior tomorrow when King Henry and Queen Eleanor come to our wedding?"

Aylena laughed, excited. "Do you truly think they will?"

"I know they will. The king suggested it. He said his mind will be easier once you and your brother are under my control, and he fain would see with his own eyes that the ceremony is done."

Aylena stared. Then she broke into laughter. "How strange! Do you think he meant that? I canna believe that I, or Ian, either, could make the king of England say such a thing. Why, we are the humblest of his subjects."

Thor grinned. "And I the happiest. Come, we'll tell Ian and the rest."